Love, Murder, and a Good Bottle of Wine

Chris Phipps

Published by Eleven Jewels Publishing

This is a work of fiction. To create a sense of place, the Sacramento-Folsom-Roseville area of California is used as a backdrop. The neighborhoods exist, but not the specific houses. The casino is fictitious, as are the restaurants, bars, and the supermarket. While the news stations, hospital, cemetery, parks and other public places exist, the characters, their names, and incidents are products of the author's imagination and experience or are used fictitiously.

Cover by Karen Phillips of Phillips Covers
Cover Photo by Kathleen Kennedy of Kathy's Images

ISBN: 978-0-9909141-1-2

For Tom

Who is always encouraging,
always believes in me,
and never complains about
the many hours I spend in my writing world

Acknowledgments

I'd like to thank the many people who helped bring this book to life:

My fellow scribes at Writers on the Storm, with whom I spent many pleasant evenings, reading, critiquing, laughing, and forming new bonds;

WOTS members Joli Roberts and Robin Rice, who later read the entire finished novel, ferreted out inconsistencies and errors and offered suggestions not only for fixing them, but for developing a better story;

My supportive fellow writers in my online Mystery Writers group, who caught any inconsistencies the other readers had missed and offered some great suggestions, especially Ron Voigts, Terry Guy and Sylvie Kaye;

Christiana Bakarich, who did all of the above, and painstaking editing;

Kathleen Kennedy for working so hard to get the cover images right;

Paddy Lawton for taking on the boring job of scrutinizing galley proofs for errors; and

All my first readers, including Windy, Kathy and Nita.

Even if I were not compelled to write, I could never leave the writing world and the people who inhabit it. I have never found more generous people, always willing to give of their time, knowledge, and expertise, as well as providing encouragement and friendship.

Thanks to all of you, for making the book so much better than it might have been.

Chapter 1

Allison turned off the two-lane highway into the casino parking lot, drove past several open parking spaces, and maneuvered the 1996 Ford Explorer onto the adjoining unpaved lot, parking out of range of the security lights. It wasn't likely he'd look for her here, but she'd rather not chance it. If it did occur to him, it would be a while, so she had some time.

She sat in the darkness for a few minutes, watching the casino, then turned on the dome light and glanced at her reflection in the rear-view mirror. God, she looked pale. And her hair had a serious case of bed head. Out of habit, she reached toward the passenger seat for her purse. It wasn't there.

"Damn him," she muttered, subconsciously rubbing her arm where he'd grabbed it.

She opened the glove compartment. Amid the usual clutter of flashlight, tire pressure gauge, and car manuals, she found a tube of lipstick and seven dollars and eighty-three cents. The lipstick tasted rancid. How long had it rattled around in the car? Well, it wasn't like she planned to kiss anybody.

Her reflection in the mirror looked like a ghost, or possibly a vampire, with straggly red-blonde hair, pale face, and lips like a bloody gash. Wiping at the lipstick, she blended a little from her fingertips onto her cheeks. Better. Not quite so pale. She ran her fingers through her hair, trying to untangle it. Impossible. It would help if she had something to tie it back. She glanced at the camping gear in the rear of the Explorer. She wasn't likely to find anything there.

She spotted an old sneaker and eyed its lace. Not exactly cutting-edge style, but better than nothing.

When she finished with her hair, she sat still for a few minutes, watching the parking lot.

Habit, long ingrained, compelled her to reach for her purse before she got out. When her fingers again failed to make contact, she automatically turned to look, and her gaze settled on the cup holder. She flipped it open, exposing the change and small bills Scott kept there for parking, netting a five-dollar bill, seven ones, and five quarters. A little more than twenty dollars, total. At least she wasn't flat broke.

After she'd turned off the dome light, locked the Explorer, shoved the keys in one jeans pocket and the money in another, she headed across the lot to the casino.

The flashing neon, clashing red and purple decor, and a cacophony of loud voices and electronic slot machines started a dull ache behind her eyes. Edging around gaming tables and heedless gamblers, she found her way to the food court and a cup of too-strong coffee. Sipping it, she tried to plan her next move. It was a little after ten; in a few hours, it should be safe to go back.

"Buy you a drink?"

"What? Oh, no thanks. I'm getting ready to head home."

A husky, tanned man slid onto the chair beside her, setting his drink on the table. He looked up at the keno board. "How'd you do? I cleaned up pretty good at the blackjack table. Sure you don't want a drink?" He leaned toward her, his leg pressed against hers. "Or we can go somewhere else."

She moved her leg away from his. "No thanks. Not interested."

"Well, okay. But if you change your mind–like I said, I've got money." He laid a hairy hand near hers, exposing ragged, dirty fingernails. His leg moved against hers again. She shifted away.

"Look. I told you I'm not interested."

Her raised voice caught the attention of a man walking by the table—one who looked like he could be a linebacker. He stopped in mid-stride. "Everything okay here?"

"I don't think he understands the meaning of the word no. I just want him to leave me alone."

The man with dirty fingernails got up, raising both hands, palms outward. "Hey, I'm leaving. I just wanted to buy the lady a drink." He turned, pushed through a group of gamblers, and worked his way toward the poker tables.

Her rescuer's gaze traveled from her tousled hair to her face, making her all too aware of her bedraggled appearance. "Are you okay?"

"I'm good. Thanks for getting rid of the jerk."

"No problem." He hesitated, gave her a brief nod and went on his way.

She took her time finishing the coffee, then found a penny slot machine. The cocktail waitress came through and took her order for water. "Could I get something for a headache, too?"

"Sure." The waitress moved on, taking drink orders from other gamblers.

"Headache?" The guy with dirty fingernails slid onto a stool at the next machine, startling her. "You look like you've had a rough night." His stare lingered on her hips and waist for several seconds, then moved up to her chest. Resisting the impulse to cross her arms across her breasts, she turned her back to him, stood and cashed out.

"Little thing, ain't you?" he said. "What are you, about five feet one or two? Don't look to me like you'd weigh much more'n a hunert pounds if you was sopping wet."

She ignored him and headed for the bar.

"What can I get you?" the bartender asked. He pointed at a rectangular pin on his lapel, black with white lettering. "I'm Alan, by the way."

"Hi, Alan. Is a guy following me? A husky guy, kind of dark? Maroon sweatshirt?"

Alan looked across the casino floor. "I don't see anybody. He give you that bruise?"

"Bruise? Oh." She raised a hand to her jaw, then dropped it. Was that what the scumbag had meant by a rough night?

"No, that was kind of an accident."

Alan raised an eyebrow.

"It isn't what you think." She stopped, impatient with herself. "Never mind."

Alan nodded like he'd heard it all before. "What about the guy following you?"

She swiveled on the stool. "He's still there?"

"No. You said some guy is following you."

"Oh. Him. Just some creep who keeps hitting on me. Doesn't understand no."

"Give me a description. I'll call Security."

He filled orders for a drink runner and waited on several customers before he came back. "Security hasn't seen the guy. Looks like he's gone, but they'll keep an eye out for him."

"Thanks." She headed for a ladies' room to check out the bruise, a darkened area spreading upward from beneath the left side of her jaw. It didn't do much for the overall image. Maybe if she tried to do something with her hair? She shook her head. Not without a comb.

She went back to the casino floor, where she strolled around, playing a few coins here and there, watching the other gamblers. She found another penny slot machine and played it slowly, just a single line at a time, not really interested, just killing time.

Was Scott still looking for her, or had he given up for the night? He was probably sprawled across the bed in a drunken stupor, only a few feet from the chair where she'd unwillingly abandoned her purse. She might be able to sneak in and grab it without waking him. But he might not be asleep. He might be sitting in that chair, waiting for her.

She had no choice. There was no way to get into Caro's house without the key. Unless...

Caro, years ago, had shown her a spare key, hanging from a tiny hook screwed to the bottom of a patio bench. "In case you get locked out again."

That was thirteen years ago, when she had been sixteen, a year after Caro had given her a home. Would the key still be there, or had Caro moved it?

She glanced at her watch. It was almost midnight, late to be calling. She hadn't wanted to get Laura mixed up in this, but she might know about the key and, under the circumstances, she wouldn't mind a late-night call from her cousin.

Now if she could just find a telephone.

Laura answered on the second ring. "Where are you? Scott called, and I kept waiting for you to phone, or to come and crash."

"Damn! I didn't think he'd bother you. He must know you wouldn't tell him anything. I didn't go to your house because that's the first place he'll look for me. For all I know, he's staked out there right now."

Silence on the other end. She could picture her cousin holding back a section of drape, peering at the cars parked along the street. "Laura, I was kidding."

At least, she thought she was. Could he really be there? No, he didn't have the patience to sit still, especially in the cramped seat of her Corolla, with binoculars trained on Laura's house. But he might drive around, looking for the Explorer.

Had he found the letter? Of course. He couldn't have missed it when he dug into her purse, looking for her set of keys. Something else for him to be angry about.

"Where are you?" Laura asked. "Are you okay?"

"I'm fine." Her hand moved up to stroke her bruised jaw. "I thought I'd go down to Caro's house and spend a day or two there, but I don't have my key. She used to hide one on the patio. Do you know if it's still there?"

"I'd forgotten all about that key. It was there two years ago. Caro called when you were in Hawaii, and asked me to go down and get some stuff to mail to her. I didn't have my key with me, and I was showing houses in Orangevale, if I remember right. Anyway, she told me about the key under the bench. It's probably still there."

"Great. I'll head on down. Thanks, Laura. Now, go to bed and get some sleep. I'm okay."

In her peripheral vision, she caught a glimpse of maroon. She turned, searching for the husky man. Had he been watching?

Listening? She didn't see anybody who looked like him. Just jumpy nerves.

She worked her way to the door, then strode across the lot, wishing she hadn't parked so far away. There was nobody close by, and only a few cars remained in the outer parking slots. She picked up her pace as she stepped off the asphalt into the unpaved lot, and squinted into the darkness for the outlines of the Explorer.

"Heading out?" The voice came from the half-lit area behind her. She glanced over her shoulder. Dirty Fingernails. He was close. It was too far to go back, and she couldn't outrun him—not with her short legs.

She had no other options, so she ran, and with every desperate step, she swore, "Damn you, Scott. Damn you to hell."

The man's hand caught and gripped her left arm, turning her to face him. His breath stank of stale beer, and he swayed a little as she turned, kicking at his knee. She missed and stumbled, his grip the only thing that kept her from falling. Desperate, she raised her right hand and thrust the key at his face, hoping to jab an eye.

"Damn." He loosened his grip enough for her to twist free. She kicked again, aiming for his crotch. Her foot hit something, a solid kick, but she didn't wait to see where the blow landed. She ran, hoping she'd gained enough time to get inside the Explorer and lock the door.

Her finger pressed the clicker. Nothing happened. *It's manual, stupid.* Everything on it was manual. She held the key ready to insert into the door lock.

He was there again. Behind her. *Stay calm.* Easier said than done. She found the keyhole, slid the key in with trembling fingers, and took it out, careful not to drop it.

His smell, an odious combination of cigarette smoke, dried sweat and stale beer, told her he was close. Too close.

She jerked the door open, scrambled inside and slammed it, not caring if it crushed his hand. Then she fumbled for the door lock switch, remembered it was manual, and jammed the lock button down.

The keys fell to the floor when she reached across the passenger seat to check the other door. Locked. She let out her breath, only then realizing she had been holding it.

He pounded on the door, cursing. She leaned down, under the steering wheel, groping for the key ring, trying to keep the man within eyesight.

Her fingers didn't make contact. She leaned over farther, losing sight of him, and touched metal. Stretching her fingers, she managed to hook the ring and pull it toward her.

The man was on the other side of the Explorer, jerking on the passenger-door handle. Failing to open it, he hammered on the window with the back of his fist.

She rammed the key into the ignition. It wouldn't turn. She tried again, harder, then twisted it the other way. Nothing. It wouldn't move.

Wrong key, stupid.

She had instinctively used the one with the black fob, like her own car key. The Explorer key was plain metal. She pulled on the key, but it didn't move; it was stuck in the ignition. She got a firm grip and yanked again. Nothing.

The car horn. She jammed the heel of her hand against it.

Where was he? She peered through the windows, but couldn't see him. Maybe the horn had frightened him away. She honked again. Would anybody hear? Was there anybody in the parking lot? Her palm came down on the horn again—and again. It sounded weak. Was the battery low?

Okay, calm down. Listen. She sat still, straining to hear. Nothing. Was he still there? Maybe he was searching for something he could use to force the door open.

She scrambled into the back, looking for a weapon, anything she could use to defend herself. A tire iron, or something from the camping gear. A tent stake. Digging through the boxes, throwing things aside, she found something better–a knife. Dull-edged, but still a knife.

Sitting on a sleeping bag, motionless, senses alert, she waited, the knife gripped in her right hand. Fifteen minutes ticked by, then another long quarter hour. Her hand ached, and she loosened her hold on the knife.

He was gone. He had to be. He was just a lecherous drunk, and she had scared him off.

She waited another half hour, then relaxed a little, trying to plan her next move. Go back into the casino and call the auto club? No, she didn't have her membership card.

Who was she trying to kid? There was no way she was going back out there. Not while it was still dark.

Even if her stalker had disappeared, other predators might be around. It wouldn't be that hard to break into the Explorer. She needed to make herself less visible.

The sleeping bag? Why not? It would hide her. Besides, it was getting cold.

By stacking some of the camping gear and tossing more into a seat, she managed to carve out enough space for her small frame. Then she crawled in, curled into the fetal position, and listened, but couldn't hear much over the sound of her own pounding heart.

He was gone. He wasn't out there. Nobody was out there.

Chapter 2

When the dispatcher called about the body Saturday morning, Dee Callender sighed and glanced at her dashboard clock. Seven minutes after six. Almost an hour until the end of shift, her last one on graveyard. She had been ready to head in, already thinking about a hot shower and bed.

She swung the black and white onto Forty-third, into the heart of the Fabulous Forties, an area of bungalows, custom-built Craftsman houses, Mediterranean villas and Tudor-style mansions, all dating from the early 1900's. She found the address, a brick Tudor, set back from the street at the end of a long driveway.

As she exited the car, a man waved his arm, drawing her attention to the shrubbery hiding the south end of the house. She looked around. Nobody else in sight. First officer on the scene. She mentally shuffled note cards from her first-responder training: lock the scene down; preserve evidence; take photos; make notes and sketches; interview witnesses and do it quickly, while their memories are fresh.

Flipping on her digital recorder, she followed a curving flagstone path toward the man, making notes about her arrival time and the layout of the property. Closer to him, she recorded, "Young, late teens or early twenties, lean build, about five ten. Has a leashed dog. Looks like a black Labrador retriever."

As she drew closer, she glimpsed part of a recessed patio concealed behind the foliage. A few more steps and the plants took shape: tall, waxy-leafed camellias and a Lady Banks rose. One branch arched over the edge of the patio, dropping delicate yellow blossoms into the red-blonde hair of the small woman sprawled face down on the flagstones. Dead. Pretty obvious broken neck.

"Looks like maybe she fell from up there." The man pointed to a second-story redwood deck. His other hand held the dog's leash in a white-knuckled grip. The dog stood, not straining against the collar, watching Dee.

Shading her eyes against the sun, low on the eastern horizon, she glanced at the section of railing that had fallen away, leaving jagged edges. A few pieces of loose wood hung from the deck, still attached to the railing. Splintered wood littered the patio.

"I'm DeAnn Callender, Sacramento Police Department," she said. "What's your name?"

"Jesse. Jesse Holcomb. I'm the guy who called it in." He licked his lip. "I was passing by, and—"

"Okay, would you mind moving back, away from the patio?"

She'd patrolled solo ever since finishing field training almost five years earlier and had seen her share of dead bodies. She never liked it, but she knew what to do.

She pulled on latex gloves and worked her way to the body, avoiding the wood fragments. No pulse. No pupil response. Not much rigor. The woman must have died within the last few hours.

Watching her steps, she reversed her path back to the edge of the grass. "I'll be with you in a minute," she told Holcomb. "There are some things I have to do."

She kept an eye on the shrubbery while making the necessary calls, but she doubted the killer, if there was one, was still on the scene. Best to be cautious, though. Who knew what went on in deranged minds?

Nobody answered the doorbell, so she hammered with her fist. "Sacramento Police Department." No response.

The deck adjoined the second story and covered about half of the flagstone patio. A set of wooden stairs led upward, and one of the French doors leading into the house was slightly ajar. She would have to wait for backup to go in. It should be only a matter of minutes.

After snapping a few pictures of the body and the deck, with its aged wood, Dee scanned the yard again. Holcomb stood ten or twelve yards away, beside a pink-flowering crab apple tree, the leashed black Lab held close to his blue-jeaned leg.

She went back to her patrol car for a roll of crime scene tape just as another officer arrived. She knew him only by sight. He looked like a high-school kid, and she suspected he would someday be doing undercover work. She searched her memory for his name. Baker? Barker? Banks...Nick Banks.

"Body's on the patio." Dee pointed. "Can you get the area secured?"

"Got it." He grabbed a roll of tape and headed for a tree at the edge of the lawn. Dee hurried back to the patio. Time to talk to Holcomb. She pulled out her notebook and pen.

"You have any ID, Mr. Holcomb?"

He pulled a worn wallet from his back pocket, flipped it open, and fumbled his driver's license free of the plastic window pocket. The photo bore a close enough resemblance to identify him. She glanced at the vital statistics. Twenty-one years old. Coloring and height and weight about right. Address eight or ten blocks away.

"You go to Sac State?"

"How did you know?" He looked down at his Hornets sweatshirt and a grin almost formed at the corners of his mouth, then trembled and straightened. He rubbed his neck. "Yeah, just out running Barney, here." He patted the dog. "He found her. About went into orbit and yanked me over here. I banged on the door, but nobody answered. I didn't know what to do. I didn't want to touch her and I thought—I called nine-one-one." He chewed his lower lip.

"You did right. You know her?"

"Nah. Don't think I ever saw her, but...her face. It's hard to tell. I didn't look very close." He swallowed. "I don't know anybody in this area. Just jog over here, maybe once or twice a week. Give Barney a run. Most of the time, we go over by the river."

Dee nodded. She often ran or biked on the American River Parkway, though not here. It bordered the river, all the way from Folsom to Old Sacramento.

"What time did you find her?"

"Don't know for sure. A few minutes before I called nine-one-one. As soon as I could think straight. I was pretty shook." He shifted his weight.

"How long have you been out on your walk?"

"How long? Let's see." He cocked his head to one side and pinched his lower lip. A light breeze carried the scent of lilacs toward them, and rustled the leaves of the crab apple tree. Pink blossoms drifted to the grass. "I think I left home about five thirty. Maybe half an hour?"

Another black and white parked behind Dee's patrol car. "Okay, Mr. Holcomb. Can you hang around a little longer?"

"Well, I've got an early class." His glance flicked toward the patio, and his shoulders drooped. "Yeah. Sure, no problem."

"Over by my patrol car, if you don't mind. We're going to have to secure this area." She followed him to her unit and greeted Officers Michaels and Joyner. Another black and white pulled to the curb. Six officers on scene now. Enough to use four to clear the house.

As Dee led the others up the wooden steps from the patio, a wine bottle and goblet on the deck table caught her attention. Empty. Had the woman been drunk? Could she have lost her balance and fallen through the railing? Dee turned toward the not-quite-closed French door, and sunlight sparkled against the glass goblet, warming the liquid inside to golden amber. So the glass wasn't empty, after all. She moved on. The detectives would check it out.

The door led into a hallway with open doors on both sides. It smelled a little musty, like it hadn't been aired out for a while. Dee crouched and went into the first open door, staying low, the sound of her pounding heartbeat reverberating in her ears. Drapes covered the windows, darkening the room. Her feet sank into thick carpeting. She wouldn't be able to hear footsteps. And there were too many shadows.

Even if somebody had pushed the woman off the deck, Dee could think of no logical reason why he'd linger in the darkened house, but she maintained her vigilance. Careless cops often become dead cops. She watched for movement, gaining only slight impressions of the contents of the rooms. One was so jammed with furniture and cardboard boxes, topped with piles of books, papers, and magazines, they could squeeze only a few feet inside. The next held only a stepladder, several paint cans, rollers, and brushes.

They worked their way through the second floor, then the first, clearing every room, every closet, every space, never leaving an unchecked door behind them. When they reached the kitchen, Banks stayed behind while Dee, Joyner, and Michaels went down the basement stairs, set into a walled space between the kitchen and living room.

Too dark. Dee pulled her flashlight from her belt, aware even as she held it to the side and flicked the switch that it would betray her position. Better that than to shoot the wrong person. The phrase "friendly fire" pulsed through her mind, triggering an image of Iraq's sun-scorched Sunni Triangle and blinding dust and sand storms, and memories she couldn't let intrude. Not now. She pushed them aside, swept the light around the area at the bottom of the stairs, and illuminated a door leading off to the right. Michaels stayed in position this time, while she and Joyner entered.

Cool air touched her perspiration-damp forehead. They faced a labyrinth of shelving, vertical rows receding into the shadows. Joyner aimed his flashlight down the first narrow aisle between them. Something dark protruded from the shelving. Bottles. They were in a wine cellar. Dee didn't see a light switch. There had to be one. Maybe back at the top of the stairs?

Joyner edged his way into the shadows and disappeared. Dee stood still and listened, facing the unexplored area, her gun ready to stop anybody who emerged from the darkened area.

Joyner reappeared. “Dead end,” he whispered. “Shelves too close to the wall. Can’t get through.” He slid into the shadows between the next set of shelves, and she moved to the opening to cover him. He returned, and they moved on, to the third aisle.

A small window set into the south wall provided enough light for her to follow his progress about halfway down the passage. She could see the tops of the racks now. They were about five feet high.

When Joyner came back, he whispered, “Problem. There’s another opening at the end.”

Dee’s mind raced. There was no way to safely clear the other aisles while simultaneously watching the new opening and the corridor leading out. Not with only two of them.

Joyner whispered, “If you move about halfway down, you’ll be able to see both ends, so nothing can move past you.”

She nodded, not saying what they both knew. If somebody lurked in one of those last corridors, he could circle around behind Joyner as he went down the one just before it, and she wouldn’t be able to see him. “I’ll go back. There’s got to be a light switch.”

But Joyner had already slipped into the shadows. All she could do was try to cover him. She waited and listened, perspiration trickling into her eyebrows, reminding herself there was little chance an intruder still lingered in the house.

When Joyner finally said “Clear,” she let out a deep breath and moved into position beside the new opening. Her flashlight beam showed a blank wall. Not until she moved closer did she realize the passage turned sharply to the right, leading to a metal door set into the left end of the wall. Joyner pushed it open, and she slipped inside, keeping her profile low.

The area, measuring about sixteen square feet, had two doors leading off the right side. Working their way through cardboard cartons, plastic bins and a discarded armchair, they reached the doors–a pantry-sized closet and a small bathroom.

“Clear,” Joyner said.

Dee lowered her gun. “After all that, nothing but a pantry and a bathroom.”

“Looks like this might have been a fallout shelter, from the sixties,” Joyner said, wiping his forehead with his shirt sleeve. “We better get back.”

They hurried to rejoin Michaels, who helped them clear the remainder of the basement. It contained nothing but some metal shelving and a rusty iron furnace, no longer in use.

“That’s a big sucker,” Joyner said. “Guess it had to be, back then, to heat a house this big.”

Banks joined them at the top of the basement stairs, and the four of them finished clearing the house.

When they emerged through the front door, the medical examiner was parking at the curb. Dee went to direct him to the patio. She turned back toward the house just in time to see Joyner and Michaels getting into their vehicle.

“Where are they going?” she asked Banks.

He shrugged. “Don’t know, but the detectives are here. Looks like we’ll be doing crowd control.”

An unmarked car had pulled to the opposite curb, driven by Al Durant, a slightly balding detective, pushing fifty. She knew him only by sight and wished she could say the same for his companion, Matt Coleman, a more recent Detective Division recruit. She nodded at both men, noting Coleman’s deep tan and blow-dried blond hair. He probably spent more time on it than she did on her own. She ran her fingers through the sides of her short hairstyle, pushing dark strands into place.

Durant offered his beefy hand. “Callender, isn’t it? Diane Callender?”

She shook his hand. “DeAnn. Dee.” She pointed toward the patio. “Body’s over there. Premises have been cleared.”

Matt Coleman glanced at the nearby vehicles. Looks like the M.E. is already at work.”

Durant peered toward the shrubbery at the end of the house. “Any witnesses?” He glanced at Jesse Holcomb.

"Not that I know about. I got here at six-oh-nine. Nobody around, except him." She nodded toward Holcomb. "He called it in. Says he spotted the body somewhere around six. I suspect it was several minutes after, because I was only a few blocks away. One of the French doors leading from the upper-story deck was open, about an inch."

Durant glanced at the shrubbery. "He couldn't have seen anything from the street."

"Dog sensed the body. Looks like the woman fell from the deck onto the patio. Jogger doesn't think he touched anything, except the front door. Couldn't rouse anybody, so he called nine-one-one. I don't think he's going to have much to offer. Says he doesn't know her. Student from Sac State, walking his dog before class."

"Okay, we'd better get at it." Durant started toward the patio, then turned back to Dee. He glanced at Banks and another officer, at the far end of the yard. "Can you guys hang around for a while and help keep the scene secure? Just 'til more back up arrives? We'll be getting some media attention, and I don't want them trampling everything. Shouldn't have to keep you very long."

Thoughts of the hot shower and bed flitted through Dee's mind. It had been a long night, and she was tired. "No problem," she said, glancing back at the street. No media yet, but any time now.

A white-haired man in slippers and a plaid robe stood in a driveway, rolled newspaper in hand, staring across the tree-lined street. A slender woman in jeans, long blonde ponytail, and a blue windbreaker pulled at a black poodle's leash, slowing as she neared the tape. It wouldn't be long until they had a bunch of gawkers, but some of them might have seen or heard something.

She took more pictures, from several angles, noted her observations, and studied the structure of the house. Shrubbery hid the adjoining patio, which faced her. Today's houses would be built with the deck and patio facing the back yard, but in this upscale area of Sacramento, the houses had been constructed at least a half-century earlier, when the builders hadn't considered privacy an issue. Now, well-established landscaping hid them and their inhabitants from public view. Unfortunately, it had hidden the body, too, and possibly a killer.

Neighbors edged closer, joined by passers-by, all of them craning their necks for a better view. They pushed against the tape. Dee and Banks pushed them back.

"Did any of you see anything?" Dee asked repeatedly, hoping to find a potential witness. She got no response, other than blank stares, head shakes, and several repetitions of the same question: "What happened?"

Crime scene technicians arrived and entered the house. A Channel 3 news truck pulled to the curb, followed a few minutes later by Channels 10 and 13. Durant emerged from the patio and walked around the house, his hands in his pockets, examining doors and windows and the ground beneath them.

A reporter pushed her way to the front, and the photographer with her aimed his camera at Dee. "What happened, Officer?"

Dee ignored them, and they worked their way over to Nick Banks. They would get nothing from him.

The crowd started drifting away, and the news crews went back to their vehicles to wait. Dee glanced at her watch.

"I think I might have heard something."

The voice came from behind her. She turned to face an elderly man who smelled of Old Spice. Something about him seemed familiar. Mentally, she sifted through the faces she'd seen that morning. The neighbor across the street, the one with the rolled-up newspaper, wearing slippers and a robe. He now wore khaki pants, a blue polo shirt and running shoes.

He licked his lower lip. "I woke up about one thirty. Sounded like a garage door opened. Strange for that time of night. I thought I heard a truck, maybe a small one."

"You're sure about the time?"

"Yeah." He shook his head. "Didn't think much about it at first. Not 'til I remembered all the recent burglaries. Then I looked to see what time it was–a little after one thirty."

"Did you see anything?"

He flushed. "It took a few minutes to get to the window. I'm a little stiff when I first get up. Anyway, I don't think I saw anything."

Dee raised her eyebrows. "You don't think you did?"

He hesitated. "Well, there might have been tail lights at the end of the block. Looked like it could be a small truck. Like one of those you rent to move? But I'm not sure. Might have been something else. None of the houses had a garage door open. At least, none I could see."

She took the man's name, telephone number, and address, glanced at her watch again and headed toward the patio to talk to Durant. As she approached, the medical examiner was rising from beside the body. "I'd estimate the time of death at around four to seven hours ago, based on body temperature and degree of rigor."

Durant stretched his back and looked up at the deck. "Hard to tell at this point what happened. Could be anything—accident, homicide, suicide, you name it. She's fully dressed. Looks like she never went to bed."

"Excuse me," Dee said. "I have a neighbor—a guy across the street—thinks he heard a small truck about one thirty. Maybe a garage door, too."

"Let's go talk to him." Durant turned and walked toward the driveway.

Coleman glanced back at the house, then followed. They angled across the deep lawn, toward the tape. "Deck's old wood, but it still seems a little modern for the house," Coleman said. "I'm wondering if it was added later. Makes for a nice setup. Shade over half the patio, and an outdoor sitting area to serve the second floor."

"Thinking about remodeling?" Durant asked.

"No. I just like the idea and the outside steps. What I'm wondering is, where's her husband?"

"How do you know she's married?" Dee asked.

"Pretty ritzy neighborhood for a woman alone. Husband's probably a doctor or lawyer or investment banker."

Dee winced. "How can you—"

Coleman waved her off. “Look, most of the houses in here run one and a half or two mil. Old money. Old families. Not single women.”

Dee shook her head. “You’re making a lot of assumptions. Sexist ones, at that.”

“Maybe, but politically correct thinking doesn’t solve cases. You keep that stuff in mind when you’re talking to the brass or media, but when you start investigating, you have to use logic and common sense. And instinct–your gut feeling–because that’s what usually solves the case.”

Durant winked at Dee. “And what, exactly, is your gut telling you about this one, Officer Coleman?”

“She’s got a husband somewhere. She is—she was a pretty woman, but too old to be a daughter still living at home, and it takes money to keep up a place like this. They’d need to hire help.” He nodded at the big lawn. “There’s maintenance. Property taxes. All that would take a good-sized chunk.”

“Meaning what?” Dee asked.

“Meaning, no matter who has the money, we’ll probably feel some heat on this one,” Durant said. “Money always feels privileged.”

“Of course, it’s possible she’s not even connected to the house,” Coleman said.

Durant grunted. “Even if she is, we don’t know in what capacity. Owner? Relative of the owner? Visitor? Housekeeper or—what the hell?”

A yellow Toyota Corolla squealed to a stop, its tires leaving skid marks and the odor of scorched rubber. The tall man who erupted from the car stared at the crime-scene tape, then shoved his way through the onlookers. Reporters, alerted by the screeching brakes, ran toward him.

He wasn’t going to stop. He was coming right through the tape, and Dee was too far away to stop him.

Chapter 3

Dee ran, cutting across the lawn toward the tape to intercept the intruder. Banks got there first and got a firm grip on the man's right arm. Dee grabbed his left. The man struggled. "What's going on?" He nodded at the yellow tape and jutted his chin toward the patrol cars. "What are you guys doing here?"

"This is the scene of an investigation," Durant said. "You need to step back and calm down. What's your name?"

The man ran a hand through his disheveled sandy-brown hair. "Wagner. Scott Wagner." He peered over Durant's shoulder, toward the house. "What kind of investigation?"

"Is this your house?"

Wagner still stared at the house, and Durant repeated the question. Dee watched his face. It was a simple question. Then she realized the man probably hadn't heard it; he looked too distraught to focus. Finally, he shook his head. "What? What did you say?"

"I asked if this is your house."

"No. It belongs to Caro. Caroline Brenhauser, my wife's aunt. She's not here, though. She's in Germany. Or maybe it was France. I don't remember." His focus shifted to the house again. "What happened? Did somebody burglarize the place?"

He shrugged off the hands of the police officers and brushed at the shoulders of his jacket. A futile gesture, Dee thought. The rumpled jacket, slacks, and white shirt looked as though he might have slept in them.

Durant frowned. "If you knew she wouldn't be home, what are you doing here?"

"Sarah—my wife. She's looking after the place while Caro's gone and I thought she might be here. She planned to check on it this week. I thought maybe she came down late last night."

"What time?" Durant asked. "And why late at night?"

"Well, we had a—kind of a disagreement. She got mad and took off. I thought she might be here." His voice broke. "I drove all over last night, looking for her, and I can't find her." He put both hands over his face.

Durant motioned to Dee, and they led Wagner away from the tape and the onlookers, to one of the patrol cars.

Durant's gaze bored into Wagner's eyes. "You said you had a disagreement. What kind of disagreement? Did it get physical?"

"No. Nothing like that. I just stayed out too late and I guess she thought I drank too much. She was mad, and we got into it—into an argument."

Durant jotted in his notebook. "Her name is Sarah, spelled with an 'h' at the end?"

"Yes. Well, no, her name is actually Allison."

Durant stopped writing. "You called her Sarah."

"That's what everybody calls her." Durant didn't say anything, so Wagner took a deep breath and started over. "She was named after her mother, Allison, but it got too confusing, having two people in the house with the same name, so they always called her by her middle name, Sarah."

"So it's Allison Sarah Wagner." Durant jotted in his notebook. "And you haven't heard from her? How long has she been gone?"

"Since last night." Wagner looked at the ground. "Around nine, I guess. Maybe a little later. I'm not sure."

"Can you describe your wife for me, Mr. Wagner?"

His head jerked up. "Why? Why do you want a description?"

"Please, Mr. Wagner. What does your wife look like?"

He took a deep breath. "Well, she's really pretty. Tiny. She's five-one, has long blonde hair—strawberry, she calls it—and gray eyes. Dark gray. What's this all about?"

The description fit. Dee felt a surge of pity for the man, for the loss he already sensed and for the grief that would soon overwhelm him. Dee knew all about grief.

"Something happened to her, didn't it?" His voice cracked. "The burglars—that's why you asked for a description."

A flurry of activity at the patio end of the house drew his attention, and he took a couple of steps in that direction. "She's down there, isn't she?" Dee put one hand on his shoulder to pull him back. He shook it off.

"Mr. Wagner, I know you're upset, but we need you to calm down."

Wagner hesitated, then nodded, his gaze riveted to Durant's face.

"I don't know an easy way to say this," Durant said. "I'm sorry. We found a dead woman on the patio. She matches the description you just gave us."

"Dead?" Wagner swallowed and stared at Durant, eyes wide. He shook his head. "No, no. You're wrong. It can't be Sarah." His voice croaked in a husky whisper, and his shoulders slumped. "Not Sarah." He put one hand over his eyes.

"Do you need to sit down?"

Wagner shook his head, his eyes bleak. "You've—there's got to be some mistake."

"Do you think you're up to viewing a photo of the body? We need identification, and the sooner we get that, the faster we can find out what happened."

Wagner nodded and Durant, low-voiced, told Coleman to use his cell phone, and to take the picture from the left side. The least damaged side, but still...

Coleman hurried away, and Durant continued to question Wagner, who apparently couldn't remember exactly when his wife had left their house near Royer Park in Roseville. His best estimate was sometime between nine and ten.

When Durant pressed him about their argument, Wagner rubbed the back of his neck and looked across the lawn, toward the patio. "It was just one of those husband and wife things, you know? It was pretty late when I got home, and I'd had quite a bit to drink. We got into a big argument."

"That's all? Just words?"

Wagner opened his mouth to speak, closed it, then opened it again. "I was just trying to keep her from leaving. She was too upset to be driving."

Dee raised her eyebrows. Wagner had already told them he'd driven around last night, despite having spent the better part of the evening drinking. Apparently he thought that was okay. Dee noted his lean build. Six-foot-one, maybe two. Big enough to easily overpower a woman, especially a small one.

"She accidentally fell and hit her head against the dresser," Wagner said. "But she was okay."

Durant stepped back a pace and started to read Wagner his rights.

Wagner held out an upraised hand, his palm toward Durant. "What are you doing? Detective, you're making a mistake. And I don't care about my rights or a lawyer. I don't have anything to hide. I could never hurt Sarah."

"You just told us you injured her."

Wagner flushed. "I only grabbed her wrist. I didn't want her to drive until she calmed down, but somehow, she...I don't know exactly how it happened, but she kind of fell against the dresser and hit her face. I wanted to look at it, to see how bad it was, but she jerked away from me and started running."

The expression on Durant's face prompted him to add, "She wasn't afraid of me. She was mad. She has a really bad temper."

"There's a Lexus in the garage. Is that hers?"

"No, that's Caro's. Sarah was driving my old Ford Explorer. We have keys to both cars on our key rings, but I'd parked behind her and—" He broke off when Coleman returned and gave the cell phone to Durant. Wagner stared at it much as he might have watched a coiled rattlesnake, his gaze locked on it as it moved from Coleman's hand to Durant's.

Durant glanced at the image, hesitated, and extended it toward Wagner. "I have to warn you, it will be difficult to look at, but we need to know if it's your wife."

Wagner nodded and held out a trembling hand. He closed his fingers around the phone, took a deep breath and closed his eyes, opened them, and stared at the photo. His eyes widened and his jaw dropped.

"That's not Sarah. It's Caro."

"Caro? You mean Caroline Brenhauser?" Durant asked. "The aunt? I thought you said she was out of the country."

"She is. She was. At least, I thought she was. So did Sarah." He swallowed. "What the hell is going on? Where is my wife?"

When Dee, relieved of further duty, finally turned toward her patrol car, she could feel Coleman's gaze on her back—probably lower. He would find an excuse to call her later. She resolved not to look back at him. A hard man to discourage. She wondered why he still bothered. Probably because she kept talking to him. He was a good source of information.

She replayed her actions as she drove back to the police station. Being first responder and the only officer on a scene was always challenging. Setting priorities proved difficult when every task was a priority. She always tried to stay focused on each step, but even that required flexibility and judgment, depending on the specifics of each case.

She hoped Durant had liked today's work. It might make a difference when she applied for the Detective Division job.

Her thoughts shifted to Scott Wagner. Did he break the woman's neck? He had behaved like a man worried, maybe even scared, not like a murderer. But she knew little about murderers. Maybe Scott Wagner was just a damned good actor.

She talked to Dave Wheeler about it when they met for dinner that night, at the Riverside Grill in old-town Sacramento. Dave was a detective assigned to Property Crimes.

A casual observer might have mistaken them for siblings, rather than friends. Both had lean builds, long legs, short brown hair and brown eyes—Dee's a color Dave described as "old copper."

She had delicate, sculpted features, while Dave's, slightly more florid and broad, betrayed the Irish in his family tree. In strong sunlight, her straight hair still looked almost chocolate-brown, while his unruly curls held a hint of red-gold.

"It was the darndest thing," she told him, as she tasted her Cabernet. "You should have seen the expression on Matt Coleman's face. In his own mind, he'd already decided that the husband had murdered his wife, then we discovered the dead woman wasn't even his wife."

"So, did Durant cut the guy loose?"

"After he got through questioning him. But if it turns out to be murder, I think Scott Wagner is going to be at the top of Durant's suspect list. He doesn't have an alibi."

"I don't get it," Dave said. "Why Durant thought the description of the women fit, with the age difference."

"Well, think about it. Both of them were petite, had long red-blonde hair, gray eyes." Dee set her wine glass on the table, a little too hard. It tilted; part of the base rested on the knife tip. She grabbed it and moved it onto the tablecloth. "She fell on her face, but the body and hands looked like a young woman's." She shook her head. "You've got to remember, she hadn't been thoroughly examined yet. She hadn't even been removed from the scene."

Dave slathered a big chunk of butter onto his sourdough bread. "So where's the wife?"

"I don't know. She hasn't been gone long enough for a missing persons report." Dee tore off a piece of bread and glanced at the butter. No, too many calories. She nibbled at the bread. It was good; it didn't need any butter.

"Maybe she's hiding out from an abusive husband," she continued. "I don't think I've ever seen Coleman so bummed out. I think he felt like Durant strung him along at the crime scene. Durant never agreed with him. Never disagreed, either. I think he was just having fun with Coleman's reactions."

Dave grinned, eyeing the bread basket. "Durant can be a real jerk sometimes, but it sounds like Coleman needed a lesson."

"He needs more than one. He jumps to conclusions. Gets an idea into his head, and you couldn't blow it out with a carload of TNT. And he can be so sexist. I don't know how he ever made detective. He's not a bad guy, really, just—"

"Just not as good as me, right?" Dave laughed. "I'll bet he was in a foul mood."

"Foul? You've never seen foul. I tried to talk to him about it, but he snapped at everything I said, so I shut up."

Dave grinned. "You're going to make a great wife for somebody, you know that? A woman who knows when to shut up? Worth her weight in diamonds. In gold. In rubies—" He ducked the wadded napkin she threw at him. "But you've got to learn to control that temper. I can see why he thinks you're a little shrewish."

"Shrewish? He said that? You think I'm shrewish? You're all alike, you—you pigs." She looked for something else to throw, considered the bread, realized other patrons were watching and changed her mind. She really needed to watch her conduct.

"Pigs? Oh, Dee." He put his hand over his heart. "That hurts. That really hurts. We cop pigs don't like to be called pigs, you know. People stopped calling us that a long time ago, and now you're starting it again? Poor Matt probably resented your smirking."

"I don't smirk. I just thought it served him right. Maybe next time he won't be so quick about jumping to conclusions."

"Maybe it's that twisted lip thing you do when you're trying not to laugh. Looks like a smirk." Dave tilted his chair back, and Dee, seeing the humor sparkling in his amber-ringed brown eyes, almost smiled.

She resisted the impulse until after she delivered her response: "I'm not smirking. I'm thinking. Something you might consider doing sometime."

He raised his eyebrows. "Oh? What are you thinking?"

"A couple of things. Durant says he doesn't believe anybody can read faces. I was watching Wagner's when he looked at that photo. I think Durant's right. Wagner reacted, but I couldn't tell whether the expression on his face was shock, anger, grief, relief, surprise—you name it."

"And the other thing?"

"I'm wondering. It seems odd. Do you suppose there's any connection between the wife going missing about the same time her aunt dies?"

Dave lowered the legs on his chair and sat up straight. "It'll be interesting to see how it plays out. Hard to get into Durant's mind. But if she doesn't show up soon, and the M.E. decides the woman was murdered, you can bet your life he'll be looking into two possibilities. One, she's dead. Two, she's the killer."

Chapter 4

The sun peeked above the horizon, casting a red glow as it climbed higher. A ray found the still form of Allison Sarah Wagner and touched her tangled hair, turning it red-gold. It inched up to her face, where it lingered, stroking her bruised jaw before it crept up to her left eye.

She stirred and stretched her legs, pushing them deeper into the sleeping bag.

Sleeping bag? Her eyes popped open. She stared at the interior of the Explorer. Dear God! Did she really go to sleep with Dirty Fingernails out there? She couldn't have; she was too scared.

But she had been so tired, and she'd lain still for a long time. Maybe she had dozed off for a few minutes. It couldn't have been long. The sky had gradually faded from deepest black to slate, to pale gray. Only then had she relaxed into the downy—and increasingly warm—cocoon of the sleeping bag.

And went to sleep. She shook her head, still not quite believing it. *Well, it's daylight now, chicken. Time to crawl out of your hidey-hole and do something.*

She climbed into the front seat and tried again to work the key out of the ignition. It wouldn't budge. She removed the key ring and the rest of the keys, put them in her pocket and eyed the rear-view mirror. The bruise had turned purple around the edges, and she had dark circles under her eyes. Maybe if she washed up, she'd feel better.

She climbed out of the vehicle and headed for the casino ladies' room. After cleaning up as best she could, she went in search of a telephone and called her cousin.

"Want to go out for breakfast?" she asked Laura.

"I thought—aren't you in Sacramento?"

"No, I never got there. I'm in the Explorer, and it won't start. I don't have my Triple-A card. No driver's license, either. I thought maybe I'd throw myself on your mercy. Could you take me home so I can pick them up? Then I'll take you to breakfast. My treat."

Laura was silent for a few seconds. "Sarah, I can't. At least, not right now. I'm on my way to meet a client. I promised to show him several houses this morning, here in Folsom."

"How long do you think it'll take?"

"Couple of hours, at least. Probably longer. I hope a lot longer. I need to make a sale."

"Okay, do whatever you gotta do. You can't call me back, so when you get through with your client, would you swing by the casino and pick me up? I'll be in the Explorer, out at the edge of the parking lot."

"Okay. I'll be there as soon as I can. I'd come now, Sarah, but I really can't afford—"

"I know." Sarah grabbed for the phone she'd almost dropped when a hefty, doughy-skinned woman bumped her. "Don't worry about it. Just don't forget me."

"Hah. Not likely."

A smile tugged at the corner of Sarah's mouth. "I don't know what I'd do without you."

"Me, neither, Cuz. Stay put, and don't pick up any stray studs."

"Yeah, right." If Laura only knew. Sarah hung up and considered her options. She wanted—no, needed—coffee. She headed for the food court, counting her change. She'd lost a little money in the slot machines but still had enough for a large coffee and a cinnamon-apple muffin.

She took them back to the Explorer, ate, and tugged at the stuck ignition key again, with no success. She needed a pair of pliers. When had she last seen the toolbox? Had it been there when she started loading the camping gear? It didn't matter; she couldn't find it now.

It would be hours before Laura arrived. Sarah didn't know what she'd do without Laura and Caro; she didn't have much family left, other than her cousin and aunt. Just her dad and grandmother—and Anna. Sarah's fingers tightened into fists when she thought about the woman her dad had married, the woman who had finally driven fifteen-year-old Sarah out of her childhood home.

It had been fourteen years, and the image was still seared into her memory—a slow-motion movie that played every time she thought about her father and Anna, who used to be their next-door neighbor. Anna, who had given both Sarah and her father quick hugs before she left the hospital waiting room the night of the accident.

"Call me if you need me," she had murmured into Sarah's ear.

Sarah had stood, motionless, trying not to flinch, wondering why Anna was there. She didn't like Sarah's mom, any more than her mom liked Anna.

Sarah had turned toward her father to ask him but changed her mind when she saw his pale face. "Dad? Are you okay?"

"What? Oh, yes, I'm okay. I just—I think I need some air. I'm going outside. I might as well make some calls while I'm out there."

"Okay. I'll be in there." She nodded toward the closed door of the intensive care unit.

She announced herself and went in, knowing her father would go to the car for his pipe and tobacco. He rarely smoked it, but tonight he needed the solace he would find in the familiar feel of the burled wood and the smell of the tobacco. Wishing she had something like that to comfort her, she watched the monitors surrounding her mother's bed.

The doctor came in, carrying a chart. Sarah stood aside while he examined her mother. She started to ask a question, then stopped, her mouth still open. She would never know how she knew—how he conveyed the message. His eyes first, she thought. That look of compassion and something else. Dread, she realized. Because he had to find the right words.

Glad she knew where to find her father, she stumbled outside, from the brightly-lit hospital lobby to the semi-darkness of the parking lot. She would have to hurry; there wasn't much time.

Angling through the parked cars, she paid little attention to her surroundings until she caught a whiff of his pipe tobacco, then the scent of his Aqua Velva. Her mind still lingered in the room with her mother and the message she had to deliver.

The parking lot lights cast shadows beyond the circumference of their pale glow, and her father stood in one of those darkened areas. Had he not held Anna so close, their bodies merged into one, Sarah might have realized he wasn't alone. Not until she was within a few feet of them did she realize he was kissing Anna—a long, deep, hungry kiss.

Sarah had escaped back into the hospital, never delivering the doctor's message: to come quickly—his wife was dying. Numb, her face frozen with shock, she stood by her mother's bed, holding her hand until she took her last breath. Then she left the hospital and went to find Caro and Laura, who had kept their own vigil, in another hospital, in another intensive care unit.

Allison, Sarah's mother and Caro's older sister, was only the first to die that night. Within two hours, Caro's husband Roger slipped away, and in the early morning hours of the next day, Laura's father, David, Caro's older brother, was gone.

Much of their family had been wiped out in that single accident. Laura still had her mother and a few relatives on that side of the family, but Caro had lost her husband and both siblings. She had only Sarah and Laura and Laura's little boys.

Sarah's face softened when she thought about Eric and Jamie, just eight and six.

Her eyes felt gritty and she considered tilting the seat back and taking a nap. She'd be too conspicuous. On the other hand, she'd had little sleep the night before and could do nothing but wait for the next few hours. Why not? She climbed into the back and burrowed into the sleeping bag.

When Laura arrived, at about eleven, Sarah was standing outside the Explorer, leaning against the driver's door, waiting. Laura pulled her faded blue eight-year-old Honda alongside Sarah and rolled down the windows "What the hell happened to you?" she asked, taking in Sarah's rumpled clothes, tangled hair, and bruised jaw.

Sarah crossed her arms on the bottom of the Honda's open window frame and laid her chin on top of them. "It's a long, long story and I don't know where to start. But for right now, could you take me home to get my driver's license and Triple-A card?"

"Do you know how strange that sounds? If you don't have your license, you shouldn't need your Triple-A card."

Sarah shrugged, and Laura said, "Yeah, I know. It's a long, long story." She leaned across the seat, a dark curl swinging across her shoulder as she opened the passenger door. "Get in."

"Kind of bossy, aren't you?" Sarah got in and fastened her seat belt.

"Looks to me like you need a boss—or a warden. But then, you already have one, don't you? Tell me what happened with Scott." Glancing behind the car, she backed out of the parking space. "It's the same old story, isn't it? The ongoing contest for Jerk of the Month. Or maybe the year. Or even the decade."

Sarah slid down in her seat. "Okay, Laura, I get it, and Scott is not the jerk you think he is. Our fight was partly my fault."

She stroked her jaw, images flooding her mind as she related the story to Laura. She'd left work a few minutes early, eager to get started on their camping trip—their time to get away and reconnect—work out some of their problems. They'd loaded most of the gear into the Explorer the night before, and as soon as Scott drove it home from work, she would add the food and other last-minute items. She had it all packed and ready to go.

He was late, probably caught in Friday night traffic. As the hours ticked by and she worried about an accident, tried his cell phone, and thought about calling the hospital, she pushed down the thought bubbling its way to the surface: there was no accident. Scott was sitting in a bar again.

He was temperamental when he'd been drinking. It would be best to avoid a confrontation until he sobered up. She was tired anyway, so she went to bed, hoping to be asleep by the time he got home.

A bump jarred her awake. Scott, stumbling down the hall. He'd fallen off the wagon again, despite all his promises.

"Hey babe, you asleep? C'mon. Wake up and let's go. Hit the road."

She didn't answer.

"Hey, get your lazy butt out of bed. We gotta get this stuff packed up." He nudged her leg, stumbled and fell, his arm thudding into her chest.

Anger surged, erasing her resolution to wait until morning. "Damn it, Scott. What the hell do you think you're doing?"

The confrontation escalated from there, her telling him precisely what she thought about his behavior, and him yelling words he never would have uttered, had he been sober. At the end, she jerked away from him and ran, grabbing his set of keys from the kitchen counter on the way out the door.

She glanced at Laura as she finished the story, but her cousin didn't say anything. Sarah untied the shoelace and ran her fingers through her hair. "I shouldn't have lost my temper. It makes him mad, and he says things he doesn't mean. I know he loves me."

"Yeah, I can see the evidence. Along with the stylish thrown-together-and-slept-in look you're sporting, you have a coordinating bruise. I've got news for you, Sarah. Good guys don't leave bruises on their wives. Even Sam, in all the time we were married, never did that." She turned out of the parking lot and headed for I-80 East.

Sarah put her hand to her jaw. "It was an accident. I fell."

Laura studied Sarah, amber-brown eyes calculating. "You know, you can tell me what really happened. It's not like I'm going to call the cops or anything–much as I might want to."

Sarah shook her head in frustration. Laura didn't believe her, and she didn't know how to make her understand. "That's really what happened. Scott wouldn't hurt me." She grabbed Laura's purse. "Do you have a comb? I'd pay fifty bucks for a comb right now. If I had any money, that is."

"They're cheaper at the shop in the casino. Why didn't you buy one there? Oh—I forgot. No purse."

"Why didn't you tell me they have a store that sells that kind of stuff?"

"You didn't ask, and I didn't know you needed one." Laura dug a comb out of her purse and tossed it to Sarah. "If what you're telling me about Scott is true, why are you sitting here in my car, bruised and gnarly, early on a Saturday morning? Instead of inside your snug little house, in your snug little life with your husband who wouldn't hurt you?"

Sarah worked the comb through the snarls in her hair—no easy task. She didn't know how to answer Laura's question. How could she make Laura understand?

But Laura didn't wait for an answer. "Because you were afraid he would hurt you. You ran to get away from him. To get someplace safe. You ran so fast, you left your money, your license, your phone."

Was that true? Sarah wasn't sure. While it was clear Scott was becoming increasingly more volatile when he drank, Sarah knew how to avoid confrontations. This time, she'd let her temper get away from her. Even as she had grabbed his keys on her way out of the house, fumbling to find her Corolla key on the ring, it was more anger than fear that drove her, and escalated when she saw the Explorer parked behind her Corolla, blocking her exit. It was a good thing she'd had to take the Explorer, though. It would have been an even more miserable night without that sleeping bag.

Laura's cell phone rang. She grabbed it and glanced at the display. "Scott. He doesn't give up. That's the third time he's called in the last hour. You'd think he'd get the hint." She dropped it back in her purse.

"I shouldn't have run away, but I have so little patience and too much temper."

Laura groaned. "Don't you dare start believing it's all your fault."

"Maybe it's not, but it wouldn't happen if I could stay calm until he's sober." She almost winced, thinking about how her words would sound to Laura. She wasn't an abused wife. Laura simply didn't understand. She didn't know what Scott was really like, how sweet he could be, always had been. They just had to get past this rough patch.

Laura sighed. "Yeah. He suddenly realizes what he's done, gathers you in his arms, tells you he loves you, asks for forgiveness–until the next time, that is—and everything is peachy."

"Shut up." Sarah's neck and cheeks felt hot. "It's just–I get mad and we fight. That's why I wanted to go to Caro's. I thought it might be good for him, me not coming home. Jolt him into thinking a little more about what he's doing."

Laura signaled and took the on-ramp to I-80.

"Then I realized I didn't have Caro's house key," Sarah continued. "It took me a while to remember the one on the patio."

"I wish you'd called earlier, before Scott did. I wouldn't have been so worried."

Sarah rested her hand on Laura's shoulder. "I'm sorry. I thought if I told you where I was, I'd be putting you in the middle of it, and I didn't want to do that. I didn't think it would occur to him to look for me at the casino, but I couldn't be sure."

Hiding the Explorer in the unlit parking area had been another big mistake. She shuddered. She had allowed her anger to overwhelm her good judgment. "Then I had to call you, anyway, about the key."

"Next time–and there will be a next time–call me, no matter what. Better yet, I'll have a copy of my house key made, so you can get in when you need to. I'll move some of Jamie's and Eric's toys, so there's room to put your car in the garage."

"Laura, you don't need to do that."

"Yeah, I do. That way, Scott won't see it, he won't know you're there, and you'll be in a safe place."

Sarah stared out the car window, fighting back tears, touched by her cousin's concern, but also frustrated because Laura could not—or would not—understand.

Chapter 5

She would never be able to make Laura see what Scott was really like. She didn't know why she still tried. Those attempts simply led to uncomfortable conversations, not the kind she usually had with her cousin. But Laura's suggestion that Sarah park inside the garage was not a bad idea.

She massaged Laura's shoulder. "Yes, ma'am. What makes you old people so bossy?"

Laura smiled, a little half-smile. "That's wisdom, child. You'll understand when you grow up a little."

"Wisdom?" Sarah grinned. "That's age creeping up on you, Cuz. Haven't you looked in the mirror lately?" she teased. "Noticed the sagging jawbone, not to mention other parts of the anatomy?"

"Hey. I can take you down, any day."

Sarah handed the comb back to Laura, appraising her thirty-two-year-old cousin. "Yeah, you do pretty well, for an old woman. A few lines around the eyes, and those deep furrows in the forehead, not to mention those crevices around the mouth."

Laura dropped the comb into her purse. "Hey, if I look tired, it's your fault."

"Yeah, I know. I'm sorry."

"No, I didn't mean..." Laura shook her head. "Well, yes, I did keep expecting you to call, or to show up, but—Sarah, I had a dream."

Sarah looked more intently at Laura's face. "What kind of dream?"

"I don't know, but it scared the hell out of me, and I couldn't go back to sleep. I saw a guy coming toward you, and you had your back turned. You didn't see him. It was all shadows, and I tried to tell you to run. Scream at you to run. But I couldn't make a sound. Or maybe you couldn't hear me. I don't know."

The hairs on the back of Sarah's neck prickled. "Dirty Fingernails." She told Laura the story.

"What I can't figure out is why he was hitting on me, the way I look? Ratty hair and—what did you call it? The latest in laundry pile chic? You gotta be kidding."

"Sarah, Sarah. Don't you know guys like that never even see your face? Or your hair? They see prey. If he had to describe you, all he'd remember is the size of your boobs." She grinned. "You know what? We should go back in there every night until we find him. You can lure him out to the parking lot, and I'll help you beat him to a bloody pulp."

Sarah laughed. "We can go into business for ourselves, hunting down and beating up the world's creeps and perverts. Make the world safe for women everywhere. Take back the night. Make use of our karate classes."

"What karate classes?"

"The ones we'll take, of course. We can write 'em off as a business expense. We'll make a fortune and quit our jobs. First California Bank of the Pacific Rim will give me a big retirement party, tell me how much they'll miss their smartest and most valuable and gorgeous—not to mention sexy—skip tracer."

Laura, eyebrows arched, assessed Sarah's body. "Right."

"You won't have to sell houses anymore, and I can tell supervisor Bertram Iverson to take a long, running jump off the bank's rooftop garden." She glanced at Laura's purse. "You got any lipstick in there?"

"Yeah, in the cosmetic bag. Not exactly your shade, though."

Sarah applied the lipstick, blotted it on a tissue, and dropped the case back in Laura's bag.

Settling deeper into the seat, she looked out the window at the housing that had been built over the last decade. Roseville looked like a flotilla of rooftops. "All California Beige," she murmured.

"What?" Laura turned her head.

"California Beige. All the developments, all the houses are some shade of beige. Dark beige, light beige, rose beige, sand beige, yellow beige–all beige. I think there must be something in the building code that requires beige. If somebody painted a house blue, with white trim, their homeowners' association would haul them into court for color pollution."

"Color pollution?"

"Yes, color pollution. We must keep our color environment clean and unsullied. We cannot allow the purity of desert beige–never mind that Northen California is not desert—to be polluted by blue, or green, or pink. How long before somebody decides to paint their house—gasp, choke—white?"

"You need to grab your neck and wheeze when you do the gasp choke bit." Laura clasped her own neck with one hand to demonstrate. "Looks like those high-school drama classes paid off. And everybody thought they were such a waste."

A few miles farther, Sarah said, "You know, I think that's what I like about Caro's neighborhood. The houses are all so individual."

"You love it, don't you? Her house?"

"Yeah." Sarah hesitated. "Partly because it was home to me after Caro took me in, after—after Anna."

Laura was silent for a few minutes, then changed the subject. "Are you planning to talk to Scott when you get there? Or just get your stuff and split?"

"I don't know. We have to talk, but I'd rather not do it right now. Maybe I'll stay at your place tonight if it's okay with you. We can make plans for our new butt-kicking business."

It would be risky. Scott would be angry if she didn't come home, but she had to get away from him for a day or two, so she could think.

"I saw you falling."

Sarah, watching the sun glint off the auburn highlights in Laura's dark, curly hair, shifted her gaze to Laura's face. "Falling? I didn't fall."

"My dream. You fell. I couldn't see anything except you, floating out through space, grabbing at something, your hair loose and flying across your face."

"That's weird. Your dreams spook me sometimes."

"Me too. I'd rather not have ones like that. I wonder why I inherited that particular little family trait and you didn't? But the dream—it seemed so real."

Sarah shuddered. All through her childhood, the family had told stories about her grandmother's dreams—dreams portending significant events in the lives of those she loved.

"I wish you didn't have that trait, either, especially if you're going to have scary dreams about me." Sarah turned to stare out the window again as Laura took the Douglas Boulevard exit, only vaguely aware of the familiar scene. They passed Roseville Square with its small shops, and turned right, toward Royer Park. "Somehow, I think I got the best of it. No strange dreams, no fear of heights, like Caro. The bars and the beam never bothered me in gymnastics, and I did get the brains, after all. I'd much rather have my brains than your dreams."

"Brains? You? That's impossible. You can't have brains. You're a natural blonde. With boobs."

"You're a natural brunette with boobs, which makes you what? A half-wit?"

Laura swung her right arm toward Sarah in a fake blow. Sarah batted it away. "Your dream was wrong. I'm okay. I didn't fall or anything." Except when she kicked at Dirty Fingernails and almost lost her balance. Only his grip on her arm had held her erect. Icy prickles crept up the back of her neck.

Laura turned right again on a leafy street and slowed as she worked her way through the neighborhood toward Sarah's house. They passed two- and three- bedroom cottages, separated from the street by short driveways and small patches of lawn decorated with bicycles and doll strollers.

Sarah knew the floor plans, though smaller, would be much like her own 1950's era home, with a living room, dining area, kitchen, bathroom and two or three bedrooms.

They passed a brick house, then a pale green stucco with forest-green trim. The white lap siding of the next house served as a perfect backdrop for the multicolored Dianthus blooming in a flowerbed by the door. Sarah smiled as they neared her own cream-colored stucco with brick trim. She loved the fireplace, the big picture window that looked out on her flowerbeds, and her backyard patio. Thinking about the two airy bedrooms and one tiny bath jolted her with the realization that she didn't want to go home. Her haven, her sanctuary at the end of a long workday, now felt more like a cage. "Want to go to Reno? Sam would probably be glad to have the boys."

Laura pulled into Sarah's driveway, next to a rock-lined flowerbed filled with pink and white carnations and blue pincushion flowers. "He's already got them. Picked them up after school yesterday."

"Then we've got the rest of the weekend. We could gamble, maybe catch a show, go to one of the buffets for dinner."

Laura turned off the ignition. "I don't have any clothes with me. Or any money, with me or anywhere else. Not for stuff like that. With the boys, money is always tight."

"I know. Ours is, too, even with both of us working. It seems like it gets worse every month." She unfastened her seat belt. At least Eric and Jamie didn't support the breweries. And the wineries. And the bars. If she had any money, she'd invest it in booze. "I have a little bit stashed away." She opened the front door of the house and put a finger to her lips. "Shhh."

She took off her shoes and tiptoed down the carpeted hall, careful to step over the creaky spot near the bathroom. She entered the bedroom, expecting to see Scott sprawled across the bed, trying to catch up on the sleep he'd lost the night before.

The room was empty. It looked much like she'd left it: the bed unmade, one corner of the blue-and-cream comforter dragging onto the carpet. Her purse still hung on the back of the blue chair. Had he even gone to bed? She checked the rest of the house, then rejoined Laura in the living room.

"Scott's not here, but that's okay. It makes it easier. I'll leave him a note." It wouldn't be okay with Scott, but right now, Sarah didn't care. "Come and help me pack."

Laura opened the door to the garage and stuck her head out. "Your car's gone." She followed Sarah to the bedroom. "I can't go to Reno, Sarah. I don't have a stash. Not unless I raid the kids' piggy banks."

"I'd report you for bank robbery. We can spend the night at your house instead if you'd rather, but Scott has an offer for a free night at the Peppermill. All I have to do is call and get a reservation. We don't have to gamble much. We could play the penny slots. Or we could go to Tahoe, if you'd rather, and drive around the lake. It's not that far, and we'd have so much fun." She pulled jeans and t-shirts out of the closet, dumped some underwear on top, and reached for her cosmetic kit.

"I'm going to jump in the shower." She pulled her shirt over her head. "Grab my overnight bag from the garage and dump that stuff in it, will you? I'll be out in a couple of minutes and finish it up."

By the time Sarah got out of the shower, Laura had the bag neatly packed. Sarah grabbed a few things from drawers and tossed them in, and picked up the tissue box beside her night stand. She worked the tip of a fingernail file under the glued flap at the end, lifted it, and pulled the tissues from the box. She removed the bills from the middle of the stack, slid the tissues back in, and pressed down the flap.

"Sneaky. But why do you hide money from Scott?"

Sarah couldn't readily think of an explanation, and it was really none of Laura's business. "Well, it's kind of complicated."

"Every time you say something's complicated, it turns out Scott is controlling it. He controls all the money, too, doesn't he?"

"It's easier that way." Sarah inspected the flap, placed the box back on the night stand, grabbed her purse and dumped the bills inside. "Ready? We can go have breakfast and get the car key unstuck, then decide."

"I've been thinking about it while you were in the shower. How long it's been since we did something fun together." Laura picked up her purse. "You have the free room, and if we get an early start tomorrow, I can be home before Sam brings Eric and Jamie back. We'd miss all the traffic coming down the hill." She nodded at the family pictures on the wall. "Maybe we could even stop and see your grandmother. I'd love to see that old house again–those hidden beds, the stamped-tin ceiling, and all that old wood paneling."

Sarah shook her head. "I don't think so, Laura. Nan's a little put out with me." Sarah opened the front door. "She doesn't think I try hard enough to get along with the wicked witch."

"With Anna? I don't understand. I didn't think your grandmother liked Anna. Especially after the way she treated you when—"

"All a long time ago. I'm not fifteen anymore, and Nan expects me to—" Sarah lifted her fingers to indicate quotation marks. "—to be a little more mature, a little more understanding, a little more forgiving. She suggested this might be a good time to get together–to try to mend fences—while Caro is gone. Want to open the trunk?"

Laura moved an assortment of softball gloves, bats, and balls, to make space for Sarah's bag. "A little more understanding? I don't think you had any problem understanding. You're supposed to forgive what you saw the night your mom died? Your world had been turned upside down, and your dad and Anna were so wrapped up in each other, in more ways than one—"

"All our lives changed that night. Not just mine."

"But I still had my mom. You didn't. You got Anna."

"And you lost your dad. I guess I did, too, really. I lost them both that night." She shook her head. Too long ago to dwell on. She put her bag in the trunk and closed the lid. "I went to see Nan a few months ago. Dad and Anna were off on a cruise—some kind of vacation Anna had won. That's the only reason I went. I knew I wouldn't run into them. Anyway, I had a long visit with Nan. She's upset because I don't have much to do with Dad anymore."

"But don't your feelings count?"

Sarah stared into the distance. "When Dad married Anna, it was like Mom never existed. I was lucky I had Caro to take me in and give me a real home."

Laura hugged her. "Caro needed you as much as you needed her. I'm not sure she could have made it without you to worry about. She didn't have much left after that accident."

"Maybe. But enough of that. Come on, let's go have some fun."

Laura took a few quick steps so she could check behind the car—a habit she'd developed after the boys got old enough to leave toys in the driveway.

A car braked at the curb and she muttered, "Uh-oh. Busted."

Chapter 6

Sarah, about to get into the passenger seat of Laura's car, turned to look. Scott had arrived, driving her Corolla. She glanced at Laura and sighed. She'd have to talk to him now; she couldn't put it off. But she wasn't ready. She needed more time. She needed to think.

He got out and strode toward them. Grim-faced, he forced his way past Laura, who had tried to step between them and wrapped his arms around Sarah. "You're all right. Thank God." His hoarse voice cracked a little. He laid his forehead against hers and stroked her hair.

She took a step back. "Of course I'm all right. What's wrong with you? Why are you acting so weird?"

"I thought...I thought you were dead and after last night, I thought I'd never forgive myself."

What was wrong with him? "Dead? Why would you think that?"

He held her away from him so he could look into her eyes, and she noticed the strain in his jaw muscles. "Honey, I have bad news—terrible news. I don't know how to tell you. We'd better go in the house."

Sarah felt the same sense of foreboding she'd experienced the night her mother died. Had something happened to her grandmother? Her father? Why didn't he tell her?

"Laura, you too." Scott unlocked the door and pulled Sarah into the living room.

"What is it?" Sarah asked. "What's wrong? Tell me."

"I couldn't find you, and I thought maybe you went to Caro's." He plowed ahead, the words coming fast now. "I drove down there this morning. The cops were...Sarah, there was an accident. A bad one."

Sarah swallowed. Her stomach felt queasy. "What kind of accident? Caro's not even home."

"She came home early. Sometime last night."

"No, she didn't." Caro would have called if she'd changed her plans. The queasiness in Sarah's stomach had moved up to her throat. She pushed away from him.

Laura said, "Scott, you're scaring us. Whatever it is, spit it out."

"I don't know how else to say this. Caro is dead. A jogger found her this morning, on the patio." He glanced at Laura. "I tried to call you, to let you know."

Sarah backed away from him, warding him off with her hands. "No. No. There's some mistake."

"I've already identified her. It's Caro. There's no mistake."

Laura gasped and reached for Sarah. Sarah's knees gave way, and Scott tried to catch her, but Laura got there first. She wrapped her arms around her cousin's trembling body, and they both stood in the middle of the living room, weeping. Scott held both of them until their sobs had subsided to silent tears, then led them to the sofa. He tore some tissues from a box, handed the box to Laura, and used the tissues to wipe Sarah's face.

"You said they found her on the patio?" Sarah asked, her voice thick with tears.

"They think she fell through the deck railing."

Laura's eyes widened. "My dream. It wasn't you, Sarah. I didn't see you falling. It was Caro. I just couldn't see her face in my dream."

"But it doesn't make any sense. Caro wouldn't have been anywhere near that railing. Not unless it was by the stairs."

"Sarah's right," Laura said. "Caro's fear of heights wouldn't have allowed her to stand that close to the edge. I should know. I inherited that same fear of open space beneath me."

"I have to see her," Sarah said. "I have to know–to be sure."

Scott frowned. "I already identified her. And she's at the morgue. I don't think it's a good idea."

"Scott, you don't understand," Laura said. "It's something we need to do. Is there any good reason why we can't?"

"Okay, I'll find out." He patted his shirt pockets until he found Durant's card, pulled out his cell phone and punched in the numbers. "Detective, this is Scott Wagner. My wife and her cousin want to see their aunt's—Caroline Brenhauser's body. They're having a hard time—" He ran his fingers through his hair. His gold wedding band glinted in a ray of sunlight shining through the picture window. "Yes. Yes, she was home." He glanced at Sarah and frowned. "I don't know. I just got here and I had to tell her about her aunt before I could call you." His hand stopped at the back of his head, smoothing down his hair as he listened. "Yeah. I never thought about that. I think you're right. I'll explain it to them."

Laura whispered, "It doesn't sound like he—" Sarah squeezed her hand. She wanted to hear Scott's end of the conversation.

"Today?" He shook his head. "I don't understand." He glanced at Sarah and Laura and shrugged, an exaggerated motion that brought his shoulders almost even with the bottoms of his earlobes.

He put a hand over the phone. "He's planning to come up and talk to you tomorrow morning, but if you're willing to drive down there this afternoon—"

Sarah nodded. She couldn't imagine trying to get through a long and sleepless night, not knowing what had happened to Caro.

Scott was back on the phone to the detective. "Okay. What time? Three o'clock? I see." He looked at Laura, his eyebrows raised in a question and held up four fingers. She nodded. "Yes, they'll be there."

He put the phone in his pocket. "We won't be able to visit the morgue. They're going to be doing an autopsy, to try to pin down the cause of death. He says it's not a good idea, anyway. She—her face was damaged in the fall. You don't want to see her until—well, until later, after they release her to the mortuary and they have her ready for viewing."

Sarah tried to swallow the lump in her throat. "I really need to see her. I'll never truly believe it until I do."

Scott drew in a deep breath. "Sarah, I know it's hard to accept, but Caro's gone. I identified her at the house and talked to the detectives, but they still need to speak to you and Laura. Detective Durant says he'll try to answer all your questions at your meeting this afternoon—you at three, Laura at four."

Sarah glanced at her watch. One ten. Almost two hours to wait, and she'd spent most of the last eighteen hours doing that: waiting for Scott to get home, waiting for the hours to pass at the casino, waiting for daylight in the Explorer, waiting for Laura to pick her up. How had her life gone so terribly wrong in less than twenty-four hours?

But it hadn't been just the last twenty-four hours. It had all started years ago, with Richie. She didn't want to think about that now, didn't want to think about any of the people she'd lost, but she'd learned over the years that each death brought memories of all the others crashing down on her.

Her little brother had been only five years old when he died of bacterial meningitis. Sarah could no longer conjure an image of his face but, strangely, twenty-one years later, she could still see the freckles sprinkled across his small nose. Maybe because they matched her own, and she saw those every day. Or maybe because they had been so much starker that day, on his pale face.

She'd been angry with him. Mom had promised to take them to see *Homeward Bound*, but Richie didn't want to go. He had fallen asleep on the sofa, and Mom had a hard time waking him.

"I don't want to go to a stupid old movie," he grumbled. "I'm sleepy, and my head hurts."

Stupid old movie? Sarah and Richie had talked about little else all week. Now, all of a sudden he didn't want to go?

"You're stupid, too, and I hate you!" she yelled as she ran for the stairs. She sulked in her bedroom until a tap on the door told her Richie must have changed his mind; they were going to the movies, after all.

It was their regular babysitter, Becca, who stood in the doorway, not Mom. "Richie got worse," she said. "He woke up vomiting, and your mom took him to the hospital. Your dad is meeting her there."

"He's really sick?" Sarah's stomach felt like it was full of butterflies.

"The doctors are taking good care of him," Becca said. "What do you want for dinner? Your mom said we could order a pizza."

Sarah didn't want to go to bed that night–not 'til Mom and Dad brought Richie home–but Becca insisted; it was already past Sarah's bedtime. Fine. She would go to bed, but she wouldn't go to sleep. She had to tell Richie she was sorry. She didn't really hate him, and she didn't care about not seeing the dumb old movie. Well, maybe she wouldn't say it was dumb. Richie might still want to see it.

Sunlight flooded the room when she awoke. The house was quiet. Richie wasn't in his room, and his bed was already made. She ran downstairs to find him, then hesitated at the bottom.

Dad was supposed to be at work, not sitting there on the sofa, both arms around Mom, whose puffy, tear-streaked face rested on his shoulder. What was wrong? She felt the queasiness again.

They told her then. The doctors couldn't save Richie; he had died in the early morning hours. Sarah hadn't been able to stop the queasiness from boiling up into a hot, burning acid that had filled her throat and spewed from her mouth, even as she ran for the downstairs bathroom.

The doorbell rang, jerking her back to the present and the new, too-raw grief. Two high school girls, on a fund drive for a science club field trip. Scott gave them a few dollars, shut the door, and went to make coffee. Laura answered the bell twenty minutes later for delivery of a book Sarah had ordered.

She walked to the window. The boys next door were shooting baskets in their driveway. Their father rinsed his just-washed car with a garden hose. How could they be doing such ordinary things on a day like this one?

She'd experienced this sense of abrupt dislocation before, first when Richie died, then when she lost her mother. Once the reality of death got past her defenses, her denial, it had bludgeoned her senses, disrupting every thought, every plan, every routine. Caught in a time vacuum, she numbly watched others go about their lives, wanting to scream, "Stop! Don't you understand something terrible has happened? That the world will never be the same?"

But their worlds hadn't changed. They would go on with their routines: getting up, going to work, keeping appointments, taking their days off, spending time with their families. It was only her world that had shattered—again.

Only Scott and Laura shared her pain, her sense of loss. But, even as the thought flashed through her mind, she shook her head. Not Scott. He didn't share her pain; he just sympathized with it. Her gaze connected with Laura's. She and Laura then, just as it had been when their parents died, just as it had always been.

She wandered aimlessly through the house, trying to collect her thoughts, and ended at the wall near the fireplace, drawn by Caro's sketches—a collage of Sarah's childhood. Standing in front of them, she could almost feel Caro's arms around her, smell her vanilla-scented shampoo.

Despite Caro's undeniable talent, her parents—Sarah's grandparents—wouldn't let Caro go to art school. When Sarah asked why, Caro had said, in a flat voice, "They didn't approve."

But Caro had found a way.

Sarah dabbed a tissue at the tears running down her cheeks and went to wash her tear-stained face. She brushed her hair, staring at her reflection in the bathroom mirror: dull, red-rimmed eyes; the light dusting of freckles across a too-pale face, like Richie's the day he died.

That's what you have to do, Sarah; find your way.

She almost dropped the brush. Where did that come from? Find her way to what? The voice sounded like Caro. Sarah shivered and brushed her hair away from her face.

"You have a bad bruise." Scott stood in the doorway of the small bathroom, looking at her reflection in the mirror. "Is that from–"

"Yeah, but it's okay. Nothing serious." She set the brush on the counter.

"Sarah, I'm so sorry. I love you. You know that." He took a step forward, put his arms around her, and drew her back against his chest. "I'd never hurt you. Never."

"I know." She leaned into him, needing the comfort of his arms.

"If you could just remember...when I come home like that, wait until the next day to say anything, okay? You know I'm not very stable when I've had too much to drink, and I could hurt you, even if I don't mean to."

She pulled away, turning to face him. "So the bruise is my fault? Is that what you're saying? I'm supposed to let you do whatever you want, not say anything until you're sober?"

"Well, it would be better—"

"I don't need this. Especially now. Not today."

His eyes darkened and somewhere in the hurt anger that flooded through her, the voice, crystal clear, echoed again.

That's what you have to do, Sarah; find your way.

Chapter 7

At three o'clock that afternoon, Sarah was at the police station, sitting in a gray metal chair, one of a set of four arranged around a matching table, two on each side, in a room with bare walls. Shivering a little, she draped her pale-green cardigan around her shoulders. Her gaze drifted to the brown plastic tray in the middle of the table. Judging by the paper cups, creamer, sweetener and stirring sticks, the metal thermos contained hot coffee. She considered pouring a cup. No, better wait for an invitation.

The door swung open, and two men entered. She guessed, from his thinning hairline, the older one might be in his late forties, maybe fifties. His rumpled gray suit and wrinkled shirt matched his countenance; he looked tired. He placed a stack of papers on the table.

"Mrs. Wagner, I'm Detective Al Durant." He inclined his head toward the younger, better-groomed man with perfectly-coifed blond hair. "And this is Detective Matt Coleman. I want to tell you how sorry I am for your loss. I know this is difficult, especially so soon after your aunt's death, but it's necessary, so we can find out what happened to her."

Sarah shook hands with both of them, and they settled into chairs across the table. Durant's eyes assessed her, finally focusing on the purple bruise. She raised her hand to her face, but at the last moment, shifted it to her hair and pushed some loose strands from her forehead.

"My husband said you found her on the patio. She fell from the deck above it?"

"We're not sure. The railing was broken, but it's old and in need of repair. A slight push might have broken it. We don't know at this point whether she fell, jumped, or—"

"Jumped?" Sarah clutched her chair arms and leaned forward. "Caro wouldn't jump."

"Sometimes family isn't aware of emotional distress, Mrs. Wagner. It's been my experience that people usually don't want to burden those they love with their problems. Was your aunt well? Did she suffer from depression?"

"No. Caro was only forty-two. She was full of life. She loved her family, and she loved to sketch and paint. She didn't have any medical or emotional problems. She would have told us."

Durant pulled a pair of glasses out of his shirt pocket, settled them on his nose, and flipped through his notes. "Any other family?"

"No children. Her husband died in a car accident. May thirteenth, two-thousand, a Saturday."

Durant focused on her face, his eyebrows raised.

"My mother and Laura's father died in the same accident. Roger had asked them to go shopping, to help him pick out a present for Caro's twenty-ninth birthday. A drunk driver–"

"Oh, I'm sorry. Sorry to bring it up again." He lowered his head and made notes. "Did you know she planned to come home last night?"

"No, and that's what puzzles me. I talked to her Tuesday–no, Wednesday. She said she might go on to Paris. Said she wouldn't be home for another week, maybe ten days. She wanted to see Monet's *Water Lilies*." Sarah felt her voice thicken. She searched through her purse for a tissue. Why would Caro cut her trip short, before she saw the *Water Lilies*? What could be so pressing?

"Was that unusual? For her to come home unexpectedly?"

"Yes. We always knew her itinerary. I don't know why she cut this trip short or why she didn't let us know. That's not like her."

Sarah looked for a place to discard the balled-up tissue. Finding none, she dropped it into her purse. "It's even stranger that she didn't call as soon as she was back in the States. Flights are so erratic and prone to delays and missed connections, she didn't always call at the beginning of a trip, but she never failed to call as soon as she landed."

Sarah reached for the coffee thermos, simply to have something to do with her hands, and poured a cup of coffee.

Durant's gaze focused on her trembling fingers. "You can't think of any reason she might have left Germany in a hurry?"

Sarah shook her head, unable to speak, afraid her voice would tremble, too.

Durant pulled a sheet of paper from the top of the stack. "She probably didn't have time to call from Chicago. Her flight was supposed to land there at four-oh-five Friday afternoon, with a connecting flight that would get her to Sacramento at eight forty, our time. But she ran into problems—lost three hours in Frankfurt when her flight was canceled. That put her into O'Hare Friday night at seven forty."

Sarah tore the corner off a packet of sweetener, poured about half of it into her coffee, and placed the packet back on the tray. "But she didn't call me."

Coleman's gaze, never wavering from her face, made her self-conscious and all too aware of her bruise.

Durant shook his head. "She had to get through Customs and she must have scrambled, because she managed to get onto a first-class standby flight at eight fifty-five."

Sarah could picture Caro pulling her luggage through the long Customs line, working her phone at the same time, to line up another flight. She would have hurried out of Customs and raced down O'Hare's miles of automated walkways, searching for the right gate. If she'd barely made the flight, maybe she had no time to call and decided to wait until she landed. That would have given her time to collect her luggage and get outside while Sarah drove to the airport. Or maybe she'd planned to take a taxi home and wait until the next day to call Sarah.

Coleman poured a cup of coffee, added a packet of sugar, and swiveled a plastic stirring stick around the dark brew, his attention still focused on Sarah.

Why was he staring at her? What was going through his mind? She shifted in the chair, wishing it had more padding.

Durant took off his reading glasses and rubbed the bridge of his nose. "She landed in Sacramento at twelve-oh-five Saturday morning. We lost track of her after that. We don't know how she got home. None of the shuttle services took her, and no taxi we can find." He slid the page to the bottom of the pile. "So we thought maybe one of you picked her up."

"But she didn't call ..." Sarah remembered then where she'd been at midnight. That was about the time she'd left the casino, and her phone had been miles away, in Roseville.

The detectives had been silent for a minute or two, Durant studying his notes, and Coleman studying Sarah. What was his problem?

Durant's voice pulled her attention back to him. "Was she traveling alone?"

"She never mentioned anybody else, and she would have. She's used to traveling alone."

She had never asked Caro why she took so many trips alone, maybe because she didn't want to give the impression she was angling for an invitation. No, that wasn't it. She had never even wondered about it. Had Caro preferred traveling alone?

Coleman interrupted her thoughts. "I'm assuming your aunt inherited the house from her husband. Was he older? The husband?"

Sarah stared at him. "Why would you assume that?" She moved her coffee cup aside. It tasted like it was at least a day old, maybe two.

"Well," Coleman floundered, looking around the room before he again focused on Sarah. "She's—she was relatively young, and it's an upscale area." He looked at Durant, who gazed back, blank-faced.

"And?" Sarah could almost taste the frost in her own voice.

Coleman shifted in his chair. "Well, she apparently didn't inherit from her family, so—"

"So you assume," Sarah made quotation marks with her fingers. "You assume she inherited from a wealthy older husband?" She rose to her feet. "You're right, Detective. Caro was fairly well-to-do, unlike the rest of us. You're also right in another respect. The house was bequeathed to her."

Coleman turned to cast a self-satisfied glance at Durant.

"Bequeathed to her until five years after she finished the last of her art classes. Then it would revert to the trust."

"What trust?" Coleman shuffled through his notes. Sarah almost smiled, wondering if he expected to find the answer there.

"The woman who set up the inheritance wanted to make sure Caro had time to finish school and get established in the art world before she had to worry about money."

"This woman, she was a relative?"

Sarah shook her head. "No. She was just a woman who loved fine art. A woman who believed in Caro."

Coleman stared at her, open-mouthed. "Who?"

Why did they think any of this mattered? What could any of it have to do with Caro's death? She glanced at Durant, her eyebrows raised.

"We know this kind of questioning is painful," he said. "You think it's none of our business, but your aunt died this morning, and the money may be an issue. We don't know at this point how your aunt died—accident, suicide, or—"

"You think somebody killed her? For her money?" Sarah put a hand over her mouth.

"We don't know what happened. That's what we're trying to find out. It might have been an accident, but if somebody killed her, there has to be a reason. It could be connected to the inheritance, so we do need to check it out."

"But it wasn't a permanent inheritance," Sarah protested.

Durant nodded. "But it was beneficial to her, and she still lived in the house."

"All right, Detective. Here's the story. Caro wanted to study art, but her parents wouldn't pay for it. They, in her father's words, didn't think she could make a living drawing pictures. They talked her into nursing, and as compassionate and caring as Caro was, she might have made a career of it, had she not loved drawing and painting so much."

She paused, gathering her thoughts. "With some help from her brother and sister–Laura's father and my mother–she managed to work a couple of art classes into her schedule. She met an instructor who was so impressed with her work, he was determined to keep her in the art world."

Coleman started to speak, but Durant motioned for him to be quiet. "Go on, Mrs. Wagner."

"He approached an elderly woman, one of the art department's benefactors, and showed her one of Caro's sketches. The woman bought several and offered to pay Caro's tuition. Later, after actually meeting Caro, the woman offered her free room and board. They had much in common and became good friends as well as housemates."

Coleman said, "Mrs. Wagner, this is all very interesting, but—"

Sarah held up one hand. "Detective, you insisted I tell you how Caro ended up with the house. I'm trying to do that. If you can be patient for a few more minutes?"

He clamped his lips together.

Sarah continued. "The woman eventually became very ill. Caro took care of her, dropping several classes to do so. Worried that Caro wouldn't continue her art classes, the woman temporarily bequeathed the house to her, along with enough money to cover tuition and books."

Coleman, who had been scribbling notes, jerked his head up. "That sounds a little suspicious. Especially with your aunt being her nurse. There might have been foul play involved."

Sarah rolled her eyes. "So another detective thought. One much like you, Mr. Coleman, until the woman's grandson explained that he had suggested the bequest to his terminally-ill grandmother." Sarah smiled, remembering the story Caro had told her. "The sketches his grandmother bought? She'd given them to her grandson Roger. He loved art–good art–and he loved

Caro's sketches. Almost as much as he loved Caro when he finally met her."

Sarah added in a quiet voice, "Roger did have money, Mr. Coleman, but after she married him, Caro did quite well with her art. I doubt you could afford one of her paintings. I certainly can't." She sat, pulled her chair forward, and smiled at Coleman. "I trust that answers your questions about Caro's finances?"

Coleman flushed and tugged at his collar. "The elderly woman. Did she have other relatives?"

"I don't know. Her will mentioned only Roger and the art trust and, of course, Caro."

"I don't understand. Why would he want his grandmother to give the house to somebody else?"

"Not give it, Detective. It was temporary. He would eventually get the house."

Coleman leaned in, his gaze boring into Sarah. "But she did get it, didn't she, through marriage? And who gets it now? And the rest of Caroline Brenhauser's estate?"

She wanted to slap the self-satisfied smile from his face. She clamped her fists tight, her nails biting into her palms. "Caro was only forty-two. I doubt she thought much about her death. She had set up college trusts for my young nephews Eric and Jamie, and some small funds for Laura and me, but she never mentioned anything else."

Coleman leaned back in his seat, sipping his coffee. "But you knew, didn't you? Logic would tell you that she'd leave her estate to the two of you."

"I–yes, now that she's gone, I suppose that makes sense." She stared at him. "But I never...what are you suggesting?"

Her heartbeat quickened. The dull headache that had been building since the interview started now pulsed in her temples, and her stomach felt unsettled. She couldn't have defined her emotions at that moment–a strange mixture of grief, despair, anger, and now a touch of fear. She concentrated on her hands, clenched into fists in her lap.

He set the coffee mug on the table. "I'm not suggesting anything, Mrs. Wagner. Just stating an obvious fact."

Durant interrupted. "Right now, we don't even know how Caroline Brenhauser died. It very well may have been an accident. We have nothing to suggest otherwise."

Then why was he asking these questions? Sarah fought back her anger. Why would they do this to her if they thought it was an accident?

Durant's next question surprised her. "How long were they married? Your aunt and Roger Brenhauser?"

She did some mental calculations. Caro had been twenty when she married, and twenty-nine when Roger died. "Nine years." She had always known the facts but hadn't put the numbers together. Nine years. It didn't seem like enough time to build the strong relationship they'd shared.

Durant nodded and cleared his throat. "And she's been widowed for thirteen years. Maybe she got lonely, depressed?"

Sarah shook her head. "Lonely? Caro? No way. She's one of the most vibrant people I know. She has so many friends, so many activities, her bridge club, her camellias. She has season tickets for the Community Theater and the Music Circus." She smiled. "She wins prizes for her camellias and belongs to a gardening club and a book club. She goes to San Francisco, to the opera, and wine tasting in Napa Valley. She sketches and paints. She's politically active. Caro isn't–wasn't lonely."

"Thirteen years is a long time. She might not have told you."

"She chose to stay single. She loved Roger. She said nobody else could ever measure up. That it wouldn't be fair to another man." Even as she uttered the words, Sarah realized she didn't feel that way about Scott. She suspected he didn't feel that way about her, either. Very few people were lucky enough to have a marriage like Caro's.

Coleman looked skeptical. "So she didn't date?"

"She saw men, socially. Several of them, in fact, but they were just friends. She said she wasn't interested in a romantic relationship–at least not a serious one."

Durant flipped to a clean page in his notebook and asked for the names. She tried to dredge them from her memory. "Les Hyatt." Caro had known him the longest, from back in her art class days. "Mark Gunderson from the Camellia Society." Who else? A doctor. George? Jeff? "Jeff Sullaway. She went wine tasting several times with Paul—I can't think of his last name right at the moment. Oh, wait. It's Wilton, like the town. She hadn't known him long."

Durant picked the next sheet off the pile. He was well organized. He knew exactly where he was going with his questions. This was an interrogation, not an interview. If she'd known, she might have been better prepared. No. There was no way she could have readied herself for this—no way she could even think logically, with Caro's death overshadowing every thought.

"What about alcohol?" Coleman asked. "How much did she drink?"

"How much? I don't know. She didn't have a drinking problem, if that's what you're asking."

"Sometimes family doesn't know, Mrs. Wagner."

"Oh, I'd know. Believe me, I'd know." Scott had taught her well. She closed her eyes briefly, willing herself not to think about her husband. When she opened them, she realized Durant's attention was focused on her clenched hands. She dropped them back into her lap.

Coleman asked, "What about employees? It's a big place. She must have had help."

"Not much. Living alone, there wasn't much to clean up. She did hire people once or twice a year for heavy cleaning, and for parties, but she didn't mind putting dishes in the dishwasher and making her bed. She liked to cook. A girl—a high school girl—came in once, maybe twice a month. I can't think of her name right now."

"What about the yard? She must have had help with that. It's a big place."

Sarah nodded. "Yes, but I don't know who. We should be able to find it in her checkbook or her address book."

"The Brenhauser name is German, isn't it?" Coleman asked. "Do you happen to know if there are any relatives living over there? People she might have visited?"

"I don't know. I'm not sure I ever heard the names of any of Roger's family."

Her mind darted back to the telephone call Caro should have made—the call Sarah couldn't have answered because she didn't have her phone. Had Caro left a message? Scott had given her the news about Caro right after she got her purse back, and after that—she had never checked for messages or missed calls!

Coleman's next question jolted her back to attention. "Where were you last night, Mrs. Wagner? Your husband said you left the house and he couldn't find you."

"I went out to the casino."

He looked surprised. "How long were you there?"

How could she explain everything that happened last night?

"Take your time." Durant gazed at her hands, and she realized she was twisting her wedding band. She moved both hands to the top of the table, one on top of the other, took a deep breath and told them about her night and morning at the casino. When she finished, Durant led her through it again, verifying the times and the people with whom she'd interacted.

"Did you see anybody, or did anybody see you after you woke up this morning?"

She closed her eyes and mentally retraced her steps. "I talked to a woman at the rewards desk when I used their telephone, and I bought a muffin and coffee at a kiosk. A few people were walking to and from the front door, but I don't know if they noticed me."

"But nobody saw you between one and three this morning?"

"Just the man who followed me outside."

"But he was gone by, what?" Durant checked his notes. "Half past twelve, or so?"

How could she know? It had seemed like an eternity at the time, but her desperate run to the Explorer would have taken only minutes, even counting the time she had fought the man off.

"I–I don't know how long he was out there after I locked myself in. It was dark. I couldn't see him."

"What about the vehicle?" Durant glanced at his scribbled notes again. "The Explorer? Where is it now?"

"It's still at the casino. We haven't had time to get it."

"Leave it there for now. Don't do anything with it until we call you. We'll let you know when you can pick it up." He placed his notebook on top of the stack of papers. "Thank you. You've been very helpful."

Sarah nodded, her mind still on the Explorer and her night at the casino. Would anybody remember her? Maybe. She looked pretty ratty. She reached for her purse, started to rise, but hesitated. "Detective, We need to make arrangements for my aunt. When will we have...When will you release..."

"Your aunt? Within the next day or two, I should think. Here." Durant fished in his pocket for a card. "Call this number. They'll be able to tell you."

"The house–will we be able to get inside? We'll need her address book, her e-mail addresses. We have to notify people."

"We're not through with the house," Durant said. "Maybe by tomorrow. We have her computers and her address book and all her notes, letters, that sort of thing. We'll be going through them over the next week, and will release them to you when we've finished our investigation. I'll see that you get copies of the address book and the e-mail addresses."

"I don't understand. Why do you need her computer?"

"Any insight we can get into her life may help us determine what happened. We'll return it as soon as we can. And Mrs. Wagner—"

"Yes?"

"Be careful if you go out on the deck. It seems to be structurally sound, but the railing should be replaced as soon as you can manage it."

Sarah shuddered.

"Again, we're sorry for your loss."

Just words. Words they say to every family in situations like this–every accident, every suicide, every homicide. Undoubtedly, Detective Durant had uttered them hundreds of times. But when Sarah looked into his eyes, she felt a sudden surge of empathy, a flash of compassion and warmth. She gripped his hand. He lightly pressed her fingers and opened the door for her. "Let's get copies of those names and addresses for you."

Chapter 8

The detectives stood in the squad room and watched Sarah Wagner wend her way through the desks, toward the exit.

"She lied about the telephone call," Coleman said, "and that's quite a story about the casino."

"Yeah. Strange enough to be true. Who could make up something like that? There are all kinds of predators out there. We'll check it out. See if a key is jammed in the ignition, and find out what we can about her visit to the casino. Check their security tapes for the times she entered and left, and see if anybody noticed her and the Explorer in and around the overflow parking lot." He lowered his beefy body into the armchair behind his desk and straightened the stack of papers.

Coleman sat in the visitor chair beside the desk. "Traffic would be light that time of night. It would take maybe a half hour each way, between the casino and the aunt's house. The aunt couldn't have gotten home before twelve thirty or, more likely, twelve forty- five. So, unless somebody can place Sarah Wagner at the casino between twelve and three thirty, she still doesn't have an alibi. As far as we know, she could have forced the key into the ignition after she got back."

"Her husband doesn't have an alibi, either, and that bruise on her face tells me he's a more likely suspect. But you're right; unless she has an alibi for that specific time frame, she could have done it. Check with the cab companies, too. See if any of them took her to her aunt's house."

"You think they're telling the truth about the bruise?"

"Hard to get at the truth in domestic cases." But it made Durant wonder. If Wagner was smacking his wife around, what would keep him from doing the same thing to somebody else? He had motive, if his wife inherited. "We need to find out how Caroline Brenhauser died before we look for suspects. Could be an accident or suicide."

"Sarah Wagner doesn't believe it's suicide."

"Families never want to believe suicides," Durant said. "Can't say I blame them."

But he thought Sarah Wagner might be right about her aunt. If Caroline Brenhauser wanted to kill herself, she could have done it in Germany and saved herself a grueling trip. And why jump off the deck? Sleeping pills would be easier. The pieces of the puzzle didn't fit. "Why would she leave a glass of wine on the deck table?"

"Maybe she was working up her courage, got to the last glass, and decided to do it."

"But if she meant to do herself in, why come home at all?" Durant shook his head. "Maybe it was an accident. If we could clear up how she got home, it might give us a lead."

He took off his glasses and rubbed the side of his nose. "We still have to talk to Laura Thornton. After that, look up the aunt's doctor in the address book. See what you can find out from him. Check the passenger list, too. See who was sitting next to Brenhauser on the plane."

"You think she had somebody with her?"

"No, but we have to check. I'll contact the attorney about the will, then I'm going out to the casino. We'll need to talk to all the men Caroline Brenhauser was seeing. Maybe one of them picked her up from the airport. Oh, and take another look at the airport video. See if you can find any way to identify that blue Honda."

"The license plate isn't visible, and we're not even sure she got into it," Coleman said. "But I'll take another look."

"Then find out if any of these people drive one."

Coleman nodded. "You think we have a crime scene?"

"No. At least not yet, but we treat it like one until we know better. It's always best to keep an open mind and look at all the possibilities. There are several people with a motive for killing Caroline Brenhauser. The nieces are likely to inherit. Wagner, too, through his wife. Maybe some of Roger Brenhauser's relatives still carry a grudge about the bequest. One of the men in her life might have felt rejected. Somebody might not have liked one of her paintings." Durant flexed his back. "But then again, maybe our victim just had a bad accident or took a swan dive."

Dee was on her way to the squad room when she crossed paths with Matt Coleman. He stopped long enough to tell her about the just-posted opening for detective.

"I know," she said. "In fact, I've already applied, but I'm not sure about the educational requirements. All I have is a communications degree and a few classes I've been taking in criminal justice."

"You're good on that score. They like communications degrees for detectives, as long as you have the experience. I can fill you in on what you'll need to know to get through the process. The test, that sort of thing. Let's get together and talk about it."

The last thing Dee wanted was an after-hours meeting with Matt Coleman. She tried to think of an excuse. Tell him Dave Wheeler would coach her?

He glanced at his watch. "I don't have time right now, though. We're still working on the Brenhauser case. Maybe a little later?"

She wanted to know what was happening with the Brenhauser case. She didn't know why. Maybe because she was first on the scene. Was it worth meeting with Coleman? Maybe, if she could do it on-site. "I think I could get together with you later, in one of the break rooms."

Coleman laughed and shook his head. "Too noisy. They never shut down. I was thinking about someplace quiet, where we wouldn't be interrupted."

Before he could suggest dinner, Dee blurted, "We could go somewhere for a quick drink. I have a—a dinner date." She did, in a manner of speaking, at her brother's house, with him and his kids, but Coleman didn't need to know that.

"Oh? Well, we wouldn't want to rush through our meeting. Maybe tomorrow night? Over dinner?"

Dee tried not to grit her teeth. "No, that won't work. Tell you what. I'll see if I can postpone my dinner date a little, and we can go ahead and do it tonight."

"Fine. I'll meet you down the street. About six?"

Her mind raced, trying to think of a way out. The little club down the street was a police hangout. If she met Coleman there, people would assume they were dating. Better somewhere away from the building. Far away.

"Can we meet somewhere else? I have an appointment this afternoon. I wasn't planning on coming back downtown. I know a little place in Old Sac. The Topaz Club. I could make it there by six- thirty."

Coleman jotted in his notebook. "I'll be there."

Dee walked into The Topaz Club at six thirty sharp, unwilling to give Matt Coleman even a fraction of a second of extra time. She would keep the meeting short and impersonal, parry every intrusive probe into her private life with a question about the job and, at the same time, find out all she could about the Brenhauser case.

He ordered their drinks and glanced at his watch. "How much time do we have before your dinner date?"

"About an hour. I figured that would be plenty of time." She looked around the room to see if she recognized anybody. Not yet. Good.

"Anybody I know? Your date?"

"No. Tell me about the exam. What's it like?"

"I could help you with that, fill you in on the kinds of questions they ask. Help you study."

When pigs fly. That thought triggered the memory of Dave's dramatic reaction to the word "pigs," and she smiled. She shouldn't have; Coleman would interpret it as encouragement. "Thanks, but I don't think that'll be necessary." She dug for her wallet. She didn't want Coleman to pay for her drink.

"Well, you might want to think it over. Some of the questions can get pretty complicated."

She pulled two fives from her wallet and placed them on the table."How so?"

"Some of the stuff on the test doesn't have much correlation to the real world." He was trying to impress her. Now he would go into a long-winded diatribe about his personal theories. She raised her eyebrows, and he flushed.

"It's like the case we're working now."

"Oh?" She leaned forward, her elbows on the table.

He hitched his chair closer. "Yeah. We don't have any evidence that it's a murder. Could just as easily be an accident or a suicide, but my gut feeling tells me it's homicide. That guy Wagner. He's violent, but I'm not sure about his motive."

"Maybe he didn't have one," Dee said. "Maybe he thought he was killing his wife. From his description, she looks like her aunt."

"Yeah." Coleman looked thoughtful. "They do look a lot alike. It would be hard to tell them apart in the dark. If Wagner expected his wife to be in that house, not the aunt, he might have killed the wrong woman. The bruise on his wife's face tells me he can get rough."

The waitress brought the drinks and Dee paid for hers before Coleman could extract his credit card from his wallet.

"I wonder, though, about his motive. They don't appear to be wealthy, so he wouldn't have much to lose in a divorce. I guess you'll be checking their financials?"

Coleman nodded. "We'll check, but I don't see it. He might like to slap his wife around, but he wouldn't kill her. Not as long as he knows she's eventually going to inherit a lot of money."

"I don't know," Dee said. The aunt wasn't that much older than her nieces. She might have outlived both of them."

"My thinking, exactly. That gives the nieces some pretty strong motivation to hurry things along." Coleman leaned in closer and lowered his voice. "We're pretty sure a blue Honda picked the victim up at the airport. One of the nieces drives one. I believe one of them either picked her up from the airport or waited for her in the house. I'm not sure which one, Sarah Wagner or Laura Thornton. Hell, maybe it's both of them." He sat back in his chair.

"Laura Thornton?"

"Yeah. The tall, sexy one. Nice build, long hair. Great legs."

Dee splashed Cabernet onto her blouse. She grabbed for a napkin and blotted at the red stain spreading across the creamy-white silk. "I have to go. Get something to take this out."

"Maybe some club soda. I'll get some."

"No. No, I have to...to change for my dinner date." She pushed her chair back and rose.

"Dee, are you all right? You look a little pale."

"I'm fine, thanks. I'll talk to you tomorrow."

She pushed through the after-work crowd and threaded her way to the door. She had to talk to Sam. Did he know?

Of course, he did. That's why he had Eric and Jamie. She tried to remember what he'd said when he called and invited her to dinner. Something about his ex-wife's aunt dying, so he was taking care of the boys for a few more days.

He didn't know she'd been first officer on the scene, and she hadn't been aware the victim was related to Sam's ex-wife. She searched her memory, wondering if she'd ever known the names of any of Sam's ex-wife's family. She didn't think so. She'd never met any of them, didn't really know Laura. She hadn't gone to Sam and Laura's wedding; she had been near the end of her military police training at Fort Leonard Wood, Missouri, and unable to get leave. She'd shipped out to Iraq shortly afterward.

Sam didn't come to Dee's wedding, either, hadn't even known about it. Nor did anybody else. She and Jason hadn't wanted anybody to know. Not after all those long months in Iraq, when regulations kept them apart. Regulations can't determine who you love, and she hadn't planned on falling in love with Lieutenant Jason Callender.

Both of them had known the consequences of fraternization between officers and enlisted personnel. Dee didn't care for her own sake; she was near the end of her enlistment, and would soon be rotating back stateside. For Jason, who planned a military career, discovery of their relationship would be disastrous.

It had developed slowly, over two years, deprived of those normal long, intimate conversations that slowly peel back the layers of the facade presented to the world. To compensate, they communicated through written journals, which they downloaded to flash drives and exchanged when nobody was watching.

They stole quick kisses and brief hugs, always watching for prying eyes. Sometimes, when only a sliver of moon lightened the sky, they sneaked into the back of a truck, to have a few minutes alone, but it was risky. A guard almost caught them one night, the scent of his cigarette smoke their only warning.

So they'd gone about their duties, keeping their engagement secret, planning to take their R&R at the same time so they could get married. They didn't want Iraqi laws to apply, so they had to get stateside. They would have only fifteen days; a few in Kuwait before they got transportation out, then a quick wedding in Reno, a honeymoon in Lake Tahoe, and the flight back.

"I wish our families could be there," Dee wrote on the document she later downloaded to her flash drive. "I'd like to meet your parents."

"You will, honey, on my next R&R," he responded. "You'll be out by then, back stateside, and it won't matter if we're married. Maybe we can plan a big bash and get all of them together."

"Do you think we're rushing it? That maybe we should wait 'til then to get married?" Dee looked at the words she'd typed, wishing she could hold his hand while she asked that question. She sighed and downloaded the file onto the flash drive.

"Only if you have reservations. I don't. I want to be married to you, Dee, in case something happens. I want a honeymoon next month, not next year, but it's your call." She read his message, smiled and wrote a return which began, "It's a date."

Jason never met her family. That "something" they tried not to think about came two months after they returned to Iraq. She came home alone, too shattered to connect with anybody else, even her brother. Only vaguely aware of his pain, of his disintegrating marriage, she had struggled to pull herself from the murky depths of her own despair. By the time she'd pulled herself from that dark, sucking void, Sam had retreated into silence. She had failed him when he needed her most.

He still loved Laura and grieved over the loss of his family, but he wouldn't talk about it, and Dee no longer even mentioned his alcoholic binges. He couldn't stop he'd told her, his eyes bleak. When the urges came, they were too strong; he couldn't control them.

What would happen to him now? How would he handle Laura being a suspect in a murder investigation, especially if she proved to be guilty? Dee shivered, afraid for him.

Matt Coleman gave every indication of being on a witch hunt, but Al Durant would keep him in check. If Durant's investigation led to Laura's arrest, it would be valid, the result of solid detective work.

Dee didn't let herself think about the repercussions. She pushed away the thought of Sam's anguished face, only to find it replaced by those of Eric and Jamie.

She sighed. There was nothing she could do. As a patrol officer, she would not be privy to information the detectives gathered. Even if she did learn something, she couldn't share it with Laura and her cousin, or even Sam, without compromising the investigation. Otherwise, she could forget about ever making detective; she'd probably be looking for a new job.

Chapter 9

Sarah had looked for Laura on her way out of the building earlier that afternoon. She wanted to warn her; the detectives might politely call their meetings interviews, but they felt more like interrogations. She glanced at her watch: two minutes until four. Laura must already be in an interview room.

Traffic had picked up. It would soon be bumper-to-bumper all the way out to the Business 80/I-80 merge. If she waited for Laura, they might have dinner together. Traffic would be a lot lighter after six.

She needed to stop kidding herself. She was just putting off her conversation with Scott. She took a deep breath and headed for the parking garage.

Her mind still on the interview, she couldn't concentrate on her driving. Why had Durant asked where she was on Friday night? Why did they want the Explorer to stay in the casino parking lot? Did they plan to check her alibi? *Alibi? My God, they couldn't think I would hurt Caro!*

A car honked behind her. The light had turned green. She accelerated through the intersection and maneuvered toward the on-ramp for the freeway.

They thought somebody killed Caro. Laura and Sarah were suspects simply because they'd probably inherit. She shuddered and shook her head. If somebody had killed Caro, it certainly wasn't any of them. Not Sarah or Laura, or even Scott or Sam. Couldn't be. Whatever happened, there had to be some connection to the unexpected flight home.

She had never checked her phone for messages.

She glanced behind her and started working her way across traffic lanes, looking for an exit. She got off onto the frontage road at Howe Avenue, pulled into a furniture company's almost-empty parking lot, and pulled out her phone.

The rhythm of her heartbeat accelerated when she saw Caro's name and number on the missed-calls screen. She'd called at eight minutes after twelve, about the time Sarah left the casino.

When she heard the familiar voice, a deep ache started in her chest. Her eyes filmed over and tears slipped down her cheeks. It took three tries for her brain to get past the sound of the voice and register the full meaning of the message. *Sarah, I'm in Chicago, on my way home. Don't tell Scott or Laura until I have a chance to talk to you. Gotta go. Love you.*

Sarah stared at the phone. Why not let Scott and Laura know?

Caro's death made the message sound incriminating, but Laura could never harm Caro. Neither could Scott. Durant and Coleman wouldn't believe that, though. She raised her hand to the bruise on her jaw. Scott hadn't hit her. But everybody thought he had.

Instinctively, her finger hovered over the delete option. No. She couldn't erase Caro's voice. She played the message again, not listening to the words this time, simply letting the voice envelop her. Tears flooded her eyes, then became a torrent. She pounded the steering wheel with her fists. Why? Why Caro?

Finally, leached dry, she wiped her face and leaned back in the seat, absently watching the freeway traffic while she analyzed every word of the message. It still made no sense.

The phone rang. Laura. "Sarah? Are you okay?"

"Yeah. I'm okay. Why?"

"I don't know. The interview. And you sound kind of stuffed up."

"Getting my real crying jag out of the way, I guess. The way things have been going, there hasn't been much time for grieving."

Silence on the other end. Should she tell Laura about the message? Caro had asked her not to, but Caro was dead. What did it matter now? She hesitated. If she told Laura, she'd have to tell

Scott, too. She couldn't keep it from him, and for some reason she couldn't define, she didn't want to tell him. Not yet.

"Did they ask you where you were last night?" Laura asked.

"Yeah. I had a little trouble explaining that one."

"I'm not much better off, being alone last night. I don't know, Sarah. It made me feel like they suspect me of something, especially after the fingerprinting and DNA samples."

"They said that's so they could exclude anybody who had a legitimate reason for being in the house."

"I know, but they even asked about my car—what kind it is and what color. Why would they do that? I found myself wishing I had a better alibi, even though I didn't do anything."

"Like either one of us would hurt Caro."

"But somebody did. We both know she didn't fall off that deck. There's no way she would have gotten close to the railing, with her fear of heights, and she sure as hell didn't jump. Somebody killed her."

Laura's voice sounded thick, and Sarah wished she could reach out and touch her—hold her. "I know. I was thinking the same thing." She shivered. "I can't stay on the phone. I'm on my way home. Do you want to get together tomorrow? Start making arrangements for the memorial service?"

"Yeah, I guess we better. We'll have a ton of stuff to do. Try to get some sleep tonight."

"You, too. Love you." Sarah dropped the phone into her purse, knowing sleep would be impossible. Too many unanswered questions clamored for her attention. She started the car, thinking about the conversation she'd planned to have with Scott.

Not tonight. It wasn't a good time. She was so tired she couldn't think straight, and she needed a clear head for that conversation, to try to keep Scott from blowing up. Maybe tomorrow, after she got a good night's sleep.

But it didn't work out quite that way.

Scott was waiting. He rose from his chair as soon as she entered the living room, her purse clutched in one of her hands, the mail in the other. He didn't move toward her, and she hesitated, just inside the door, trying to collect her thoughts. Or maybe read his.

"Where the hell is the Explorer, Sarah? And where did you spend the night?"

She told him.

He stared at her for a moment, open-mouthed. "The casino? Why? Why would you go there?"

She looked through the mail, not really seeing it, trying to formulate words that would make him understand without angering him. She studied his face and saw no indication he'd been drinking, so she took a deep breath and plunged in. "I didn't have a lot of options. I didn't want to pull Laura into it, and I didn't have the key to Caro's house. It was here, in my purse." She paused, watching his face. "So was my phone. Did it ring after I left? Did anybody leave a message?"

He shook his head. "Did you...did you talk to anybody at the casino?"

It was a question she hadn't expected, but she should have. His unreasonable jealousy always unnerved her. She'd never given him a reason to distrust her. Yet, he was always suspicious, reluctant to let her go anywhere without him, even resenting the time she spent with Laura. She tried to keep her face blank. She'd learned long ago that nothing she said would allay his suspicions.

He stepped closer. "I had to look in your purse, to get the key to the Corolla. I found this." He slapped the envelope against his leg. "When were you planning to tell me about it, Sarah? After you left?"

The letter. She'd tucked it away, waiting until Caro got home, then forgot all about it. "Scott...this isn't the time. I can't deal with any more right now. I just can't. I'll talk to you about it later."

"You're the one who brought the subject up."

"No. I was asking about my phone."

He never answered her question. Was he purposely evading it, or simply overriding anything she said, as he so often did, intent on his own line of thought?

"And I was asking about the letter."

The rhythm of the slapping envelope increased, and Sarah took a step backward. "I was waiting to talk to Caro. To see if—"

"So Caro was behind it. Meddling again. I should have known. Was she going to pay for this—" He glanced at the envelope. "—this graphic design school?"

"Caro didn't know anything about it. It was just something...Scott, you know I've been interested in design for a long time. I wanted to see if a good school would accept me, that's all. If I'd qualify."

"Then why didn't you ask me about it? And why did you apply to one in Los Angeles? Did you think I'd let you go to L.A.?"

She sank into a chair, trying to tamp down her anger, already weary of the conversation. "You haven't been easy to talk to lately. But, since you ask, Los Angeles is the closest school for what I want. To be honest, I don't even know why I sent for the information. I knew you'd object, no matter where I went. You've made it clear you don't want me to go to school."

"We can't afford it. The dealership is losing money, and we need your paycheck."

"But I'd eventually earn a lot more in graphic design. You might be able to leave the dealership, do something else." She took off her shoes and rubbed the sole of one foot against her other instep. "I know you're miserable there. How bad is it? The finances?"

He ran his fingers through his hair. "We're losing a lot of money. With this economy, people aren't buying cars. Dad doesn't see that. He blames me. Says I can't manage anything. That he shouldn't have put me in charge." Scott hesitated, then forged ahead. "He says I can't even manage my marriage. Or my wife."

Sarah's pulse quickened and her foot stopped rubbing. "I'm something to be managed?" She couldn't lose her temper. That always made things worse.

Scott flushed. "He means well. He knows I want to start a family. He can't understand why you don't."

"First of all, it's none of his business, and you shouldn't be talking to him about it. Second, as you said yourself, we've got financial problems. We can't afford to have another—a baby." She hesitated, watching him. "Third, we have some serious problems to work through before we can even think about starting a family. I don't know what's happened to us. Your drinking–"

He stared at her. "Did it ever occur to you those are the reasons why I drink?"

"Then we have a real problem, don't we?" She rose to her feet. "I can't do this. Not now. Maybe tomorrow. I'm going to soak in a hot bath, and crawl into bed."

"No, wait. I'm cooking dinner."

Scott? Cooking dinner? The closest he ever got to the kitchen was the liquor cabinet.

"Just steaks. I already put some potatoes in the microwave and made a salad." He reached for her hand and pulled her toward the kitchen. "You need to eat, and I need to...well, I guess I need to start this conversation all over again. To say I'm sorry. For everything. Not just for Caro, but for last night, too. I screwed up. I know that, and I hope you'll forgive me."

"Scott, I'm too tired for this."

His face contorted; he looked close to tears. She closed her eyes briefly, trying to summon strength. "I can't talk about it right now. I'm too tired to think straight, but you're right. I do need to eat. Thank you for doing this." She nodded at the table, set for two, a bud vase in the center, holding two King Alfred daffodils.

He pulled out her chair. "Okay, I'll get the steaks off the grill. Want a glass of wine? Or would you rather wait and have it with a hot bubble-bath?"

She sank into the chair, trying to rein in her whirling thoughts. Scott cooking dinner? Scott offering wine and a bubble bath? Caro's message: don't tell anybody. Durant. Being a murder suspect. Caro murdered. She closed her eyes, trying to pull it all together, and felt her body sway. She opened her eyes and grabbed for the edge of the table. Scott, searching for the steak knives, never noticed.

Later, while she dumped a generous portion of bubble bath into the tub and filled it with hot water, Scott brought a glass of Merlot to the bathroom.

"I think you can use this tonight. And, Sarah, for what it's worth, I meant what I said. I'm sorry. For Caro and, well, everything. You're the best thing that ever happened to me. I know I don't deserve you, but I'm going to do better, I promise."

She reached for the wine and tried to smile, remembering all the broken promises he'd made in the past. Searching for words she couldn't find, she welcomed the sound of the ringing telephone.

Detective Durant, telling her they could pick up the Explorer.

"We can get it in the morning," she told Scott. "I can take you out there before Laura gets here. Or even after. We could all go. Have breakfast, or lunch."

"No. Better do it tonight. It's been there too long already. No telling what'll happen if we leave it 'til morning." He grabbed his phone. "I'll call Triple-A. Have them meet us."

She glanced at the waiting bath bubbles, sighed, pulled the plug, and slipped her feet back into her shoes. So much for understanding.

Chapter 10

Scott talked as he drove, telling her how much he loved her, how much she meant to him. She tried to respond, to reassure him, but felt so numb she couldn't dredge up the words. He didn't notice. His voice droned on, complaining about his micro-managing, unreasonable father, and boring job.

"Have you thought about looking for something else?"

"I can't quit. You know that. We need the money."

"But I thought—didn't you say you're losing money?"

"Not me. The dealership. I'm still getting my salary. A reduced one, like everybody else. At least, I am for now." His voice sounded bitter. "Until the old man decides to cut me loose."

She touched his arm. "Scott, if you're that unhappy, you can't stay. It's destroying you. It's destroying us. We can work something out. We'll find a way."

He pulled into the casino parking lot. The tow truck's light bar blinked at them from beside the Explorer.

"We'll talk about it." He hugged her and kissed her cheek. "You go on home. Take your bath and get a good night's sleep. I'll take care of this." He slid out of the car, his mind already on the Explorer and the tow-truck driver.

Sarah drove home from the casino in a stupor. She couldn't think; stress and lack of sleep had overwhelmed her brain's thought processes. Aching with fatigue, she thought only of home and a hot bath. But, by the time she got there, she no longer even thought about the bath; she simply crawled into bed.

She awoke the next morning with a vague sense of unease that deepened into awareness, then despair as her mind came fully awake. Caro. Caro was dead. Sarah lay motionless. Tears trickled down the sides of her face. She hadn't thought she had any left, but the tears for Caro would never stop, just as they had never stopped for Richie or for her mother, and it had been thirteen years since her mother died. Thirteen years in which Caro had tried to fill that void. Now she had lost her, too.

Richie, Mom, Caro, all gone. She knew people who had lost more. A coworker had lost her husband and two children in a boating accident a few months after her mother had died of cancer. How had she borne it? Sarah couldn't survive losing anybody else. Scott and Laura and the boys were all she had.

She tried to go back to sleep, unable to imagine doing anything else. Weariness washed through her body at the thought of dragging herself from bed.

The door opened, and Scott stuck his head in, reminding her Laura was coming over. She glanced at the clock. Ten twenty. She hadn't set the alarm, never dreaming she'd sleep so late.

As she headed for the shower, Scott asked, "Want me to fix some breakfast?"

She shook her head. "No. No time. Laura will be here any minute."

"I probably shouldn't have let you sleep so late, but you were so tired last night, you'd already conked out by the time I got back from the casino. I thought maybe we could talk some more this morning, over breakfast."

She'd almost forgotten about their conversation. His conversation. She had been too tired to contribute much.

He was trying, and she needed to meet him halfway. Her mother had always told her marriage was hard work and compromise, and divorce wasn't an option, at least in their family. "Do you want to go out for dinner tonight?" she asked. "Some place nice, where we can talk? Around seven?"

"Sounds good. But Sarah? Don't invite Laura to join us, even if she stays too late. Okay?"

By the time Sarah got dressed, Laura was having coffee with Scott in the kitchen. She could hear their voices as soon as she stepped into the hallway: cautious, well-considered remarks and overly polite responses. She stopped in the doorway, feeling the tension between them. Scott moved around the kitchen, putting away dishes, making toast, pouring coffee—all while evading Laura's gaze. He needn't have bothered. Had he glanced her way, he would have seen her, straight-backed, sitting at the kitchen counter, staring into the depths of her coffee.

Scott noticed Sarah first. "Hi, sweetie. I have your toast and coffee ready." He put the plate of toast on the counter, beside a mug of coffee, and steered her toward the stool. There, he held her for a moment, kissed her cheek, brushed back her hair, and glanced at Laura. It was all a show, for Laura's benefit.

"Change of plan," Laura said. "Detective Coleman called. He wants us to meet him at the house at one."

"That's short notice," Scott said. "I need to go in to the dealership."

Laura favored him with a cool, appraising stare. "Not you. Sarah and me."

Sarah reached for the sugar. "You go. I'll wait for Durant. I don't like Coleman."

"I don't think we get to choose our cop. Coleman wants us to do a walk-through at the house. See if anything's missing."

Sarah's hands stilled. "They think it was burglars? That Caro might have surprised them in the act, and they killed her?" Her mind leapt ahead. "We're no longer suspects?"

"How can you possibly be a suspect?" Scott asked.

Laura ignored him. "I think the detectives are simply going through the motions, ruling things out. I don't know how hard they're looking for anybody else." She looked pensive. "But, Sarah, what if there's something there, in the house, that will prove somebody else killed her?"

"Then both of us had better look hard when we walk through." Sarah turned to Scott. "Think about it. Laura and I are at the top of the suspect list. We'll inherit from Caro, and neither of us has an alibi."

"But both of you loved Caro."

"Yeah? Why don't you try convincing Detective Coleman of that?" Laura said. "And, by the way, I think you're third on the list."

"Me? Why would I be a suspect?"

Laura looked from him to the bruise on Sarah's jaw, then back to him again, without saying anything. He flushed. Laura pushed her coffee cup aside. "We'd better get moving. There'll be lunch-hour traffic by the time we get to Sacramento."

Sarah kissed Scott. "Would you mind unloading the camping gear while I'm gone? We may need to haul some stuff. I feel nervous about leaving all Caro's paintings and sketches in the house, with nobody there. Especially now that people know the house is empty."

"Uh—yeah, I need to do that. If it's okay with the cops, maybe we can pick up some of the stuff tomorrow. If we can get in. How long will they keep us out of the house?"

She shrugged. "Maybe we'll find out today. But, please, unload it. In case we need it?"

"Okay. And Sarah? Be careful."

"I will. We'll talk about everything tonight." She followed Laura out the door and, a few minutes later, while Sarah still fumbled with her seat belt, Laura backed out of the driveway and picked up speed as she headed for Douglas Boulevard.

"Easy, Cuz," Sarah said, bracing her arm against the dashboard. "I don't know about you, but I don't want to be pulled over for speeding or an unfastened seat belt. Not today. It might be a little awkward, explaining to Coleman why we're late. We still have time."

Laura eased off the accelerator. "What, no sense of adventure?" Neither of them could muster a laugh.

"I've got to run by Sam's when we get through," Laura said, "to take some more clothes for Eric and Jamie. He's going to keep them this week." She stopped for a red light and turned to look at Sarah. "Do you mind? Dee, Sam's sister–I think I told you about her? She's going to be there."

"I always love seeing the boys. Sam, too, but I don't remember anything about Sam's sister. Maybe you'd better fill me in."

"Dee's a cop. I guess she was the one who—she was there when they found Caro."

"I don't understand. Is she working with Durant and Cole man? They already interviewed us."

"No, she's not a detective, and she's not working the case, but Sam seems to think she might help us."

"Okay, but I promised Scott I'd be home in time for dinner."

"That shouldn't be a problem."

They neared Caro's house, and Sarah's chest tightened as Laura drove through the familiar neighborhood. A gentle breeze ruffled tree leaves, casting dancing shadows onto the pavement. Sarah had loved walking here during those years she'd lived with Caro—on her way to the Sac State campus, to her part-time job at the pastry shop, or just to stroll the leafy streets.

The yellow tape surrounding Caro's house fluttered across the driveway, blocking it. Matt Coleman leaned against an unmarked car parked at the curb. Laura pulled in behind him.

Sarah instinctively glanced toward the patio, then averted her eyes. She recognized the impulse as irrational; she couldn't see the deck or the railing from the street, and Caro was not there. The stillness of the house, of the yard, of the street, suddenly seemed oppressive, as though all of it had died along with Caro. She didn't want to get out of the car, didn't know if she could force her feet to step through the door of the house that had always felt welcoming.

She trudged behind Coleman and Laura, her mind filled with images: Caro painting, her eyes squinted a little, focused on the canvas, oblivious to everything else; her quick strides as she came to greet Sarah, her smile almost as wide as her outspread arms.

The door swung open, and even knowing Caro wasn't there—couldn't possibly be there—Sarah's pulse quickened. She faltered, closed her eyes for a few seconds, and stepped into the entryway. The brooding silence inside didn't help. The house seemed to be grieving, too, missing its owner.

"Take your time," Coleman said, sounding bored. "Just walk through and look for anything missing or out of place. Anything unusual."

Sarah grasped Laura's hand and felt an answering squeeze. This was going to be hard. Harder than she had expected, but she had to concentrate. They had to find something that would lead to the killer.

Her gaze swept the room: the rose silk curtains and burgundy swags pooling onto the thick rose-beige carpeting, the antique furnishings and brocade chairs, the artwork. Nothing big missing. She moved forward a few feet, studying every surface, every wall, every corner. She had no idea what she was searching for, but there had to be something.

She saw nothing on the first floor, and by the time they reached the stairs, her spirits had plummeted. Coleman looked at his watch for the third or fourth time. "If you don't see anything down here, we need to move on." He led the way up the stairs and turned to look at Sarah when she caught her breath. She shook her head. They stood at Caro's bedroom door, and she'd caught a faint scent of vanilla. Caro's shampoo.

She glanced at the walls and furniture, her line of vision settling on Caro's floral comforter—a mix of greens, yellows and golds—and its coordinating pillows. Reluctant to enter, she shook her head and looked down the hall, her gaze faltering at the French doors leading onto the deck. She turned and headed for the little room Caro used for an office, the one most familiar to her, and her last hope for finding something. Beyond it were only the almost-empty room where Caro sketched and painted, a bathroom, and a spare bedroom.

The office contained nothing but a folding ladder, paint-spattered roller-tray, new rollers and brushes, and several paint cans. Plastic sheeting covered most of the floor. Sarah stared at the bare walls where the sketches had hung. Executed in delicate pencil strokes that shaded and delineated, they had captured perfect images of Sarah's mother and Laura's father. Caro had promised to give them to her nieces. "But not yet," she had said. "I'm not quite ready to part with them."

Where would she have put them, and all those other things she had kept here, in this private room where she spent so much of her time?

"You didn't know she was redecorating?" Coleman asked.

Sarah shook her head, still thinking about the sketches. "She never mentioned it."

"We found the contractor," Coleman said. "He started before she left, but she couldn't make up her mind about colors and put it on hold 'til she got back." He opened the door to Caro's paint studio. "It looks like everything was stored in here."

The room contained a jumble of boxes and furniture, jammed in so tight it was impossible to walk between them, their surfaces overlaid with draperies, lamps, books, and a variety of decorative items. A computer printer rested on the floor, alongside a wastebasket and a tangle of cables.

Sarah walked on, to the last door—the spare bedroom that had once been hers. It looked sterile and unused, the bed neatly made, no posters on the walls or textbooks stacked on the desk.

On the top closet shelf, Sarah found a video game and two CDs by artists she didn't recognize. She almost smiled, remembering the steamy books she'd hidden on that same shelf, behind more innocuous things. At her engagement party, Caro had whispered, "I hope the books in your closet taught you everything you need to know." Then she had erupted into peals of laughter.

"Find anything?" Coleman leaned against the door frame behind Laura, who stood just inside the doorway.

"Not much." Just memories. She held up the video game and CDs. "They belong to Angie, a high school girl who helped Caro. She sometimes used the room if it was dark when she finished up and Caro wasn't here to drive her home."

"How do you know they're hers?" Coleman asked.

"She labeled the video game. See? Her name and telephone number are on it." Sarah entered the number into her phone. "I'll call and let her know they're here."

"We'll want to talk to her," Coleman said.

"I'm sure the number is in Caro's address book. The one you took," Sarah said.

He yawned and looked at his watch again. "To the best of your knowledge, there's nothing missing from the premises. Is that correct?"

Sarah, close to tears, protested. "How can we be expected to know that? I don't live here. I haven't lived here for years."

Laura frowned. "There may be things missing from her office."

Coleman raised his eyebrows. "Moved, so the contractor could paint. I just showed you where they're stored. Do you think a burglar would bypass everything else in the house, climb the stairs and root around in there for something to steal?"

Laura took a deep breath. "Detective, you showed us where you *think* everything was stored. We don't know that she moved all of it in there. Maybe some of it is missing. We have no way of knowing what was here." She spoke slowly, much as she might have explained something to six-year-old Jamie.

Coleman flushed. Sarah's lip quirked, then straightened. *Probably not a good idea to irritate the cop who suspects us of murder, Cuz.*

"That may be," Coleman said. "But I don't see anything that points to a burglary. There's no sign of forced entry. No broken windows or doors. Your aunt must have trusted the person she let inside. Not a burglar, but a killer." He stared at Laura, then Sarah. "Maybe more than one."

Chapter 11

Sarah and Laura stopped for a late lunch at a little coffee shop in the neighborhood, one that specialized in desserts and fresh-baked bread.

Laura opened the menu. "Their salads look good, but I'm so used to eating at fast food places, anything else looks wonderful."

"I suppose this isn't Jamie's and Eric's style, is it?" Sarah stirred her coffee, trying to find the right words. "Do you ever worry about them when they're with Sam? You know, that they're safe. I do, sometimes."

Laura reached across the table and clasped her hand. "Oh, no, Sarah. You don't have to worry about Eric and Jamie. Sam's drinking isn't like Scott's. Sam's always been a binge drinker. He knows when it's coming on, and he'd never keep Eric and Jamie with him. He's brought them home early, because when he feels that urge, nothing—and I mean nothing—will keep him from the bars. One time he climbed out a bathroom window when I thought he was taking a shower."

Sarah stopped stirring. "You're kidding."

"Nope. He even left the water running, to throw me off. But once the binge is over, he's fine until the next one—two weeks, a month, sometimes a little more. During that time, he's sober, and he's never, ever been violent. He gets quiet, moody." She looked over the rim of her coffee cup at Sarah. "So, no, I don't worry about the boys."

"I'm glad. I always liked Sam, but I felt bad for you, that he made you so unhappy."

"I liked him, too. Still do. Sometimes I wish—" She shook her head. "No, I don't wish to be back in that destructive cycle." She laughed, a far-away expression in her eyes. "It was bad, really bad, while it was going on, but now I can laugh at some of it. I remember one night in particular when he finally called me. He'd been gone for three days, and wanted me to come and pick him up."

"What did he do with his car?"

"That's what I wondered. He thought he'd left it at home. I asked him where he was, thinking if I could find him, I might get him home and worry about getting the car later. He had no idea where he was–just that he was on a corner. I asked him if there was a sign. He said there was, but he couldn't read it. So I asked him to spell it out for me."

"Where was he?"

"Damned if I know. He spelled out the letters very, very slowly, only a little slurred: T- e - x - a - c - o."

Sarah burst out laughing, something she hadn't done since Saturday. It felt good. "How did you find him?"

"He ended up in jail. I had to go down and bail him out the next morning. Drunk in Public." She picked up the check. "It wasn't very funny at the time. We always leave out the boring parts of the stories, like me not sleeping all night, up pacing the floor, wondering if he was all right."

Sarah knew all about pacing the floor, waiting for somebody to call. "Oh, wait, Laura. I forgot to call Angie. It'll just take a minute."

The girl answered on the second ring, and Sarah told her about Caro's death, the video game and CDs. "We'll be back at the house next week if you'd like to pick them up. Just call before you come, to make sure we're there."

Just before she ended the call, it occurred to her that Angie might have helped Caro pack the things in the office. "I was wondering. We've been looking for some sketches Caro did. They're missing and we think they might have been stolen—that Caro surprised the thief in her house the night she died."

"I don't know where they are. They were hanging on the wall with a bunch of other stuff. The cops think she was murdered?"

"I'm afraid so. Do you know where she might have put the sketches when she packed up the things in her office?"

"No. Maybe they're in one of the boxes."

"Okay. Thanks, Angie." Sarah put the phone in her pocket and told Laura what Angie had said.

They took Folsom Boulevard back to 80 East, speaking little. Sarah suspected Laura's thoughts were in the past with Sam, but Sarah's were firmly rooted in the present and kept circling back to Detective Coleman's parting words.

They passed East Lawn Memorial Cemetery, and Laura said, "We still have to make funeral arrangements."

"Maybe tomorrow?" Sarah closed her eyes, trying to picture the kind of service Caro might have liked, but the only image she could summon was that of Detective Coleman and his cold, accusing stare. She suspected that image would haunt her in the days and nights to come. Her lunch felt heavy in her stomach, like a rock she couldn't dislodge, and she shifted in the seat, trying to get more comfortable.

Laura crossed under the freeway at L Street and continued downtown, working her way over to the Memorial Garage at Fourteenth and H. She pulled into a space on the second level. "Dee will be parked in Sam's visitor space, but it's only a few blocks from here, so we won't have to walk far."

Sarah didn't mind walking. She loved this area.

They grabbed the bags of clothing for Eric and Jamie and took the elevator down to street level, exiting the garage directly across from the Music Circus Pavilion. No lines at the box office now. The summer season wouldn't start until mid-June. They walked on, past the deteriorating Clarion Mansion Inn, with its vine-covered walls, and the old Governor's Mansion. Sarah had taken field trips there, as a kid.

"Tell me again," she said. "Why are we talking to Sam's sister?"

"It's Sam's idea. She's a cop, and he thinks she may be able to help us. She knows Durant and Coleman, and she's familiar with how the system works. That may give her some idea of what they're planning, where their investigation is going."

"Kind of like having a spy on the inside? I like it."

They turned on E street, toward Sam's apartment. If she were ever single, Sarah would live on one of these leafy streets. She would buy season tickets for both the Community Theater and summer stock productions at the Music Circus and walk to the performances. She would sample all the surrounding restaurants and catch light rail to Old Sacramento for the annual Music Festival.

In her dreams. She could never afford it.

The next thought came so quickly it appalled her. She could now, with the money she'd get from Caro's estate. She pushed it away, trying to tamp it down, bury it deep inside her subconscious from where it had so unexpectedly erupted.

It wouldn't go back. It bubbled right beneath the surface, waiting to tease and torment her with possibilities. Tears stung her eyes, and she blinked them away. Did Laura have any of those same thoughts? Did Scott? No. She shook her head. Matt Coleman's suspicions were infecting her own mind–making her suspect those she loved. She couldn't let that happen.

She followed Laura up the wide steps to Sam's apartment building.

"Mom! Auntie Sarah!" Eric and Jamie launched themselves from the bottom step of the interior stairwell. Their sneakered feet landed on the tiled floor with solid thumps. Sarah took a quick side-step to avoid a collision, then exchanged hugs with both boys.

"What took you so long?" Jamie asked. "We've been waiting and waiting."

"Dad's gonna take us to the park while you're talking to Aunt Dee," Eric chimed in. "And maybe to the capitol building or Sutter's Fort."

"We're gonna get ice cream, too. Don't forget the ice cream." Jamie charged back up the stairs, Eric close behind. "They're here, Dad. They're here. Can we go now?"

Sarah followed the boys. She tousled Eric's mop of sandy brown hair. "I don't think the capitol's ready for you two." She hugged their father. "It's been too long, Sam. How are you?" She'd forgotten how blue his eyes were, a clear sky blue that accentuated the silvery streaks in his dark hair. More silver than the last time she saw him.

He wrapped his wiry arms around her waist. "Good, Sarah. I don't have to tell you how sorry I am about Caro."

"I know. Thanks." Blinking away tears, she turned toward the tall, dark-haired woman who bore a faint resemblance to Sam. "This must be Dee."

The woman smiled and held out her hand. "I've heard a lot about you. It appears I've got some real competition in the favorite aunt contest."

Sarah returned her smile. "That sounds like one of the most worthwhile and fun competitions I can imagine."

Dee turned toward Laura. "If I can help any with—"

"Thanks, Dee, I appreciate it." Laura hugged Eric and Jamie again before they ran out the door.

"Hang on, guys," Sam yelled to the boys. He put his wallet in his back pocket. "There's fresh coffee and some tea in the cupboard, and sodas in the fridge. Beer too, and wine, if you want it. Help yourselves. We'll probably be gone a couple of hours."

Laura's gaze followed Sam and the boys down the stairs. Then she closed the door and turned to face Dee. "I appreciate this, especially since Matt Coleman has already made up his mind one of us killed Caro. He's just not sure which one."

Dee turned toward the living room, so she wasn't facing either of them. "I'm not sure what you're thanking me for, Laura. Unfortunately, it's a proven fact that most murders are committed by family members or other people close to the victims. So you have to understand where Coleman is coming from. It's logical you would be suspects. Especially with your aunt's wealth. So Cole man is not being unreasonable."

Laura followed Dee into the living room and sank onto the sofa. "Kind of a self-fulfilling prophecy, isn't it? Think about it.

You're related, so the cops assume you're guilty. They concentrate so hard on proving you guilty, they don't look at other possibilities."

Sarah, on her way to the kitchen, paused in the doorway. "And they get enough convictions—right or wrong—to raise the statistics on people being killed by those closest to them. So the cycle goes on."

Dee shrugged. "They're just starting with you because you're the most obvious suspects. If they find other evidence, they'll certainly take a hard look at it. They have to begin somewhere."

Sarah leaned against the doorframe. "Is anybody really considering anything else? From where we're sitting, it doesn't seem like it."

"I know Al Durant's reputation. He's a good cop. He'll be looking at everything—not once, but two or three times—and there's very little he misses."

Sarah tried to hide her disappointment. Dee had already drawn her own conclusions about the case. There would be no help there. "Why did you agree to meet us today? I thought you were going to help."

Dee frowned. "I don't—"

Laura stared at her. "Sam didn't even talk to you about helping us, did he?" She covered her eyes with one hand. "Oh, God. I'm going to kill him. I should have known—" Her shoulders slumped. "He set this whole thing up, then chickened out when it came down to asking you about it. Typical Sam."

Dee's dark eyes flashed. "He did talk to me, and I told him the same thing I'm going to tell you. I don't have any information, other than what I'm trying to collect on my beat, and if I did, I couldn't share it with you. Worse, if you were to tell me something that might incriminate you, I'd have to report it."

Laura's eyes widened. "You would actually—"

Dee raised a hand, palm outward. "You might not even know information you shared was incriminating. You would be putting yourself at risk by talking to me about anything connected to your aunt's death, and I'd be putting myself and my career at risk if I shared information with you."

Laura glanced at Sarah, eyebrows raised. Sarah shook her head and turned toward the kitchen. She needed to think about Dee's words, and she had to get her emotions under control. She had counted too much on Dee.

Her step faltered when Laura said, "We're willing to take that chance. Even if you can't share information with us, something we say may help you find the real killer. You would at least listen, and not discount everything we tell you. Sarah and I have nothing to hide, so there's no way we could incriminate ourselves."

Sarah stood in the middle of the kitchen, her back to Laura and Dee, and struggled to catch her breath. She'd waited too long; she should have told Laura about Caro's message before they came here.

She pushed her phone deep into her pocket and reached for two coffee cups.

Chapter 12

Dee looked up as Sarah came back into the living room carrying two mugs. She set them on the coffee table and settled onto the sofa beside Laura, who handed her a pillow. Dee realized that Sarah needed the pillow behind her back to push her forward so her knees would meet the edge of the sofa. Laura was so attuned to her cousin's needs, she didn't even think about it before she offered a pillow.

Sarah's hostile stare unnerved Dee. She looked so much like the dead woman on the patio, it was like watching a ghost. *What am I doing here, risking my job for people I don't even know? I should walk out the door and not look back. But then I wouldn't be able to face Sam.*

She chose her words carefully. "As I said, Al Durant is a good cop, a fair one. I have every confidence he'll sort all this out." She kept her misgivings about Matt Coleman to herself. She didn't think he was going to make a good homicide detective, but right now, he was the detective on the case and he could cause them serious problems by overlooking clues or failing to pursue leads.

She hesitated. "If you're sure you want to do this, probably the best place to start would be with what you've told Detectives Coleman and Durant. That way, you can't tell me anything they don't already know."

"They talked to us separately," Laura said, "so I don't know what Sarah told them. They called it an interview, but it seemed to me more like an interrogation. They even wanted to know all about my car."

So it was Laura who had the Honda.

"And they seemed to be insinuating that Caro had a drinking problem—that she might have been drunk when she fell off the deck." Laura shook her head. "Caro didn't drink that much; I don't care how many bottles and glasses of wine were on the deck table."

Sarah frowned. "What are you talking about?"

"They didn't mention it to you?"

"They asked if Caro had a drinking problem, but they didn't tell me why they were asking." Sarah turned to Dee. "Do you know?"

Dee was convinced. Sarah either hadn't known about the wine or she was a good liar. Was there a reason why the detectives had told Laura and not Sarah? No. They knew the cousins would discuss those interrogations.

She tried to recall her climb up the patio stairs that morning. She had been distracted, her focus on clearing the house. "There was a wine bottle," she said, her voice halting, "and a glass on the deck table. I thought it was odd, for that time of the morning."

Sarah leaned forward, attentive and perhaps even a little friendlier. "We didn't go out on the deck today."

Dee studied her face. *She's grieving, but she's scared, too, probably with good reason.*

Dee had to be careful. Telling Sarah about the wine was okay; Laura already knew, but she'd best steer the conversation to safer ground. "Why don't you tell me about the interviews?"

She interrupted as little as possible while Sarah and Laura summarized their meetings with Coleman and Durant.

"Is there anything you didn't tell them that might be relevant? Because if there is, and you have nothing to hide, you need to tell them. Or, if you're in doubt, tell your attorney."

Both women looked puzzled.

"It's stressful," Dee said. "People are nervous. They forget things, or just don't think something is important. Worse, they sometimes withhold information—extramarital affairs, petty crime, that sort of thing. It always comes out, and makes the person look guilty."

Sarah opened her mouth, then closed it, and chewed on her lip. She dug into her pocket and pulled out her cell phone. "There is one thing. I didn't really keep it from them—"

Dee rose to her feet and held out her hand as a signal to stop. "Don't—"

"Caro did call me," Sarah said.

"—tell me." Dee finished, her voice trailing off to a whisper as she sank back into the chair.

"I didn't know about it," Sarah said. "Not until after the interview." She darted a quick glance at Laura, who drew in a sharp breath. Sarah rushed her words, as though she wanted to get them out before she changed her mind. "I didn't have my phone. After I did get it, I never had a chance to check my messages. Not until last night."

She played the message: *Sarah, I'm in Chicago, on my way home. Don't tell Scott or Laura until I have a chance to talk to you. Gotta go. Love you.*

"She can't mean what it sounds like," Laura said. "Play it again."

Sarah complied, and Dee concentrated on the length of the message. "Would your aunt have called from her cell phone?"

"Yes, once she was back in the States. And she wouldn't have had time for anything else. Detective Durant said she barely made it onto her California flight. She probably called about the time she was boarding."

Durant would check Caroline Brenhauser's calls and know she had phoned Sarah. Could he be certain she'd left a message? It was a short one. If he did know, he would wonder why she hadn't mentioned it.

"Why wouldn't Caro want me or Scott to know she was coming home?" Laura asked. "I don't get it. And I don't understand why you didn't tell me, Sarah."

"I didn't know about it until last night, and we've been rushing around all day. Laura," Sarah pleaded, "I needed some time to think about it. Not so much about you, but about Scott. And Caro asked me not to tell anyone."

"Before she was killed. That changed everything." Laura leveled an unfriendly look at her cousin. "I can't believe you didn't trust me enough to tell me. You've had all day, and not a peep out of you. No wonder Coleman suspects us. You're keeping information from them. What else have you kept from them? From me?" She jumped to her feet. "Oh, I get it now. You think Scott—" Her jaw clenched. "How far will you go to protect him, Sarah?" She grabbed her coffee mug and strode into the kitchen. Her heels clicked hard on the tile floor.

"Scott would never hurt Caro." Sarah raised her voice over the sound of banging cabinet doors. "And he had no reason, but Durant and Coleman won't believe that. They've already decided he's a—a wife beater."

"The problem is, you may have made them suspect you," Dee said. "They'll track your aunt's calls. Even if they're not sure she left a message, they'll be suspicious."

Laura carried her mug back to the coffee table and settled onto the far end of the sofa, not looking at her cousin. Sarah shifted on the other end, leaning away from Laura, and pulled her bent legs up beside her on the cushion.

"The message makes no sense to me, and I've gone over it so many times, I've memorized it. I thought when Laura and I went through the house today, we might find something to explain it, but that didn't pan out, either. Not unless there's something in Caro's studio, in that jumble of stuff. With Coleman there, we didn't have much time to look. I didn't even know about that wine on the deck."

"Maybe it's been there since the night of the party," Laura said. She shook her head. "No, Angie would have cleaned it up."

"Who is Angie?" Dee asked.

"She's a high school student," Sarah said. "Caro hired her on a part-time basis to do light housework. She would have helped Caro clean up after the party."

Laura added, "It was sort of a bon voyage gathering Caro threw for herself before she left for Europe. She loved to entertain."

Sarah swung her legs to the floor and sat up straight. "Do you suppose something that happened at the party might be important? I'm wondering because..." She sat forward, one elbow on the arm of the sofa, that hand pinching her bottom lip. "It's probably nothing. I was outside, in the garden, and I saw a couple out there, half hidden by the roses. At first, I thought they were guests, but I got a glimpse of white—a tunic, maybe, or a white apron–and I thought they might be some of the help. Before I could check into it, they disappeared, swallowed up in the darkness. Maybe they heard footsteps, because the next thing I knew, another couple showed up."

She shook her head and laughed, a sound so brittle Dee wondered what Sarah's normal laugh sounded like. "I guess it was a night for arguments because they were really going at it."

"You said arguments. So the first couple was arguing, too?" Dee asked.

Sarah looked at the floor, let out a deep breath, lifted her mug from the coffee table and stared into it. "No. I couldn't hear what they were saying. When I said 'arguments,' I was thinking about Scott. We'd quarreled earlier. That's why I was in the garden." Dee waited. Finally, Sarah said, "It's...Well, Scott has a drinking problem."

Laura snorted. "There's the understatement of the year."

Sarah glared at her and continued. "He was taking full advantage of the open bar, and I was afraid he'd drink too much."

"The couple who were arguing—what was that about?" Dee asked.

"Hard to tell. When you come in at the middle of an argument, it doesn't tend to make much sense. It sounded like the woman was accusing the man of seeing somebody else. Maybe having an affair. She was using some pretty strong language. I got the impression the woman in question was at the party."

Dee leaned forward. "And the man? What was he saying?"

"Mostly, he was trying to shush her. He sounded embarrassed. Maybe even a little desperate to shut her up. I couldn't see, but I think he may have clapped his hand over her mouth. She stopped talking all of a sudden, and her voice was muffled. They struggled a little, and he pulled her away."

"Back toward the house?"

Sarah thought about it. "You know, I really don't think so. I think they walked off toward the street."

"And it wasn't your aunt?"

Sarah shook her head, not answering. Dee watched her face. "Sarah, is it possible the woman was talking about Caro? Accusing the man of having an affair with her?"

"Caro wouldn't—"

"I'm not saying Caro had an affair, but if the woman even thought she was, that could be a strong motive for murder. You need to tell Detective Coleman—"

"Right. I'm sure he'll fall all over himself checking it out," Laura said, "he pays so much attention to everything we say. I don't think there's anything there, anyway. It doesn't sound like Caro, and if there was a jealous woman, I can't imagine who it would be."

"Maybe there's a guest list?" Dee said.

Sarah shifted on the sofa. "If there is, the detectives probably took it, but I can talk to some of Caro's friends, see if I can piece one together." She glanced at the wall clock. "I've got to get going. I hadn't realized it was getting so late."

"Don't forget to tell somebody about the message, Sarah," Dee said.

"I won't. I'll take care of it tomorrow."

Just as Sarah and Laura rose from the sofa, Eric and Jamie burst into the room, followed by Sam, carrying two pizza boxes. "Dinner," he said.

"That pepperoni really smells wonderful," Sarah said, "but I promised Scott I'd have dinner with him."

"Please. Please, Auntie Sarah. Stay and have pizza with us." Jamie clutched her leg.

Sarah glanced at Laura, one eyebrow raised. "I can stay for a while if you want to eat with the boys."

"No. I need to get going, too. I get to eat with them every night."

Sarah knelt beside Jamie. "Maybe we can have pizza sometime next week if it's okay with your mom." She cast a hopeful glance toward Laura, but her cousin didn't respond.

It was going to be a chilly ride home.

Later that evening, Sam checked on his sons, sleeping in the spare bedroom. Eric lay facing Jamie, the cap he had insisted on wearing to bed now turned so the bill, along with the *River Cats* logo, stuck out over his left ear. Sam smiled, reached to remove the hat, changed his mind, and turned his attention to Jamie, who sprawled, his right leg uncovered, the sheet twisted around it. Sam untangled the bedding, maneuvered Jamie back under the blankets, and tucked them around both boys. He lingered for a moment, watching them, before he went back to the kitchen and popped the tab off a can of beer. He opened a bottle of wine, poured a glass and took it to Dee, in the living room.

"Sam, the bon voyage party Caro threw before she went to Germany—did you go?"

He snorted. "Not likely. Caro didn't invite me, and I wouldn't have gone if she had. I despised Caro. If it hadn't been for her, Laura and I might have made a go of our marriage."

His words surprised her. Sam kept his feelings close—so close that, like an unopened wound, they sometimes festered into something uglier and deeper than the original injury. He hadn't talked about the collapse of his marriage. Maybe he should have.

"Be careful with remarks like that, Sam, especially around Durant and Coleman. They haven't talked to you yet, but they will."

"Why would they talk to me? Surely they can't think I'm a suspect." Dee didn't say anything, so he added, "If I am, I have a problem, because I don't have an alibi, other than Eric and Jamie, and they were asleep. And, for the life of me, I can't figure out what my motive would be. If I'd planned to kill Caro, I would have done it years ago, not now, when it no longer matters."

She stared at him, speechless for a moment, then said, "It will matter to the detectives. When you make statements like that, you're giving them all the motive they need."

He crushed his beer can, shrugged and pointed at her wine glass. "Want another?"

She shook her head; she'd taken only two or three sips of the Cabernet. But she'd grown accustomed to Sam's beer chugging. He had built up a high tolerance and held his liquor well.

He came back from the kitchen with another beer. "I think I may have a clue why Caro came home early."

"Really? You'll have to tell Durant and Coleman."

"I figured that, but I want you to know, too. Maybe you'll be able to help—"

"Laura?"

"Maybe. Or Sarah." He turned the beer can in his hands, as if he was studying the logo. "Owen Hardesty—that's Caro's accountant—I've known him for a long time. Anyway, back when I married Laura, Caro wanted me, or at least my firm, to manage her money. I didn't think that was a good idea. Conflict of interest. So I recommended Owen."

Sam tipped his head back and drank several swallows of beer. "He's independent, but he has a solid reputation. He works in my building, and I've gotten to know him over the years."

The part of Dee that was Sam's sister didn't want to ask the next question, but the part that was cop asked, "Have you ever discussed Caro's finances with him?"

Sam flushed. "I didn't want to know anything about Caro's finances. Or anything else about her." He finished his beer. "I appreciate her setting up trust funds for the boys, but I can take care of my sons. We didn't need her meddling in our lives. She'd done enough damage."

Dee, impatient now, raised a hand to stop him. "You're better off to leave that alone. Do you understand me?" She stared into his eyes, hoping to hammer home the message, and realized he hadn't answered her question. "And that's not what I asked you.

What I'm asking is, did this Owen Hardesty ever tell you anything about Caro's finances?"

Sam went to the refrigerator and came back with another beer. "He told me something he thought I should know, because of the boys, the family connection. Something was off with some of the accounts. He tried to tell me about it." He raised his head and met her gaze. "But I wouldn't let him."

"And that's all you know? That there was something wrong? Did he tell you which accounts and what they were doing about it?"

"No, but it was difficult for Owen. The decision to tell me. He was—well, it was obvious he was struggling with it, so I thought it might be the boys' trust funds. Or maybe the ones Caro set up for Sarah and Laura." He looked past her. "I don't know anybody who would have access to the boys' accounts, other than Laura. But why would she do anything with them?"

"Laura and Sarah have accounts, too?"

Sam shrugged. "Nothing big. Caro wanted them to have some funds available for emergencies. In case she wasn't around. I think there's about five thousand in each of them."

"Must be nice." Dee took a sip of her wine. "How often did she replenish them?"

"Not that often. At least not while Laura and I were married. She considered it kind of a security blanket, knowing it was there. I don't think either of them wanted to take advantage of Caro's generosity, and they knew she would replenish the funds without saying a word. Of course, she might not have if either of them had abused it."

"Did you talk to Laura about Owen's misgivings?"

Sam shook his head. "I didn't know how to bring it up. It's not information I should have, and I didn't want Owen to get into trouble. Nobody could do anything with it except Caro anyway. I thought Owen would tell her as soon as she got back, but now I think he might have called her. I think that's why she came home early."

Should she tell Sam about the message Caro had left on Sarah's phone? No. Durant and Coleman hadn't interviewed him yet, and when he got that information, she wanted it to come from Sarah or Laura, not her. She was getting too involved; she needed to back away.

Sam's voice rose. "My God, do you think that's why Caro was killed?" He stood and paced a few steps. "But that can't be it. Nobody knew she was coming back."

Dee thought about the message: *Don't tell Scott or Laura.* Why not tell Laura? How could Scott do anything with the funds, unless it was through Sarah? Yet Caro sent the message to Sarah, seemingly the person she trusted most. Could Scott have somehow used Sarah, without her knowledge?

"Would Sarah have access to those accounts?" Dee asked, still thinking her way through the problem.

Sam sat and studied his beer can again. "Only if she had the passwords and access to the computer. I know Sarah and Scott are hurting financially, but I can't see Sarah doing anything like that. Especially with the boys' trust funds."

Dee didn't doubt Sarah's affection for the boys or theirs for her, and she and Laura shared an unusual closeness, for cousins. Yet Sarah had risked alienating Laura by not telling her about the phone call. Why? Did she know more than she was divulging? Was Laura right? Was Sarah trying to shield Scott?

"How far do you think Sarah might go to protect her husband?"

"Protect him?" Sam snorted, lifted his beer can to his lips, realized it was empty and rose to get another. "I think Sarah is the one who needs protecting, not Scott."

"Is she afraid of him?"

"Sarah? I don't know. He can be a real ass when he's drunk. Sarah is—I don't know. Insecure, maybe? Scott is a control freak and Sarah's always done pretty much what he wants. Tries not to rock the boat." He paused, shaking his head. "Sometimes I think she's afraid to let him go. I don't know why, but I somehow got the impression she doesn't believe in divorce."

"You're describing some of the symptoms of an abused wife."

"Abused?" Sam closed the refrigerator and stood for a moment, beer in hand. "She's never had any injuries I'm aware of." He shook his head. "I can't see Sarah sticking around if Scott started pounding on her. She has other options. She's attractive, smart, fun—"

"Intelligence has nothing to do with it, and I'm talking about abuse that is emotional, rather than physical. It can be insidious, almost like brainwashing. The partner who appears to be so caring at the beginning of the relationship gradually becomes more and more manipulative and controlling."

Sam frowned but didn't say anything, so Dee elaborated. "It works well on women with low self-esteem or somebody like Sarah. If she's had a lot of losses in her family, that could make her insecure."

Sam was silent for a few minutes. "You've described Scott pretty well, and Sarah, too, I guess. I haven't seen much of her since Laura and I split up, but she seems different somehow. That may be Laura, rubbing off on her." He met Dee's gaze. "Laura is definitely not timid or insecure."

"No, she's not." Dee, seeing the pain reflected in his eyes, wondered why she was putting her job at risk for Laura. After the evening she'd just spent with them, she didn't believe either Sarah or Laura were involved in Caroline Brenhauser's murder, but she had to leave it to the detectives. Al Durant was good. He would find the killer.

She spoke the next words without thinking. "Sam, I can't do this. I'm risking my career to try to help Laura. I know you still care for her, and I wish I could help, but I have to tell my boss I have a connection to the case. If I don't, and they find out—"

"I know. It's too much to ask of you, and you've already helped." He was silent for a few moments. "But you're my sister. They can't keep you from talking to me, can they?"

"No, they can't do that." She rose and hugged him. "Sam—be careful when you talk to Coleman. Don't give him any reason to suspect you."

She left the apartment doubting Sam could tamp down his bitterness long enough to get through the interview.

She couldn't worry about that right now. She had to figure out how she was going to tell Durant about her involvement in the case.

When she went to see him the next day, he didn't seem troubled about the connection. "I don't see a problem," he said. "You're not a detective, and you have nothing to do with the case, so you're not privy to any information you can give the suspects. As long as you keep your distance, work your beat, and report anything you do learn, I don't see a conflict."

He obviously didn't know about Coleman's running mouth disease. At least, not yet.

"There was a message from Caroline Brenhauser," Dee said, "left on Sarah Wagner's cell phone. I just found out about it last night. She said she didn't find it until after the interview. She's going to call you about it."

"Yes, I know." Durant seemed distracted. He glanced at his watch. "Coleman will follow up on it." He stuffed papers into his briefcase and stood. "I'm not going to be spending any time on the case for a while. I have to go to court. Jury trial. One that could last for days. Maybe a week or more. Matt Coleman will be handling the case until I get back."

Chapter 13

Sarah unfastened her seat belt as soon as Laura turned into the driveway. "When do you want to get together to make the arrangements?"

Laura didn't look at her. "Whenever you're ready." Her voice was cool, distant. "It doesn't matter to me."

"Fine. I'll call you," Sarah said, and by the time she unlocked the front door, Laura was gone, without a hug or even a wave. Once inside, Sarah leaned against the door, eyes closed.

"Sarah, is that you?" Scott called from the kitchen. "What are you in the mood for, Italian or Chinese?"

She didn't want to go out for dinner. She wanted to burrow deep into her blankets and never crawl out. But it wasn't Scott's fault. He was trying, and she needed to meet him halfway.

She perked up a little when they entered Alphonso's, and her stomach complained—loudly—that it was hungry when she breathed in the aroma from the surrounding tables. They sat near the window, and despite her protests that they couldn't afford it, Scott ordered a bottle of Merlot.

"You have to splurge a little sometimes, Sarah, and I think this is one of those times."

Maybe it would help with the conversation. They needed to talk about so many things she didn't quite know where to begin: his job, his father, his drinking, the design school, Caro. She took a deep breath. "Caro left a message on my phone."

He took another bite of cannelloni and waited for her to continue.

"She was in Chicago, on her way home, but she said I shouldn't tell you or Laura. Do you have any idea why she wouldn't want you to know? It doesn't make any sense to me."

He swallowed, picked up his wine and took a long sip. He was stalling, and whatever he told her, it was going to be a lie. She wasn't sure how she sensed that. She never had before but didn't doubt the sudden revelation. She sipped her own wine, studying his face: the sudden stillness, followed by a watery smile.

"Who knows what went through Caro's mind?" he asked. "She could be a little paranoid sometimes. This is the same woman who tried to convince you I was gambling our money away, remember?" His voice had changed; it was light, almost bantering. "Maybe she'd planned a nice surprise for me."

"Yeah, right, she's so fond of you." Sarcasm wasn't going to help. "She didn't want me to tell Laura, either, and I can't think of any surprise that would include the two of you."

He dabbed a napkin at the corner of his mouth, then clenched it in his fist. "Did you ask Laura?"

"She didn't know, either, but it had to be important, for Caro to call from Chicago."

He threw his napkin on the table. "What the hell do you want me to say, Sarah? I already told you I don't know anything about it. Why do you keep harping on it?"

She opened her eyes wide, trying to contain tears that threatened to overflow. "I didn't realize I was harping. I think you're overreacting." She stood. "I have to go to the ladies' room."

By the time she got her hurt feelings under control, squashed down her anger, and returned to the table, Scott held the dessert list. "These crepes look good. Apples and pastry cream, gelato and caramel sauce. Or the chocolate mousse with fresh raspberries." He talked fast, one word almost tripping over another.

"I can't eat any more. How about I finish my wine while you're having dessert?"

He smiled. "How about we both skip it and open another bottle when we get home, where we'll be nice and cozy? Finish our conversation there? I've got a lot of ideas about some of the things we can do now." He signaled for their check.

"Now?"

"Well, not right now. But later. After—you know—after the estate is settled."

"That's what you want to get cozy and talk about? Caro's money?" She reached for her purse. "I don't think so. Not now. Maybe not ever."

He tried to apologize on the way home. "I know it's too soon to talk about it. You're still grieving. You're in a lot of pain. I just...I guess I finally saw a way out of some of our problems and got carried away. I'm sorry. Let's pretend the subject never came up. Tell me about your day. It must have been difficult, going into the house. Are they going to release it, now that you've had the walk-through?"

She had stopped listening. His apologies no longer held much meaning. What had happened to change him so much? More important, would he ever again be the man she had married—the one she had loved and admired because he had been so much fun, so caring and thoughtful and charming? He could still be all those things when he tried, charming friends and acquaintances, people who didn't know him well. Had he changed, or had it all been a facade he couldn't maintain for extended periods of time?

He was gone when Sarah woke the next morning, grief washing over her again as she became fully conscious. She wished she could lose herself again in the depths of sleep and, not for the first time in her life, understood why people took too many sleeping pills.

The rift with Laura over Caro's message played in her head, over and over. She should have handled it better, told both Scott and Laura about the message right away. Now, she didn't know how to repair the damage.

As she showered, dressed and made breakfast, unwelcome thoughts coursed through her mind. Why did Scott go to Caro's house Saturday morning? He claimed he was looking for her. But he knew she didn't have Caro's house key with her. She couldn't get into the house.

Was there a connection between Caro's call and Scott going to her house? Had he listened to Caro's message, known she was on her way home, and gone to—do what? He would never have harmed her. But he never answered her question, either, about whether he had heard her phone ring or listened to Caro's message.

Laura's stricken face—was that because Sarah had kept something from her? Or was it the message itself?

Sipping her coffee, she looked at Caro's sketches. They didn't have their usual calming effect. If only Caro could talk to her, help her understand. But the sketches didn't talk, nor did Caro's photograph. Where was the voice she'd heard Saturday? The voice so like Caro's? The one that told her she had to find her own way?

Too restless and distracted to concentrate, she wandered through the house, coffee cup in hand, and finally settled, cross-legged, on the living room carpet, a pile of scrapbooks and photo albums in front of her.

Lost in the past, she wasn't aware of the hours slipping by until Scott came in the door with bags of take-out food. He paused long enough to drop a kiss on the top of her head before heading to the kitchen with their dinner.

"I got Mexican," he said. "Didn't think you'd be up to cooking. Want a beer with it?"

"Yeah, that sounds good." She slid the albums back into the bookcase and rose to her feet. "Thanks for thinking of this." She nodded toward the food. "I got lost in old memories."

He hugged her. "Maybe that's good for you. A catharsis. Are you up for a movie tonight? I can look for something. Maybe a comedy?"

"That sounds nice." She didn't want to watch a movie, but maybe he was right, and he was trying.

Long after he went to sleep that night, she lay awake, thoughts still churning and twisting into knots she couldn't untangle.

She threw back the covers and went to the kitchen for a cup of tea. While she drank it, she pulled up the word processor on her computer. Maybe if she could see the questions in black and white, she could shift them around and bring some order to the chaos. She worked for almost an hour, but when she finished, that's all she had: just a series of unanswered questions and observations. *Well, it's a start. Maybe if I do some brainstorming? Some free flow writing? Throw everything on the page, without allowing myself to stop and edit?*

What she had, after the better part of another hour at the computer, was not increased insight, but the nucleus of an obituary for Caro. She saved the file, read through it again, made a few edits, deleted portions of it, elaborated on others, and changed the wording from first person to third. It was good. Really good. She saved it as a new file. The e-mail to Laura was harder, but the best she could do:

> *Laura, here's what I have, so far, on Caro's obituary. Feel free to make changes. I'm also attaching a couple of photos. If you have better ones, send them to me, along with your notes on the text. Maybe we can take it to the Sacramento Bee as soon as we have a time of service set up. Sarah*

She crawled back into bed about one o'clock, drifted off to sleep sometime after two, and came awake fighting the blankets, trying to reach the alarm. She punched the button twice, but it didn't stop ringing. *The phone. It's the phone, stupid.*

"Sarah, it's beautiful. I wouldn't change a word. And either of the photos will work."

"Oh. Laura." Sarah rubbed her eyes and peered at the clock. Six thirty. The obituary. Laura was calling about the obituary.

Scott grunted and burrowed deeper into the blankets.

Sarah slid out of bed. "Um, thanks. I'm glad you like it. Which picture do you think would work best?"

"Doesn't matter. They're both good. Sarah...I'm so sorry. I shouldn't have reacted the way I did yesterday. I know I hurt you, and I apologize."

Sarah paused at the bedroom door. "I'm sorry, too. I should have told you."

"Not 'til you had a chance to talk to Scott. I realized that later—how difficult it was going to be."

If she only knew. Sarah turned toward the kitchen. "Do you want to take care of those arrangements—at least what we can—this morning?"

"We can do it all. Coleman called. They've released the house, and they'll release Caro's body Wednesday. We just have to let them know which mortuary."

"Then we can take care of the memorial service today." Sarah was glad. She managed better when she had something to do.

"Yeah. Let's get it done early, then go over to the house and tackle that room. Do you think we should plan to spend a couple of days? It's going to take a while to sift through everything."

Sarah's stomach churned at the thought of spending a night in the house where Caro had died, but they had to clear out the room and find out if anything was missing. Eventually, they'd have to pack up Caro's paintings and the rest of her things and decide what to do with the house. It wasn't the house that killed Caro. They had to find out who did before Matt Coleman decided to arrest one of them.

"I'll pack a bag," she told Laura. At least for one night, she wouldn't have to listen to any more of Scott's fake apologies.

"Okay, I'll pick you up in about an hour."

Sarah tiptoed back into the bedroom to grab jeans and a polo shirt, and the suitcase she'd packed Saturday morning for the trip to Reno. She showered and dressed, added her cosmetic bag to the case, and checked on Scott. He was still sleeping. She wrote a note, asking him to please unload the camping gear from the Explorer. She underlined the word "please."

Laura was a few minutes late. "Sorry. I ran by a new listing on the way so I could snap a few pictures."

"Great. Do you have a buyer in mind?"

"Maybe. I'm hoping to get back early enough tomorrow to give them a tour."

They got to the mortuary in time for their appointment and made arrangements to hold the memorial service on Thursday. When they finished, they took the obituary to the Sacramento Bee on Twenty-first Street.

Sarah's stomach grumbled loud enough for Laura to hear. "No breakfast? I think I remember a coffee shop on Alhambra."

Sarah mentally counted her money. "No, let's stop for groceries so we can eat at Caro's. We can get enough for dinner, too, and breakfast tomorrow. There's a supermarket on the way."

They moved through the store at a brisk pace, taking their cue from overhead aisle signs.

"Crunchy or smooth?" Sarah asked, holding up jars of peanut butter.

"We're having peanut butter sandwiches for lunch?"

"Why not? It's quick, and I want to get started on that room." Sarah pushed the cart toward the dairy section. "We'll be tired tonight, so let's keep it simple. Maybe an omelet and a salad?"

She opened an egg carton. "One is missing."

"You mean broken. Cracked."

"Nope, see?" Sarah held the carton open so her cousin could peer in. Laura picked up another. "There's an egg missing from this one, too."

"Why would anybody take one egg?" Sarah asked.

"I don't know. Egg burglars? Do I look like the egg police? Better ask somebody who knows." She found a full carton and put it in the grocery cart.

The clerk at the checkout counter shrugged when Laura asked about the missing eggs. "Happens all the time."

"Really?" Sarah asked. "Only one? Why?"

"No clue. I just work here."

Laura wheeled the cart out of the store. "That's the trouble with the world. Nobody cares. They just do their jobs and go home. No curiosity. I'll miss that about Caro. She was so interested in everything, so full of curiosity." She opened the trunk. "Damn. I forgot about that stuff. We'll have to put the groceries in the back."

Softball gloves and mitts nestled between a cooler and boxes of flyers featuring houses for sale. The grip end of a bat poked out of a nest of real estate signs.

Sarah opened the back door of the Honda. "Yeah, you're right about Caro. It's too bad she never found somebody after she lost Roger. She was still so young—"

"She said Roger was the love of her life, and she'd never find another. I like to think that they're finally together again, happy."

"I like that." Sarah pictured Roger, waiting for Caro, his face lighting up when he saw her. "Do you think there's only one? Love of your life? If there is, how much chance do we have of finding him? I thought you and Sam were good together, but you couldn't make it work. And I like Sam. Scott and I—" Sarah felt warmth creeping up her neck and into her cheeks. "I didn't mean we're not making it work."

Laura placed the last bag into the car. "You don't have to dance around it. I know what you mean. Even if you and Scott work things out, you'll never have what Caro and Roger had. I don't think many people find that."

"Maybe we didn't wait long enough. Didn't try hard enough to find the right one." Sarah slid into the car and fastened her seat belt.

"Strange thought, isn't it?" Laura asked. "That the right people might still be out there, looking for us? Wondering where we are, if they'll ever find us?" She started the car. "And I'm still too afraid to look, after Sam, and you're afraid, too. I think you're afraid to be alone."

Laura was wrong. Sarah didn't mind being alone. In fact, her favorite time of the year was the annual, week-long camping trip Scott took with his dad. She never told him that, though, and she didn't want to tell Laura, either.

"Well, on that profound thought," she said, "let's get going. I want to get started on that search. We've got to prove there was a burglar in that house."

Chapter 14

They put the groceries away and, without discussing where they would sleep, unpacked their overnight bags and pulled out the lower section of the trundle-style daybed in Sarah's old room. While they bantered about having a sleepover, Sarah eyed the too-firm bottom section of the bed. It would be uncomfortable, but she would sleep better there than in Caro's room. Not so much because it was Caro's—the vanilla scent might even be comforting—but because she would be alone, and she didn't want to be alone in this house tonight.

"Oh, Laura, I forgot," she said. "There's something else. We have to choose a dress." Laura, looking puzzled, opened her mouth to speak, and Sarah hurried on. "For Caro. For the service."

Laura closed her eyes for a moment and took a deep breath. "Okay. Let's do it now. Get it out of the way."

Sarah opened Caro's closet. Laura ran her hands over the hangers. "What do you think about the one she bought for Julie Vaughn's wedding?" She pulled out a rose-pink chiffon dress with a flared skirt and embossed top.

"Oh, yes. That looked so good on her. The pink tones really brought out her coloring." Sarah clapped a hand over her mouth. "Oh, God, what am I thinking?"

Laura hugged her. "It's okay. The dress will be fine. Caro already sent it to the cleaners, so all we have to do is drop it off at the mortuary on our way home."

"And if we plan to get home anytime soon, we'd better get started on that room."

"I've been thinking about that," Laura said. "We're not sure the sketches are even in there. Why don't we start downstairs? It won't take long, and if we find them—"

"We won't have to worry about the room full of stuff. Good thinking. And you're right; it won't take long. Caro wouldn't have stored them in the basement or kitchen, so there's just the living room, dining room, entry way and library alcove."

"And not too many places to stash them away, other than the cubbyhole under the stairs. I'll tackle it and the hallway if you want to start with the library."

It didn't take long. Sarah checked the china cabinet in the dining room, then moved on to the coat closet in the entryway, and from there to the library alcove.

"Find anything?" she asked Laura, who was putting boxes back into the cubbyhole under the stairs.

"No, and Caro was so organized, everything is labeled–mostly Christmas stuff. How about you?"

Sarah shook her head. Not many places to store things down here."

Laura closed the cubbyhole door, moved into the living room and started opening drawers. "Looks like we have to clear out that room, after all."

It wasn't going to be easy. Even with her petite frame, Sarah couldn't squeeze between the furniture and boxes. "We're going to have to move it all out. But where?"

"Back where it came from? Caro's office?"

"You know, that's not a bad idea," Sarah said. "If we put everything back the way we remember it, it might be easier to see what's missing."

"We'll have to get help. There's no way we can move all that stuff."

"Sure there is. The boxes will be the biggest problem, at least those stacked on top of the furniture, but we can partially unpack them if we need to. Come on." Sarah led her cousin to Caro's bathroom. "Get the big throw rug. I'll get one from the other bathroom." She showed Laura how to slide the furniture by placing a rug, bottom-side-up, under each end.

"Wow. That makes it so much easier. Where did you learn to do that?"

"When you're as small as I am, you find ways. Just because I look like the proverbial ninety-pound weakling doesn't mean I am. You're forgetting all those muscles I developed in gymnastics."

Laura smiled. "No, I was trying to be kind and not mention your manly, muscle-bound arms and legs."

Sarah laughed. "Shut up and get to work, weakling."

Caro's office gradually took shape: the furniture back where it belonged, draperies hung from the windows, lamps, and books back in place.

They found nothing to hang on the walls—not even the family photographs.

Laura stretched and rubbed the small of her back. "You're right, Goliath, I'm a weakling. I've got to take a break."

"I thought you'd never ask."

They had almost emptied Caro's studio. An easel stood in the corner, a cloth covering its canvas. Several more, unframed, were leaning against a corner wall. Laura separated them, one by one, propped them against the wall, and backed up, studying each in turn.

"These are wonderful. I don't know which are best, the sketches or the paintings. She had so much talent."

"So do you. Caro just had a lot more training."

Laura shook her head. "It wouldn't matter. I could never have done anything like this."

"You never tried oils. Your sketches are really good."

Laura hugged Sarah. "I appreciate your somewhat biased opinion, but my sketches don't begin to compare to Caro's. Those she did of Dad and your mom—Caro was so young when she did them. She established her artistic reputation early, and she kept getting better and better."

"Laura," Sarah spoke slowly. "Maybe that's it. Her reputation as an artist, not a random burglary. Thieves might find out her studio was here, in the house, and suspect her work would be here. What if Caro surprised them while they were looking for it and...they killed her?"

Laura's eyes widened. "That's why they didn't take anything from the bottom floor, why they came upstairs. They were looking for the artwork, but the canvases were hidden back here, behind all the other stuff." Her shoulders slumped. "Detective Coleman isn't going to believe that because the thieves didn't take anything."

"If we can't find the sketches of Mom and your dad, and all the other things we know are missing, we'll have some proof, won't we? And if they're here, they've got to be in some of those last boxes."

Laura sank into a chair. "Right now, I'm almost too tired—and too grubby—to care. It's going to have to wait until tomorrow. I'm bushed. I could go for an ice-cold beer about now, but I don't suppose Caro has any?"

Sarah shook her head. "Just wine."

"Is there a store nearby? Where did Caro shop?"

"Nordstrom, Macys, Paris—I don't know. Want to go back to the supermarket?"

"No, I don't have the energy. I'm going to take a quick shower and, if I'm still on my feet after dinner, maybe have a glass of wine."

"Go ahead. I'll wait and take a hot bath before I go to bed, to work out some of the aches and pains so I'm not so sore tomorrow. In the meantime, I'm opening a bottle of wine."

She found a bottle of Sangiovese, one of Caro's favorites. "Here's to you, Caro," she whispered, her voice husky. A warm presence enfolded her. Of course. This was the room where she would feel the closest connection to Caro–this room where they had shared so many meals, so many bottles of wine, so many long, intimate conversations. The room where Caro had shared childhood memories, including stories about her big sister,

Sarah's mother. The room where they'd planned Sarah's wedding—and where Sarah had told Caro about her miscarriage. A loss so devastating at the time, in those early, good years of her marriage, she hadn't been sure she could survive it. Now she rarely thought about having children.

She sat still, tracing her fingers over the bottle's label, letting the memories wash over her, tugging her into the past and the years she had spent in this house with Caro, a woman who had been so young, she'd been as much a friend as a loving, nurturing aunt.

Caro had clearly delineated living zones, the upstairs rooms her private world, where few people were ever invited. She entertained on the bottom floor, sometimes with a few friends for dinner, and at other times, big parties, like the last one before she left for Europe.

Sarah set the unopened wine bottle down and rose from her stool. Maybe Caro kept beer on hand for some of those guests.

A search yielded little: the fresh vegetables and fruit they'd just bought; catsup, mayo, mustard, jelly and some soft drinks; eggs and cheese for the omelet. No beer—and no butter. How could she have forgotten butter? She couldn't make an omelet without butter. She couldn't even make toast.

There had been a little store a few blocks away, one Caro had often used. Sarah could be there and back in a few minutes. She scribbled a hasty note, grabbed her purse and Laura's car keys and headed for the Honda.

The store was gone, probably long closed, along with the pastry shop where Sarah had once worked. There would be another neighborhood grocery somewhere in the vicinity, but she didn't know where, so she went back to the supermarket.

After collecting the beer, she walked down the length of the dairy case, searching for butter. She passed cheese, eggs, milk, cream, but no butter. When she looked around for somebody to ask, she noticed that the case curved to the right. There she found it: boxes of butter, tubs of butter–solid butter, whipped butter, low- fat butter, low salt butter, almost-butter. She grabbed a box of the real stuff and glanced back at the long side of the dairy case, mentally calculating the shortest distance to the checkout stands.

A woman stood in front of the egg case, an open carton in her hands. She looked in both directions, turned her head and glanced behind her. Odd. What was she looking for?

Sarah almost missed the transfer of the egg to the woman's coat pocket—a very ragged pocket in a man's suit coat, so old Sarah couldn't determine the color. Gray hair straggled from the woman's scarf, and a skirt of some dark material hung unevenly beneath the coat, the hem loose on one side.

The woman closed the carton and placed it back in the case. She opened another and studied the eggs, ostensibly searching for cracks. With another furtive glance in both directions, she slid an egg into another pocket. Only when she turned to leave did she glimpse Sarah. She paused, her head tilted a little, sharp hazel eyes staring, assessing. She lifted a pointed chin and turned toward the front of the store.

Sarah grabbed a dozen eggs and pushed her cart to the checkout counter just as the woman went out the door. By the time she got outside, the woman had disappeared. Sarah drove around the block and halfway down another before she saw her, pushing a grocery cart loaded with what appeared to be junk. Sarah slowed the car and pulled to the curb.

"Wait," she called. The woman walked faster. Sarah parked and ran after her.

"Here," she said, thrusting the eggs at the woman. "Take these."

The woman stopped, her toes peeking beyond holes cut into frayed and dirty tennis shoes. She glared at Sarah. "What you want?"

"I saw you." Sarah nodded toward the store. "Back there. You took two eggs."

"What business is it of yours, missy?"

"What? No, you don't understand. I—"

"You deef or something?" The woman raised her voice. "What business is it of yours, what I do?" She looked at Sarah's leather sandals, her gold watch. "Ain't never been hungry, have you? You think that store's gonna miss a couple eggs? Ain't hurting you none, so leave me be. You keep sticking your nose where it don't belong, you're like to get some more bruises on that pretty face."

Sarah stepped back. "I'm–I'm sorry. I didn't mean...I just wanted you to have these."

Without a backward glance, the woman turned and trudged down the street, pushing the cart. Sarah stared at the carton of eggs she still held in her hands. It looked as though they'd have eggs for breakfast. Maybe lunch, too.

Her phone rang. Scott. "Why did you take off like that?" he asked. "I planned to go with you today."

"You never said anything." She walked back toward the car.

"I thought it was pretty obvious. You said there were a lot of boxes and furniture to move. You and Laura can't move them by yourselves."

"We already did." She nestled the eggs next to the beer, behind the driver's seat, and closed the car door. "It's all moved, and we just have to go through a few more boxes."

"I could still come down and help. Maybe hook up the computers and printers."

"They're not here, Scott. The cops took them."

Silence. Was he still there? "Scott?"

"Yeah." He sounded tired. "I guess there's nothing else I can do then, is there?"

Chapter 15

A black SUV occupied Caro's driveway—parked in the middle, leaving no room for the Honda to get into the garage. "Inconsiderate jerk," Sarah muttered, pulling to the curb.

A man burst out the front door of the house. Sarah caught a glimpse of Laura's pale face behind him before she slammed the door shut. The man ran toward the parked SUV. Afraid to get out of the car, Sarah punched Laura's number. Busy. Laura would be calling nine-one-one. *Think, Sarah, think. This might be the man who killed Caro.*

She aimed her camera phone at him, but a billed cap hid the upper portion of his face. She couldn't get a clear image. The license plate? She swung the phone toward the SUV and leaned out the window. Too far. She leaned a little farther. He veered away from his SUV, toward her. She pulled her arms inside and jabbed the window and door buttons. He slowed, looked around the yard and trotted toward the landscape rocks bordering a tree well.

As she pulled away from the curb, he ran to the SUV and backed out of the driveway. He was getting away. She grabbed her phone and punched in nine-one-one. Even if Laura had already called, Sarah could give them more information.

"He's medium-height and weight, dark-haired, looks dark-skinned," she told the dispatcher. "I don't know the make or model of the SUV. It's black. He's in it now, backing into the street. Oh, God, he's not trying to get away. He's coming after me!"

She accelerated and passed two cars. He followed, gaining on her. She had to settle down. He couldn't do anything except follow her. She just had to get somewhere safe. She glanced in the rear-view mirror. He was right behind her. She punched the accelerator and tried to see the front license plate, but could see only the top of a gold cross. "It's a Chevy, maybe a Tahoe or a Suburban," she told the dispatcher. She rose in her seat, trying to see the number. He was too close and getting closer, looming in her rear-view mirror. Her hands and legs shook. "He's going to ram me." She veered around a pickup. "Oh, God, there's not enough room. I'm going to hit him!"

She skimmed past and slid between him and another SUV. The driver of the pickup punched his horn in an angry blast.

Her pursuer came around the pickup. The idiot! He didn't have enough room. He squeezed in front of it, anyway, forcing the driver to brake and veer off the road.

Her hands were so clammy they slipped on the steering wheel as she turned right. She had to get free of the traffic, to gain some space to maneuver.

He followed, moving alongside, on her left, inching closer to the dividing line. She flinched, holding in a scream as he came over, forcing her toward the shoulder. The only space she had was straight ahead. She stomped on the accelerator.

Had she turned onto Thirty-Seventh or Thirty-Eighth? She didn't know; she'd been too busy watching her rear-view mirror to pay attention, but both led to J Street and Mercy General.

She swerved around a car and a motorcycle, the SUV right behind her. Where was a cop when she needed one?

She approached J Street on a green, changing to yellow. She slid into the intersection holding her breath, bracing for a collision. She made it through, straightened the Honda's wheels and picked up speed. The SUV would be stuck at the red light.

She reached for her phone. "I'm on J, a few blocks from Mercy," she told the dispatcher, talking fast. "The guy chasing me is stuck at a red light on Thirty-Seventh or Thirty-Eighth. By the time he gets through it, I think I can be at the hospital, and I'm hoping he won't see me turn off."

Honking horns and squealing brakes drew her attention to the rear-view mirror. She caught a strangled breath. “He ran the light, and he’s working his way over into my lane!” She threw the phone down, grasped the steering wheel with both hands, and slowed enough to skid through the entrance to the hospital. The Honda slid to a stop in front of the emergency room. She unfastened her seat belt and opened her door, to run for it.

The SUV followed her into the entrance, coming fast, narrowly missing an ambulance. The driver straightened his vehicle and drove directly at her. She slammed the door and ducked under the steering wheel, waiting for the collision. He swerved, and by the time she raised her head, he was gone.

An EMT opened the Honda door. “Are you all right, lady? I thought that guy was going to ram you. Do you need help?”

“Not anymore,” Sarah said and collapsed into his arms.

When she opened her eyes, the EMT was taking her pulse. At the rate her heart was pounding, she doubted he’d had any trouble finding it.

“I’m okay. I—just let me catch my breath.” She reached for her phone, but it wasn’t in the dashboard holder or on the passenger seat. She felt a little dizzy when she turned her head, so she tilted it back against the head rest. “I’m okay. Just a little stressed out. Give me a few minutes, okay?”

He stepped back and nodded. “If you’re sure. But you can’t stay here more than a few minutes.” He nodded toward the emergency room doors.

Sarah sat, listening to the drumbeat in her chest. Her hands still felt clammy, and her fingers shook when she turned the key in the ignition. She drove a few yards, but her leg shook so hard she wasn’t sure she could keep it on the accelerator, so she pulled to the curb and stopped. She tipped her head back and closed her eyes, taking deep, even breaths. It took a while, but finally, she felt her heartbeat slow to its normal pace. She could drive now.

“Sarah? Are you all right?”

Sarah opened her eyes. “Fancy meeting you here,” she said to Dee Callender, too surprised to think of a more appropriate greeting. How had the cop found her? Then she remembered. This was Dee Callender's beat. She was the one who had found Caro.

Dee stepped back, wrinkled her nose, and asked, "Have you been drinking?"

"Drinking? No, not yet, but I'm about ready to start. Do you see my phone anywhere?"

"I can smell alcohol—beer."

"Oh, that." Sarah looked over the seat, at the thick shards of glass scattered over the wet carpet. "That's Laura's. And there's the phone. It must have hit one of the bottles, or knocked some of them together." Sarah turned, knees in the driver's seat, and tried to reach the phone. "I haven't had anything to drink. Ask the EMT."

Dee opened the door, fished out the cell phone, and handed it to Sarah. "You don't smell like beer. The car does. You probably lost the phone at the same time the dispatcher lost the connection." She nodded toward the back seat. "It would be better to put alcohol in the trunk."

"You haven't seen Laura's trunk." Sarah turned the phone around, almost dropping it. "She's going to be freaking out. I've got to call her." But Sarah's fingers, small and usually so agile, refused to cooperate. She could barely hold the phone in her trembling hand. So much for being able to drive.

Dee took it from her, called Laura, and handed it back to Sarah. "Make it quick. Tell her you're okay, then we need to talk."

"You don't understand. The guy was in the house. He might be going back, and Laura is all alone."

"She's not alone. She called nine-one-one, and some officers are with her. She's not hurt. Just shaken up a little, and worried about you. She'll be okay, once you talk to her."

Only then did Sarah become aware of Laura's voice on the phone, demanding an answer. "Sarah? Is that you? Sarah, answer me."

"Yeah, it's me. I'm okay. How about you?"

"He got in through the back door," Laura said. "Broke one of the little glass panels and reached through and unlocked it." Her voice rose. "While I was in the shower. He broke in while I was in the shower, Sarah. It took me ten years to get over *Psycho* and take a shower when I was alone in the house. Ten years. Now I'm never going to be able to do it again. I'll see Janet Leigh every time—"

"Janet Leigh? Not the guy who played Norman Bates?" *Way to go, Sarah. Creep her out even more.* "Never mind. You're okay, and so am I. A little egg- and beer-splattered, but okay."

Laura giggled. "Eggs and beer sound like a batter, not a splatter." Her nervous giggle dissolved into a sob. "Oh, God, what am I saying?"

Somebody took the phone from her. "Sarah? This is Emily Rafferty, Caro's next-door neighbor. We—Herb and I—we've been keeping an eye on the place since, well, since Caro's accident. Trying to be good neighbors. We knew you girls were here. Saw you drive in. So when Herb saw the police cars, we were afraid something might have happened. We came right over. Laura's fine, just shaken up, and Herb is fixing the door."

"The door?"

"Well, it's temporary. He's hammering boards across it. You won't be able to use it, but nobody's going to get in, either. Herb says you'd be better off to get another door, though. A good solid one with no glass panels."

Sarah could hear another voice in the background. Then Emily's came back. "He says to get some better deadbolts, too."

"Okay. Thanks, Emily. Tell Laura I'll be there as soon as I can."

She sat for a few minutes, concentrating on her breathing again. Long breath in, let it out. In, out. Dee had moved away, to give her some privacy, Sarah supposed, and stood by a nearby patrol car, talking to another officer.

Sarah found a plastic bag and started collecting glass shards from the backseat carpeting, her motions choppy and mechanical. She'd have to vacuum to get the small slivers, and she couldn't do that until it dried out. She lifted the dripping egg carton just as Dee returned.

"Want some eggs? They're already scrambled." Sarah dropped the carton into the bag and looked for something to wipe her hands on.

Dee handed her a tissue and pulled out her notebook and recorder. "Tell me what happened."

"A guy broke into the house. Laura was in the shower—"

"I mean what happened to you. I already know about Laura. She called nine-one-one, too."

Sarah started slowly, trying to recapture every detail, but her voice accelerated, along with her heartbeat, when she described the car chase. "I don't know why he came after me. I thought he would jump in his car and take off, but when I tried to take a picture of his license plate, he went ballistic. I think he was after my phone."

Dee held out her hand. "May I?"

She flipped through the photos. "Not much here. Not surprising, under the circumstances. No license number, but you did get a face. It's blurry, but it might lead to something." She swiped at the screen a few times. "I sent it to one of our guys to see if he can find a match. We've had reports of several burglaries in the area lately. Maybe this was the guy. I'll run it by our Property Crimes people."

She handed the phone back to Sarah. "I'll call with whatever we find, but I don't think you have to worry. These burglars have a routine. They find a place that looks like nobody's home and ring the bell, just to be sure. If nobody answers, they look for a way to get in. With the shower running, Laura couldn't hear the bell, and the burglar couldn't hear the shower running upstairs."

Sarah shuddered, images of Janet Leigh's shower scene from *Psycho* projecting onto the back of her eyelids.

Chapter 16

Dee closed her notebook. "I don't think he's likely to come back, now that he knows somebody is staying in the house, but we'll increase our patrols, keep an eye on the place. Are you staying there overnight?"

Sarah didn't want to stay. Not now. Maybe, if they rested for an hour or so, they could finish their search tonight and go home.

Dee studied Sarah. "Are you okay to drive? You look pale."

"I'm fine now. Thanks."

Sarah drove back with a new awareness of her surroundings, glancing at the mouths of alleys and watching her rear-view mirror. By the time she turned off J Street, she realized she wasn't "fine" after all. The beer fumes, made stronger by their enclosure in the warm car, engulfed her. She waved her hand in front of her face and rolled down the windows, but the queasiness crept from her empty stomach toward her throat. Only one more block. She could see the house.

She pulled to the curb, jumped out and leaned against the car. She was about to get sick in a lovely residential area, just about the time its occupants would be coming home from work.

The nausea passed. Sarah waited a few more minutes, not wanting to get back in the car, but it was only a block, and Laura was going to be worried.

A woman wearing blue jeans, a red polo shirt, and white sneakers trotted across the street, pulling off her sunglasses. "Sarah? Is that you? I thought I saw you in that car, earlier."

A red baseball cap covered most of her short, sun-bleached hair. She looked familiar, but Sarah couldn't place her.

"Oh, Sarah, I know you've just got to be so devastated. We all are. It's just so unexpected. I've been trying to think of what I can do—how I can help. I know you must be just overwhelmed. I thought—well, a few of us got together and we wondered—for the memorial service, have you arranged for food after, some sort of appropriate gathering?"

Sarah's mind, trying to follow two tracks at the same time, ground to a halt. A gathering. What gathering? And what was the woman's name?

"Uh, well, I haven't had much time to think about it."

"Exactly. That's what I thought. You've just got so much to do. I...we thought maybe we could do the reception for you, after the service. Maybe there, at Caro's house?"

The reception. She hadn't even thought about a reception, and she didn't think Laura had, either. How could they have forgotten? What else had slipped their minds?

"Laura and I want it to be relevant. Something Caro would have liked."

The woman nodded, and now that Sarah's brain was back in gear, it registered the way the ball-capped head bobbed up and down.

"I'd have to talk to Laura first."

"Oh, yes, of course." The woman's head bobbed down, then up. "Talk to her and let me know."

"Okay. It sounds like a wonderful idea. Could you write down your number for me so I can call you later?"

The woman waved Sarah's words away. "Oh, just look in Caro's book. It's there."

"I know, but we don't have it." It wasn't really a lie; they had a copy, not the actual book. "The police are keeping Caro's address and phone books until they finish their investigation." Sarah opened the glove compartment and dug out a small notebook and ballpoint pen. "So, if you wouldn't mind writing it down for me? Oh, and put your name on it, too, so I won't get it mixed up with somebody else's number."

The woman scribbled on the notepad and handed it back to Sarah. "I never thought about the police and...and all that." Her head bobbed again. "It's all just so terrible. What have they found out?"

Sarah glanced at the notepad. Marge. One of Caro's bridge group. The highlighted hair was new. "Oh, you know how it is. They don't tell us anything. The service is on Thursday at two, and the house is a mess. Caro was doing some redecorating, and the place hasn't been dusted for a while."

"Oh, that's no problem. I know a wonderful woman, a combination maid, housekeeper and cook who can accomplish miracles on short notice. She already knows Caro's house. She's worked for her before. You could leave a key somewhere."

Sarah tore off the page, folded it, and put it in her pocket. She placed the notepad and pen back in the glove compartment. "Is that how Caro handled it? Leaving a key for household help?"

Marge pursed her lips. "I don't know. It's what I do." Her head bobbed. "You could leave it with me if you want. That is, if Laura agrees. I hope she does because we just want to do this. It would be our goodbye present to Caro. A real Caro-style farewell."

Sarah slid into the driver's seat. "I'll give you a call. I appreciate the offer. It's very generous of you—all of you." She waved and drove the rest of the way down the block.

Laura stood in the doorway, waiting. "Where have you been? I've been worried ever since the cops left."

"Dee doesn't think the guy will come back. He was just looking for an empty place to rob. Can you take some of these?" She tilted her chin toward the beer bottles cradled in her arms.

Laura took the beer, two in each hand. "Where's the carton?"

Sarah retrieved the tub of butter from the crook of her arm. "In a garbage bin, along with a dozen broken eggs and a lot of soggy cardboard. And your car—Laura, it smells so bad, I had to get out on the way back so I could breathe."

"You don't think we can drive it back tonight?" Laura put the beer in the refrigerator and reached for the butter. "Sarah, I have to take clients out tomorrow."

"I know, but I almost got sick on my way back to the house." Sarah took a deep breath. "What about using Caro's car? It's in the garage, and the keys are here."

Laura recoiled. "Caro's car?" She put up her palms, warding away Sarah's suggestion. "No. Sarah, I know it sounds stupid, but I can't."

Sarah hugged her. "Never mind. It was just an idea. How about this? You can borrow my car while I get yours cleaned up."

"Borrow yours? When's the last time you even saw your car, much less drove it?"

"Good point." Scott might not even be home when she got there. He'd be angry because she hadn't cleared it with him before she came back to Caro's. They needed to talk, but right now, it would help if he gave her some space.

"We'll have to find a car wash," Laura said. "One that stays open late. If they can scrub it out tonight, it'll have time to dry before I have to pick up the clients. And we can drive it home tonight. The front will be dry; the mess is in the back."

A tall, lean woman with short, orange-red hair strode into the kitchen. "Sarah. There you are. It's good to see you again." She gripped Sarah's hand so hard it hurt. "I don't have to tell you how sorry we are about Caro."

Sarah had forgotten the neighbors were there. She pulled her hand free. "Thank you."

The woman—Emily Rafferty, Sarah assumed—plowed on. "I know it's difficult for you girls, and Herb and I want to help. That's why we stayed here with Laura. Now that you're finally back, we have to go." She looked around for her purse and grabbed it from the kitchen counter. "We're late for a meeting, one we simply cannot miss."

"All right, and thank you."

Emily had already turned to join her husband, who waited by the front door.

Sarah locked it behind them and went back to the kitchen, rubbing her throbbing hand. "She's a little overpowering, isn't she? Probably the head of neighborhood watch." She took a few steps into the adjoining dining room, cocked her head to one side and studied the back door. "Looks like he did a thorough job." Several solid pieces of wood covered the glass panes, extending into the frame on each side. "Nobody's getting through that."

"Not pretty, and not permanent," Laura said. "I'll call tomorrow, and see if we can get somebody to replace it. Right now, we need to take care of the car."

Sarah ran one hand over the boarded-up glass. "Laura, I think we'd be okay here tonight. The front door's pretty sturdy."

"Maybe we won't have to stay. Let's get the car taken care of first. Then we'll see if we can finish up here."

Ten minutes later, with the Honda's windows rolled down, they found the car wash. A coffee shop occupied the same strip mall, and Sarah's stomach whimpered that she'd put nothing in it all day, other than a peanut butter sandwich.

"Want to grab something to eat while they're working on the car?"

"What about the omelet we were going to cook?"

"Somehow, eggs no longer sound very appetizing. I don't know if I'll ever be able to look at them again without smelling stale beer."

While they ate, Sarah gave Laura a detailed description of the car chase and its aftermath. "And," she said, "when I stopped the car to get some fresh air, I talked to one of Caro's friends. They want to do the reception after the memorial service at Caro's house."

Laura groaned. "We forgot about a reception. It never even entered my mind."

"They want to do a Caro-style farewell. They'll even get the house ready."

"At Caro's house? I don't know. Seems weird. I can't remember. Is that the way it's usually done? Can't they do it somewhere else?" Laura frowned, and Sarah knew she was searching her memory for details of her father's funeral, just as Sarah was trying to remember her mother's. But Sarah had been so young and so traumatized she couldn't remember anything but the raw, tearing pain that had engulfed her, pain which still lay too close to the surface for her to stay in that dark section of her memory for long.

"I guess it's normal to have it at the house of the...the deceased," she said. "But you're right. It seems off somehow, considering the way Caro—what happened to Caro. On the other hand, they want to do it, and it would be impossible for us to pull it off by Thursday."

"Maybe they can do it at one of the other houses?"

"I'll ask her." Sarah pulled out her phone and the slip of paper with Marge's number.

Laura glanced out the window. "Looks like the car's ready."

Sarah made the call while they walked over to the car wash. "Marge says her living room isn't big enough for a crowd," she told Laura. "She'll ask around and get back to me."

"Okay. Surely one of her friends has a house with enough space." Laura opened the Honda door and took a deep breath. "Much better. Maybe a slight scent of Eau d'Brewery, but it should be gone by morning."

Sarah got in, fastened her seat belt, leaned back in the passenger seat, and almost fell asleep during the short drive to the house. It had been a tiring day: less than four hours sleep the night before and several hours of hard work, topped by a tense car chase. She yawned when Laura pulled into the garage beside Caro's Lexus. "After we get those last boxes unpacked, I'm all for opening a bottle of wine and taking a hot, soaking bath."

"In the wine?"

"No, I'm going to bathe the inside of me with wine."

"I don't get any?"

Sarah unlocked the kitchen door. "Are you kidding? After what I went through to get you that beer, you'd damned well better drink it."

"I wish I had a deep bathtub like Caro's because I don't think I'll ever be able to take another shower—at least, not when I'm alone. I'm going to have nightmares about *Psycho* tonight."

"You're going to be so tired when we finish with those boxes, you're going to sleep like a hibernating baby bear." But Sarah knew she, too, was going to have nightmares. Maybe worse ones than anything the Bates Motel had to offer.

Chapter 17

Sarah's phone rang. Dee Callender. "I thought I'd check in. Make sure you and Laura are okay, and you got the house secured."

"That's thoughtful of you, Dee. Way beyond the call of duty."

"Actually, I'm off duty right now and just finished having dinner with a friend. He's from Property Crimes and intrigued by your theory about the missing sketches. He knows your aunt's work and thinks he might be able to help. I was wondering if it's too late to stop by?"

Yes, it was too late. It was after eight, and she was tired. She needed to finish the job so she could go home and get a hot bath and some wine.

She pushed a strand of limp hair out of her face. "No, it's not too late." She ignored Laura, who was shaking her head, mouthing *no*. "How long will it take for you to get here?" Laura scowled at her. "Twenty minutes? Okay, we'll be expecting you."

She summarized the call to Laura. "They're cops, and with Coleman on our backs, we need all the help we can get." She headed for the stairs. "I have to get a quick shower."

It took a few minutes to dry her hair, and by the time she started down the stairs, she could hear voices from the living room. Dee stood there, beside a slender, well-built man, admiring Caro's paintings. Sarah slowed her steps and studied him. Tall, long legs, with dark hair. He looked up at her, his eyes warm and friendly, and walked toward the stairs, matching his pace to hers, so they met at the bottom.

"You're Sarah." His wide smile displayed even, white teeth. "I'm Dave Wheeler." He grasped her hand. "I'm sure I'm not the first person who has told you that you look remarkably like your aunt. I've admired her work for a long time but wasn't aware she did sketches. When Dee told me about them, I had to come." He still held Sarah's hand. "I hope you don't mind?"

Sarah tried to shake her head without losing eye contact with the deepest, softest brown eyes she'd ever seen. He smiled and slowly released her hand.

"I thought, if I knew what they looked like, I could search for them in the pawn shop database."

"The what?" Heat crept up Sarah's neck. Absorbed in the sound of Dave Wheeler's soothing baritone, she hadn't registered the meaning of his words. Something about a database.

"I'm sorry," he said. "I should have explained. It's an inventory of items taken in by pawn shops. Stolen goods sometimes end up there."

Laura waved a hand toward the top of the stairs. "We're not sure yet that they're missing, but Caro has—had some similar ones in her studio if you'd like to see them."

He said he would, so Sarah turned and led them back up the stairs and down the hallway, to Caro's studio. "Laura and I think there's a connection between their disappearance and Caro's death."

"What does Detective Coleman say?" Dave asked.

Laura motioned them into the studio. "Him?" She snorted. "He's too busy trying to pin her death on one of us to consider other possibilities."

Dee didn't comment. Dave, who had glimpsed the canvases propped against the studio wall, whistled. "These are wonderful." He walked around the room, hands clasped behind his back, studying them. "Which sketches are most like the ones that are missing?"

"None of them," Sarah said. "The ones that are missing—she did those when she was young, and her work has evolved over time. Laura and I have some at home that would give you a better idea."

Dave suggested a visit to one of their houses to see the sketches, but Laura shook her head. "I live in Folsom, and Sarah lives in Roseville. It would be better if we brought them down here."

"We're not even sure the sketches are missing," Sarah reminded them. "We've been rummaging in boxes all day and unearthed those." She nodded at the canvases. "But the ones we're trying to find are smaller, and framed." She pointed at a stack of large cartons against the wall. "We still have to unpack five or six boxes."

"Why don't we look through them now?" Dave asked. "It won't take long. That's the only way we're going to know if they're here."

"Dave—," Dee said, but his attention was on the boxes.

Sarah took a deep breath, trying to draw in energy. She couldn't remember when she'd ever felt so tired. But Dave was right. They needed to know whether the sketches were gone, and she didn't want to turn down an offer of help.

Laura grabbed one side of a box and tugged on it. Dave helped her drag it to the center of the room and opened it. Laura pulled out a stapler and a small desk calender. "Looks like this is all small stuff from Caro's desk." She handed them to Sarah and tried to dig a little deeper into the box.

"Why don't we move it to Caro's office and unpack it there?" Sarah asked.

"Good idea. Maybe you can put it away while we sort through the rest of the stuff." Laura inclined her head toward the other boxes.

"It's been a long time since I lived here," Sarah protested, "and Caro must have shifted things around over the years, so I can't be sure where all of it goes."

"Yeah, but you're the best we've got," Laura reminded her. "I'll take a look at it, too, once we have everything in place."

Sarah, noting Dee's raised eyebrows, explained. "We're trying to re-create Caro's office, as nearly as we can, hoping that will help us see—or rather, not see—anything that's missing."

In a little over an hour, they had finished. Sarah stood back and surveyed Caro's office and its bare walls.

"Where are all the pictures?" Laura asked, from behind her. "Our wedding photos, your graduation picture, the ones of Eric and Jamie and Roger?"

"You've unpacked all the boxes?"

Laura opened a desk drawer and looked through the contents. "Every one of them. She must have put the pictures somewhere else." She closed the drawer and opened another.

"I already went through all those," Sarah said. "They're not here."

Dave glanced around the small office. "Family photos would obviously have no value to a thief." He studied the objects in the bookshelf and brushed his fingers across the books. "But they were probably the most valuable things in the house to your aunt, so she would have taken extra care with them when she packed up her office. The sketches, too, from what you've told me. So we have to figure out where she would have put them for safekeeping." He cocked his head to one side to read a book title, displaying a firm jaw line.

"Maybe they're not lost, after all," Dee said, but Sarah's attention was focused on Dave's head. Nice hair—thick, a little curly. An amused smile creased Dee's lips and Sarah, flustered, tried to concentrate. What had Dee just said?

"The sketches," Dee smiled again. "Maybe she stored them somewhere else while she was gone. Did she have a secure place where she stored her artwork?"

"I don't know," Sarah said. "And you—the police—took all her paperwork and her computer." But Sarah had never heard Caro mention storing them somewhere else.

"Call Al Durant and ask him," Dee suggested, "or her attorney might know."

Sarah tried to swallow the lump in her throat. The sketches were gone, but they'd proved nothing. Neither Dave nor Dee believed a thief had taken them.

Dave's voice was soft. "I can still check the database." He pulled a book from the shelf. "And I'd like to see your sketches."

Sarah needed to change the subject, at least for right now. "You like Michener?"

He glanced at the book he held, *Centennial*. "I do. And, yes, I know. Nobody reads Michener any more. But I find him so—"

"Knowledgeable?" Sarah asked. "At least, that's how he comes across to me. But maybe he was simply exceptionally good at research. He obviously did lots of it."

"You read him, too. Do you find his books hard to get into?"

Sarah smiled, a wide smile. "Caro liked him, and they were here, so I started when I was in high school. I read *Hawaii* for a book report. It had more than I needed, but by the time I realized that, I was hooked."

"Ah, yes. The early settlers. The missionaries, the sugar plantations—"

"And the leper colony on Molokai," Sarah said. "And, yes, I do find him hard to get into. All that beginning of time stuff. It's too much. But I learned, reading him. Before I read *Hawaii*, I knew little about the Japanese, Chinese and Filipino cultures, and nothing about their influence on Hawaii."

She had to stop babbling. He would think she was an idiot. But his open, expectant expression led her to add, "The Chinese woman, the matriarch, fascinated me. I can't remember her name." That was lame. She pulled *Hawaii* from the shelf and leafed through it, trying to find a reference to the woman, and as an excuse to stop talking before she made a complete fool of herself.

Dave sank into a chair. "What about *The Source*, the one about Israel? What did you think of it?"

Laura rolled her eyes and exchanged a glance with Dee. "I didn't know we were having a book club meeting. I, for one, am much more interested in a glass of one of Caro's wonderful wines." She turned to Dave. "There's no reason why you and Dee can't join us for a drink, is there? It seems like the least we can do, after all your hard work."

"No reason at all," he said before Dee could respond. He rose to his feet and put the book back in place. "We're both off duty. But I'm more of a beer man, myself. Do you happen to have any cold?"

Sarah laughed and headed for the stairs. "I just happen to have a few bottles." Dee chuckled, Laura joined in, and Sarah found herself giggling as she could only do when exhausted. Dave's glance caught her gaze, a puzzled look that matched his bemused smile. Dee must not have told him about her disastrous beer run.

He had nice lips, curving, sensuous. God, why was she noticing a man's lips? She tried to generate an image of Scott's mouth, but managed only a blurred oval, with thin lips twisted in anger.

She busied herself with the drinks, pulling goblets from the cabinet, finding the corkscrew, selecting a bottle. Dave's fingers brushed hers when he took the Cabernet from her, heightening her awareness of his closeness. She took a step back but found herself watching his hands as he opened the bottle. She turned to the refrigerator to get the beer and almost collided with Laura, who stared at her with disapproving eyes.

Sarah bit her lip. "You'll have to excuse me for a few minutes. Laura, there are some nuts and crackers in the pantry, and some cheese in the fridge." She bolted for the upstairs bathroom.

After she'd splashed water on her face and dried it, she stared at her reflection in the mirror—a tired woman, her hair caught in a straggly ponytail, wearing jeans and a t-shirt, and on her jaw, a faded purple blotch enhanced by an uneven border of dull greenish-yellow. She felt washed out, her defenses down, her emotions raw.

She pulled out her cosmetic kit, worked on the bruise, applied some blush and lipstick, and combed her hair. A little better, but not much. Maybe a glass of Cabernet would help. She detoured to the kitchen for the wine before joining the others in the living room.

Laura and Dee sat together on a small brocade love seat, Laura telling Dee about an outing with Jamie and Eric. Dave strolled around the room, sipping his beer while he looked at the artwork hung above cherry wainscoting. He paused to listen to part of their conversation.

"We're sisters-in-law," Laura told him. "Or ex-sisters-in-law."

"That's what I understand. Dee talks about Eric and Jamie all the time."

The carpeting, deep and plush, urged Sarah to kick off her sandals. She resisted the impulse and sank into the nearest chair, glad the draperies were closed, so the warmth of the dimly-lit room cocooned her. Strange that she could feel so safe here, where somebody had killed Caro, but this house had always been a haven for her.

"What do you read besides Michener?" Dave asked, lowering himself into a chair beside Sarah. "Who is your favorite author?"

Sarah took a sip of wine. "Mmmm, not sure. There are so many it's hard to choose. I like David Baldacci, Ken Follett—"

"Ah, yes. *Pillars of the Earth, Fall of Giants*—"

"I was thinking more about *Jackdaws*."

"*Jackdaws?* I don't think I've read it."

"It was one of his early books. A thriller, set during World War II, about Englishwomen recruited to go into France to help the Resistance. Based on a true story."

"Dave," Dee called, "Come and look at these."

He set his beer on the cherry drum table. "Back in a minute."

Sarah joined them in front of one of Caro's paintings, the one she'd worked on the spring Sarah was sixteen. She had loved the soft blue-violet shade Caro had worked into the sky. "That's the color I want for my dress," she'd said.

"For the prom?" Caro had studied the color, then looked up at Sarah. "It would suit you, I think. But it might be hard to find. Maybe, if we went to San Francisco? We could make a day of it. Go to the Top of the Mark for lunch. Or maybe Fisherman's Wharf?"

"What do you think, Sarah?" Laura asked, breaking into her thoughts and bringing her back to the present.

"You need to do something," Dave said. "The paintings are too valuable to leave here, unprotected. Especially with no alarm system. Have you thought about having one put in?"

"I guess it's time," Laura said, "after everything that's happened." Caro always thought the deadbolts were enough. She'd lived here for years, and it had always been a safe neighborhood."

"The burglaries just started recently," Dave said, "so maybe she wasn't aware of them. But I'd advise you to put in an alarm."

"Okay, we'll see what we can do," Laura said, "but to be honest with you, money is a little tight right now, and we don't know what we'll have in expenses for the reception and everything."

Dee frowned. "I thought you had—" She bit her lip. "Never mind. I should think your aunt's attorney would release funds for the memorial service and to protect the paintings."

Laura tapped her forehead with the heel of her hand. "Duh. I never even thought about that. I'll call him first thing in the morning. We need to talk to him about the will, anyway."

Sarah reminded her that she had to meet a client in Folsom the next morning. The cousins exchanged glances. It was late, and they had both drunk more than one glass of wine. They would have to spend the night in the house.

"I'll call him," Sarah said. "I'll have to come back, anyway, to let the house cleaner in. I'll arrange for the alarm installation, some new dead-bolt locks, and a door replacement." *And get out of here before dark.*

Dee glanced at her watch. "You have to wake up early, and it's getting late. We'd better go."

Sarah saw them to the door.

"Why don't you bring the sketches with you when you come back tomorrow?" Dave asked Sarah. "Call me when you get here, and I'll come by and take a look at them."

Sarah nodded, saying nothing, all too aware of her quickened pulse. She needed to get home—back to Scott—before she made even more of an idiot of herself. She showed them out, locked the door, and stopped in the kitchen long enough to get her unfinished glass of wine before she started up the stairs. "I'll clean everything up tomorrow," she told Laura. "Right now, I'm going to crawl into bed and sleep until you drag me out."

She reached the landing and walked down the hallway, toward her old room—and the doors leading to the patio. She couldn't see anything but darkness through the glass panes, but her imagination soon filled the void. How could she sleep with those doors just a few yards away?

She went back to the bathrooms for the rugs. Once inside the bedroom, she and Laura used them to slide a heavy dresser across the door and the adjoining wall.

"Help me get the rugs out from under the edges," Laura said.

"No. Leave them. That way, we can easily move the dresser to get out, but nobody can get through from the other side."

"You're right. I may get some sleep after all."

Sarah spent a restless night dreaming about car chases and smashed windows and intruders. She finally fell into a deep sleep and dreamed the man who had broken into the house was trying to catch her, intent on sending her to the lawless leper colony on Molokai. She ran through volcanic ash, avoiding flowing streams of lava. She stumbled over a broken beer bottle, but strong arms caught her, and she looked into the smiling face of Dave Wheeler. The face changed to the shadowed, blurry face of the burglar. She struggled, trying to break free, and awoke to find herself tangled in the sheet.

The dresser had been pushed aside, and Laura's voice floated up the stairs. She sounded happy. What was the song she was singing? How long had she been up? Sarah drew a deep breath. Long enough to make coffee. Only half awake, she crawled out of bed and staggered downstairs for a cup. She could drink it while she dressed.

Laura leaned against the counter, eyeing Sarah over the rim of her coffee mug.

"Why are you up so early?" Sarah grunted. "And why are you so damned cheerful?"

"I'm up early because nobody could sleep with you thrashing around all night. And I'm cheerful because it's a beautiful day, the coffee is good, and I've accomplished something this morning. Look." She raised a sketch pad and displayed the image of a man's face.

Sarah moved closer. "It's the burglar, isn't it?" Laura had sketched clear features onto the pad, filling in Sarah's memory of a blurred face—a face that somehow didn't look as ominous in the early morning sunlight of Caro's kitchen. She remembered the car chase and shuddered. "Maybe the detectives can identify him from this. Did you call Matt Coleman?"

"I think I might have better luck working with Dave Wheeler."

Sarah handed the sketch back to her. "You're probably right. Matt Coleman would toss it in a drawer and forget about it. Or the wastebasket. Dee's guy will try to find out who he is. If you want, I can give it to him when I show him Caro's sketches."

"When **I** show him the sketches," Laura corrected. She grinned. "I'm going to call and invite him over as soon as I finish up with my client. And he's not Dee's guy. They're just friends." She put down the coffee cup and grabbed Sarah's hand. "I'm pretty sure he's interested in more than the sketches. We had so much fun, bantering back and forth, while you were putting the stuff in Caro's office last night. Later, when you were upstairs, he was...well, let's say he was pretty attentive. Sarah, he's the first guy I've met in a long time that I really like."

"But about the sketches. When he left, he said—"

Laura pulled a strand of her long, dark hair back and fastened it into her hair clip. "I know. He's here because of the case, and I just met him. But I've got a good feeling about this. You've got to admit he's one attractive man."

Sarah poured a cup of coffee, muttering, "Yes, he's certainly that, a very attractive man." She had to set Laura straight. "Last night, before he left, he asked me to bring my sketches back down here. He said he'd drop by and look at them."

Laura flushed and stared at her with narrowed eyes.

"I'll call him, Laura, tell him I can't bring them."

"I should have known. You were flirting with him all evening. Did you forget you're married? Or did you take off your rings so he wouldn't know?"

Sarah glanced at her ringless finger. She had taken them off when they started moving furniture, and she'd forgotten to put them back on. "That's ridiculous. You know me better than that."

"It's just...never mind." Laura turned toward the window above the sink and stared into the small side garden. Sarah stood, looking at her cousin's back, not knowing what to say. Finally, she picked up two empty wine bottles from the night before. She would take them out to the recycling bin. Maybe that would give her time to think of something.

A memory almost surfaced, and she looked at the bottles in her hands. Had they been the trigger? She closed her eyes, trying to think. It was something Dee had said—but not last night. It was earlier, when they were at Sam's apartment. They were talking about the party Caro threw before she left for Europe, and Dee had mentioned a wine bottle and a glass on the deck table.

Sarah had forgotten about it. She had avoided the deck, had averted her eyes from the doors leading to it. Would the bottle still be there? She raced up the stairs.

The only thing she found on the table was a powdery residue. Of course. The crime scene technicians would have taken the bottle and glass as evidence. Disappointed, she turned back toward the French doors. Out of the corner of her eye, she caught a blurred image. A man was at the top of the stairs coming up from the patio where Caro had died.

Chapter 18

Sarah screamed, thoughts tumbling through her mind. She had to run. Get inside, off the deck. Lock the door. No, he was too close. She turned toward him, her arm already swinging, trying to knock him off balance, to gain some time. Maybe he'd lose his footing and fall down the stairs.

Her fist connected, and she turned to run but her legs felt rooted to the deck. He spoke as he reached for her, but she couldn't hear the words over the roaring in her ears, and she couldn't stop her flailing arms, even after she recognized Scott's voice.

"Sarah. Sarah, be still. It's me." He looped both his arms around her, holding hers tight against her body. Her second scream trailed off to a strangled whimper.

Anger surged through her, drowning the fear, and she twisted, struggling to free herself. Scott moved with her, tightening his hold. His back was to the French doors when Laura charged through, already swinging one of the wine bottles at his head. Sarah ducked, and for one tiny instant she hoped the bottle would connect with its target. Then she threw herself to the deck, pulling him with her.

He glared up at Laura. "What the hell is wrong with you?" He untangled his legs from Sarah's, scrambled to his feet, and held a hand out to help her up.

"Me? What's wrong with me?" Laura lowered the wine bottle. "Sarah's scream scared the hell out of me. That's what's wrong. Why are you skulking around up here? Why didn't you ring the bell like a normal person?"

Sarah pulled her hand away from Scott's. "That was a stupid stunt, grabbing me like that. Especially this morning. Laura's on edge. We both are. A man broke into the house yesterday, while she was taking a shower."

Scott gaped at her, and she tried to reassure him. "I wasn't here. I'd gone to the store—"

"Broke in?" He looked at the French doors, then back at Laura. "But you're all right?" He turned to Sarah, the shock on his face morphing toward relief. "You weren't in the house?"

It was not the time to tell him about the car chase. "Why are you here? We were just getting ready to leave. To go home."

"I thought I could help." He jutted his chin toward the railing. "That needs to be fixed. It's dangerous. Somebody could have an accident."

Laura winced. Sarah shut her eyes and took a deep breath, trying to block images of Caro falling. Scott, seemingly oblivious to their strained silence, rambled on. "I climbed up here to take a look. I can tear out the damaged and weak wood, but you need a carpenter to rebuild it. I should think Caro's lawyer would okay the cost."

Sarah stared at the railing, seeing for the first time the jagged edges of wood. Her anger deflated, she shuddered and grabbed Scott's sleeve to stop the torrent of words. "We know. I'm going to call him this morning."

"We'll need enough for ongoing maintenance."

"We?" Laura's voice was low, with a sharp edge. "I didn't realize you were included in the 'we' of Caro's affairs, Scott."

Sarah squeezed his arm, trying to send a signal to stop talking, to stop feeding Laura's animosity. Her hurt feelings over Dave Wheeler's attention to Sarah were spilling over onto Scott.

"I'm not," he said. "But there is a 'we' in my marriage to Sarah, so whatever is going on in her life is part of mine, and I'm here to help her any way I can."

Sarah tugged his arm again. She wanted to get away from the railing, into the house, with the doors shut.

Laura snorted. "Yeah, right. You're always so thoughtful that way. Where were you yesterday, when we really needed help?"

"At work. I manage a car dealership, Laura, and with Sarah taking this week off, I need to earn some money. But I'm here now, and I'm going to help her, whether you like it or not. You know as well as I do, if you and Sam were still married, he'd be doing the same thing. And you wouldn't object to that, would you?"

Laura took a step back. Her eyes darkened. "Leave Sam out of this. Sam and I are none of your business. Just like this is none of your business."

Sarah put her hand on her cousin's arm. "Laura, he could help. Think about it. There's so much to get done, and you have to pick up clients. You don't know how many houses you're going to have to show them. It could take you most of the day. This way, I don't have to go home to get my car and come back to get everything ready for the service on Thursday, and Scott will be here to help. And we are going to have to fix that railing."

Laura took Sarah's hand. "The problem is, Scott has a way of disappearing. If he does that today, you'll be alone here, and after what you went through yesterday—"

"Went through?" Scott's voice rose. "You mean the man who broke in?" He placed a hand on Sarah's cheek. "I thought you said you weren't here."

So much for not telling him about the car chase. *Thanks a lot, Laura.* Sarah led the way back into the house, telling him the story. She paused while Laura closed and locked the doors. "Laura and I believe, more than ever, that Caro interrupted a burglar when she came home so unexpectedly, and he killed her."

"What do the police think?"

"That one of us did it," Laura said.

Scott stood still. "How do you know that? They're probably still trying to figure it out."

"Detective Coleman has made it pretty clear," Laura said. "We're family. We inherit. Thus, we must have done it. He's not looking at anything else."

"It's true," Sarah said when Scott still looked doubtful. "So, if we don't want to eventually be arrested, we have to figure out who did it. Some things are missing. It has to be a burglar."

"How do you know the stuff is missing? Maybe she got rid of it. Gave it away, donated it."

"No." Sarah pulled Scott inside Caro's office. "See? The sketches are gone, and all the family photographs. She would never have gotten rid of those. And the clock Roger bought for her in Switzerland on their honeymoon, and the little painting they bought in Point Reyes—"

"But nobody would take that stuff." Scott walked around the room, randomly picking up objects and setting them down. "They don't have any value."

Laura sank into a chair. "That's what the cops keep saying. I agree that they wouldn't want photographs, but the sketches are matted and framed and look expensive. If all of it was in a box with the sketches on top, they might not have even seen the photos. It had to be burglars. Why else would anybody kill her?"

Scott laughed, a harsh half-snort. "You might be surprised, Laura dear. A lot of people had strong feelings about Caro, including me. Probably Sam, too, if Caro interfered in your marriage as much as she did in mine."

"Scott! Caro never interfered in our marriage," Sarah said. "Never. She wouldn't do that."

"Oh, she interfered, Sarah. She certainly interfered. Maybe not openly. But she didn't try to hide her disapproval of me, did she?"

Laura's face paled, and she opened her mouth, but Sarah spoke first. "She never, ever said anything."

"She didn't have to. You knew she didn't think highly of me, and Caro's opinion was important to you." He stood with his legs a few feet apart, his arms crossed. "Important enough to sway you toward her viewpoint, no matter what I did."

"But you can't call it interfering if she never said anything. Whatever her feelings might have been, she kept them to herself."

Scott's voice rose. "That's just it. Don't you see? She didn't have to say anything to manipulate you."

"Manipulate? Caro?" Where was all this coming from?

"Exactly. Think about it, about the whole damned family. You and me, Sam and Laura, your dad and you and Anna, your grandmother. Whose fine hand has been in all this? Manipulating, controlling, having things her way, just because she had enough money to do what she damn well pleased."

"That's not fair. She had nothing to do with Nan or Anna or—"

Laura jumped to her feet. "You are way out of line, Scott. Based on your reasoning, I guess I interfere, too, because I don't like what you do to Sarah. I like you even less after that little outburst. I don't know how you can stand there and accuse anybody of manipulating and controlling when you're the world's expert. It's what you do to Sarah every single day."

Sarah couldn't stand any more. "Laura, that's simply not true. You don't know what you're talking about. Scott, you don't either. You're being terribly unfair."

Laura turned toward the door. "You know something? I don't feel very comfortable here anymore. I'll grab my bag and get going."

"Laura, wait." Sarah ran down the stairs after her, unable to match her cousin's long stride. Laura stopped at the bottom and turned back long enough to say, "You're not going to want to hear this, but I'm telling you anyway. He controls you. He controls your money. You don't even get to spend your own paycheck. Where does all of it go? The two of you are always broke."

Sarah opened her mouth to protest, but Laura hurried on. "You'd better keep an eye on him, or next thing you know, he'll have his sticky fingers on Caro's paintings, and anything else he thinks he can get away with."

Sarah gasped. "Laura, how can you even think anything like that? Scott wouldn't—"

Laura shook her head "Wouldn't he? He doesn't mind taking everything you earn." A stony expression settled across her features. Only her lips moved. "You don't get it, do you? It's Caro's phone message all over again. You didn't tell anybody about it because it would implicate him. You didn't even tell me. Worse, you withheld information from the cops, making them even more suspicious of us. You're going to protect Scott, defend him, no matter what he does, no matter what it costs us, who it hurts. How can you possibly be so blind, so incredibly stupid, Sarah?"

She strode across the kitchen and slammed the door on her way out to the garage. Sarah turned to face Scott. "Why did you say those things?" Her lips felt stiff, but her voice shook, her ears still ringing with Laura's last words. "Those awful, hateful words," she whispered.

He lifted both hands. "You know something? I'm getting tired of having somebody getting pushed out of shape every time I open my mouth and say what I think. We were having a conversation. Laura asked why anybody would want to kill Caro. I tried to give her some reasons. Neither of you want to hear them."

"No, I don't want to hear them." Her voice was rising, and she tried to get it under control. "And I would think you'd have the decency to keep them to yourself. Especially now. It's only been three days since Caro died, and Laura—" Her voice rose again and broke. "Laura and I are both grieving, and you—you—" She slumped into a chair and covered her face.

He knelt beside her and tried to pull her into his arms, but she stiffened and pulled away. His tone softened. "You're right, and I'm sorry. What do you want me to do?"

She couldn't think, couldn't get past Laura's words. She didn't want to look at him, didn't want to talk to him. "Just—I don't know. The railing. Take care of the railing."

He reached toward her again, and she shrank away. He sighed, rose, and trudged back up the stairs. Sarah sat still, trying to think, but her mind wouldn't cooperate. She went to the kitchen desk, trying to push Laura's words out of her mind, but, like a church bell's repetitive gong, they crashed and reverberated through her head: *Stupid Sarah. Stupid Sarah. Stupid Sarah.*

She tried to drown them out by making a list of things to do. Call the lawyer. Call the alarm company. Call a locksmith. Call Marge. Call Dave Wheeler to let him know she didn't have the sketches. Call a carpenter to fix the door and the railing.

When she finished, she pressed her hands to her forehead, trying to still the cadence of ugly words that still beat in her head. Sighing, she picked up the phone and called Robert Gibson, Caro's attorney. His cool tone surprised her. She didn't know him well, but she had expected more warmth, more sympathy. In clipped words, he told her he would approve the costs of the railing and the new door, the installation of an alarm system and new locks, and temporary storage of Caro's artwork. "And the costs of her service, of course, provided you adhere to her wishes."

"Her wishes? I don't understand." Would they be different from what she and Laura had already planned? Sarah's pulse quickened. She didn't have time to make changes.

"They're very simple. She left detailed instructions. I can e-mail them to you."

"The police took all her office equipment. Maybe it would be better if you read it to me, and I'll take notes."

Her heartbeat gradually settled into its regular rhythm as he read. They wouldn't have to make any changes. They'd known Caro would be buried beside Roger and had instinctively chosen the same mortuary.

"A reception afterward," Mr. Gibson said, "at her house." He paused and cleared his throat. "In her own words, a last bon voyage."

Laura had made it clear she didn't want that, but it was no longer Laura's decision. Maybe it would provide closure, help them get past what had happened here. After all, they–or at least somebody–would eventually live here again. Life would go on.

"I'll have the accountant deposit additional money into your trust account, so you'll have working capital," Mr. Gibson said. "Save your receipts, and bring them with you when you come in to hear the terms of the will."

"We'd like to do that as soon as we can."

Silence, then the sound of shuffling papers. “I can do it at two on Friday if that’s agreeable?”

Sarah said it was and ended the call. If she had to, she could call back and change the appointment time.

She hadn’t thought about using the trust account. Caro had kept five thousand dollars in it for Sarah to use in emergencies, but Sarah seldom drew from it. Would she need more than that? She didn’t know. She had no idea what the reception alone would cost, but she and Laura could have managed everything from their combined accounts.

She found a handyman on her copy of Caro’s telephone list. He could come that morning. The alarm company would send a representative sometime between two and six that afternoon. The locksmith would be there before six o’clock.

She called Dave Wheeler.

“Sarah.” His voice held the warmth she’d remembered. She liked the way he drew out the first syllable of her name for one tiny extra beat. He sounded disappointed when she explained that she hadn’t yet picked up the sketches. She promised to get them to him later in the week, not remembering until after she hung up that Laura planned to do that today when she took the sketch of the burglar to him.

Laura hadn’t taken the sketch, though. It still lay on the counter. Sarah picked it up and studied the face, then took a photo of it, so she could compare it to people she might see around the neighborhood.

She called Marge, to let her know they would have the reception at Caro’s house.

“Your timing is wonderful,” Marge said. “Nellie, that’s the housekeeper I told you about, is finishing up here. She says she can come right over if that’s okay.”

“That’s fine. I’m glad she can come on such short notice. I have to go to the store, but my husband is here, working on the deck.”

Marge was silent for a moment. “Do you think it would be all right if we used some of Caro’s camellias for centerpieces? I know they’re in bloom right now.”

“I think that’s a wonderful idea,” Sarah could hear the huskiness in her own voice. “You can come over and get them anytime you’re ready, and I can be here in the morning, before the service, to let you in and lend a helping hand.”

Finished with the telephone calls, Sarah ran upstairs and opened the door to the deck. “Scott, I’m going to the supermarket to pick up some sandwiches for lunch. You’ll have to stay here, because the housekeeper and a handyman are coming over, and maybe somebody to get some flowers from the garden.”

She didn’t go out on the deck. She’d rather not be that close to him right now.

Chapter 19

After Sarah ordered sandwiches, she headed for the dairy section. Scott liked either beer or milk with his sandwiches, and for now, it had better be milk.

The old woman stood in front of the eggs, and Sarah scrutinized the worn coat for bulges around the pockets. A store employee also watched. Sarah edged forward, fearing the woman would be caught.

She needn't have worried. The woman turned and walked away.

Sarah grabbed a jug of milk and a carton of eggs, hurried through the express checkout and ran outside. She caught up with the woman about halfway across the parking lot.

"Here," she said, thrusting the eggs at her, "I had to buy a whole carton just to get a few for breakfast. I can't use all of them, and they'll go to waste. Do you want some?"

The woman hesitated. "You live hereabouts?"

"For a few days, off and on."

"Well, I guess I could take two, maybe four off your hands." She picked them out of the carton with gnarled fingers, settled them into her pockets, and turned to weave her way through the parked cars, toward the street.

"Wait. I'll be coming to the store every so often, for the next week or so. When I buy groceries there's always too much—eggs, bread—they don't package them small enough, and I don't like to waste food."

"Yeah?" The woman squinted at her.

"If I knew where to find you, maybe you could use some of the stuff."

"I don't live nowhere."

Of course, she didn't; she was homeless. Sarah extended her hand. "I'm Sarah. Sarah Wagner. What's your name?"

The woman arched her eyebrows, ignoring the hand. "Nobody cares no more if I got a name." She studied Sarah. "I—never mind; it don't matter none. You can call me Maudie."

"Okay, Maudie, is there a place where I can find you?"

The woman laughed, almost a cackle. "You're new 'round here, ain't you? Ever body knows old Maudie hangs out down there." She nodded toward a small strip mall down the street.

"I'll look for you. I won't be here long, though." She didn't want the woman to become dependent on her. "I'm just taking care of my aunt—my aunt's memorial service."

"Well, that's what we all do, die." Maudie took a few steps toward the street, hesitated and turned back toward Sarah. "That why all them cops was all over the place the other morning?"

"Probably. Why?"

"Nothing. Just wondered. I gotta go."

Sarah thought about the woman as she drove back to Caro's house. What chain of events had made the difference between Caro's life and that of the street woman? Caro had married well, but even more than that, she had found people who helped her develop her talent. Had Maudie always lived in poverty or had circumstances led her there? Had she endured a string of hard luck, things she couldn't have prevented?

Without Scott, Sarah would have a difficult time managing. Her paycheck wouldn't cover the cost of her house, her car, her food, and clothing. She could always depend on Caro for shelter, but what about all those who didn't have a Caro in their lives? Many of the people Sarah knew were just a few paychecks shy of a park bench, no matter how hard they worked.

Marge was in the kitchen, arranging masses of flowers. "The housekeeper is dusting the living room. I told her she'd better wait 'til the handyman replaces the door before she does the dining room. He's up there now, with your husband."

Sarah put the eggs and milk in the refrigerator, set the bag of sandwiches on the dinette table, and headed for the stairs. "Scott, time for lunch." He didn't respond until she was almost at the top.

"Yeah, I'm here." He came out of Caro's office.

"What were you doing in there?" She led the way back into the kitchen.

He looked puzzled. "Where?"

"Caro's office."

"Oh, that." He walked to the table and opened one of the bags. "I had to answer the phone. Somebody calling about the time for the memorial service. Did you get any milk?"

"Sure." Sarah turned back toward the refrigerator in time to see an odd look cross Marge's face, an expression so fleeting Sarah couldn't pinpoint it, but her glance followed Marge's, to the kitchen phone. Had Scott lied? Had the phone not rung?

When the man arrived from the alarm company, a few minutes after two thirty, Sarah took him into the kitchen to go over the contract agreement. But Marge and her helpers had created a workshop there, complete with long, low crystal vases, and an assortment of floral supplies. Camellias, baby's breath, wisteria, and other flowers Sarah couldn't identify filled vases and cascaded over the counters and table.

She considered Caro's office, but construction noise from the deck would make it impossible to hear. Finally, she led the man to the dining room and closed the door. But even without the noise, she had difficulty concentrating on his words. The system was wireless, so it would operate even if the telephone line were cut. When it was set, an alarm would ring if a door or window opened. She would have just a few minutes to enter a four-digit code to turn it off. If she failed, the alarm company would call. If she didn't respond, they would try Scott or Laura. If any of them gave an incorrect code word, the police would be dispatched.

She signed the contract and told him to go ahead with the installation.

The locksmith came about an hour later. He could install new locks and deadbolts throughout the house but recommended replacing the doors leading to the patio. “Too easy to open, with all those glass panes.”

“But, without them, the hallway would be so dark, even in the middle of the day.”

He shrugged. “Your call, but you said you wanted the house secure. That means a good, solid wooden door.”

Sarah was conflicted. She wanted a strong door, but she also wanted the light. Worse, the change wouldn’t fit the architecture of the house.“Isn’t there something else we could do? Maybe some grillwork or something?”

The man pulled off his hat and scratched his head. “I dunno. Maybe. Or, if you have that kind of money, some security glass.”

“How much would that cost? The security glass?”

“Depends on the grade, I guess. Not my area of expertise. I’d guess at somewhere around twelve to fifteen hundred for each door. But that’s just a guess. I can refer you to several people who do good work and are reasonable, if you want to go that way.”

“Okay. Leave that information with me, so I can check it out. Meantime, go ahead with the rest of the doors.”

She called Robert Gibson to get his approval, but he was out of the office. She left a message.

Late in the afternoon, the carpenter finished. He showed Sarah the new door leading into the back yard, and the work he’d done on the deck. “It’s not finished, but it’s all I can do in one day, and it’s safe.”

Sarah nodded, wrote a check, and told him she’d call when they were ready to finish the job.

Scott, at loose ends, went to inspect the yard. A few minutes later, the drone of the lawn mower replaced the handyman’s hammering and sawing. Slowly, as the hours ticked by, the noise diminished. The man finished the alarm installation, showed her how to work it, and left. Robert Gibson called to approve installation of the security glass, but he suggested installing it in all the downstairs windows, too, to provide better protection for Caro’s paintings. That job would have to wait; it was too late to do it today.

The house settled again into its cocooning silence, and Sarah would have liked nothing better than to sink into Caro's deep tub for a hot bubble bath, followed by a glass of wine and a good night's sleep.

"Want to grab something to eat on the way home?" Scott asked. She'd forgotten he was there and realized she hadn't heard the mower for hours. Where had he been?

"Sounds like a good idea. I'm too tired to cook. But it will have to be something quick because I've got to call Laura when I get home. I still need to find something to wear tomorrow, and I have to be back down here early in the morning."

She fell asleep before Scott merged onto Eastbound I-80, and didn't awaken until he slowed for the Douglas Boulevard exit in Roseville. She straightened in the seat and rotated her head, trying to relieve the ache in the back of her neck.

Scott patted her leg. "You're beat, but we're almost home."

She didn't say anything, and he waited until he'd executed the turn off Douglas before speaking again. "Do you have any money stashed away, Sarah? If you do, I need it. I wouldn't ask, but it's—well, it's important."

What could he possibly need money for this time? She started to ask, but didn't have the energy to fight with him. Better to let it go until after the memorial service, when things had settled down, and she wasn't so emotional.

Her mind still a little fuzzy from her short nap, she tried to think. She had taken money from the tissue box when she and Laura had planned to go to Reno on Saturday. Before she knew about Caro. After that, she couldn't remember. But it didn't matter. "I can get some out of the trust fund. I'll transfer it over as soon as we get home. How much are we talking about?"

"No. No, don't do that." He pulled into the driveway. "You've never touched that money. I don't want you to start now. Not for me. I'll figure something out. Don't worry about it."

Wide awake now, Sarah had a sudden image of Laura's still face, her lips thin, saying, "He doesn't mind taking everything you earn." Scott wasn't taking her money; he was refusing to take it. Why, then, did she feel so uneasy? Because Laura had put doubts in her mind, and she couldn't let her do that.

She kicked off her shoes as soon as she entered the house. Even as she poured a glass of Merlot, she knew she shouldn't. She was drinking too much, fortifying herself for unpleasant tasks. Was that the way alcoholics got started? She left the wine on the kitchen counter.

She would call Laura first, get the toughest job out of the way, then the others wouldn't seem so bad.

"Everything is under control at the house," she told her cousin. "The railing is fixed and the back door replaced, with a new deadbolt lock. The alarm system is installed. I called the attorney, Robert Gibson. He'll put enough money into my trust account to pay for everything." She paused and took a long breath. Laura didn't say anything. "I made an appointment for us to see him at two on Friday."

Laura's voice was cool. "Who is supposed to be there? You and me and who else? Scott?"

Sarah bit her lip. "He didn't mention anybody else, so I suppose it's just the two of us."

"But you'll bring Scott, won't you? He'll insist."

"Laura, what is your problem? What difference can it possibly make whether Scott is there or not? It won't have any bearing on the terms of the will. He's sorry about the things he said. He's going to apologize."

Laura didn't respond.

"If it makes you feel any better, I'll ask Scott not to go with me."

"Sarah—never mind. I can make it at two on Friday."

Sarah swallowed and plunged ahead. "The reception—it's going to be at Caro's house. But I think it will be fine. Marge and her friends have made some beautiful centerpieces."

Laura's voice went from cool to icy. "I don't want to have it at the house. I told you that."

"I know you did, but when I called Mr. Gibson, he—"

"Forget it. I suppose you're doing the best you can. I'll talk to you tomorrow." Laura hung up, and Sarah stared at the phone. The best she could, because of her stupidity?

She decided she'd have that glass of Merlot after all.

Chapter 20

Dave Wheeler looked over the rim of his beer mug. "You're a cheating woman, Dee Callender."

"Cheating? I'm not—"

Larry, the bartender, stood a few feet from them, taking his time wiping up a spill, a grin pulling at the corners of his mouth. They were in Barney's, a small club around the block from the police station.

Dee waited, but Larry didn't move, so she lowered her voice to a whisper and leaned toward Dave. "Look, all I'm asking you to do is call. You don't even have to say anything. I just want the phone to ring."

Dave studied his beer. "I don't know. It just sounds dishonest to me–almost sleazy. After all, I am an officer of the law. I have certain standards to maintain. How do you think it would look—ow." He rubbed his shoulder. "No hitting! You're assaulting a police officer."

"It's going to escalate to premeditated murder if you don't knock it off. It's bad enough I have to see the jerk."

She had called Matt Coleman to tell him about the break-in at the Brenhauser residence. He dismissed it as a random breaking-and-entering. Then he asked her to dinner. She'd almost said no. She'd rather be stalked by a mountain lion than spend an evening with Matt Coleman. She could legally shoot the cougar.

She felt uneasy about the Brenhauser case, especially with Durant inactive. She suspected Laura and Sarah were right, that Coleman had closed his mind to the possibility of other suspects. She had no intention of getting involved, but she'd feel better if she could be sure Coleman was looking at all the leads. She had agreed to have dinner with him, suggesting the Topaz Club again, because there was little chance they'd be seen by anybody they knew. Then she had gone to find Dave.

"I only need a couple of hours," she said. "He's so egotistical, once I get him started talking, he won't shut up. By the time you call, I'll know more about the Brenhauser case than he does."

Dave turned on his barstool to face her. "Dee, seriously, do you think this is a good idea? You don't have any business in this case, especially with your sister-in-law involved. You were pushing it, going to the house last night."

Dee raised a hand, palm outward. "That's where you're wrong. Last night had nothing to do with the murder. I was following up on a B and E and the car chase. Besides, I was off duty, visiting a family member."

Dave looked dubious. "An ex-family member, and if anything goes wrong, it could seriously damage any chance you have of making detective."

"Why? I'm just having dinner with a detective, and he asked, not me. I can't help it if he has running-mouth disease. Dave, Coleman is so focused on family as suspects, he's not even looking at other possibilities. I'm a cop. I have to do something."

Dave turned his beer mug, keeping it perfectly aligned in the damp circle it had made on the bar. "Yeah, I guess you do. I'll help. But be careful. Coleman isn't stupid. He's just close-minded and a little lazy. You don't want to get on the wrong side of him. You're probably going to have to work with him some day."

"You really know how to cheer a girl up, don't you?" She blew him a kiss and headed for the door. "Just call me."

She glanced at her watch as she walked into the Topaz Club. She was five minutes late. Coleman was waiting in the bar.

"Sorry," she said. "I was buried in paperwork from that break-in at the Brenhauser place."

He turned around on the barstool. "Punks taking advantage of an empty house. Happens all the time. Want a drink?" He held a half-filled cocktail glass aloft.

"No, I'm ready to eat." She turned toward the dining room. He followed, and she waited until they were seated before continuing the conversation. "You could be right, and it was a random crime of opportunity, or at least, an attempted crime. But Laura Thornton was in the house alone when it happened. Luckily, she wasn't hurt. The guy ran. But what's really strange is, he chased her cousin when she tried to take a picture of him. That, with Caroline Brenhauser's death, makes it seem like more than a random burglary, doesn't it?"

Coleman drummed his fingers on the table while Dee told him about the car chase. "Dirtbag probably has a mug shot and didn't want to be identified."

"Maybe. But they think it has something to do with the missing sketches. They cleared out the aunt's studio, and still haven't found them."

The waiter took their orders, and Coleman asked for another drink. "The sketches could be anywhere. If they even exist. Most likely, they're trying to throw us off track. This thing has family written all over it. You want a glass of wine with dinner?"

"Yes. Cabernet, please. So no fingerprints or other evidence of somebody who didn't belong in the house?"

He grunted. "The woman had a party a little over a week before she left. She cleaned the house afterward, but there were fingerprints all over the patio and the furniture out there. So far, we haven't found any that don't belong to family, guests or workers. I don't figure we will."

"Did she have someplace where she stored valuable things, like her paintings, when she traveled? She didn't have an alarm system."

Coleman shrugged. "Nothing I've seen yet."

"You're about ready to wrap the case up, then? And you've done it so quickly." She smiled, hoping it didn't look as fake as it felt.

It was as easy as that. Encouraged by a few admiring phrases and well-placed questions, he talked about the case all the way through dinner.

Caroline Brenhauser's doctor had confirmed she was healthy and, in his opinion, not suicidal. Nor did it make sense that she would travel from Germany to Sacramento to kill herself.

The wine on the deck table raised the possibility of an alcohol-related accident, but she would have had little time to drink any of it. Her plane landed at twelve-oh-five. It would have taken from forty-five minutes to an hour to get off the plane, reclaim her luggage and get to her house, and she died between one and two a.m. The autopsy showed no alcohol in her system.

"Funny thing is, the attempt to make it look like an accident is one of the things that points to a murder."

Dee raised her eyebrows and sipped her Cabernet, trying for another encouraging smile.

"It was an inexpensive white, something Caroline Brenhauser wouldn't have served to guests, according to her friends. They were positive she wouldn't drink it herself. She preferred reds. When she did drink white wine, it was exceptionally good stuff, so we figured the wine on the deck came from the kitchen, something she used for cooking. The killer poured most of it down the drain, to make it look like she drank it, and left an almost-empty bottle and full glass on the table."

"It checked out?"

"Yeah." Coleman grinned. "Killer should have run some water down the drain. The trap or elbow or whatever they call it still had white wine in it. So we have a murder scene."

"But wouldn't the nieces have known she wouldn't drink that wine?"

"They probably never thought about us checking it out."

Dee didn't agree. The nieces weren't stupid. They would have used Caroline Brenhauser's favorite red wine if they had staged a scene. "Do you have a cause of death?"

He shrugged. "Broken neck, consistent with the fall. Tox report won't be back for a few weeks, but we don't expect it to give us anything." He leaned in closer and lowered his voice. "The crime scene techs say she went through the railing with a lot of force."

"So she didn't jump. Probably didn't fall, either."

"Nope." He sat back in his chair, a self-satisfied smile playing across his lips. "We're looking at a murder, and I'm betting on the nieces. Of course, we have to follow all the other leads, see if anybody else has a motive."

Dee glanced at her phone. She still had five minutes before Dave called. Coleman started talking again. The man couldn't keep his mouth shut.

"We pulled all the names from the Brenhauser woman's address book and checked them out. Even tried to find some relatives in Germany. Nothing panned out." Coleman signaled for the check. "We're working on some other angles. Interesting looking stuff, but it's over my head. We'll know more within the next day or two."

"Really?" Damn. Where was Dave? Why hadn't he called?

"Would you like to go somewhere else? I know a place that's quieter."

Dee's phone rang. Finally. "Dee Callender." She didn't wait to see who was on the other end of the line. "Oh, Liz, hi."

"So now I'm Liz?" Dave asked. "You've hurt my manly pride. And I much prefer Elizabeth. Her Majesty, to you."

"How long is he going to be gone?"

"Who? Prince Philip? Or Prince Charles? Or do you mean Prince William? Harry? I didn't realize you were on such familiar terms."

Dee grabbed her purse. "You sound awful. I'll be there in fifteen minutes, okay?"

"But, Dee, calling Queen Elizabeth 'Liz.' Do you think that's appropriate?"

Dee cut him off before she started laughing. "A friend," she told Coleman. "All alone and not well. Not well at all. I have to go." Before he could protest, she was out the door, on her way back to Barney's.

Dave was leaning over a pool table, lining up a difficult shot on the eight ball, so she slid onto a barstool to watch. He called the corner pocket. From Dee's position, it looked like a scratch shot. He sank the eight. Ever so slowly, exactly as she'd envisioned, the cue ball slipped into the side pocket. Dee grinned, waiting for the collective moan from the onlookers to subside before she said, "I hope you didn't have any money riding on that game."

He racked the cue stick. "You win some, and you lose some. I was getting tired of playing anyway." He slid onto a stool beside her. "How was your dinner date?"

"He's a pompous ass."

"Well, when you're accustomed to consorting with royalty—"

"Right now, the only royalty I'm consorting with is a royal pain in the ass. So knock it off, *Liz*. Did you get any dinner, by the way?"

"You think I sat here for more than two hours while you were enjoying a fine dinner?" He lifted a full mug of draft beer. "I got back about fifteen minutes ago."

"Lost the game that fast, huh?" She glanced at Larry, waiting to take her order, and dug into her purse for her wallet. "Cabernet."

"I see your romantic dinner left you in a glowing mood," Dave said. "Must have been something special."

Dee snorted. "If I have to do much more of that, I may reconsider being a detective." She dug out a twenty-dollar bill and laid it on the bar, beside her napkin.

Dave eyed the money. "You're planning on drinking more than one, are you?"

She made a face at him. "He's honing in on the nieces, Dave, because he doesn't have anything else. He talked about some information they're expecting, but he was pretty vague about it. I don't think he's digging around much beyond that. The victim may have got into a blue Honda at the airport. One that looks a lot like Laura Thornton's."

"Seems pretty thin."

The bartender set a glass of Cabernet in front of her. "Yeah," she said, "but they're pretty sure it's a murder, and with the inheritance angle, he thinks he's got a sure thing. How about you? Did you get a look at those sketches?" She picked up her change and dropped it into her purse.

"No, Sarah called and said she didn't get back home to pick them up. She'll get them to me sometime this week. Probably after the aunt's service."

Dee swiveled her stool around to face him. "Sarah?"

A reddish tinge crept across his jaw. "Wagner. Sarah Wagner."

"You always did have a thing for pretty little blondes." Dee hesitated. "You know she's married, don't you?"

He glanced up, startled. "Never thought about it. It's not like that. We just clicked somehow, you know?"

Dee knew. A wave of melancholy swept over her, along with something else. Grief? No, it had been too long for that. Sadness then, a longing for what might have been, and beneath all that, maybe a sense of impending loss? Or jealousy?

She couldn't be jealous of Dave. Their closeness wasn't romantic. He was her best friend, but would another woman understand that, be willing to share him? Much as she wanted happiness for Dave, wanted him to find the right woman, she liked things the way they were. If either of them got romantically involved with somebody, their relationship would change.

"What about Laura Thornton?" she asked.

"She seems nice enough. I certainly wouldn't peg her as a murderer. But what do I know about murderers? My realm is filled with thieves, and while they aren't as attractive as your murder suspects, they seem to be every bit as cunning."

"No luck with the recent rash of robberies in that area, hmm?" Dee sipped her wine, glad Dave wasn't drawn to Laura. That would be awkward, her brother's ex-wife with her best friend.

He turned the mug around the wet circle on the bar. "The burglars seem to know exactly what houses to hit. They go in fast and get out with high-end stuff. The owners are never home. How do they know what's in the houses they hit? That nobody will be home? How do they get in and out so fast?"

"Sounds like an inside job. Household help, that sort of thing."

He shook his head. "I've looked at that, but it never pans out. I can't find a connection between a burglary and the people who have worked in a house."

"Something else, then. Lawn service, newspaper delivery?" She turned the stem of her glass on the counter. "But they wouldn't have access to the inside of the house, would they?" She was silent for a few minutes, thinking. "They're smart, really smart. Not run-of-the-mill crooks. Have you checked other jurisdictions for the same sort of thing?"

"Yeah. Nothing there. I can't figure it out."

She patted his arm. "You will. They may be smart, but you're smarter." She slid off her barstool and picked up her purse. "Do you think it would help if you could get into one of the houses while they have an event going on? Observe without anybody knowing you're a detective?"

"I don't know. What do you have in mind?" He picked up his change from the bar and followed her to the door. He opened it and asked, "Where did you park?"

She pointed down the street, and they headed in that direction. "I have to go to the memorial service for Caroline Brenhauser tomorrow. Since Laura is my ex-sister-in-law, Sam wants me there."

They stopped at Dee's car. She unlocked it. "The reception is going to be at the house, and I'm sure Laura wouldn't mind if you went with me."

"Sounds like a good idea. If I just go as a guest, I might learn more than I can as an investigator."

Dee suspected he had another motive for agreeing so readily. A small, blonde motive.

Chapter 21

Sarah, still in her robe, hair damp from the shower, stood at her closet Thursday morning, trying to find something to wear.

"What about that black dress with the little straps?" Scott asked. "It has the jacket you can wear over it, and it looks good on you."

No. The black crepe spaghetti-strap with the fitted jacket was one of her favorites. She had made that mistake once before, worn a favorite dress to her mother's funeral. She'd never been able to wear it again and had eventually given it away, to get it out of her sight.

She pushed the hangers across the rod, one at a time, until she found a black skirt. She pulled out a tailored gray blouse and a pair of black pumps, things she liked, but not so much she would mind giving them away.

"I always liked that blouse on you," Scott said. "It brings out the color of your eyes."

Her gaze met his in the mirror. "Thanks for calling and apologizing to Laura, Scott. I know it wasn't easy. But things are tough for her right now, too."

"We were all a little emotional. I'm still not sure why I was asking her to forgive me when she was the one who—" Sarah opened her mouth to speak, but he hurried on. "It doesn't matter. I did it for you, so you can patch things up with her."

He brushed a hand over his hair and leaned toward the mirror to get a closer look. "I need a haircut, and I have to go by the dealership. We don't have to be down there until two, right?"

She closed her eyes; her fingers curled into fists. "The memorial service is at two, but I told you last night–I have to be at the house by nine, to let Marge and the others in. They need to set up the flowers and the food in plenty of time to change and get to the service themselves."

"But that means you'll have to leave by what? Eight fifteen? Earlier, with commute traffic. I can't get everything done in an hour. I have to pick up my suits from the cleaners—"

She watched his mouth, not hearing the rest of his excuses. Thin, firm, but not sensuous like Dave Wheeler's. She bit her lip. "No problem. I'll drive down early, and you can come later, in time for the service." She didn't have time to worry about what was going on in Scott's head. Thinking about Dave Wheeler had made her remember she had to take the sketches with her. What else? She grabbed a pair of jeans and a t-shirt.

"Why do you need those? You're not planning on spending the night again?"

"I'm putting them on. I have no intention of wearing a skirt, pantyhose and heels all day. I'll change for the service and reception, and change back again to help with the clean up." She threw an extra set of underwear into her overnight case, followed by the pumps and another pair of pantyhose, and searched her jewelry box for the earrings that went with the gray blouse. "You can either come to the house and ride over with me or go directly to the mortuary, but I need to know what you have in mind."

"Um. Depends on whether I have time to get the Explorer unloaded. I don't want to drive it out to the cemetery loaded with camping gear." His grin faltered and collapsed at the look she gave him. "I haven't had much time," he protested. "I spent all day yesterday helping you."

"What about the rest of the week? Were you busy then, too?" She zipped the overnight case shut. "That's all I asked of you. Just that one thing. To unload the Explorer."

"I know, and I meant to. Time just got away from me. I'll get it done." He tried to kiss her but she turned her head.

"I don't have time for this." She picked up the bag and walked toward the door. "Call and let me know whether I should wait for you at the house or meet you at the mortuary." She walked out, slamming the door behind her, then glanced around to see if any of the neighbors had heard. That was childish. She had to keep a tighter rein on her temper.

The drive softened her mood. Grass, still green from the winter rains, carpeted the roadside. Thick clumps of native oaks left little room for the occasional redwood, maple or Deodar Cedar to nestle among them. Patches of blue and yellow wildflowers bloomed, along with a few California poppies.

The grass wouldn't be green long, now that the rainy season had ended. It would dry to a ripe-wheat color and stay that way all summer. But the poppies would multiply and bloom for another month or two.

Caro wouldn't see them this year. She loved the wildflowers, especially poppies. Sarah had a fleeting thought that, once all this was over, she would pick some and take them to Caro's grave. No, she couldn't take the state flower from public areas. Maybe she could grow some for Caro.

She got to the house in time to make a pot of coffee before Marge arrived, followed by the caterers, and finally Nellie and her husband, Tony. Busy helping them, she lost track of time until Marge said, "We're through. How do you like it?" She waved a hand at the flower arrangements, lush with camellias, decorating the tables.

"It's beautiful." Sarah glanced at her watch. "I need to run up and change. It's almost time to go."

Scott didn't call, so she drove to the memorial service by herself. She looked for him there but, surrounded by scores of taller people, couldn't see him. She'd forgotten how many friends Caro had, and every one of them seemed intent on speaking to her, offering their condolences. She wished they would wait until later, at the reception, because their tears served as a primer for hers.

Laura slid onto the pew beside her, but didn't speak. Sarah longed to reach out for a comforting hand, but Laura held hers clasped in her lap. Sam, on the other side of Laura, gave Sarah a brief smile and turned his attention back to his ex-wife, who reached an arm toward him. He took her hand and held it between both his larger ones.

What did that mean? Were they working into a relationship again, or was it just a temporary thing? Sarah had no way of knowing; Laura wasn't confiding in her any more.

About twenty minutes later, the door at the back of the room opened, disrupting the service. Laura looked back and stiffened, telling Sarah the latecomer was Scott. Had it taken him that long to run his errands and unload the Explorer? He slid onto the pew behind her and touched her shoulder. She ignored him.

The service ended. Sarah waited while the chapel emptied. After the minister directed his last words and prayer to the family, Sarah gathered her things and stepped into the aisle, Scott close behind—so close he bumped into her when she abruptly stopped at the door of the chapel. The Explorer was parked in the green twenty-minute loading zone just outside the door, still full of camping gear. "You didn't even wash it."

He followed her down the steps, trying to take her arm. "Don't," she hissed, between gritted teeth. "Stay away from me." She hurried down the walkway, toward her Corolla, and almost collided with Laura, who raised an eyebrow. Sam held a car door open, and without saying a word, her cousin slid onto the passenger seat.

The crowded house was too warm. Sarah worked her way toward the thermostat and ran into Marge, who handed her a plate. "Here. You need to eat something."

Sarah took it. "I can't thank you enough for this, Marge. It's lovely, exactly the sort of thing Caro would have done."

"It's nothing. I'm just glad we could get the caterers on such short notice." She nodded toward the housekeeper. "But Nellie did most of it. She and Tony are real treasures."

"You said they worked for Caro before?"

"Yes. I think it was the party she threw right after the camellia show last year." Marge's head bobbed up, then down, a characteristic Sarah had forgotten. "She was looking for help, and I told her about them."

"Where did you find them?"

"You mean originally?" Marge set her coffee cup on a nearby table. "You know, I don't remember. It might have been Janice Riverson. No, she was out of the country most of the year. Maybe Estelle." She frowned. "I don't know. I'll have to think about it. Is it important?"

Sarah smiled. "Probably not. I guess I'm just a little curious about why you'd take a chance on people you don't know very well, instead of using well-established agencies." She wasn't hungry, so she set her plate on the table where Marge had put her coffee cup.

"Oh, they're fine. Lots of us use them. The agencies are just so terribly expensive, you know." Her voice was low, confiding, including Sarah in the circle of people who could afford caterers and household workers. "These people don't cost nearly as much. We kind of share them, I guess. So when we find workers like Nellie and Tony, word gets around."

"But you don't hire them full time?"

"No, just for special events. They're willing to stay late, to clean up, or come early, if they have to." Marge didn't seem embarrassed by the revelation, and Sarah wondered if she, or any of them, even saw the connection between the "long hours the couple wanted" and the low pay rate. Before Sarah could think of a way to ask, her attention was drawn to a raised masculine voice somewhere in the vicinity of the front door.

A blond-haired, red-faced man was trying to shake free of a woman who grasped one of his arms with both hands.

Sarah had seen the woman before. She recognized the pale, oval face framed by long, auburn hair. Even though she couldn't see the woman's eyes, Sarah remembered that they'd matched the blue-violet dress she'd been wearing.

"What's her name?" she asked Marge.

"What? Oh, the woman. That's Julie. Julie Seeley. And the guy with her is Steve Richlin. I'm surprised he showed up here today."

"Caro didn't know him?"

"Oh, yes, she knew him. She just didn't like him, especially after that business about the painting."

The front door slammed as the man left. Julie Seeley winced, then turned to face the onlookers, who averted their curious faces. She saw Marge and Sarah and worked her way over to them.

"You're Sarah," she said, offering her hand. "You look like Caro."

They'd never met, then. Yet, Sarah knew she'd seen the woman somewhere. She studied her face, trying to place her.

"I apologize for the scene," Julie said. "I just couldn't figure out why Steve was here. I decided to ask him and didn't think he'd react so strongly."

"It was one of Caro's paintings." Sarah didn't realize she'd verbalized the thought until she saw the other women's questioning glances. "I've been trying to remember where I saw you before," she told Julie, "and I just realized it was in one of Caro's paintings. We've never actually met."

Julie nodded. "And I thought that might be why Steve showed up—to see if he could get his hands on that painting."

"Steve and Julie were engaged," Marge explained, "and as I understand it, he's the one who commissioned the painting of Julie."

"But then we broke up," Julie said, "and Caro hadn't been paid for the painting. My mom said that wasn't a problem. She and Caro were good friends, and Mom wanted the painting, so she paid Caro. Steve was furious. He said he'd commissioned the painting, not my mom; he had a right to it, and he wanted it. That just seems creepy to me, and I didn't want him to have it. But it's like an obsession with him now. I thought he might be here to take it."

"And your mom has it?" Sarah asked. It wasn't among those she and Laura had found hidden away in Caro's studio.

"I don't know. The last I heard, Caro wanted to do some finishing touches. She said she might need me to come back and sit for an hour or two, but wasn't sure. I never heard anything more, and I don't know if Caro finished the painting before she left."

"Did Steve think your Mom had it?"

"I don't think so. I'm pretty sure I mentioned that I might have to go back for another sitting. I can't ask Mom and Dad about it, either. They're in Italy."

"Do you have a way to contact them?"

"Why? Is the painting missing? Because if it is, I wouldn't be surprised if Steve stole it. He's become obsessed with it. He swore he'd get it back, and he knew Caro was gone."

Chapter 22

Sarah was walking across the living room, trying to locate Dee Callender, when a hand touched her arm. She turned to a plump woman in her late forties or early fifties, wearing a navy print dress. Sarah searched the round face, trying to place it. "I'm sorry, I don't—"

"No, of course not, dear. We've never met." The woman held out her hand. "I'm Valerie Weston. I saw the obituary, and I had to come."

Sarah took her hand, wondering how soon she could extricate herself. She was tired, her feet hurt, and she still had dozens of people to greet. Then the woman said something that caught her attention.

"I couldn't believe it. I just saw her, and this was so sudden."

"You just saw Caro? Where? When?"

Valerie Weston's bright blue eyes peered at Sarah through square, rimless glasses. "On the trip to Germany. We were staying at the same hotel and connected when we took a local tour together. We met for dinner and planned to get together the next day. But my husband got a call from his office. Something about a business deal gone wrong."

"Sarah?"

She jerked at the sound of the familiar voice and the touch of her father's hand on her shoulder. What was he doing there? Anger threatened to undermine her fragile composure, and she tried to tamp it down, to stay calm. "I didn't expect to see you today."

Valerie Weston patted Sarah's arm and edged away.

"I thought...I hoped ..." Sarah's father let out a deep breath and dropped his hand to his side. "I knew today would be a hard one for you and I wanted to be here to help."

It had been three years since she'd seen him. Three years, and he decided to show up today to help. Where had he been all those years when she needed him?

She tried to think of something to say, but her mind was blank. Better that than let it replay the scenes imbedded in her memory: the hospital the night her mother died, him holding Anna in the parking lot. She didn't want to remember any of that. Especially not today.

"I'm sorry, Sarah, for, well, for everything." He cleared his throat. "I didn't handle it well, and I'm glad, grateful really, that Caro was there for you."

"Because you weren't?"

He looked much older, grayer, and more stooped than she remembered. The years–or perhaps his marriage–hadn't been kind to him. She supposed she should feel sorrow, some sense of impending loss, but her father had slipped away from her a long time ago, not long after she lost her mother.

He shifted his weight and cleared his throat again. "Sarah, I want to make things right again. Between you and me."

She tried to imagine what his words would have meant ten or twelve years ago when she needed to hear them. Now, she felt nothing, not even regret.

"A little at a time maybe, feeling our way?" His eyes pleaded with her, bringing back memories of those same pale-blue eyes reading bedtime stories or examining a scraped knee. Or accusing her of being disrespectful to Anna, refusing to believe the things Anna said about Sarah's mother.

"There are some things that simply aren't forgivable," she said.

He flushed, whether from anger or embarrassment, she didn't know, and took a half-step away from her. "What I did was wrong, and I regret the way I did it. But it's time you stopped blaming Anna. She tried. She did everything she could."

Sarah stared at him in disbelief. “The only thing Anna ever tried to do, besides destroying our family, was to drive me out of the house.”

He shook his head, his mouth opened to speak, but she hurried on. “You didn’t believe me when I was fifteen, and you won’t believe me now. But she was vicious and cruel and said awful, hateful things about Mom. I will never forgive her for that and I will never ...” Sarah gaped at the woman teetering down the stairs on too-high stilettos, in a sheer black dress. Anna flashed her best fake smile, raised her hand and fluttered it in their direction.

“What is she doing up there?” In Caro’s private area?

Her father shifted to look. “Oh. The powder room down here was occupied, so she went to look for a bathroom upstairs.”

“Get her out of here,” Sarah hissed, her voice low, “and don’t ever bring her near me again. Not ever.” She fled, her goal only to put as much distance as possible between herself and Anna. But well-meaning mourners blocked her way, holding out their hands, offering their condolences, their quiet goodbyes.

Sarah didn’t see Valerie Weston. Maybe the woman was gone. The reception was winding down; several groups had already left. Laura stood by the front door, seeing people out. Did she see Dad and Anna? Talk to them? Sarah longed to share her feelings about their sudden appearance but doubted that Laura would be receptive.

Sarah had tried, when she got back from the cemetery, to explain that Caro had wanted the reception at the house, that it hadn’t been Sarah’s choice. But Laura, her shoulders stiff and unyielding, had walked away without speaking.

Sarah ached all over. She longed to kick off her pumps and sink her toes into the thick living room carpet. If only she could find so simple a remedy for her aching heart. She headed for the stairs. She had to get away for at least a few minutes, had to pull herself together.

She washed her face and applied fresh makeup, working a little extra foundation over the fading bruise, and lingered long enough to check her hair and find something for her headache. Taking a deep breath, she started down the stairs, ready to face the last of the mourners.

Dave Wheeler waited at the bottom. "We've got to stop meeting like this." He motioned at the stairs, a smile curving his lips—the lips she'd been thinking about just this morning. He took her hand and led her around the corner, to the little alcove off the entryway that Caro had used as a library. "Just for a few minutes," he said when she looked back at the guests in the living room. "They won't miss you for a while, and I need to talk to you. Besides, you look like you could use a drink." He nodded toward a goblet of red wine and a bottle of beer on a nearby drum table.

"How did you know I'd be here?"

His baritone washed over her, the deep tones like a soothing lullaby. "I was working my way over to you when you went upstairs. I knew you wouldn't stay up there long, so I got the drinks and waited. I hope that's all right, that I'm not intruding."

"No, not at all. I was just wishing I could escape for a while."

He smiled, that wonderful, sensuous smile, and glanced at the bookshelves. "With Michener or Follett?"

He'd remembered the books she liked. "Neither. Just for a few minutes to sit still, away from all that." She motioned toward the living room.

He handed her the wine. "You've been through a lot the last few days, and it eventually catches up with you." He took a sip of his beer. "I'd say you're holding up remarkably well."

"I brought the sketches. The ones my aunt did of me. I'll go up and get them."

"Maybe a little later. Right now, I'd like to talk to you about the household help. How well do you know them?"

Sarah sank into the chair. "The caterers? I didn't hire them. Some of Caro's friends did all this." She kicked off her shoes, curled her legs up under her, and took another sip of wine. "But it's an interesting question. Do you think it has anything to do with my aunt's death? Because I just learned how these people hire their workers."

He leaned in closer, listening, and Sarah almost lost her train of thought. Her gaze flicked away from his mouth to his eyes, but they were so warm and attentive, she shifted her attention to the safety of his left eyebrow while she told him about the conversation with Marge.

"Do you have any record of your aunt's employees?" he asked.

"I don't know. I suppose that information would be somewhere in her paperwork, and the police took all that. They gave me a copy of her address book and e-mail contacts. I can check those if it would help."

"Okay, do that." He handed her a card. "My phone and e-mail. Let me know what you find out."

She slid the card into the drum table's shallow drawer. "There's something else I discovered. There may be a missing painting." She told him about her conversation with Julie Seeley.

He remained silent until she finished, apparently thinking about what she'd said. He rubbed a thumb against the corner of his bottom lip, drawing Sarah's attention to it. Sensuous. She looked away until he spoke again. "Sounds like it might be worth checking into. If this guy broke in the night your aunt died, he wouldn't have found the painting, even if it had been there. It would have been hidden away in the back of all those boxes and furniture. He might have thought he'd have a better chance of getting it today. It wouldn't be hard to take it out on the deck and down the patio stairs."

"But it wasn't there, Dave. I remember the painting, and it's not here. Maybe the mother has it, and Steve Richlin didn't know that, because I can't think of any reason why he'd be at the service today, other than to look for the painting."

"But you're sure you remember it in Caro's collection?"

"I know she painted it, but I don't know when she last had it at the house."

"Your aunt was a businesswoman. She must have kept an inventory of her work, along with records of sales and commissions. I'll check with Durant and Coleman—see what they have."

Sarah took another sip of wine. "Oh, I almost forgot. There's something else I discovered."

He smiled. "Maybe you'd better re-think your line of work and become a detective."

She returned the smile and he watched her face, absently turning the beer bottle as she went on to tell him about her encounter with Valerie Weston. "She said she saw Caro in Germany."

Laura appeared in the archway. "Sarah, why are you hiding out in here? I could use your help." She took several steps toward them, then recoiled. "Oh, Dave. I didn't realize it was you, the light is so dim." She took a step backward, turned to leave, and spun around again. "I thought you were Scott." She paused for dramatic effect and added, "Sarah's husband."

"Laura? Did you say something to me?" Scott walked toward the archway. When he got close to Laura, he glanced over her shoulder, then edged around her, glaring at Dave. "Who the hell is this guy?"

Dave rose and held out his hand. "I'm Dave Wheeler, Mr. Wagner, from the Sacramento Police Department. Property Crimes. I've been talking to your wife about items missing from the house. Items she thinks were stolen. She and Mrs. Thornton." He nodded at Laura.

Scott ignored Dave's hand. He looked around the alcove, taking in the wine glass and beer bottle, and Sarah's shoes on the carpet. "Looks like a pretty cozy meeting, here in a dark room."

Sarah unfolded her legs from beneath her and put on her shoes. "It may be a little dim right now, but it's not dark. It's a library. It doesn't have many windows."

"You took off your shoes," Laura said.

"Yes, I took off my shoes." *Not my blouse or my skirt.* "And I'm drinking some wine. I'm tired, I'm emotionally beat, and my damned feet hurt. Now, if you two don't mind, I'll go upstairs and get those sketches to show Detective Wheeler." She brushed past Laura and Scott and ran upstairs.

When she came back down, they were gone. "Where did they go?" she asked Dave, who sat in his chair, waiting for her.

"They didn't say. Sarah, I'm sorry if I caused a problem for you."

"You didn't cause a problem. They did, making something out of nothing. They were looking for a fight long before you arrived. So don't worry about it." She pulled the sketches out of the plastic bags she'd wrapped them in. "I hope you don't have to take these with you. They're precious to me, and I don't think I could bear it if anything happened to them."

"I can see why." He studied the sketches, glancing from them to Sarah's face. "I don't need to take them." He pulled out his camera. "A few photos and a description to enter into the database. That's all I need."

When he finished, Sarah told him to find Laura, that she had drawn a good likeness of the man who had broken into the house. After he left, she carried the sketches back upstairs and put them away. She went into the bathroom and stared at her reflection. Her headache was gone, replaced by a hollow feeling in her stomach, and she didn't think there was anything she could take for that.

She passed Caro's bedroom on her way back downstairs. They'd never searched it for the sketches. At least, not after the quick walk-through with Detective Coleman. Sarah had subconsciously marked that space off-limits, knowing she wasn't strong enough to handle Caro's things. But what better place for Caro to keep the possessions she especially treasured?

Sarah's steps slowed. No, she couldn't search it now. Maybe tomorrow, when she came back to take care of the cleanup.

By the time she got downstairs, the last of the guests had gone, and Marge and her crew were picking up the floral arrangements. Two young men, part of the catering crew, carried plastic tubs around the room, gathering glasses and china.

The doorbell rang—a man from the mortuary, with a white box containing leftover leaflets from the memorial service, blank thank-you notes and envelopes, and the cards taken from the flower arrangements. Another chore to add to her list.

She couldn't find Scott and felt a quick rush of anger. No matter how mad he was, he shouldn't have left her there alone. Not today, of all days. Both he and Laura should have cared enough not to do that.

But the surge of anger was a ripple compared to the fury that washed through her when she went out to load her bag into the Corolla. Scott had taken it, leaving her with the dirty Explorer, still loaded with camping gear.

She considered going back inside, slamming the door, and never going home. But that wouldn't solve anything. She stood in the open doorway, staring at the Explorer until she figured out what she wanted to do.

Smiling, she took her bag back inside the house and went to start the Explorer.

Chapter 23

It took forty minutes to find Maudie, a half block from the grocery store, pushing her shopping cart across the road. Sarah drifted to a stop and parked. "Hey, Maudie."

The woman approached the car. "You got eggs?"

"Nope. But I've got a lot of other stuff." Sarah climbed into the back of the Explorer. "Canned goods, if you can use them. There's a can opener." Maudie nodded, and Sarah continued. "I have a sleeping bag. It's almost brand new and really warm."

Maudie's eyes gleamed. "Why you giving good stuff away? You could sell it. Get some money."

"Yeah, but that wouldn't piss my husband off as much."

Maudie laughed, a deep, belly-shaking sound. "That's the best damn reason I ever heared for giving stuff away. Give it to me, girl."

Her arms were too frail to handle the box of canned goods, so Sarah removed half the contents, lugged the box to the shopping cart, then went back for the rest of the cans. She topped off the box with the sleeping bag. "Can you handle all that?"

But Maudie was eyeing the contents of the Explorer. "Whatcha gonna do with the rest of that stuff?"

Sarah grinned. "What do you think? But you don't have room for it."

Maudie's gaze searched Sarah's face, her eyes unblinking. Finally, she turned and pointed to the strip mall down the street. "They's an alley behind them stores. You can't get in from this side. Drive 'round the block. You'll see it. Wait there." She grabbed the cart and headed toward the stores.

The alley was lined on one side with wide, roll-up delivery doors and punctuated with dumpsters, some of them overflowing. Chain-link fence bordered the other side, decorated with wind-blown plastic bags. Dry weeds poked through the bottom, littered with cigarette wrappers and other trash Sarah didn't want to get close enough to identify. It was too late in the day for delivery traffic. Sarah locked the doors of the Explorer and waited, watching the entrance to the alley.

She saw them from the corner of her eye, only a faint motion at first. A man pulled back a section of the fence and came through, reaching back for a shopping cart. He pulled it through the opening, parked it on the dry grass, and looked around the alley. He ducked his head at Sarah, then helped Maudie pull her cart through. She, too, glanced around the alley before she pushed the cart toward the Explorer. The man limped behind her, the tongue of one worn-out, laceless shoe sticking straight up. He had an unshaven face; narrow, hunched shoulders; and long, slightly graying hair, tied in a loose ponytail.

"This here's Danny," Maudie said, offering nothing more. Danny grinned, exposing a gap between two lower molars.

Sarah opened the back of the Explorer. "Take the tent and stove, too, if you want, and all the boxes." She slid one a little closer to the door.

Danny grabbed it and shifted it to his cart. "Take a trip or two."

Sarah wanted to get out of the alley, so she got out to help. They had one of the carts loaded in a few minutes, and Danny took it back toward the opening in the fence.

"Camp ain't far," Maudie told Sarah, perhaps sensing her unease. "He'll be right back."

Sarah helped Maudie fill her cart and get it through the fence, climbed back into the Explorer and pushed the rest of the gear toward the back, so it would be easier to unload.

Twenty-five minutes later, Maudie and Danny were back with the empty carts, and Sarah helped them transfer the last of the Explorer's contents.

"Thankee, Sary," Maudie said. A grin cracked her seamed face. "And thank your man, too. Come find us if you want to get rid of some more of his stuff." She followed Danny through the fence, and, while he was still fastening it back into place, Sarah drove out of the alley.

She was hungry, and she hated eating in restaurants alone. She could get her things and be home in thirty-five to forty minutes, or she could stay at Caro's house long enough to fix a sandwich and eat it while she did a quick search of Caro's bedroom. Then she'd know, once and for all, whether the sketches had been stolen. A glance at the dashboard clock confirmed that it was a couple of minutes until seven. It wouldn't get dark until after eight, and she could be gone by then.

A side street beckoned. She took it and was turning around before she realized she'd already made a decision.

She unlocked the door leading from the garage into the house, turned off the alarm, and made sure both the lock and deadbolt were in place before she reset it. She stood, letting the quiet enfold her, a little surprised that it didn't feel threatening–perhaps because the alarm was set. Eyes closed, listening to the humming silence of the house, Sarah could almost feel Caro's presence, her warmth.

She hesitated at the entrance to Caro's room, reluctant to invade this vanilla-scented space. But Caro would want her to do this, not somebody else.

She started to work.

At first, with every drawer opened, every shelf searched, she felt like she was violating Caro's privacy. Gradually, the feeling diminished, but after almost an hour of searching, she still hadn't found the sketches or the photographs.

Tired and thirsty, she went to the kitchen but decided against a glass of wine. She still had to drive home. Maybe she should go now, get a good night's sleep, and come back tomorrow. She shook her head. It wouldn't take long to search the closet. She found a bottle of water in the refrigerator and carried it upstairs.

She'd worked her way around less than half the closet when Caro's robe slid off the hook and settled on the floor. The vanilla scent overwhelmed her and, without warning, tears streamed down her cheeks. Wiping them away with the back of her hand, she took a deep breath, broke into rib-cracking sobs, and sank to the floor, holding the robe pressed to her chest.

She had cried before; when Scott first told her Caro was dead, at night when she tried to sleep, when she heard Caro's message on her phone, and at the memorial service. But she had never cried like this. Sarah gulped, trying to catch her breath, and scrabbled her way to Caro's bed, where she curled into a tight ball, drowning in tears. When they finally subsided, she lay still, too exhausted to move, staring at the ceiling, thinking about all the times she'd sat in this room, on this bed, sharing something with Caro—a good test score, the cool new guy in her Algebra class, or getting a good part in the school play.

Her eyes burned, and she closed them for a few minutes.

She was dreaming about the baby; the little girl she might have had, with Scott's curly dark hair and her own gray eyes. But Caro, holding the baby, said, "She looks like Allison, like your mother, exactly like her. I'll get the sketch and show you." Caro carried the baby to her office and tried to pull the framed sketch off the wall, but every time she pulled a corner loose, another slammed down. Caro, intent on pulling it free, let the baby—Sarah's beautiful baby—slip. Sarah tried to yell, to tell Caro not to drop the baby. The sketch fell to the floor with a soft thud.

Sarah jerked awake, sat up and listened. The house was quiet. She sat still, her ears searching for whispers of stealthy movement, but finding only the ghostly voices of years past, and a strange reluctance to venture beyond the closed bedroom door.

She wasn't a child. There was nobody else in the house. There couldn't be; the alarm was set. It was wireless. There had been no sound of breaking glass from the patio doors or from a window. Either would have set off the alarm. She was alone—except for the disembodied spirits of Laura and Caro. Laura's face was cool and distant, but not her eyes. They pleaded with Sarah, and she wished she had her cousin's clairvoyance. Right now, she would welcome one of those illuminating dreams.

How long had she been asleep? She glanced at Caro's bedside clock. A quarter to four.

She slid off the bed and stumbled over the water bottle. She must have knocked it off the bed in her sleep. That explained the thud. Good thing or she'd have been there all night.

I have been here all night, she realized. The sun would be up in a little over an hour. She had spent the night alone in Caro's house, on Caro's bed, and she felt at peace, more than she had in days, maybe weeks.

Scott must be worried, though, wondering what had happened to her. She reached for her phone, hesitated. The phone worked both directions, and he hadn't been concerned enough to call her. Or not sober enough, if he'd gone home and started drinking—a strong possibility, considering how angry he'd been when he left. But not as angry as he was going to be.

She couldn't help grinning. He had really liked that flannel-lined sleeping bag. She was going to enjoy watching his face when she told him she'd given it away.

It would have to wait. The housekeeper wouldn't arrive until eight, and Sarah saw no reason to drive home to Roseville, then fight the commute traffic to get back.

She went back to sleep.

The phone woke her at half past six. Scott, angry because she hadn't come home. "Where did you spend the night, and who—"

"At Caro's, searching for the sketches," she interrupted before he could finish that question. Not because she had anything to hide; it just made her uncomfortable, maybe even a little guilty, because it brought Dave Wheeler to mind.

"You should have called," he said, "I was worried." His voice held a note of petulance.

"But not worried enough to call me?"

The silence stretched out for a full half-minute before he answered. "Okay, I was mad."

She got out of bed, pushing hair out of her face. "I meant to drive home, but I fell asleep on Caro's bed. I guess I was really tired."

"You spent the night there? In her house?"

"Yes, I did, and got a good night's sleep." He hadn't minded leaving her alone here yesterday, so why the big fuss now? "I have to let the housekeeper in at eight, and I can't leave until she finishes."

"You have to see the attorney this afternoon, don't you? Am I supposed to go with you?"

"No. Why would you?"

"I don't know. Maybe because I'm family?"

Not part of Caro's family. Surely he didn't think Caro would leave him anything. "You do too much for him," she'd told Sarah, "and he does too little for you."

Like not unloading the Explorer.

"I gave away the camping stuff." The words slipped out. She had wanted to tell him in person, to see his face. She did the next best thing and closed her eyes, trying to imagine the expressions playing across his features.

"Why the hell? Sarah, my sleeping bag was in that stuff. I had a hard time finding one I liked. What right did you have to get rid of it?"

"You didn't unload it. I asked you to, several times, and you didn't. I couldn't. Most of it was too heavy. You kept dumping the Explorer on me, taking my car, so I was the one who had to listen to that stuff rattling around. I got tired of it."

"You got tired, so you gave it away? What got into you? Do you know what it'll cost to—"

She waited, her eyes still closed, wondering how he'd finish that sentence. He didn't. He started a new one. "Well, I don't suppose it matters. We don't need that old stuff. After everything has settled down, we'll buy something better. That's if we even want to go camping. Probably not. We can afford to travel ..." His voice trailed off. He'd finally noticed her silence.

"Is that all Caro's death means to you, Scott? The things you can do with her money?"

"No, of course not. Don't be stupid. You know that's not what I meant. You always twist what I say, put words in my mouth. But, be realistic. We will inherit a lot, won't we?"

Stupid? She took a long breath. "I don't know. I haven't thought about it. For all I know, Caro willed everything to the Camellia Society."

"To the–" His breath caught. "You're joking. Aren't you?"

"No," she lied. "The Camellia Society was important to Caro. She worried about it being underfunded." He didn't say anything, and she smiled. "I've got to get going, Scott. I'll talk to you later."

By the time Nellie arrived at eight, Sarah had showered, eaten breakfast, and finished searching Caro's room. She didn't find the sketches and didn't know whether to feel sorrow over their loss or elation over what that loss meant. Somebody had taken them, probably the night Caro died. She called Dave Wheeler, to let him know.

"I'm sorry to hear that," he said, "because I didn't find anything in the pawn shop databases."

"Where else could somebody sell them? Craigslist or eBay?"

"Some stolen property ends up there, but not much. If the thief is a crack addict needing a fix, he'll get rid of it as fast as he can—trade it to his dealer for drugs, or sell it to anybody who will take it."

Sarah tried to conjure an image of the man who had chased her in the SUV. He'd been alert, a skillful driver. "And if he's not a crack addict?"

"Depends. If he's experienced, he may have a buyer beforehand. If he steals a lot, he might have a fence who disposes of the goods for him."

Sarah felt hollow in the pit of her stomach. Somehow, even as she'd searched for the sketches, she'd been sure they would eventually turn up wherever the thief had disposed of them.

"But the fact that they're missing does prove that a thief killed my aunt, doesn't it?" Even to her own ears, her voice sounded thin, pleading.

"Sarah." The void in Sarah's stomach expanded. "I'm not a homicide detective. You need to talk to Detective Coleman about that. But, so far, I don't see any solid connection between your aunt's death and the missing sketches. I even checked out your caterers. They were all working a party the night your aunt died. And Tony's and Nellie's neighbors say they were home that night—at least, they were when a pinocle party broke up around eleven forty-five, and their car was still in the driveway at two a.m."

Sarah tried to speak, but her throat felt tight.

"I'll talk to Dee Callender," Dave said, his voice gentle. "Maybe she can help. I'm sorry. I know the sketches were precious to you."

Sarah croaked a hasty "thank you" and disconnected.

While Nellie was cleaning, Sarah went in search of an iron. She would keep the appointment with the attorney before driving back to Roseville, but she'd have to press the skirt and blouse she'd worn for the memorial service; she had nothing else with her.

Matt Coleman called. He wanted to talk to her again.

"I have an appointment at two," she said. "Could I do it after that?"

"What are you doing right now?"

"Now?" Why did he care what she was doing right now? What did that have to do with anything? "I've been closing up my aunt's house. I'm tired and dirty, and just getting ready to clean up."

"We all get tired working murder cases, Ms. Wagner." His voice sounded smug, self-righteous.

Well, he wasn't the only one trying to find a murderer. "Right. I've been searching for the missing items. Which are not in the house." She enunciated the last sentence slowly.

He made no comment.

"I can be there in forty-five minutes. I hope that's soon enough." She bit her lip. It wouldn't help to irritate him even more.

"I'll be waiting." He sounded so self-satisfied, her fingers trembled when she started the car again. What did he want to talk to her about?

It didn't take long to find out. He knew about the telephone call and wanted to know if Caro had left a message. Sarah played it for him.

"Why didn't you come forward with this?"

"I didn't know about it at first, when I came in to talk to you and Detective Durant. I was out at the casino, without my purse, when the call came in. When I did get my purse back, I'd just learned about my aunt's death. I was so shaken by that, I never thought about checking for missed messages."

"And when did you get around to checking them?"

Her mouth felt dry. "That evening—Saturday."

His gaze bored into hers. "And why didn't you call us then?"

"I did. I mean ..." Her voice trailed off. She hadn't been able to reach Durant. Reluctant to talk to Coleman, she'd left a message for Durant to call her back. He'd never called, and with so many other things competing for her attention, Sarah had simply forgotten about it.

She told Coleman that. He wasn't satisfied but would have been far less pleased if she'd told him the rest: that he was so intent on finding one of the family guilty, she hadn't wanted to give him more ammunition.

He let her go, but not before he threatened to arrest her for obstruction of justice if she ever withheld information again.

Chapter 24

Robert Gibson's law office felt chilly, but Sarah attributed it to Laura's stiff greeting and Gibson's cool nod and brief handshake. The three of them sat around the small wooden table in his office, surrounded by shelves of neatly aligned legal reference books.

Sarah pulled an envelope from her purse. "Here are the receipts for the alarm system, the railing repair, and the new door." She paused to make sure Laura heard the next words. "And for the reception at the house. We tried to do it the way you said Caro wanted."

He took the envelope without comment. Sarah glanced at Laura, hoping she would finally understand the reception at the house had been Caro's wish, not Sarah's. Laura blinked and pressed her lips together, but said nothing. Gibson cleared his throat and read the will.

Caro had left her entire estate to Sarah, Laura, Eric and Jamie. The boys' inheritance would be held in trust, managed by Robert Gibson until their twenty-fifth birthdays. Sarah's would be held in trust until her thirty-fifth birthday, or until she was no longer married to Scott Wagner.

Sarah gasped, and Laura smirked. Gibson barely paused before turning to the next page of the will. Sarah dipped her head so they couldn't see her face, hot with embarrassment. Why had Caro done this? Lumped her in with Eric and Jamie, all of them children who couldn't be trusted to manage money. Except, the boys were apparently more trustworthy than Sarah; their money would be released on their twenty-fifth birthdays, hers not until her thirty-fifth.

Gibson was still reading, finishing a section Sarah had been too upset to hear. He looked up at the end, giving each of them a questioning glance. Apparently, Sarah's blank look led him to fold both hands on top of the page and launch into an explanation. Caro had considered it unfair to leave a portion of her estate to Laura's children and none for any Sarah might have. To compensate, she left Sarah the house and furnishings, in trust.

Sarah glanced at Laura and caught a look of dismay, quickly replaced by one of cool reserve.

Laura didn't understand; Caro had known how much Sarah loved the house. It had been her home, her haven during those traumatic years after her mother's death. Laura, not having that emotional connection, might want to sell it, and Caro would have wanted it to be there for Sarah, as a refuge. Caro wasn't treating Sarah like a child. She was trying to protect her.

"I want to make sure I understand," Sarah said. "The house is mine? I can live in it, but I can't sell it?"

Gibson nodded. "Except the artwork, of course. That belongs to the estate, to be divided between you. But the trust conditions still apply to your portion of it, and to the house and furnishings, as well. If you don't have children, either natural or adopted—" He flipped through several pages. "—by your fiftieth birthday, half the value of the house reverts to Ms. Thornton. However, you have the option of buying her portion, if you wish, at the appraised value at that time."

"But in the meantime, if I don't actually get the money, how will I pay the taxes? The insurance?"

Gibson pushed his glasses down his nose and peered over them, his look quizzical. "I must not have made myself clear. You will not be penniless. You will have whatever funds you need. Within reason, of course."

Whose reason? Her face must have reflected her doubt because he riffled through the paperwork for another document.

"I doubt money is going to be a problem. Roger Brenhauser had a sizeable estate, which he invested wisely. Caroline never touched the principal. She could have lived quite well on the interest and dividends, even without the earnings from her artwork. Right now, excluding the artwork, which has yet to be fully appraised, the estate is worth approximately nine million dollars."

Nine million dollars. One million to each of the boys, with an equivalent amount in the value of the house and furniture to Sarah. That left over five million to split between the cousins. Sarah couldn't imagine what that much money looked like. Not that she was likely to see much of it anytime soon. In the meantime, it would keep her at the top of the suspect list, cause more friction with her husband and, by throwing in the house, make her cousin hate her. Not a fair trade-off.

Gibson's voice droned on. "Caroline had her assets protected in a trust, but with this large an estate, there will be some tax liability. The accountants can give you more information. I suggest you set up a meeting with them as soon as possible."

He stood and shook their hands. Laura, stiff-lipped, left without speaking. Sarah watched her walk away. Would they ever get past all this?

The attorney was gathering papers and aligning them into a perfect stack.

"Mr. Gibson, I need a few more minutes of your time. Perhaps you can clarify what you mean by 'reasonable expenses.' Can you tell me what I might expect as a monthly allowance, if that's what you call it, from the trust?"

He explained that the accountants would have to determine her net worth, decide how best to invest it and calculate the expected return. Only then would they know how much she could safely spend without endangering the principal. The entire process could take several months. "In the meantime, I can replenish the five thousand dollars you have in your trust account on a monthly basis.

"So there will be no problem if I spend five thousand dollars each month?"

"No more than there has been in the past, Ms. Wagner, unless probate should take much longer than we expect. If, for some reason, you should need more than that, call me. I would strongly advise that you keep the money in a separate account, in your name only. As long as you do that, it will not be considered community property, nor will anything you use it for."

He stood. "And now, if there is nothing more I can do for you?" He picked up the perfectly-aligned rectangle of papers and, with great care, slid them into his briefcase.

Still a little dazed, Sarah walked to the parking lot, oblivious to her surroundings. She slid into her car and sat, staring out the front window, at the concrete pillars and low ceilings. But she saw only Scott's and Laura's faces, both of them cold, angry and accusing. What had Caro done to her?

Scott would be furious when he heard the terms of the will, but he was always angry, anyway. She would simply be adding a little more tinder to coals that never seemed to quite cool, that Scott kept banked, always ready to flare into a red-hot rage.

When had he become so angry? She searched her memory for the last time she had seen him laughing, smiling, his eyes tender. All that came to mind was an image of Dave Wheeler's sensuous lips and his warm brown eyes. She shook her head, trying to dislodge the image. Dave wasn't for her.

Finally, she shifted in the seat and dug out her cell phone. If she told Scott now, he'd have the rest of the afternoon to cool off. The next thought came unbidden: It would also give him time to plot ways to get around the provisions of the will.

He surprised her. While he sounded tired, perhaps a little disheartened, he didn't get angry. "Sounds like pure Caro," he said. "But I'm glad you got the house. You have a connection to it that Laura doesn't have. It's almost like it's a part of you. You're different when you're there, more centered, more at ease. Maybe even happier. I want you to be happy, Sarah. The rest of it doesn't matter."

If he meant that, did it follow that he would be okay with her quitting her job, going back to school? "I'll be getting about five thousand a month from the trust. More if there are extenuating circumstances. If Robert Gibson approves, that is."

He was silent, and when he finally spoke, he seemed distracted. "We'll figure it all out. I've got to go, got a customer waiting. I should be home by six. Sarah, I'm sorry for all this. I love you."

She sat for a few minutes after he disconnected, thinking about the call. There was something in his voice she couldn't define. Worry? Or was he just tired or distracted? The past week couldn't have been easy for him, either.

Maybe she could make it up to him. She could cook something he especially liked, and open a bottle of wine. They could talk and maybe understand each other a little better.

It was three thirty-five. Time to get out of town, before state workers converged on the parking lot and freeways, intent on escaping to the suburbs. But even as she drove back to Roseville and her local grocery store, her thoughts drifted back to Scott's comments about Caro's house. Sarah's house now. Did she want to live in it? Or had she relished her time there this week simply because she had some time alone, away from Scott?

She detoured to a bank that had branches all over the country and opened separate checking and savings accounts, in her name only. She wouldn't tell Scott about it just yet.

When she pulled into her driveway, she sat for a few minutes, wondering how the money would impact her life. Her gaze drifted over the house, her flower beds, the neat lawns of her neighbors. She loved Caro's house, but she loved this one, too.

It took her twenty-five minutes to make the lasagna and put it in the oven, and another twenty to prepare the garlic bread and mix a salad. While she waited for the lasagna to cook, she unpacked, changed into jeans and a t-shirt, and leafed through the mail. He should be home any minute.

After she set the table, checked the lasagna, and slid the garlic bread into the oven, she opened a bottle of Merlot and held it over her glass for a moment. Maybe one quick splash? No, she'd wait for him.

A half hour later, she had turned off the oven, put the salad back in the refrigerator, and settled into a chair with the newspaper, absorbing little of what she read, because she was listening for the sound of the Corolla. Scott wasn't answering his phone, so he must be driving.

The white box from the mortuary caught her attention. She might as well work on thank-you notes while she was waiting. But she found it awkward. Should she sign them only for herself, or for Laura, too?

Laura was not acting like herself. The petty jealousy she was displaying was out of character for the woman Sarah had so admired for her self-confidence, a quality Sarah knew she lacked.

A memory flitted through her mind of a night, before Laura's divorce, when Sarah had driven her around Folsom, searching for Sam, who was off on a three-day bender. They had finally found him in a little dive—she couldn't remember the name—that smelled of stale beer and sweat. He was in the middle of the room, dancing a slow shuffle, his partner a middle-aged bottle-blonde with racoon-like eyes in shades of green. Glitter sparkled on her pancaked makeup.

Laura had muttered, "Sam does love to dance. Even if all he can find is bimbos." She had strolled across the dance floor, caught his arm and said, "Come on, Twinkle Toes, time to go home."

Sam, despite his startled expression, apparently had dulled his senses with so much booze his brain didn't flash danger signals. He explained, in slurred but careful words, that he couldn't go home; he had two or three full glasses of beer on his table, drinks people had bought for him. It would be rude to leave them. He wobbled his way back to the table. When Laura and Sarah followed, he motioned for them to sit.

He sank onto the chair with the beer mugs in front of it. Laura still stood, surveying the beer, both in the mugs and spilled on the table. She lifted one, surprising Sarah, who thought Laura was going to drink it. Instead, she held the mug over Sam's head, tilted it, and let its contents dribble through his hair, over his ears, and down his neck.

"What the hell?" Sam scrambled to his feet, brushing wet hair from his eyes.

Laura placed the mug back on the table. "There's one gone. Ready for another? Or do you want to come home?"

He stood for a moment, looking at Laura with a somewhat quizzical expression.

Sarah, all too aware of the stunned silence in the room, later told her cousin, "I couldn't believe you'd do something like that."

"Well, he made me mad. He didn't mind leaving me home, wondering. For three days I didn't know where he was or if he was okay. I had mental pictures of him in a car wreck or rolled by some thief, lying in an alley somewhere. But did he care about that? What he did to me? No, he cared about being rude to his drinking buddies."

Laura had her way. Sam had gazed longingly at the glasses of beer on the table, almost as though he was counting them, but walked out the door.

Scott wouldn't have done that, wouldn't have followed Sarah out of a bar. She shuddered to think what he would have done if she'd poured beer over his head.

"I always wished I had that much nerve," she had told Laura. "But I never had enough courage. I would have been too embarrassed."

"That's because you worry about what people think, and I didn't care what those barflies thought. You're a nicer person than I am."

"No. No, I'm not," Sarah had said. "I don't have as much guts as you do. I'm not as strong."

"But you're getting there, Sarah, you're getting there. And when you do, I hope to hell Scott's ready for it."

A tear splashed on Sarah's hand. She hadn't realized she was crying, tears generated by the memory of Laura and the closeness they'd shared, and maybe lost forever. Would they ever get that back? Or had Caro's will destroyed it?

She poured a glass of wine and stood in front of the window, watching as cars slowed, turned onto her street, then drove past her house. No Corolla. Where was he? Why hadn't he called? Why didn't he answer his phone?

How many nights had she stood at that window, staring into the darkness, watching for his car and wondering where he was, trying to decide whether she should go to bed or call the hospitals to see if he'd had an accident?

He should be home by now. Maybe he'd really had an accident this time.

The thought stirred no emotion, and she realized that, for the first time, she felt no tremor of fear at the possibility. Before she could explore that thought or chide herself for her calm acceptance, for feeling nothing, emotion finally came, in the form of bitterness. With her luck, he'd do just enough damage that she'd have to take care of him for the rest of his life.

Chilled, she wrapped her arms around her waist. What was happening to her? What kind of person was she becoming?

The doorbell rang. Oh, God, she didn't mean it. She couldn't lose Scott. He was all she had left. She opened the door, bracing herself for the police officer, his face betraying by its detached stillness the devastating news he had come to deliver.

But the only officer at her doorstep was Dee Callender, accompanied by Sam, and there was nothing detached about the expressions on their faces.

Sarah's legs felt like cooked spaghetti. She reached for the door frame. If she clung to it hard enough, maybe she wouldn't fall. "Is he—is he—" Dark shadows gathered on the periphery of her vision, and she felt her grip loosening. Sam's face wavered, and then it was floating away. Or maybe she was; she couldn't tell.

Then Scott was there. He had a strong arm around her, guiding her to a chair.

"Get a wet cloth," Dee told Sam.

Sam hurried to the kitchen while Dee lifted Sarah's legs onto the ottoman, murmuring words Sarah couldn't quite decipher through the buzzing in her ears. Something about Laura.

Sam sloshed a too-wet cloth against Sarah's face. Water trickled down her neck, into her collar, and she jerked, pushing the cloth away. "Laura? What did you say about Laura?"

"She's been arrested," Sam said, panic creeping into his voice.

"Not really arrested," Dee said.

Scott spoke at the same time. "For what? What did Laura do?"

"Not arrested," Dee said again. "Matt Coleman has taken her in for questioning. But there's a good chance she will be held."

Sarah looked from Dee's face to Sam's, trying to grasp what they were telling her. "Questioning for what?" But even as she asked, a void opened in the pit of her stomach.

"For murder," Dee said.

So many thoughts whirled through Sarah's head, she couldn't organize any of them into a coherent question.

Because she didn't speak, Sam apparently thought she hadn't heard. "For murdering Caro," he said, and slumped into the opposite chair.

Chapter 25

Sarah sat for a long time after Sam and Dee left, trying to force her brain into a task it was incapable of performing. Had Caro's telephone message triggered Laura's arrest? She should have lied. Told Coleman Caro didn't leave a message. But they might have found out, and that would be worse.

Laura didn't kill Caro, and Sarah had to prove it. But she couldn't get beyond that, didn't know how she was going to do it. She was too emotional, too drained for cohesive thought.

Despite the sleeping pill Scott gave her, she spent a restless night, besieged by strange dreams. Scott's alarm jarred her from an image of Caro flying, soaring through the air. In the instant before she crashed onto the patio, she morphed into Laura, who looked upward, beating her arms like wings, in an effort to climb back onto the deck. No, above the deck, where Matt Coleman leaned over the railing, reaching for her.

The dream had been in vivid color, so real it took a few seconds for Sarah to detach from it, to anchor herself in reality. She shuddered and pushed deeper into the blankets.

She'd lost them, all of them. Richie, Mom, Dad, Caro, and now Laura. And her marriage was so broken she couldn't fix it. She had nothing left. Despair settled over her, and she wasn't sure she could drag herself out of bed.

Almost like another dream, the voices came, her mother's first. "So, you're just going to give up?"

"With Laura in trouble?" Caro added.

Her mother again: "You're going to stay in bed with the covers pulled over your head?"

Caro: "You're a big girl, Sarah. It's time you started acting like one."

That stung, and they weren't going to leave her alone until she did something, so she threw the covers back.

Before Scott finished his shower and starting dressing for work, Sarah had finished packing her overnight bag. She set it by the door, and when Scott came back to the bedroom to dress, grabbed some underwear, a pair of jeans and a knit polo shirt and headed for the bathroom.

When she came out, Scott stood by the bed. He nodded toward the suitcase. "Where are you going? Sarah, I told you how sorry I am about last night. I had a client, a sale I needed, and I didn't get a chance to call. Then it was too late, and I was afraid you'd be mad."

Sarah wasn't listening. None of that mattered now. "I've got to go back to Caro's. That's the only way I'm going to find answers."

His hands trembled a little as he straightened his tie. Nerves? Repressed anger? More likely a hangover. "Sarah, you can't do that. It's not safe. You're not a detective. Leave it to the professionals."

"What professional? Matt Coleman? You think he's going to do anything to help Laura? He wants her convicted."

Scott placed his hands on her shoulders and looked into her eyes. "I know you don't want to hear this, but don't you think they must have good reason for arresting her? Some kind of proof—"

She twisted away from him. No, all they had was that damned voicemail message. "They don't have proof because Laura wouldn't hurt Caro. She loved her too much. My God, don't you remember the fight you two had over her, just a few days ago? How angry she got when you said those things about Caro?"

He grabbed her shoulders again and turned her back to face him, leaning in close, his face almost touching hers. "I was wrong, and I apologized. I should never have said those things. But that doesn't mean Laura is the paragon you seem to think she is. If you recall, she made some pretty nasty accusations about me, too."

He was right. Both he and Laura had uttered words better left unspoken—barbs that had sunk deep, caused too much pain, and started the rift between Laura and Sarah. "But the point is, you did say them, and it hurt. I never knew you disliked Caro so much."

He dropped his hands from her shoulders and took a deep breath. "There are a lot of things you don't know about the way I feel. You never bother to find out." He put a hand on her cheek and looked into her eyes. "I love you, Sarah. You're the best thing that ever happened to me. I'm sorry. Not just about what happened between Laura and me, and about Caro, but about us and things never coming out right when I say them."

She had heard it all before. She reached for the bag, but Scott pulled her around to face him again, more gently this time. "I didn't hate Caro. I kind of liked her. I just wished she liked me better. But somewhere along the way, I realized it didn't matter." He brushed a lock of Sarah's hair away from her forehead and tucked it behind her ear. "Caro would never have liked anybody you hooked up with, or Laura, either. But especially you. She'd never think anybody was good enough. Nobody could ever give you what her precious Roger had given her."

"That's not true. Caro was happy for me. She helped plan the wedding. She paid for most of it."

"Yeah, but then life got real," Scott said. "I wonder if the love of Caro's life would still have been so wonderful if he'd lived a few more years. Long enough for a little of the shine to rub off his armor."

Heat surged through Sarah's body. She took a deep, steadying breath. "They were married for nine years, plenty of time for the shine to rub off, if it was going to. We've only been married for six, and look what's happened to us. Are you saying our marriage–the fights, all of it–that's real life? Because I can't live like this, Scott."

"No, I'm not saying that. I know I've got a problem. I drink too much and don't treat you right. I don't call and let you know where I am, making you worry too much. I did it again last night. Not call you, I mean. But you have problems, too. You lose your temper. You fly off the handle too easy. Even worse, you always put your family ahead of me."

"How do you expect me not to lose my temper when you get drunk, don't come home, don't call, and won't even answer your phone? How do you think that makes me feel? And I don't put family first, Scott. I just have to depend on them because I don't feel like I can depend on you."

"I'll try to start answering my phone," Scott said. "It's just that—when it gets late, and you call, I know you're already mad, so there doesn't seem to be much point in answering. But I'll do whatever it takes. I love you too much to lose you."

Sarah didn't want to lose him, either. Caro was gone, and her relationship with Laura was on shaky ground. Maybe he was right; she'd depended on them too much. "Okay, maybe I've been too close to family. But I need to be close to somebody, and sometimes I feel like you're deliberately doing things to push me away."

"That's exactly what I'm talking about. You can't see your part in any of this. Everything is my fault."

"So, what do you want to do about it? Counseling?" Sarah looked directly into his eyes, challenging him. He would never agree to that.

He hesitated. "A shrink?"

"No, a counselor. And what, exactly, did you have in mind when you said you'd do anything?"

He rubbed the back of his neck. "I don't know. I thought maybe I'd look into AA. Find out something about it. Then we could talk some more."

"We've done enough talking. All that ever gets us is more broken promises. But Alcoholics Anonymous sounds like a step in the right direction if you're serious about it."

"Yeah, okay. I can do that. I'll check around, see where they have a group, and go to a meeting. But if you think we need a marriage counselor, too, I'm game for that."

"I'll see if I can find somebody. I can do that from Caro's."

He was full of surprises this morning, and she wished she could believe him—that he would follow through. But within a few days, he'd drink too much and not come home, leaving her wondering where he was and why he didn't answer his phone.

She grabbed the overnight bag.

He put his hand out, as though he wanted to take it from her, then dropped his arm. “You’re running away again.”

“I’m not running away. This is something I have to do. Don’t you understand? The answers are there, and I’m the only person who is looking for them. I can’t let Laura go to prison for something she didn’t do.”

“I’ll go with you. You’ll be safer with me there.”

“No. You need to run the dealership.”

He didn’t say anything more, and looked so miserable she added, “I’ll try to find a marriage counselor, and you look into AA. Scott, if our marriage means enough, we can save it without throwing Laura away. We have to because I could never forgive myself if I did that.”

Finally, he nodded and kissed her forehead, his mouth gentle. “Okay, we’ll do it your way. But you have to call me tonight and every night you’re there. I have to know you’re safe. Keep the alarm set. Don’t answer the door unless you know—”

Sarah smiled. “—who’s on the other side. And don’t accept any rides from strangers. Yes, Papa.” She looked directly into his eyes. “Now you know what I feel like when I don’t know you’re safe.”

She grabbed her purse and headed for the door. “I’ll call tonight.” Maybe he’d even be home. At least for a night or two. Or maybe not. The bars always beckoned.

She backed out of the driveway and headed for Douglas Boulevard and the on-ramp to I-80, wondering if she should call and ask for more time off work. She shook her head; she didn’t know how much time she would need. She didn’t like the job. She’d like to quit and go back to school, but Scott would never agree to that.

She glanced behind her and switched lanes. Traffic was light this time of the morning, and she enjoyed driving.

How would Robert Gibson react if she quit? Did it really matter? She couldn’t imagine needing more than five thousand a month to live on.

She stopped at the supermarket for groceries but didn’t see Maudie. She considered tracking her down but decided against it.

The woman would show up eventually, and Sarah had more important things to do right now.

It took her less time to unpack than to decide where to put her belongings. She finally settled into her old room. Eventually, she would have to pack up Caro's things, but not yet. She needed more time. Maybe she could have the housekeeper do it, or Angie, if she was still available to work.

Caro had complained that the girl had changed over the last year since she'd become a high school junior. "She's always disappearing, not sticking with her chores. I find her out in the garden, or in the kitchen. Not working, just walking through."

"Maybe she's coming up from the basement after nipping at some of your wine," Sarah had teased. Then she had confessed. "I used to sneak out the back door and meet boys in the garden." She had laughed at the surprise reflected on Caro's face.

Another memory to cherish. There would be more, long forgotten ones, stirred by her presence in the house. While she welcomed them, she didn't want them to overwhelm her, especially now, when she needed a clear, uncluttered mind.

She opened her laptop on the kitchen desk and connected Caro's printer, ready to make a list of every unresolved question, every lead, every possibility. She came up with five items:

1. *Why did Coleman arrest Laura? What evidence did he have?*
2. *Who was the man who broke into the house and why did he chase me?*
3. *Who took the sketches? Was it the same man?*
4. *Why did Caro come home early? What was the meaning of the message she sent me?*
5. *Did Steve Richlin break into the house to steal a painting that might—or might not—be there?*

Sarah stared at the screen, appalled at its brevity, and added another line. It probably had nothing to do with the murder, but she would have to check it out.

6. *Who were the couples in the garden the night of the bon voyage party?*

Dee didn't know why Coleman had arrested Laura, but she had promised to let Sam know if she found out. So, skip that one for now, and go on to item two.

The only lead Sarah had to the man who had broken into the house was Laura's sketch. Both Dee and Dave had tried to match it to profiles in law enforcement databases, without success. What more could she do? Make copies and plaster them around the neighborhood?

She moved on to item three. Dave had found no trace of any of the missing items. It was unlikely she'd see any of them again, so that was a dead end.

Item four, Caro's message. Why did she come home early? Was the reason connected in some way to her death? Why had she asked Sarah not to tell Laura or Scott? Sarah felt a sudden chill and shivered. She rubbed her arms and moved on to item five.

Had Caro interrupted Steve Richlin in the act of stealing a painting? Had it even been there to steal? It didn't matter, as long as he thought it was there. Sarah had told Dee about it. For the time being, she could only hope Coleman would follow through. Sarah shook her head and moved on to item six, the last one she'd added to the list.

She doubted the couples in the garden had anything to do with Caro's death. She'd remembered them only because she had dredged up every memory of those last days before Caro left, but, right now, that's all she had to work with.

She walked through the kitchen and stepped from the new dining room door onto an eight-foot-square concrete slab, bordered with herb beds. Beyond that, a high fence, mostly hidden by plant growth, enclosed an expanse of lawn, studded with colorful flower beds. Flagstone paths wound around and through them, to a wisteria-draped arbor in the back.

None of that would have been visible the night of the party. Unless the guests knew where the arbor, the benches, and the bistro set were located, they would have stumbled upon them only by accident as they strolled, guided by the path lighting. Sarah had glimpsed the couple in the arbor only because a sliver of moonlight had reflected off their white clothing. That's all she had seen—blurred white patches against the darkness. Now she could see only the wisteria, the edges of the arbor, and part of the dark, shaded interior.

She looked toward her right, where the large gates, now locked, had opened onto the patio beneath the second-floor deck. The couple she had seen arguing had exited through those gates and continued across the patio, toward the street. To pinpoint the spot, Sarah walked along the path until she could see their route. That put her several yards from the bistro set, nestled into a widened bulge in the path, between her and the gate. Had the couple been sitting there when their disagreement started? That would mean they could have been outside for a while—long enough for people to think they'd left much earlier than eleven when Sarah had seen them.

She went back inside, fixed a sandwich and ate lunch, thinking about the couple. Had they attended Caro's memorial service? The garden had been too dark for her to see their features, but they had both been tall and slender. She closed her eyes, trying to recall every mourner who had greeted her at the chapel and the cemetery. That proved fruitless; she had been so absorbed in grief and anger, she hadn't paid much attention.

She had the guest book and the box from the mortuary. If she had to, she could piece together a list. Then what? Visit every single one of them to see if they looked like a couple she saw in the dark who probably didn't even have anything to do with Caro's murder?

She cleaned up the kitchen, opened the guest book and scanned the handwritten pages until she came to the name of Valerie Weston—the woman who said she had seen Caro in Germany.

Sarah couldn't find her in the online white pages. She might not have a landline, might not even live in Sacramento. At least two dozen communities were within reasonable driving distance of the capital. Sarah tried one of the "find anybody" sites on the internet. Valerie Weston lived in El Dorado Hills.

As she was scribbling down Valerie's information, Sarah's phone rang. She didn't recognize the number. The voice on the other end sounded familiar, but she couldn't quite place it.

"Sarah, it's Sam. I was wondering how you're doing?"

More likely he wasn't doing well and needed somebody to talk to, somebody who shared his own despair.

"I'm okay. Trying to go over everything again, to figure out who really killed Caro. I'm at her house for the time being. Do you know, has Dee learned anything new?"

He was silent so long, Sarah thought she'd lost the connection. When he finally spoke, his voice was strained. "Dee's not supposed to know anything about the case, much less talk about it. That could get her into a lot of trouble. They can't expect her not to talk to me, but she has to be careful."

"I get it. Has your sister told you anything you can share with me?"

The voices of Eric and Jamie came through the receiver, bickering with each other, then Sam telling them to knock it off. "Sorry," he said. "Seems like every time I get on the phone, they start acting up. Anyway, Detective Coleman has been suspicious of both of you because of the inheritance, but especially Laura, since they think somebody in a blue Honda picked Caro up from the airport. Then Caro's message, the one she left on your phone, seemed to implicate her, and maybe Scott, even more. They started digging into the financials, and they claim Laura has been siphoning money through your trust fund and transferring it into an offshore account."

Chapter 26

Sarah sat still, trying to absorb Sam's words. Her mind whirled with so many thoughts she struggled to form a rational question. Even as she blurted, "That's impossible. Laura wouldn't do that," she was thinking of all the safeguards in place to keep the accounts secure. Laura would need Sarah's passwords—and there were two of them—and she would have to make the transfers from Sarah's computer. At least, that's what she'd been told when she questioned the security on the account. What would happen if somebody tried to access the account from a different computer? Probably a list of security questions. She tried to think of how long it had been since she'd looked at her trust fund account. Months. She never drew from it.

"Sarah? Are you okay?"

"Yes. I just...I'm sorry, Sam. I'm trying to think. I don't see how she could have done that."

"I know, but they've traced the transfers, Sarah. They were made through Caro's computer, from your trust fund to Laura's, and from there to the offshore account."

"But it has only five thousand dollars in it," she protested, at the same time she realized Caro would have replenished it. *My God, is that why Robert Gibson acted so cool toward me? He thought I was taking advantage of Caro's generosity.* "I don't care what they think they've found. You and I both know Laura wouldn't do this."

"Yes, but other than you and Laura, who else had access?" Unspoken, under the surface, was a name Sam was too much a gentleman to speak, at least to Sarah. Scott.

"If someone used Caro's computer, there are lots of possibilities. Think about it, Sam. Most people don't memorize their passwords.

They write them down and keep them near their computers. Anybody who had access to Caro's house might be able to get into her accounts, and from there, it would be easy to transfer funds from one to another. A lot of people knew when Caro was gone."

"You may be right, though I should think Caro would have been especially careful with those particular passwords. And why channel the funds through yours and Laura's accounts?"

Sarah could think of only one reason. "If Caro had our accounts set up so the funds were electronically replenished when they fell below five thousand, the transfers wouldn't be noticed as anything unusual. At least, not for a while."

"But who else would know that? And why make the transfer through yours first, into hers, and out again?"

Sarah didn't have an answer.

Eric's voice in the background demanded his father's attention. Sam, his voice muffled, said, "I'll be there in a minute," then came back to Sarah. "I've got to go, but I wanted to ask—could you watch the boys for me for a few hours tomorrow, around ten? I want to try to see Laura, and with it being the weekend and no school, I don't have a place to take them."

"Bring them over. I'll be glad to have them."

"You might regret it. They can be pretty demanding."

Of course, they were. Laura was gone, their routine upset. They would sense something was wrong and need reassurance. "We'll be fine," Sarah said, wondering when the boys would see their mother again.

After Sam's call, Sarah put her list of questions aside and started a new one. Who had access to Caro's house? The person who had transferred the money would have needed sufficient time to work with the accounts and fairly frequent use of the computer. That meant they had to have a key or some other means of entry, probably while Caro was not home.

Sarah and Laura had keys for emergency use, and so Sarah could check the house during Caro's absences. Laura rarely used hers, so she kept it locked in a desk drawer at home. Sarah kept hers in her purse, which was either with her, locked in her desk drawer at work, or in her closet. It wouldn't have been difficult for Scott to make a copy. She shook her head. She couldn't believe he would do that.

Caro had the only other key—unless there was still one hidden under the bench. Sarah hadn't been on the patio since Caro died, and she didn't want to go now, but she had to know whether the key was still there, so she went out the door leading to the upstairs deck.

Muddy footprints had dried on the floor. She looked at the tread pattern. Had Scott made them the morning he'd startled her with his unexpected appearance on the deck? Or the carpenter, when they worked on the railing?

From the top of the wooden stairs, she could look down into the patio and out over the shrubbery, to the long driveway and front yard. She didn't see anybody, so she headed down to the bench.

Kneeling, she peered underneath and glimpsed a black spider—a big one, inches from her face. She jerked, bumping her head against the bench leg, scrabbled away, then took another look. No key hung on the hook. Had Caro removed it, or somebody else?

She rose to her feet and dusted off the knees of her jeans. Who, besides she and Laura, had known about the key? Had Caro shown it to Angie, in the event the girl got locked out, like she'd done with Sarah a decade earlier?

Sarah called her.

"Hello?" The girl's voice was hesitant, and Sarah hurried to identify herself. "This is Sarah Wagner. I called you earlier, about the video game and CDs."

"Oh, yeah. I'm sorry I didn't call you back. I got busy and couldn't get over there to pick them up. I got them the day of the memorial service. You were busy, and I didn't think you'd mind."

Sarah didn't remember seeing the girl, but that wasn't surprising, considering the number of people who had been there. "That's all right. I understand. I was calling to see if you might be available to do something for me. There's no set time frame."

"Uh, I don't know. I'm pretty busy with school right now."

"This won't take long. It's...I need to pack up the things from my aunt's bedroom, and it's...well, it's too difficult for me to do. I thought maybe you wouldn't mind. I'll pay you, of course."

"I don't know." The girl sounded reluctant. Maybe it was too much to ask of her. But then she said, "I might be able to do it Tuesday. I don't have any classes that day."

"Sure. Whatever is convenient for you. Do you happen to have a key, or did my aunt leave one somewhere for you?"

"No, she was almost always home when I got there. If she wasn't, she left a key hidden on the patio. She didn't do that very often, though, and I always left it on the kitchen counter after I used it."

"And you didn't tell anybody about it?"

A moment of hesitation. "No, not about the key," leaving Sarah wondering what she had told somebody about.

"Okay, why don't we do it this way? Call and let me know what time you can make it Tuesday, and I'll make it a point to be here."

If Angie didn't have a key and there wasn't one on the patio, that meant only Sarah and Laura, and possibly Scott, had access to the house. Angie was the only employee Caro hired on a regular basis. If she hadn't given Angie a key, she wouldn't have given one to anybody else who worked in the house. If she'd left one with a neighbor or friend, she would have had them check on the house, rather than asking Sarah to drive down from Roseville.

Sarah considered the men in her aunt's life. Caro had valued her privacy too much to give any of them the freedom to enter her house at will—unless her relationship with one of them was much deeper than Sarah thought. Even if she did give one of them a key, the same question applied: Why ask Sarah to drive down?

She stared at her list: Sarah, Laura, Scott—unless the key had stayed on the patio and somebody else knew about it or found it. She wadded up the paper. Maybe the person who had accessed Caro's computer didn't need a key; maybe he knew how to pick locks.

Frustrated, she rose and paced the room. She was missing something, but what? She'd been gnawing away at the problem for hours. Maybe a break would help—a glass of wine and a few minutes out in the garden. Was it too early for a drink? She looked at the kitchen clock. Five thirty. It couldn't be. It must have stopped. But her watch confirmed the time. Hours had zipped by while she had tried to untangle the puzzle.

Just as she was wondering what to make for dinner, Scott called. "How are you doing, honey? It's got to be hard for you, being alone there in Caro's house."

"It's not too bad, but a little frustrating because I don't think I'm getting anywhere."

"Maybe there's nothing you can do." He hesitated, then asked, "Did you have any luck finding a marriage counselor? I can go to one down there, if it's easier."

She'd forgotten about it. "No, not yet. I got sidetracked. Coleman arrested Laura. He says she was transferring funds from my trust into hers, and then to an offshore account."

"Wow, I didn't see that one coming. Are they sure it's Laura?"

"Coleman is always sure, as long as the evidence points to one of us. But Laura didn't kill Caro. I got caught up in trying to figure out how somebody got access to Caro's computer and lost track of time."

"Making any progress?"

"No, not really. I figure he had to have a key, so he must have copied mine or Laura's, or Caro's."

He was quiet for a moment, then spoke so softly, she had to strain to hear him. "I know you don't want even to think it, but isn't it possible that Laura did this? Who else would have known the funds would be replenished?"

"Maybe he didn't know, the first time. Then when he came back, looking for something else to steal, he found money in my account again."

"Seems a little far-fetched. And there's no indication anybody broke into the house. You and Laura are the only ones who ever believed that."

"The sketches are missing. We looked."

"You can't know for sure that they were stolen. Maybe Caro took them someplace else for safekeeping. They're not valuable, Sarah. The family photos are gone, too. Why would anybody steal those?"

She closed her eyes, pushing down a mix of emotions: some anger, impatience or irritation, and, yes, fear. "Scott, you're beginning to sound like Matt Coleman. What if all the missing things were together, in a box? Thieves wouldn't go through the contents. They'd see the sketches and think they were valuable."

"I'm sorry. I don't mean to sound like Coleman." He was silent for a few moments. "I hope Laura appreciates your loyalty and everything you're doing for her. I worry about you, in that house alone, especially at night. I wanted to come down, spend the evening with you. But I have an AA meeting at seven, and that wouldn't give me much time, with the drive down and back."

He'd actually done it. He'd found a meeting, and he planned to go. "That's great, Scott. Maybe you can come down tomorrow night." She would be sure to find a marriage counselor the next day.

She put the phone down and riffled through the sheets of paper she'd printed. Was Scott right? Was she letting her love for Laura cloud her thinking? No, she knew her cousin better than that.

Right now, she needed a break; she couldn't think straight.

The white box from the mortuary caught her attention. She'd never finished the thank-you notes. That might clear her mind. But as she addressed envelopes, she also made a list of the names. Marge and some of the others would have telephone numbers or e-mail addresses. Somebody had the answers she needed, and she intended to find them.

Scott called again while she was getting ready for bed, excited about the AA meeting he'd attended. "You'd better hold off on the marriage counselor, at least for right now. This kind of support is exactly what I need, and I plan to go every night until I get a handle on this thing."

"So I'm not going to see you for a few days?"

"I'm off on Monday. I thought maybe we could spend it together. Forget about all the rest of this stuff for one day."

She bit her lip. She had so much to do, so many people to see, and she wouldn't get much done the next day, once Sam dropped the boys off. But she had to do whatever she could to save her marriage. This might be their best—and last—chance. "What did you have in mind?"

"Well, I thought about Napa Valley, but with all those places for wine tasting, I decided that wasn't a good idea. What do you think about spending the day in San Francisco? Or we could drive up the Pacific Coast Highway or take a drive through Yosemite."

"No, San Francisco sounds good. Maybe Chinatown? We haven't been there in ages."

His voice softened. "We'll have a great time. Maybe we can think of something to do next week, too. We're going to make this work, Sarah. I love you. Have a good night, honey."

"You, too." Sarah put the phone back on the night stand and went to bed, wondering if she could believe him. He'd made and broken so many promises in the past, she wasn't sure, but he'd never gone to AA before, and he'd never agreed to a marriage counselor.

The real question was, did she still care enough?

Chapter 27

On Sunday, Dee met Sam for lunch, a few blocks from the jail. He had dark, puffy circles under his eyes and a grim expression on his face. "They're going to charge her," he said.

Dee hadn't believed Coleman would do it, didn't think he had enough evidence. Certainly not enough for a conviction. She could only hope Al Durant would finish his trial work soon and come back to manage the case.

She didn't know how to help, but she offered anyway. "What can I do?"

"Help me find a good criminal attorney."

"I don't know of any, offhand, but I can make some calls." She rose from her chair. "Give me a few minutes. Order the pastrami melt for me, on rye, and a glass of water."

She came back to the table fifteen minutes later with a handwritten list. It contained three names and telephone numbers. "These guys are expensive. If you need money, I can help a little—"

He rubbed his forehead. "God, I'm an idiot. It will take weeks, maybe months, for the estate to be settled, but I thought if I could scrape up enough money for the retainer, the attorney would wait for the rest. I should have realized–Laura is not going to get any of that estate until she's cleared of complicity in Caro's death."

Dee put her hand on his arm. "I'm sure her cousin will help. They're close."

Sam shook his head. "Laura tells me Sarah's share of the money is tied up until she's thirty-five. She might not be inclined to give Laura anything, anyway. They're not speaking to each other." He peeled back the bun on his hamburger, added mustard to the patty, and topped it with the pickle and onion slices on his plate. "Laura thinks Sarah is shielding Scott, that he's the one behind all this."

Laura had accused Sarah of protecting Scott before—something about the telephone call from their aunt—but Dee had sensed an unusual closeness between the cousins.

On the morning of Caroline Brenhauser's death, Scott Wagner had given every appearance of being a frantic, worried husband. That, and his anguish when he thought the body might be Sarah's, would be hard to fake.

Dee had never seen him after that. Sarah rarely spoke of him, and when she did, Dee had never noted a change of tone, a softening of features, or any other indication of warmth.

"From what I've observed, I assumed they weren't a tight-knit couple."

"They're not and I don't believe for a minute Sarah would sacrifice Laura for Scott. But Laura—I don't know what happened, but she doesn't even want to see Sarah right now."

Dee didn't know what to say, so she took a bite of her sandwich. Not bad.

"And speaking of Sarah," Sam said, "she's taking care of Eric and Jamie for me today. I was supposed to pick them up this afternoon, but I need to find an attorney. Sarah says she doesn't mind keeping the boys for as long as it takes, but she does need some time to get out and do some investigating on her own."

Curious about what leads Sarah could possibly be following, Dee said, "I can go by and get them. What time are we looking at?"

"Sometime late this afternoon? Or maybe even after dinner, if that works better? But she's had them since ten this morning, and they can be a handful. Especially now."

"How much do they know?"

"Nothing yet. I told them their mother had been called away for work. But that's something they're not used to. And normally, when I have them, I'm with them all the time, doing fun stuff, not sending them off to babysitters. I think Eric senses something. He's been a little quieter than usual."

"What are you going to tell them if the police decide to hold Laura?"

"I don't know." His eyes looked bleak. "I've never lied to my kids, but I may have to now."

"Sam, there's something really weird about this entire case. Coleman knows they're not going to indict Laura for murder. Not unless he has something we don't know about, and I can't figure out what that could be."

She hoped to hell she didn't have to make another date with him to find out.

She had to pass Dave's apartment on her way to pick up the boys, so she stopped to tell him they'd probably have to skip dinner that evening. "I'm on my way to pick up my nephews, and I may be babysitting for a while."

"That's okay. I'm deep in the middle of something." His enthusiastic tone told her whatever he'd uncovered was significant.

"About to catch some thieves, are you? Don't you know it's Sunday?"

"I may have a lead, somebody I want to talk to again." He rolled his chair back. "So let me get this straight. You're dumping me so you can take on a babysitting job? Back in my high school days, it used to be the other way around. Girls would rather go on a date than babysit."

"Unless the boy came to babysit with her. But that was a long time ago, and you know how it is. You guys get older, and the younger men start looking much more appealing." She picked up her purse. "I might be able to squeeze you in tomorrow night, though."

He looked up at her, frowning. "Is there anything I can do to help, Dee?"

"Nothing I can think of, but thanks for asking. Things don't look good." She patted his shoulder. "I'll fill you in later."

She got to Caroline Brenhauser's house a little after four and could hear Eric and Jamie laughing as soon as Sarah led her into the kitchen. The boys galloped up the stairs from the basement into the kitchen, Jamie lagging behind his older brother.

"Auntie Dee!" Eric grabbed her around the waist. She brushed back his sandy-brown hair, so much like Sam's had been as a child. He tugged her toward the stairs. "Come and see our fort. It's really neat. Aunt Sarah showed us a great hiding place."

"It's a castle. Isn't that right, Aunt Sarah?" Jamie tugged at Sarah's arm. "We're gonna pretend there's a moat. We'll have a dungeon and big dragons flying up at the top." He widened his eyes and pulled down the corners of his mouth, showing his teeth. Stretching his arms out on each side, he raced around the two women.

Dee laughed. "Aunt Sarah looks a little tired. I think you wore her out. Maybe we should go and let her rest. You can build a castle another day."

Sarah picked Jamie up and swung him around. "Yeah, Dragon, let the human rest." She glanced at Dee. "I promised them a snack—if it's not too close to dinner time?"

"I think dinner is going to be a little late tonight, anyway," Dee said.

"Okay." Sarah turned back toward the boys. "You guys ready for some milk and cookies? Oh, I guess not. Dragons don't eat cookies, do they? Maybe some nice, juicy raw meat?"

Eric bobbed his head up and down. "Yeah, real bloody."

Jamie clambered onto one of the counter stools. "Not me. I want cookies and milk."

"They're playing down there?" Dee nodded toward the basement stairs, thinking about the labyrinth of shelving leading into the former bomb shelter. "I was there when we cleared the house, after ..." She bit her lip.

Sarah nodded and reached into a cabinet for a plate. She kept her back turned while she poured milk into two plastic glasses and put the jug back into the refrigerator. By the time she turned back to face Dee, she was smiling. "It's okay. They play in the old bomb shelter room. The rest of the basement is off limits. All the really good wine is at the top of the racks, above their heads, and I told them they're not to climb on the shelves or touch the bottles." She put the glasses on the counter. "And you guys follow the rules, right?"

"Right," they said in unison.

"Aunt Sarah said we might get cut if we break a bottle," Eric added, reaching for a cookie.

Sarah touched the back of his hand. "Go wash up first. You, too, Jamie."

"C'mon." Eric grabbed Jamie's hand, and they took off for the bathroom.

"They're really little buddies, aren't they?" Dee asked, watching them. "And they look so much alike."

"Eric does a pretty good job of looking after Jamie, for an eight-year-old." Sarah's voice trembled a little, and she blinked several times. "They're great kids. They know something is wrong, and they don't deserve this."

"No, they certainly don't," Dee said. Sarah obviously loved those kids and, no matter what Sam said, she was tight with her cousin. Dee stepped closer. "You're right. They're really good kids, and I think you're a pretty good aunt." Then she did something so out of character, it surprised her. She put her arms around Sarah.

Sarah relaxed against her for a moment, then raised her head and moved her lips in a quavering half-smile before she stepped away. "Thanks." Her voice was soft, almost a whisper, and she glanced toward the bathroom before asking, "Have you seen Laura? How is she?"

"I haven't talked to her. Sam is trying to get the best attorney he can find, and raise some money."

"But she has money now. She...but she won't get that for a while, will she?" Dee didn't respond, and Sarah plunged on. "If the lawyer knows she's going to get it, that he'll be paid, he'll take the case, won't he?"

Dee didn't know how to tell her Laura might never get the money. "Sam is checking that out. Maybe he'll know something by tonight."

"Do you happen to know—if you can tell me—did the police find Caro's passwords in her paperwork? I'm curious about how easy it would have been to get into the accounts."

A good question, one Dee hadn't considered. She wondered if Coleman had. She would have to find out.

The thought made her answer more cryptic than she would have liked. "I don't know. I'm not working on the case, and I don't have access to that kind of information."

"Oh. I'm sorry I asked. Sam told me that. I just forgot." Sarah turned to watch the boys as they ran back into the kitchen. "Cookies and milk are on the counter."

"After that, will you show us the flip back again?" Jamie asked.

"Backflip, you dork," Eric said. "You should see her, Aunt Dee. She can flip frontwards and backwards without even stopping."

Sarah smiled. "I used to do gymnastics," she told Dee, "and there's a place in the back yard that's perfect. There's a high fence so the neighbors can't see me making a fool of myself. I was showing them how to do backflips." She shrugged and smiled. "To be honest, I was running out of ways to entertain them."

She tousled Jamie's hair. "Did you guys get all your stuff? Did you leave anything down in the basement?"

"The fort," Eric said.

"No, the castle," Jamie insisted.

"But you got everything?"

They nodded, and Sarah hugged Eric, then Jamie. "Don't burn anything down with your dragon breath. Okay, buddy?"

He giggled. "Bye, Aunt Sarah. Can we come back and do flip backs? And play in the basement?"

"Yeah, that was cool," Eric chimed in.

"Of course you can come back. I need somebody to keep the monsters away." She walked with them to the door.

Dee checked to be sure Eric and Jamie were securely buckled into their booster seats before she waved at Sarah and slid into the driver's seat. She looked in her rear-view mirror when they were halfway down the block. Sarah still stood outside the doorway, waving at the boys.

Dee had planned to spend part of her weekend catching up on the never-ending paperwork, but Sam's needs and those of the boys had taken precedence.

"Is it okay with you guys if I make a quick stop at work?" It would take her only a few minutes to grab a stack of folders to work on later that evening.

"At the police station?" Eric's eyes widened. "Can we see the jail?"

"No, I'm afraid not. It's in a different building."

Jamie frowned. "Are there bad guys in there, where you work?"

"No, they're over at the jail." At least, the ones they'd caught were. She parked, shepherded the boys inside, and steered them toward the front desk.

"This is Officer Patterson. You're going to stay with him for a few minutes while I pick up some things. Joe, meet Eric and Jamie, my nephews."

"Hi, guys," Joe said. "You gonna be police officers like your aunt?"

The boys nodded, staring at his shield and holstered gun. Dee settled them into chairs close to the desk and supplied them with pads and pencils. "Here, draw something for me while I'm gone."

She took the elevator upstairs and hurried to her work area, wending her way through desks and law enforcement personnel. After gathering a stack of file folders and cradling them in one arm, she worked her way back to the hallway and the elevators. Just as she pushed the downward arrow, one of the doors opened, and several people stepped out, Matt Coleman among them. He lingered beside the door while the others stepped around her and hurried down the hall.

She didn't have time to talk to him—not with the boys waiting downstairs. She gave him a friendly smile and lifted her free hand in a half-wave, but before she could speak, he asked, "How's your friend?"

Dee's mind went blank. What was he talking about?

"The one who wasn't well?" Coleman prompted. "Liz, if I remember correctly."

"Oh, right, Liz." Dee smiled as Dave's reaction to the name flashed through her mind. "Much better, thank you." She moved toward the open elevator door.

Coleman stepped in front of her. "What was wrong? It sounded serious, the way you rushed off."

"Yeah, it was. But it's–well, it's a little complicated. And private. Something she wouldn't appreciate me talking about." Disconcerted, she added, "Thanks for asking, though."

"That's odd," Coleman said, his words slow and precise, "because I heard you were having a glass of wine with Dave Wheeler shortly after you left me."

Barney's. She should never have met Dave there, although she couldn't imagine why anybody would consider it gossip-worthy. She stood, looking at Matt Coleman, trying to think of something to say, but her brains had turned to mush. "Is it okay if we talk later? My nephews are waiting downstairs."

"No, it's not okay." He grabbed her arm.

She jerked away, then had to grab for the files, which were sliding across her arm, toward the floor. Once she'd righted them into the crook of her arm, she turned to glare at him. "What the hell do you think you're doing?"

"Getting your attention." He stepped closer, so his face was only a few inches from hers. "I had an interesting conversation with Al Durant last night, all about your relationship to one of the murder suspects in the Brenhauser case."

"I've already reported that relationship to him," Dee said.

"Yeah, and he didn't see a problem since you weren't working the case and weren't privy to details of the investigation." His gaze bored into hers, and she involuntarily took a step backward. "But he didn't know about you cozying up to me, going on dates, trying to solicit information to help the suspect."

His emphasis on "solicit" left no doubt about his connotation of the word. His gaze moved down to the breast not hidden by the folders, lingered for several seconds, then moved to her waist and hips before coming back to her face.

"Date?" she said. "In your dreams. If you didn't shoot your mouth off so much, trying to impress people, you might get a clue."

Two men in plainclothes appeared at the end of the hallway, walking toward them.

Coleman lowered his voice. "You tried to use me, and you're not going to get away with it. You can forget about making detective. By the time I get through, you'll be lucky if you still have a job."

Chapter 28

The silence that settled over the house after Dee and the boys left seemed heavier than usual.

Sarah had never lived alone. She had shared a house with her parents and Richie until he died. Their house had been unnaturally quiet after that, not just with grief, but with the diminished sounds of an only child without a playmate. After her mother had died and her father married Anna, Caro's house had been her refuge. Sarah had lived first with Caro, then Scott. She had become accustomed to having somebody around who talked to her, ran water in the shower, clattered dishes and cutlery in the kitchen, and answered the phone. Now, alone in the house again without Eric and Jamie, she realized just how oppressive silence could be.

What must it have been like for her father, to lose his wife and only son? Is that why he was so blind to the things Anna had done, so deaf to Sarah's complaints? Had he, like Sarah, lost so much he couldn't bear the thought of losing Anna?

The thought startled her. She tried to suppress it, but it refused to slink back into her subconscious.

Surely her father couldn't have been so desperate to keep Anna that he let her alienate his only child. Even now, Sarah had to blink away tears when she remembered the way Anna had taken over the house, confiscated her mother's things, even the necklace that had been handed down through several generations of her mother's family, and the gold locket holding her grandmother's and grandfather's photos.

Those pieces had been promised to Sarah. Where were they now? Had Anna sold the locket and bought something more to her liking? Sarah couldn't imagine the woman ever wearing the old-fashioned piece, but Anna would love the intricate setting of the necklace, with its tiny emeralds and diamonds. Sarah had never seen either of the pieces of jewelry around Anna's neck. Was she just careful about wearing them around Sarah? Not likely. Experience told her Anna would be more inclined to flaunt them. Maybe she had even been wearing one of them at the memorial service. Sarah didn't see her up close.

Something was niggling at the edges of her consciousness, but she couldn't quite grasp it. The harder she tried, the more it receded. She needed to relax, stop thinking about it for a while.

Her phone rang. Scott. "Hey, how about opening the door and letting your husband in? I've brought dinner."

She punched the security code into the alarm and opened the door. Scott stood on the doorstep, holding several bags of California-Asian takeout. Sarah took one from him. "I thought you were coming down in the morning."

He leered at her. "And miss spending the night with my girl? I don't like sleeping alone."

"Then maybe you should have checked out the sleeping accommodations before you came. The daybed pulls apart into two singles, and the bottom mattress is a little hard."

He put the bags on the dinette table. "What about the master bedroom? I thought you slept in there the other night."

"Caro's bed? I did, but just for that one night. It was—different." She couldn't explain the serenity that had filled her when she awoke, the sense that Caro had been with her one last time as she slept, watching over her. She would never feel Caro's presence as strongly in that room again. She didn't want to sleep in there, especially with Scott. "I know you won't understand this, but I don't want to use the room until I've packed Caro's things."

Scott nuzzled her neck. "I know. They bring back too many memories. We'll manage fine on the daybed. We'll just have to snuggle closer."

That wasn't really it, either. The house was full of memories. It was more a sense of desecrating Caro's space, and it would be Caro's until all her things were packed up and her vanilla scent no longer lingered.

Sarah and Scott spent the night on the daybed, and she awoke to the smell of fresh-brewed coffee. She stretched, reveling in the satiny feel of her nude body against the warm sheets.

Scott was making breakfast. She smiled. This was the man she'd fallen in love with. She slid out of bed and picked up her nightgown, puddled beside the bed, as she headed for the shower. She was more than ready to get away from the house and its mysteries and spend the day in San Francisco.

She enjoyed the drive across the valley almost as much as the city. They had lunch in Chinatown, and she looked for souvenirs for the boys. She found a red t-shirt for Jamie, imprinted with a dragon so impressive, she knew Eric would want one too, so she bought him a black one. Scott held up a gold-plated abacus, inspecting its jade-green base.

"Tired of counting on your fingers and toes?" Sarah teased.

"I just like them. They're so—so—"

"Chinese?" She grinned at him. "I like the wooden ones, or maybe the one with the gold-veined marble base."

"Ah, but this one is special." He took it to the register and paid for it. "Gold and jade. A gift for a very special lady." He handed it to her, and just for an instant, as their fingers touched, she wondered which Scott was real—this one or the one she'd grown so accustomed to.

"What do you say we head out of town before the rush hour starts?" He opened the shop door for her.

She tried to slip back into light bantering, annoyed with herself for her doubts. He was trying; she needed to meet him halfway. "Ah, romantic to the core, I see."

He put an arm around her waist. "If it's romance you want, we can stop somewhere nice for dinner, once we get out of the worst of the traffic."

She sighed. "Too bad the Nut Tree's gone. I loved that place."

"Yeah." He glanced at his watch. "If we wait 'til we get back to Sacramento, the timing will be about perfect for dinner."

"I need to go by the supermarket on the way to the house," Sarah said. "I need some boxes. Angie is coming tomorrow to pack up Caro's things."

"What are you going to do with the room?"

"I don't know yet. I just need to pack everything up. Right now, I can't walk past that room without catching a scent of vanilla, and it all comes crashing down on me again. I've tried closing the door, but that makes it worse."

"I hope you won't be there much longer. I'd like to have my wife back." He reached for her hand. "In our house."

When they got to the entrance of the grocery store several hours later, Sarah glimpsed Maudie, pushing her shopping cart around the side of the building. The woman started toward them, but stopped when she saw Scott. She raised one hand a little, grinned and turned the cart in the opposite direction.

"Seems to be a lot of homeless people around here," Scott said.

"A few." How many people occupied the camp Maudie and Danny had mentioned? "I haven't seen any around Caro's neighborhood, though."

"Makes me a little uneasy about leaving you. I think I'll spend the night, go back in the morning."

"But you have an AA meeting."

"I'll go tomorrow night. Looking on the bright side, my commute tomorrow morning should be a snap, going against the incoming traffic."

So he stayed. Sarah made popcorn, and they watched an old movie, laughing at Tony Curtis and Jack Lemmon in *Some Like it Hot*. In the odd way that the brain works, her thoughts jumped from the image of Tony Curtis to his wife, Janet Leigh, to *Psycho*, to the man who had broken into the house and chased her in the car. She would have liked a glass of wine, but out of deference to Scott, opted for iced tea, instead.

She woke during the night, a little crowded by Scott, curled around her on the daybed. She tried to free a numb leg, but he pulled her closer. She drifted back to sleep and didn't awaken until he kissed her on the forehead. "Don't get up, sweetie. I'll grab some coffee on the way to work. Be careful today."

"Scott? Take the Corolla. I have to take Caro's things to the thrift shop."

"Don't they come and pick up stuff like that?"

She stretched and yawned. "Not anymore. At least, I don't think so. Anyway, the Assistance League was Caro's favorite charity. They do a lot of good in the community, and I know she'd want her things to go to them. They provide clothing for needy kids, scholarships, backpacks for high school students, women's outfits for job interviews—"

"Okay, gotcha." He leaned over to kiss her again. "I'll call you later."

She would miss him. Yesterday had been a good day. Scott was behaving like the man she had fallen in love with and married. She hugged him and pushed deeper into the covers, missing the warmth of his body but relishing the space to stretch her legs. She would have to get up soon. Angie would be here to pack up Caro's things.

A few minutes later she sat upright, the thought that had been niggling at her finally breaking to the surface.

Anna. Anna going through her mother's carved wooden jewelry box, taking the emerald necklace and gold locket and the pearls her dad had given her mother on their fifteenth wedding anniversary. There had been a key in that box, too—a key to Caro's house. Her mother had been the caretaker back then, checking on the house when Caro and Roger traveled.

Sarah mentally added Anna's name to the list of people who had access to a key: Sarah, Scott, Laura, Anna. She liked the addition, but would Anna have known Caro was gone? Maybe. Sarah had told Nan. In fact, Nan had suggested Sarah might take advantage of Caro's absence to try to reconnect with her dad and Anna.

Logic forced its way through Sarah's self-satisfaction. Much as she relished the idea of Anna as a suspect in Caro's death, there was no motive. Nor could Sarah find a single reason for Anna to use the key, even if she knew it unlocked Caro's house and Caro was gone.

Angie arrived while Sarah was eating breakfast. Sarah took her upstairs and pointed out the things she wanted packed. When she went back to her cereal, she took one soggy bite, dumped it down the garbage disposal, poured a cup of coffee and headed back upstairs.

Angie stood beside a small desk, holding a sheaf of papers. “I didn’t think you’d want me to pack these, too. I mean, before you look at them. Are you just storing everything?”

“I’m donating it. And you’re right. I don’t want any paperwork mixed in. Good catch.” Sarah held out her hand. “I’d better see if it’s anything I need to take care of.”

The papers were receipts for paint.

The desk was small, about the length of a yardstick, with only a landline phone and a green banker’s lamp on top. It had several drawers she hadn’t searched because they were too small to hold the sketches. Now would be a good time to go through them, while she supervised the packing.

It didn’t take long to determine that this desk was devoted to social functions. It held old seating charts; photographs of table arrangements and floral centerpieces; advertisements for caterers, party supply rentals, bands and musicians, photographers, florists, bartenders and alcohol suppliers. There were no lists indicating which, if any of those services, Caro had used, and there were no guest lists.

“Angie, do you know if my aunt kept guest lists in here?”

“Oh, yes. There should be a blue folder in there for her bon voyage party.”

Sarah found no blue folder. It was probably in a box at the police department, gathering dust. She would have to try to reconstruct the list. But maybe there was an easier way.

The neighborhood snoop would be the best source for the kind of details Sarah needed, so she called Emily Rafferty. Neither she nor Herb were home, so she called Marge, and got the names of eighteen people.

“There were more than that,” Marge said, “but I can’t remember all their names right now. Call Emily Rafferty and some of the others. They’ll probably be able to fill in the rest.”

"There's one couple I'm especially interested in. I saw them in the garden that night. In fact, I think I saw two couples. One in the arbor and another close to the bistro set. But I'm most interested in the one at the bistro set. They were arguing and left early. I didn't see them at the memorial service, and I thought you might know who they are."

Sarah closed her eyes, creating a blackboard for the images. It had been dark, with just a sliver of moon. A soft glow had spilled from the patio and the windows, lightening the areas closest to the house. "The woman had pale hair. Blonde, I think, and long. She was wearing a full-length, light-colored dress—or maybe matching pants and top."

Marge laughed. "Oh, I forgot about them. Janice and Seth Carver. They were arguing before they went out there. In fact, I think that's why he steered her outside. They didn't come back. She seemed to think Seth was flirting too much. Or maybe somebody was flirting with him. I can't remember."

"Did Caro know them well?"

"Oh, yes. But Jan is something of a drama queen, especially when she drinks too much, which she does all too often. She's a little insecure, I guess. Always thinks somebody is hitting on Seth. He's a good-looking man, but I've never heard a peep about him fooling around."

"Do you know who catered that party?"

"No, I don't, but Nellie and Tony did a lot of the work."

Sarah couldn't think of anything else to ask, so she thanked Marge and hung up, only then aware that Angie stood motionless, her arms full of folded clothing.

"It was me in the garden." She blushed. "Me and my boyfriend. In the arbor."

She explained that Caro had asked her to stay that night to help with the party and to clean up the next day. "I knew what kind of wine to bring up when it got low, and where to find stuff, so she liked to have me here." She put the folded clothing in a box.

"And your boyfriend came to see you while you were working?"

"I wasn't working. Not full-time until the next day, when I cleaned up. It was part-time that evening, helping out a little." She pulled several semi-formal dresses from their hangers and carried them to the bed, keeping her face averted as she spoke. "Manny just wanted to see me. My dad doesn't like him, doesn't let him come around. So it seemed like the perfect chance to get together. He wasn't even supposed to be working that night. He had to trade shifts with Roberto."

"So he was supposed to be working when he was out in the arbor with you?"

"Well, yes. But we weren't out there that long." She picked up a navy chiffon dress and folded it, not looking at Sarah.

"Seems like a lot of trouble to go to, for just a few minutes in the arbor."

"We weren't...we just needed to figure out when we could really get together. Like, you know, after the party." Sarah tried to see the girl's face, screened by a fall of dark hair.

"In your room?" Sarah asked.

Angie lifted her head. "No. We didn't want Caro to find out." A dreamy look crossed her face. "Manny is romantic. He found a place we could go, where nobody would bother us."

Sarah had no doubt he did. "How did Caro feel about all that? A boy your parents didn't approve of coming here? Taking you some place to—"

Angie ducked her head again. "She didn't know. I didn't tell her. And it wasn't like that. Manny loves me."

Right. Sarah let out a long sigh. That solved the mystery of the couples in the garden. Another dead end. Just a couple having an argument, helped along with a little too much booze, and two kids sneaking around. "Did you ever tell Manny about the hidden key or show it to him?"

"No. I don't think so."

Sarah rose from the desk. When she turned, she glimpsed a section of Caro's closet, emptied now of clothing, and in the wall, her safe. She'd forgotten about it. It was too small to contain the sketches. Caro had always kept some cash there, along with a few documents and her more expensive jewelry, mostly pieces Roger had bought for her. She hadn't been in the habit of locking it, but she might have, before leaving the country.

She couldn't open it now. It would have to wait until after Angie was gone.

Sarah grabbed one of the boxes. "I'm going back downstairs. Let me know when you've finished, and I'll help you carry the boxes down."

"Are you getting the house ready to sell?" Angie looked around Caro's room. "I mean, I wouldn't want to live in a big place like this all by myself. Especially after..." She glanced toward the patio.

"No. I've just got to take care of a few things here, then I'm heading home. I've got a husband and a job I need to get back to."

She set the box in the foyer just as Scott called. While she walked to the kitchen, opened the refrigerator door and pulled out a bottle of cold water, she told him about her progress–or rather, lack of it. "The only lead I have left is the guy who broke into the house. I'm thinking about taking Laura's sketch of him around the neighborhood, to see if anybody recognizes him."

"You can't do that, Sarah. If he found out...he knows where you live. He chased you once. The cops should be doing all that, anyway, not you." She didn't say anything, so he continued. "Yeah, I know. Matt Coleman's not going to do it. How much longer before Al Durant is back on the job?"

"I wish I knew. I hope it's soon because I don't know what I'm doing."

"You're cleaning out Caro's room now?"

"Yeah, I hope to be through by tonight or early tomorrow."

She said goodbye to Scott, turned to go back into the living room and almost bumped into Angie.

"Whoa! Where are you going in such a hurry?"

"I ..." The girl's gaze shifted to Sara's water bottle. "I needed a drink."

Sarah didn't think so. Angie's steps had been aligned with the back door or basement, not the refrigerator. Caro had mentioned that she often found Angie here when she was supposed to be working in other parts of the house. Had she arranged a rendezvous with Manny? She watched as the girl got a bottle of water and went back up the stairs, then opened the door and surveyed the yard. She couldn't see anything.

She checked both the lock and the deadbolt, then opened the bottle of water and settled down at the desk. The pad of paper she pulled toward her had a telephone number scribbled on it. Valerie Weston. She'd never called the woman. Sarah picked up her phone.

"I'm sorry we didn't get to finish our conversation Thursday," she said after she identified herself. "You were telling me you saw Caro in Germany?"

"Oh, yes. We hit it off right away. Jack–that's my husband–and Caro and me. From the first minute of the tour we took together, after we found out we were all from the Sacramento area."

Sarah didn't think she'd need to take notes, but she pulled out a pen, just in case. "Did she, by any chance, tell you why she decided to come home early?"

"Oh, no, dear, she didn't. We met for dinner that night, and she kept going on and on about Paris and the *Water Lilies*, and we were having so much fun, Jack and I thought about going with her. We were even talking about extending our trips a little–the three of us, and going on to Monte Carlo. None of us had ever been there. But Jack got a call from his company later that night–some big problem, and that changed everything. We had to come home."

Sarah sat up straighter. "Caro came home early, too, instead of going on to Paris."

Valerie laughed, a soft, warm chuckle. "I know, dear. We flew back with her. That morning, when we all met for breakfast, and Jack said we had to go home, Caro said she thought she'd better go, too. I was surprised because she'd never said anything before that. It seemed—well, to be honest, it seemed a little strange."

"And she didn't say why." Sarah doodled on the pad. "That is a little odd."

"Yes, but we talked about getting together later for the trip to Paris and Monte Carlo. It wasn't an easy trip home, especially out of Chicago. But it worked out okay. We shared a cab to the airport, and had lots of time to visit, with the flight delays and all, and on our way home from the airport."

"You shared a cab again in Sacramento?" Sarah stopped doodling. Maybe Valerie or Jack had seen something—or somebody—when the cab dropped Caro off.

"Oh, no cab that time, dear. We were in long-term parking. So Jack took the shuttle out to pick up the car while Caro and I got the luggage, and we dropped her off on our way to El Dorado Hills."

Sarah's chest felt tight, and she took a long breath. "What kind of car do you drive?"

"What kind? Oh, it's a Honda. Jack always buys Hondas. It's an Accord, so we had plenty of room for our luggage."

"What color?"

There was a short silence on the other end. She could hear the question in Valerie's voice when she said, "It's blue, dear. Why do you ask?"

Chapter 29

Sarah wanted to call Matt Coleman, to let him know he'd just lost one piece of his evidence against Laura—the blue Honda. But she hesitated. The man was so intent on convicting her cousin, she didn't trust him. She would tell Sam. He could pass it along to Laura's attorney, who would know how to use it to Laura's advantage.

Angie came down the stairs holding a cardboard box, canted a little to the side so she could see the steps. "All that's left is the costume jewelry and cosmetics and some paperwork. You didn't want me to pack the stuff in the bathroom, did you? Or the lamps and clock?"

"No, you got everything." Sarah rose and led the way up the stairs, hoping there weren't too many cartons to carry down.

When they finished, Sarah collapsed into a chair in the living room. "Let's take a break before we haul these boxes out to the car. Then I'll write you a check, so you can get out of here and hit your books. Or maybe you're seeing the boyfriend?"

"No. Manny has to work. We're planning to get together later this week." The girl blushed, and Sarah wondered if she should talk to the parents. Maybe later. Right now, she had too many other things to worry about.

"I may not go back to school next year, anyway," the girl continued. "Manny says I won't need it after we get married. He'll take care of me."

"Angie, it's none of my business, but you should finish school. Your senior year will be a lot of fun. And what if things don't work out between you and Manny? You'll need some way to support yourself. What kind of job can you get with no high school diploma?"

"You don't understand. He loves me, and he doesn't like those guys at school hitting on me all the time."

Manny was clearly manipulating the girl, but she was too young and naïve to see it.

Angie nodded toward the stack of cardboard boxes in the foyer. "I'll get some of those loaded up." Her voice was stiff. Further discussion would be useless, maybe even alienate her more.

Sarah rose and grabbed a carton. "Thanks for coming on short notice, Angie. I appreciate your help."

Angie nodded and strode to the car, carrying a box.

So much for chit-chat. Sarah had better just shut up, at least for now.

When they finished loading the vehicle, Sarah wrote a check and told the girl goodbye. Angie had spoken only when necessary, and then in monosyllables.

Sarah was going to have to call Angie's parents, but not until she had a chance to think about what to say. She didn't want to make matters worse. The problem was, she had too much to think about, and Laura had to come first.

Sarah's only remaining lead was the man who had broken into the house. He had some connection to Caro's death, or at least to the missing sketches. Otherwise, he wouldn't have chased Sarah. Despite that, Detective Coleman showed no interest in Laura's sketch of the intruder.

Once Dee and Dave had searched and found no matches for the sketches in their databases, Sarah didn't think they had pursued it any further, either. She got the impression they were humoring her when she mentioned a burglary in connection with Caro's death.

Sam had asked Dee to help Laura, but Sarah could see no evidence Dee was doing anything, other than occasional babysitting. Laura was in jail for a crime she didn't commit, and nobody, other than Sam and Sarah, cared.

She had to do something, but no matter how often that thought had crossed her mind, she shied away from the only thing she could think of–finding the man on her own. He scared her. He'd broken into the house, chased her in his SUV, and tried to kill her. At least, he'd done a pretty good job of convincing her that was his intention. She didn't want anything else to do with the man; never wanted to see him again.

But what about Laura? Wasn't she worth some risk?

Scott was being overly protective. She could limit the danger by being selective about who saw the sketch. She would start with the busybodies, Emily and Herb Rafferty.

She printed some copies so she could give them to the neighbors, put them on the passenger seat of the Explorer, and set off for the thrift shop.

As she drove, she tried, without success, to think of something more she could do. Maybe go home. She missed Scott. That surprised her a little. It had been a long time since she'd missed him, wanted to be with him. They'd had a wonderful day together in San Francisco. She smiled at the memory of his gentle goodbye kiss that morning.

She unloaded the boxes at the thrift shop and, before she left the parking lot, called him. He sounded pleasantly surprised. No wonder. How long had it been since she called him just to hear his voice?

"I'm working with a customer right now," he said. "But I have a couple of minutes. Is everything okay?"

"Yeah. I'm just leaving the thrift shop, and I was thinking about you."

He was quiet for a moment, and when he spoke, his voice was husky. "I've been thinking about you, too. A lot. I love you, and I'll be glad when all this is behind us, and you can come home to stay."

"Me, too." Even as she uttered the words, Sarah felt her tiredness, both physical and mental, and the hopelessness of her task. "Maybe I can wrap everything up by tomorrow."

"That would be great. It gets a little boring, just working and going to AA meetings–not like having you to come home to."

She should be there, supporting him. "I had a wonderful time yesterday, Scott. Thanks for thinking of it. We need to do things like that more often."

"Sounds good."

"Let's plan on it. But right now, you have a customer waiting, and I'd better get back if I want to beat the traffic. Call me tonight, after your meeting."

"I will. Stay safe. I love you."

She drove back to the supermarket and bought some groceries for dinner and breakfast the next morning, and possibly lunch. Anything she didn't eat, she would take home to Roseville. She doubted there was much in the kitchen there.

When Sarah came out of the store, Maudie was standing by the Explorer, peering in the window. Sarah was glad she'd already dropped off Caro's things at the thrift shop. They would have been of no use to Maudie, but the woman's eyes would have lit up at the sight of them, and flattened with disappointment when Sarah explained what the boxes held.

"I've got eggs I need to get rid of," Sarah said, opening the car door. Maudie stared at the sketch on the passenger seat. She looked around the lot, then back at Sarah. "What you doing with that stuff, girl? You looking for trouble?"

"Do you know him, Maudie?"

The woman backed away. "I know he's nothing but bad news. Real bad. You don't want to get mixed up with the likes of him, Sary."

"I have to. The police have arrested my cousin for killing my aunt, but I think he did it." She nodded at the sketch. "He broke into my aunt's house and chased me in his car. Finding him is the only way I can clear my cousin, prove she didn't do it."

Maudie's hands trembled on the handle of the shopping cart. "The only way, Sary? That's the only way, girl?" She looked around the lot, furtive now. "Give me some of the eggs. Do it slow."

Sarah opened the egg carton, removed two eggs and handed them to Maudie.

"He's a bad one," Maudie said, her voice low. She settled the eggs into separate coat pockets. "He just showed up around here one day a few weeks ago. Runs with some no-accounts. They rip off houses and whatever else they can get their hands on." She nodded at the sketch. "You best take that to the cops and let them handle it."

Sarah closed the egg carton and reached for a box of crackers. "You don't know his name? The cops aren't doing anything, so I thought I'd just show his picture to a few people, see if they know him." She opened the crackers and handed a packet to Maudie.

Maudie slipped it into one of her pockets. "Don't mess with this stuff, Sary. Go home. Make things right with your man."

Sarah put the cracker carton back into the Explorer, on top of the sketch, and crossed her arms against her waist to ward off a sudden chill. "I can't. I have to find him."

Maudie blinked and used one hand to shade her eyes from the sun. "Can you wait a few days? There ain't no big rush, is there? Courts is slow. Maybe old Maudie can find out something. Me and some of the boys."

"I can't let you do that. Put yourself in danger."

The woman cackled. "He won't even see us, girl. Who pays any mind to homeless folk? Danny even got his rig running. It ain't much, but it'll get us 'round. Give us a few days. If we don't have nothing by the weekend, you can try it on your own."

"Are you sure you'll be safe?"

Maudie snorted. "Been taking care of old Maudie long afore you come along, missy. You git, now. Don't worry yourself 'bout us."

Sarah pulled three twenty-dollar bills from her wallet and held them out to Maudie. The woman batted her hand away. "I told you, I don't need your charity, missy."

"No. No, Maudie. Not charity. For gas. You'll need gas for Danny's car, if you're going to look for this guy." Sarah gestured toward the sketch.

Maudie nodded and took the bills. "Expense money, then." The bills followed the eggs and crackers into the folds of the jacket.

How deep were those pockets? And how many did she have in that coat?

Sarah stood for a moment, watching Maudie push her cart down the street. The woman's words had scared her, and she intended to follow her advice. She'd see what Maudie and Danny could find out before she did anything else.

Anxious to explore the contents of Caro's safe, she went back to the house and climbed the stairs to Caro's room. The locking mechanism was a wheel with four columns of numbers. Four digits. She tried Roger's birthday, first, the month and day, then the month and year. No luck. She tried their anniversary and finally got it by reversing the year and month.

Besides the documents and an envelope containing almost a thousand dollars, Sarah found seven large jewelry rolls, some in black velvet, others in silk jacquard. She carried them to the bed, untied and unrolled them. She was familiar with most of the pieces. Lifting one of Caro's favorites, a tourmaline necklace Roger had given her on their first anniversary, triggered a memory of Anna.

Her stepmother had stood before a mirror, admiring a necklace she'd fastened around her neck, this one of topaz, one of the pieces that had belonged to Sarah's mother.

Sarah tried to think about something else. Bad enough to be haunted by an image of Anna on the night Sarah's mother died. She didn't need this memory, too, seared into her subconscious, ready to surface at will.

The image persisted. Was Anna's greediness a motive for murder? How could it be, when Anna wouldn't inherit?

She put the jewelry back in the safe and locked it. She would show it to Laura later, and let her choose the pieces she wanted.

Restless, she roamed the house, trying to think of something more she could do. Maybe call Angie's parents? She didn't know them, didn't know how they'd react to a call from a stranger, but somebody had to intervene before Angie quit school.

Once Sarah made up her mind to call, she found she had only Angie's cell phone number, and couldn't remember the girl's last name. She went back to her copy of the check. Jones. Just her luck. And she didn't know either of the parents' first names.

She tried the white pages on her computer for addresses in the area but found so many, it would be daunting to try to call all of them. She printed the pages, then found herself researching "manipulative men," hoping to find out more about Angie's relationship with Manny.

Her search engine turned up hundreds of articles, most of them with links to other websites or blogs. Finally, blurry-eyed and tired, she printed several of the most interesting ones and shut down the computer. It was time for a glass of wine and a warm bubble bath. She would read the articles in the tub, then get a good night's sleep. Her head might be clearer by morning.

Her phone rang, and she glanced at the display. The number looked familiar, but it took a few seconds for her to recognize it as her father's. She might not have answered it at any other time, but tonight she needed to hear a familiar voice. "Dad?"

"No. It's Anna. Your dad's not here right now. We're going to be in town tomorrow, and I was wondering if we might drop by? He misses you, Sarah. He's been miserable ever since he tried to talk to you at Caro's memorial service and you pushed him away."

"Tell Dad to call if he wants to talk to me, and I'll listen, but I have nothing to say to you, and I don't want you in my house."

"Sarah, I'm sorry you feel so bitter toward me. We got off to a bad start years ago, and I'd like for us to try to get on better terms, for your father's sake, and your grandmother's. She's getting on in years, you know."

Sarah pulled the phone away from her ear and stared at it. Was she joking? The money was all she was interested in. Anna's one talent was in figuring out how to get her hands on things that belonged to somebody else.

When Sarah put the phone back to her ear, Anna was still talking.

"After all, with your aunt dead and your cousin in jail, you don't have much family left." Anna took a deep breath, hesitated, and asked, "How strong is the evidence against her? Do you think she's going to be convicted?"

Sarah hung up on her. What was that all about? What did Anna have to do with Laura? But Anna was right about one thing. Sarah didn't have much family left, and she'd never felt more alone. Grasping the handrail with one hand and her glass of wine with the other, she trudged up the stairs.

When her phone rang again, she hesitated, sure it was Scott. The articles she'd been reading had planted a seed of doubt, made her question Scott's motives, his sudden metamorphosis. Was Laura right? Was he manipulating her? She shook her head. Caro's death was making her paranoid, suspicious of even those she loved.

The call was from Emily Rafferty. "Sarah? Is everything all right?"

Confused by the question, wondering if something had happened outside the house, Sarah said, "Yes, I'm fine. Why do you ask?"

"You sounded—I don't know—a little down." Emily took a deep breath. "I'm sorry. Of course, you are with everything that's happened, and now with this thing about Laura. I...well anyway, you left a message for me to call you."

"Oh." It took a second or two for Sarah to remember. She had called about the guest list for Caro's bon voyage party. It no longer mattered.

"It was kind of you to call back," she told Emily. "I was trying to find a couple who attended Caro's bon voyage party, but I already got the information from Marge. Janice and Seth Carver. Thank–"

"Oh, yes, Jan and Seth. They had a big fight that night and left early. But that isn't unusual for them. I don't know why they stay together. How are you holding up, dear? You've had so much to deal with. We were so shocked when Laura was arrested. It's just so hard for us to believe, and I know it's got to be much worse for you. We're a pretty close-knit group around here, and everybody liked Caro. So we're here for you if you need anything."

The woman was trolling for information to spread around the neighborhood. "Thank you, Emily," Sarah said, trying to end the conversation.

"I just wanted you to know, it was so good to see you with those sweet little boys of Laura's the other day, and with your good-looking husband. I was glad the two of you got away from everything for a day. I know he's a busy man and doesn't have a lot of free time, but I do wish he'd dropped by to say hello. Herb would have enjoyed visiting with him. We haven't seen much of him this last week or two."

Last week or two? Scott hadn't been at the house for months. Not until the day Caro was killed. "You must be mistaken. Scott hasn't been here—"

"Oh, I know. Not lately. Even when he was coming down to check on the house, he wasn't here that often. Although I've got to say, he did a good job. He stayed long enough to check everything out."

Why was Scott visiting the house during Caro's absence, especially without Sarah's knowledge? How did he get inside? What was he doing when he stayed so long "checking things out"?

Unlike Sarah. She just checked the doors and windows and went inside long enough to see if there were any strange smells or leaking water.

Sarah could think of only one answer. She fought to keep her voice composed, even as something inside her shattered. She sucked in her breath. "I have to go. Something's burning." She threw the phone on the bed and stared at it, as though she expected it to reach out and grab her.

Chapter 30

Sarah sat, holding herself together with arms wrapped tightly across her waist. She kept turning the facts over in her mind, trying to make sense of them. What reason could Scott possibly have for being in the house, other than the obvious one—getting access to Caro's computer and passwords? She couldn't believe he would do that. Following close behind that thought was another: He always needed money. Why?

Yet, when he called a little later, seemingly light-hearted and playful, telling her about the AA meeting, she didn't ask him to explain. She wasn't sure why, other than a sense of foreboding.

"You sound tired, honey," he said. "Did I keep you up too late last night?"

She spoke through dry lips. "I'm not feeling very well. I think I'll go to bed early."

"Are you sick? Do you need me to come down? I couldn't stay, but...maybe you should come home. There's not much more you can do there."

"No, I'm not sick. I'll be all right after a good night's sleep."

"Okay, but I worry about you. You've been under a lot of stress. Go to bed, and I'll check in on you tomorrow. I love you."

The words caught in her throat. She couldn't say them, so she faked a yawn instead. "Okay, I'm off to bed now."

Going home was not an option now. Not until she found out what was going on.

She went back to her computer, but couldn't get into her trust account. Access required two passwords, one assigned by the bank and one she had chosen. It had been so long since she had used them, she could remember only that the bank's was comprised of eight numbers. She knew where to find them: in the address book in her desk drawer, disguised as parts of the telephone number and address of a non-existent friend. She would have to go home to research the account.

She went to bed but couldn't sleep and, during that long and restless night, she formulated a plan. Scott would be at work all day, giving her plenty of time. Once she had her passwords, it wouldn't take long to go through all her trust account transactions. The financial records would take longer because she didn't know exactly what she was looking for, and was unfamiliar with them. Scott handled all their finances.

Why had she trusted him to do that? He'd never exhibited any skill in handling money. Still, she had let him do it, because it was easier than fighting about it. Scott needed to be in control of everything, including her, something she hadn't known when she married him. He saw her as another of his possessions—a loved and treasured one, but still a possession.

Laura was right. He had manipulated Sarah, the same way Manny manipulated Angie.

Too agitated to sleep, Sarah went back to the web sites she'd visited earlier. This time, though, it wasn't a generic study of manipulative men; it was specific to her relationship with Scott. Some of the passages described it so well, she might have written them herself. She never saw this, never felt it happening. Maybe she hadn't wanted to. Scott had been so charming, so caring and attentive when they dated. After they married, those qualities had gradually turned into possessiveness and jealousy, and finally into a need for control. She had let it happen, let herself get sucked in, because it was easier than dealing with his anger.

The last few days had been wonderful. He was more like the man she'd fallen in love with. Had it all been an act?

She felt more lost and alone than she ever had in her life. She cried herself to sleep, but woke a few hours later, her mind churning with unanswered questions. She got up again and paced the floor, finally coming to a decision. Only then did she fall into uninterrupted sleep.

When the alarm woke her the next morning, she lay in bed, not wanting to get up and face the day and what she might discover. But she had worked out the timing so she would arrive at the house a few minutes after Scott left. She needed to stay on schedule.

The drive against the early morning commute traffic went smoothly, and twenty-five minutes later she pulled to the curb a half-block away from the house. From there, she could see the Corolla in the driveway. Scott's route would take him the other direction, so it wasn't likely he'd look her way.

She hadn't counted on curious glances from homeowners. She knew most of them, at least well enough to say "hello." What logical reason could she possibly have for sitting there? Should she pretend a car problem? No, they'd offer to help, drawing attention. She willed Scott to hurry up, to get going.

Finally, the front door was opening. Scott got into the Corolla, backed out of the driveway, looked her way to check for traffic, and turned the other direction. Just in case he came back for some forgotten item, she waited five minutes before driving to the house. It would help if she could hide the Explorer in the garage, but there wasn't room.

The house was still, with unwashed dishes piled in the sink, a coffee cup on the counter, and an unmade, rumpled bed. Maybe his night had been as restless as hers.

She got the address book, found her passwords, and went to work.

It took several hours, but she finally pieced it all together. He had started with transfers from her trust fund into their checking account. From there, he'd written checks for hundreds—sometimes thousands—of dollars, most of them to somebody named Don Randolph.

Sarah sat back, marveling that Caro had never mentioned how regularly she replenished Sarah's trust fund. Had the deposits been automatic when the trust fund dipped below five thousand dollars? Had Caro not been aware until somebody brought it to her attention? Did that explain the message from Chicago and her unexpected trip home?

What did Scott spend the money on? They were always broke, trying to make each paycheck stretch to the next. Surely he couldn't run up drink tabs that high. He had said something recently–about

Caro having once accused him of gambling away their money. She looked up the number for the casino.

"Is Don Randolph there?"

"Is he somebody you're trying to locate on the casino floor? A visitor?" a pleasant young voice chirped.

"No. I thought—he's not an employee?"

"Not here. Are you sure you have the right number?"

"Maybe not." Sarah ended the call. Who was Don Randolph, and why would Scott be writing checks to him?

She would try to find out more about him when she got back to Caro's house. Right now, she had more pressing things to do. She went back to the computer.

Without their passwords, she couldn't access Caro's or Laura's accounts, but she found the first transfer from her own account to Laura's, made six months ago. Had Caro been away then? Yes, to Sedona. She'd wanted to go in the fall, when it wasn't so hot, and had returned just before Thanksgiving.

Sam said the money went to the offshore account from Laura's. Why had Scott changed the pattern, no longer simply drawing funds from Sarah's account? Because it had gone on too long, and he was afraid Caro would start asking questions. He had to cover his tracks, and rather than cast suspicion on Sarah by transferring the money directly from her account to the one offshore, he had used Laura. She, like Sarah, rarely looked at her account, and the funds wouldn't have been there for long.

According to Sam, the owner of the offshore account was untraceable because it was set up through a dummy corporation, with an attorney as trustee. The attorney could then claim client confidentiality to avoid revealing the name on the account.

Sarah dug through some more paperwork before she called Sam. "The offshore account—do you have the name of the corporation, or the name of the lawyer?"

"I've got a folder here, somewhere. Hold on a minute." There was a slight thump as he set the phone down, and a rustle of papers. "Abacus Jade Financial Services."

"Abacus Jade?" She closed her eyes for a long moment. Well, she'd always heard it was the thought that counted. "Do you have the lawyer's name?"

"The registered agent on the account? That's one Daniel Buchanan, Esquire."

Sarah stared at the piece of paper in her hand: a statement for a five thousand dollar retainer for legal fees, marked "paid." It was on the letterhead of Daniel Buchanan, Esq., and addressed to Scott Wagner.

She thanked Sam, ended the call, and sat, motionless. There had to be some other explanation. Yet, no matter how she shifted the facts, tried to find a different answer, they all led to one inescapable conclusion. Scott had taken the money, not Laura.

Without warning, bile rose in Sarah's throat. Barely making it to the bathroom, she vomited until there was nothing left in her stomach. Still, her body heaved, trying to rid itself of the fear and revulsion that had settled deep inside her. When it finally stopped, she rose, weak and shaky, and splashed cold water onto her face and neck. Her reflection in the mirror looked pale and drawn.

She made a copy of the statement from Daniel Buchanan and the computer print-outs. She folded the originals and put them in her purse. Arranging the others in chronological order on the dining room table, she tried one last time to find a different conclusion. There was none.

She slid her wedding and engagement rings off her finger and set them alongside the documents. It was too bad she didn't have the jade and gold abacus. It would add a nice finishing touch—a little melodramatic, but nice, and there would never be a better time for a little melodrama.

She looked around the house she had so lovingly decorated and furnished, at the cherished items they'd bought together or received as gifts. She'd have to leave it all. But she was tired of him dumping the Explorer on her. She wanted her Corolla.

If she switched cars, it would have to be at the dealership. Once he left there, she couldn't be sure where he'd go: home, an AA meeting, or somewhere else. Possibly a bar. He'd lied to her about everything else.

It would be easier to make the switch at the car lot, anyway. Scott parked at the curb, on the street at the back. He would be working on the other side, in the area at the front of the building. Once she found a parking slot for the Explorer, which shouldn't be difficult on that particular street, she could transfer a few things to the Corolla and leave before Scott even noticed the switch.

Selecting a few of her favorite outfits took only minutes. A big suitcase would be too cumbersome to handle in the quick transfer to her Corolla, and her overnight case was at Caro's house, so she opted for a kitchen trash bag instead. It would hold the clothing and her jewelry box.

She fastened the top, grabbed her purse, took a last look around, and headed for the door just as the Corolla pulled into the driveway.

She froze, her heart pounding. Why was he home so early?

It didn't matter. She had to get moving.

Could she get out the back, through the dining room, before he got inside? Only if she abandoned the bag. She dropped it, ran for the door, got through it, and eased it shut. The Corolla was in the driveway, parked behind the Explorer.

He would be looking for her. She had to wait until he was in the bedroom, then run for it.

She eased forward far enough to peer through the kitchen window, then jerked back. He was there, his back to her, bent over her display on the kitchen table. She pulled her keychain from her purse, positioned the one for the Corolla between her thumb and index finger, and ran.

She yanked the door of the Corolla open about the same time he burst out of the house. She hit the lock button, but her hands were trembling, and it took two tries to get the key in the ignition.

The door locks clicked. She looked up, her heart pounding, as Scott opened the passenger door. He slid into the seat beside her, still holding his key to the Corolla. He pulled her key out of the ignition.

She opened the door. He grabbed her arm.

"Scott, let go. You're hurting me."

He released her. "Go ahead, then, get out. But when you do, you're going back in the house. I have all the car keys, and there's no way you can outrun me—not this time."

She looked across the nearby lawns and out into the street. The neighborhood was quiet, most of the homeowners still at work. A few children played in their yards, some of them supervised by their mothers. She would be safer here, in the car, than in the house where nobody could see them.

"I'm not going back inside with you. Whatever you're planning to do, it will have to be right here."

"What do you mean, whatever I'm planning to do? I just want to talk to you, to explain." His face was pale, enhancing the intensity of his eyes. "You have to listen to me. This is not what you—"

"—think it is. Isn't that what every husband says when he's caught in a compromising situation?"

Where did that come from? Why was she spouting stupid gibberish? Because she didn't have a rule book for the situation and her brain didn't know how to process it.

He stared at her, pain reflected in his eyes. "I'm trying to explain, to make you understand."

"Oh, I understand. It's perfectly clear. I'm married to somebody I don't even know. Our entire marriage has been a lie." Why was she so calm, her thoughts so clear? "You gambled and drank away my money, Caro's money, and when you thought you were going to get caught, you set Laura up to take the blame. When Caro found out, when she came home, you...you..."

Calm though she was, she couldn't utter the words to finish the sentence. She took a deep breath and tried again. "You knew she was on her way home. You listened to my message, the one she left on my phone."

"I didn't even see Caro. Sarah, you have to believe me. I didn't know she'd left a message. I didn't know she was coming home." He put a hand on her shoulder, and she shrugged it away, cringing at his touch.

"I don't believe you. Everything you've told me has been a lie."

He put his face in his hands, the car keys dangling between his fingers. "Okay, you're right," he said. "I screwed up big time. I got in over my head at the casino. I had to borrow money from some loan sharks, and they were putting a lot of pressure on me to pay up."

"Don Randolph."

"He's the one I dealt with, but I think they're a big outfit with a lot of resources because they found out all about me. He told me I had to come up with the money or—"

"So you decided to raid my account."

"No." He raised his head and looked at her with liquid eyes. "I... well, not then. I borrowed some from the dealership. But then Dad found out."

"So that's why you were having trouble at work. No wonder your father was riding you so hard. You stole from him, too." Disgust flooded through her when she thought about their conversation the night they'd driven out to the casino for the Explorer, the way he'd whined about his unreasonable, micro-managing father.

"I didn't steal it. I was going to pay it back."

"With what? The money from my account?"

"I was just going to borrow it. You're my wife, so technically, I wasn't doing anything wrong, and I figured I could win enough to replace it."

"So you kept gambling and drinking, and you got in deeper, and you took some more money."

Tears leaked from his eyes and dribbled down his cheeks. Sarah wasn't moved.

"I had to. Randolph was threatening me. He said they had people who didn't mind hurting families, that they'd get to mine. I was afraid if I took more money, Caro was going to mention it to you. I couldn't chance that, so I had to do something different."

Sarah couldn't bear to look at him any longer. She turned her head and watched a little boy riding his bike down the street. She wanted Scott to shut up, so she didn't have to hear the sound of his voice.

"I had to copy your key," he said, "so I could get to her computer and passwords. But all the transfers took time, and Randolph was calling me every day, threatening me—and my family. When Caro was killed—Sarah, I think they did it."

Sarah's head whipped around, her eyes staring at him in disbelief and horror. "You think you know who killed Caro, and you didn't tell the police? You let Laura go to jail?"

He hung his head. "I'm not proud of what I've done, but I was trying to protect you. I was going to tell the cops once I'd paid the loan sharks back, so they wouldn't hurt you."

"Is that why you were prowling around Caro's house the day before the memorial service? Looking for things to steal?"

He flushed. "I had to do something. I couldn't let you look at your account."

"My account? Oh, that's right. You didn't want me to transfer money out of it for you. Now I know why. You're pathetic. It's everybody's fault but yours." She plucked her car keys from his hand. "You weren't forced to do anything. You brought all this on yourself. And I was so stupid, I didn't see."

"I was doing it for you—to keep you safe."

"And the gambling? That was to keep me safe?" Scott's story didn't make sense. Now that Sarah had a few minutes to think it through, the pieces didn't fit.

"How did the loan sharks even know about Caro? She's not related to you, so it doesn't make sense that they'd kill her over a debt you owed. If they had the resources to find out about her, they'd know you didn't like her, so there was no point." She paused, thinking. "How would they know she was coming home? They would know she was in Europe. In fact, Scott, they would know she was your cash cow. Why kill her?"

He frowned and raised a trembling hand to rub his jaw. "It doesn't make much sense when you put it like that," he admitted. "But I didn't kill Caro, I swear."

"And these last few days...it was because of the money, wasn't it? It was all an act. Scott, get out of my car. I'm leaving. If you insist on staying, I'm driving you straight to the police station, where you can tell them your sad story."

He slid out. "I can't do that. I'd go to jail for taking the money, and probably for killing Caro. I didn't hurt her, Sarah, and I would never harm you." His tone was pleading. "You know me better than that."

She shook her head. "I don't know you at all."

Sarah backed out of the driveway, turned, and headed for Douglas Boulevard. Frequent checks of her rear-view mirror told her he wasn't following her. There was no need; he knew where to find her.

She wasn't afraid of him anymore. She didn't doubt he loved her, at least as much as he was capable of loving anybody.

Her hands trembled, and she concentrated on keeping her foot steady on the accelerator. Just nerves, an aftermath of all the tension. She shouldn't be driving. At least, not until she calmed down, which shouldn't take more than about six months or a year. It wasn't every day that you proved your husband guilty of embezzlement and possibly murder.

Tears slid down her cheeks, and she mopped at them with the back of her hand. She concentrated on the road. All she had to do was get home.

It was the first time in years she'd thought of Caro's house as home. Once again, it was her refuge.

She would finish clearing out Caro's room, get that color wheel out and decide on colors, put in new carpeting, new drapes, make the room her own.

Then what? She couldn't live Caro's life.

Chapter 31

That evening, wrapped in a fleecy sofa throw, her feet curled under her, Sarah huddled on the sofa in Caro's living room, trying to will her mind to function. She needed somebody to talk to, but who? Caro was dead, Laura behind bars, and Scott out of her life. That effectively wiped out her family, at least the ones she cared about, and she couldn't share this with anybody else. Certainly not Sam or Dee or Dave.

She thought about calling her grandmother. No, it had been too long; she'd lost that once-close connection. Nan couldn't help; she would just be distressed. Her father? An image of Anna dispelled that idea. Anna's only interest was Caro's money. If Laura were convicted she would lose her part of the estate, leaving more for Sarah and potentially more for Anna, if she could worm her way back into Sarah's life.

Scott called, and she stared at the phone display, not even considering picking it up. Her hold on self-control was thin; she might lose it if she heard his voice again. He called a second time, and a third, before she turned the phone off, rose and paced the room, trying to decide what she should do.

She needed Laura. All her life, from infancy, Laura had been there, more like a sister than a cousin. Sarah couldn't imagine her life without Laura's unfailing love and support.

Despite the embezzlement, she couldn't believe Scott had killed Caro. Hidden beneath his need for control and quick flashes of irrational anger, Sarah had sometimes seen an inner sensitivity, a tenderness he didn't show to others. He wasn't capable of murder, but neither Matt Coleman nor Al Durant would share her conviction, once they saw the evidence she'd discovered. Scott's acts had been so despicable she felt nothing but revulsion, but she couldn't be the catalyst that sent him to death row for a murder she didn't believe he'd committed.

Her stomach rumbled, and she tried to remember the last time she ate. Not that it mattered; she felt like she'd lost everything she'd ingested that day. She started for the kitchen, but her stomach rebelled at the thought of food. She might as well go to bed. Maybe she could think better after she got some sleep.

Her body felt heavy, so weighed down she used the handrail to pull herself up the stairs, step by slow step. Once there, she fell onto Caro's bed and lay sleepless until early morning light crept through the edges of the drapes. She slept then and awoke feeling so drugged she at first thought she had a hangover or the remnants of a migraine. Memory hit her again, so hard she buried her head in the pillow, trying to sink back into the mindless void of sleep.

The hope had been there all along, she supposed, hidden in the recesses of her mind, that a new day would bring insight. Instead, she felt even more lost and confused, more alone. How do you condemn your husband to prison or death? Betray your marriage vows? For better or worse—and it didn't get any worse than this.

Her phone showed seven missed voicemails, six from Scott and one from Sam. She deleted the messages from Scott. She couldn't talk to Sam. Not yet.

Neither Scott nor Laura had killed Caro. Sarah had to find the burglar, and she had to do it soon, before the police unraveled the financial mess Scott had created.

She would have to wait a few more days, to give Maudie and Danny the time they needed. She would drive to the store every day. Twice a day. She would buy a sandwich for lunch and eat it there, then go back around dinnertime and drive around the area.

What would she do with the rest of her time? She couldn't just sit and wait. She had to find something to keep her busy.

She took a shower, put on clean clothes, and made a cup of hot tea and some dry toast, hoping it would settle her stomach.

Restless, she wandered back upstairs. If she planned to make Caro's house her home, she had to do something about the bedrooms—either buy a more comfortable bed for the spare room or refurbish Caro's so she could use it.

She went back to Caro's room. The vanilla scent, not quite as strong as before, floated toward her as she entered. She studied the large, airy space. The antique maple furniture fit well in the room. She would keep it and change the color of the walls and drapes, and maybe the carpet. What colors would coordinate best with the maple's soft, golden glow?

Caro used to have an elaborate color wheel, but Sarah hadn't seen it in her search. It might be boxed up in the basement. No, Caro would have used it recently, to choose the paint for her office. It would be in the cubbyhole under the stairs. Sarah went to find it.

Caro had neatly labeled almost everything: Xmas—Outside Lights, Xmas Tree, Xmas Interior, Florist Supplies, Decorating. Two boxes on the top of the stack had no labels. Sarah pulled them out so she could get to the one marked "Decorating." The flaps on one of them hadn't been tucked in because the contents poked above the edges of the box. She pulled it out of the cubbyhole, opened it and stared at the missing sketches, the painting Roger had bought, the family photographs. She opened the other box. More photographs, the clock, and several other small items Caro had especially treasured. Caro had obviously stored the boxes here when she packed up the contents of her office.

Why hadn't Laura found them when she searched? The boxes were scarcely noticeable among the others, except for their lack of labels. It would be easy to miss them, but not when they were searching so hard. They had divided the rooms, Laura doing the living room and hall while Sarah worked in the library and foyer. Sarah had seen Laura open the door to the cubbyhole, watched her stack boxes back inside.

Everything was there, had been all along. Nothing was missing.

There had been no theft, no burglar in the house when Caro came home. Had Laura known that? No, she couldn't have. Beyond that, Sarah couldn't think. Her mind was shutting down, its last defense against the unthinkable crashing down on her.

Maudie! The woman was endangering herself to find a man who had no connection to Caro's death.

Sarah scrambled to her feet, but even as she pulled her car keys from her pocket, she knew it would be futile to search for Maudie.

There was little chance the woman would be pushing her cart around the streets by the grocery store. She had said Danny had his car fixed. The two of them would likely be in it, looking for the man in the sketch. Sarah didn't even know what the car looked like. She could do nothing but hope and pray Maudie would be safe.

Sarah turned her attention back to the boxes. She could think of no logical reason why Laura hadn't told her they were there. Was she too close to Laura to think clearly? How would somebody else see this? Somebody like Matt Coleman?

Laura was his prime suspect in Caro's murder. If Laura could keep Sarah—and through her, Dave and Dee—believing the sketches were missing, it kept open the possibility that a burglar had killed Caro, deflecting suspicion away from Laura.

Dee and Dave were professionals. They had checked out the possibility, even helped Laura and Sarah unpack boxes, looking for the sketches. They had run Laura's drawing of the burglar through their databases. When they found nothing, they had discounted that theory. They'd done it gently, still humoring Sarah and Laura, and sympathizing with their loss, but they had stopped looking.

She had been critical of them because they were doing nothing about it. She owed both of them an apology. A silent one. She'd never tell them what she'd been thinking.

Should she call one of the homicide detectives and let them know what she'd discovered? No. It was pointless; it wouldn't mean anything to them. She couldn't think of a single person, other than Laura, who believed a burglar had taken the sketches. Now she couldn't even be sure Laura had believed it.

She had to let at least Dave and Dee know what she'd found. Her first inclination was to call Dave. He had always been interested in the sketches, and his voice would wrap her in a warm, comforting cocoon. For that reason, because she didn't need more complications in her life right now, when she was so vulnerable, she called Dee instead. "I found the sketches," she said. "They were here all the time."

Dee was silent for a few seconds. "I don't know what to say. I'm glad you have them, that you haven't lost them. But if a burglar didn't take them—"

"What about the man who wanted the portrait? Steve Richlin?"

Dee's voice was slow, hesitant. "We don't have anything to tie him to the scene, Sarah, other than the fact that he wanted the portrait."

"What about fingerprints, fibers, all that sort of thing?"

"Apparently, there's a lot to sift through. Your aunt liked to entertain; she had that big party right before she left. Then you have to add in the caterers and other help. To make matters worse, the girl who cleaned didn't do a very thorough job. Even if the technicians find traces of Steve Richlin, it won't mean anything; he was in the house several times while his fiancee was sitting for the portrait."

Sarah closed her eyes and took a deep breath. "But if there was no burglar, somebody else killed Caro, so it had to be him."

"He has an alibi, Sarah. He was at a bachelor party that night."

Sarah looked for a tissue, didn't find one, and blotted her tears with a napkin. She hadn't realized she was crying.

Dee's voice was soft. "Do you need me to come over?"

"I don't think I ever realized how much I depended on Laura for emotional support. Now she's the reason I need her, and I can't talk to her." Sarah's voice thickened, and she stifled a sob.

Dee was silent for a few seconds. "Sarah, you and Laura have an unusually close connection, and nobody can replace her. But if you need somebody to talk to, I'm here."

Sarah blew her nose on the napkin. "I'm all right, but I'm not sure what to do next, and I don't know how I'm going to tell Sam." Her voice broke on the last word.

"From your viewpoint, this looks bad for Laura," Dee said. "But it's not going to make any difference to Coleman. He never believed the burglar theory, anyway."

"I know. He thought the only attempted burglary was the guy who broke into the house, assuming it was vacant. I guess Coleman was right. But I can't understand why a petty thief would chase me."

"Sarah, if he was a crack head, there's no telling what he was thinking."

Sarah sniffled. "I was so sure a burglar had taken the sketches and murdered Caro. I thought, if we could just prove it to Coleman, it would change everything. Now, I don't know what to think." She hesitated, not wanting to tell Dee the rest. "Laura searched the cubbyhole where I found the sketches. I watched her. And she didn't tell me they were there."

"Maybe she didn't see them. You two had worked hard, searching for those sketches, moving furniture, unpacking boxes, and putting that room back together. You were both exhausted when Dave and I dropped by. She might have been so tired she simply overlooked them. Or she could have been distracted."

"Maybe." Sarah didn't really believe that. Despite the barriers she tried to throw up, doubts about Laura were already creeping around them, like a tidal wave about to overwhelm her.

Scott had taken the money, not Laura, so why would she kill Caro?

Scott was weak and dishonest, but she didn't think him capable of murder. No, he must have listened to Caro's message, known she was coming home to tell Sarah about the embezzlement, and gone to the house to talk to her. He would have been overconfident, depending on his ability to charm, manipulate and control.

Caro wouldn't have listened, would have been angry, and Scott–Sarah put her hands over her face. Scott had been drinking that night, so out of control Sarah had run from him, a little afraid of what he might do. Had he also frightened Caro? So much she ran blindly and plunged through the railing?

Dee was still on the phone. "Sarah? Are you still there? Don't let your discovery of the sketches convince you Laura is guilty. There's probably another explanation. Just be glad you have them back. I don't think Matt Coleman has enough evidence to convict Laura. She'll be out on bail soon and eventually be released and back with Eric and Jamie, where she belongs."

In that instant, with the thought of Eric and Jamie, Sarah knew what she had to do.

"Dee, I think you need to come over, after all. I have copies of some documents you'll want to see."

Chapter 32

Things happened quickly after she turned the documents over to Dee, at least for everybody except Sarah. She felt like she moved in slow motion, her legs treading molasses, her mind wrapped in cotton batting. While aware of events unfolding around her, she couldn't connect to them, couldn't get through the all-enveloping fog.

Al Durant, finally back on the case, had arrested Scott for Caro's murder. That surprised Sarah, who had expected her husband to bolt as soon as she discovered his complicity, possibly to the Bahamas, or wherever he had the offshore account. On reflection, she realized he had probably used the money to pay his gambling debts. There would be nothing left.

Laura was released from jail, and Sam brought her to visit. Her face looked thinner, and she had dark circles under her eyes.

"Sarah, I'm sorry." She sat beside Sarah and pulled her close. "Sam and Dee told me about everything you've done to help me. I should have known...I can't believe I accused you of protecting Scott. I was so angry with you, and I'm not even sure why."

Sarah knew why: jealousy, partly over Sarah getting the house, and partly over Dave Wheeler. She didn't say what she was thinking. She couldn't, with Sam standing behind the sofa, his hands gentle on Laura's shoulders.

"You two, are you—" She didn't know how to finish the question, but she got an answer through Sam's quick grin and Laura's blush.

"I started AA," Sam said. "It seemed like Scott ..." He hesitated, pressing his lips together, then went on. "It seemed like he was doing so well, I thought I'd give it a try."

"I realized how much Sam meant to me," Laura said, reaching a hand up to his cheek. "He's been like a rock through all this, taking care of the kids, finding a lawyer, scraping up the money. I don't know what I would have done without him."

I would be glad for them, if I could feel anything. I know I would.

"Sarah, if it helps any, I don't think Scott intended to kill Caro," Sam said. "I've been thinking about that message Caro left on your phone. Even though it looked like Laura was transferring the money, I don't think Caro was sure. For some reason, she was suspicious of Scott. So she flew home to find out and surprised him in her house, possibly using her computer. He would have panicked, maybe tried to talk her into being quiet."

"I know. I figured all that out, but Caro is just as dead, whether it was intentional or not." She clapped a hand over her mouth, her eyes wide. "Oh, my God! I could have been here. If I'd had my key, if I hadn't gone to the casino, if I'd remembered the key I thought was on the patio–" She looked at Laura. "Maybe I could have stopped it."

Laura hugged her. "Or you could be dead, too. Sarah, there's nothing you could have done. Let it go."

Easy for Laura to say. Her husband didn't kill Caro. But Laura was right; there was nothing she could do now, except regret that she'd married Scott, that she'd brought him into the family. Because she had, Caro had died.

The room was silent then, except for the living room clock, ticking the seconds away. Sam spoke again, probably trying to change the subject.

"Sarah, if you think you'll be okay, I'd like to get Laura away from here Saturday, just overnight, to Monterey. The boys have to be back in school Monday, and I've already taken too much time off work—"

Sarah glanced at her cousin. Laura needed some time with Sam, alone. "Why don't you leave Eric and Jamie with me? I'm not very busy these days."

Laura squeezed Sarah's hand. "We couldn't ask that of you, Sarah. You've been through too much these last few days."

"I think the boys might help take my mind off all that. That is, if you think I'm stable enough emotionally to take care of them."

"You know there's nobody I'd trust more," Laura whispered, brushing a lock of hair off Sarah's cheek. "But they can be a handful."

"I can help," Dee said. "I have to work part of the day on Saturday, but I can relieve Sarah after that."

"It's settled, then," Sarah said, smiling at Dee. "Now, tell us all about your plans."

Sam grinned. "They may change a little bit, if we don't have the boys. Maybe a drive up the Pacific Coast Highway, and a bed-and-breakfast instead of a motel. What do you think about the Seventeen Mile Drive, Laura?"

His expression, when he looked at Laura, was so tender, Sarah blinked back tears.

"Sounds wonderful. I'd just add dinner at one of the good seafood restaurants. What's the name of that one on the wharf, with all the sea lions?"

Sam turned to Sarah. "I can't thank you enough. Laura will be able to relax and enjoy herself so much better, knowing the boys are with you and Dee. We'll be back Sunday afternoon, if you're sure you're up to it."

"You two go and enjoy yourselves. Eric and Jamie and I are going to have fun together."

Maybe they will make me feel something again.

They did. It was impossible not to feel love when they ran into the house and hugged her that Saturday, and amusement when Jamie asked her to teach him to do "flip backs."

Sarah spent almost an hour teaching them to do backflips, and when Jamie finally did one, his wide grin made her smile.

"Now show me how to do it like you do, frontwards then backwards."

"Not until you get really good doing backflips. Then I'll show you how to work them together."

Another fifteen minutes, and Eric was tired of gymnastics. "Let's go play in the castle."

"Okay, but I need my dragon shirt." Jamie barreled past her, Eric close behind. Both of them ran upstairs to find the t-shirts Sarah had bought for them in San Francisco, in the same shop where Scott bought the abacus. She bit her lip, trying to will the memory away.

The boys came back downstairs, headed for the basement.

It was getting late; she should be thinking about dinner, but she didn't know what was in the kitchen, didn't even remember the last time she'd shopped. Yes, she did. It had been the day she bought eggs and bread, on her way home to Scott. Her eyes filled with tears of frustration. How could she ever get past all this if every memory led back to him?

The doorbell rang, and she went to answer it, brushing away tears. Dee and Dave stood on the doorstep.

"Look who I brought with me," Dee said. "We thought maybe you could use a break. After an afternoon with the boys, we decided pizza would be great for dinner. Then maybe a movie for the kids and a little wine for the adults?"

Dave smiled with the curve of his lips that always made Sarah feel too warm. "The booze was my idea. I opt for pizza and a movie for all of us, with milk for the boys, wine for the girls, and beer for me."

"Pizza?" Eric asked. "What kind?"

"My, what big ears you have," Dee said to the boy who had materialized at the top of the basement stairs, his little brother standing beside him. "Want to go with us and choose for yourself?"

"Yeah. Can we get ice cream, too?"

Dave nodded.

"Not me," Jamie said. "I gotta finish my hideout in the castle. And Auntie Sarah needs some company."

Sarah was still trying to swallow the sudden lump in her throat when Jamie turned to his brother. "I bet you won't be able to find me when you get back."

"I have to run by my office for a few minutes, too," Dave said, "so it may be a while."

"That's okay. Jamie and I will have fun together. Just bring lots of pizza. We'll be hungry by then."

"And ice cream," Jamie said. "Don't forget the ice cream."

After Dee and Dave left with Eric, and Jamie went back down to the basement, Sarah caught a glimpse of herself in the mirror as she passed the downstairs bathroom. Her hair was wild, after all those backflips, and Dave had seen her that way. She went upstairs to comb her hair and added a touch of color to her too-pale face.

She didn't have any popcorn. They had to have popcorn, if they were going to watch a movie. She called Dee and asked her to pick some up, finishing the call just as she reached the bottom of the stairs. She glanced at the time. She'd called a landscaping service to have the lawn mowed, and the guy was ten minutes late.

Jamie raced up from the basement. "Auntie Sarah, look what I found." He carried a rose-colored box that looked as though it might once have contained gift chocolates. The worn edges suggested heavy use. Sarah had never seen it before.

"Where did you find this, Jamie?"

"In the hideout room. You know. Where the castle is."

The old bomb shelter room. It had a bathroom and a pantry-like storage room. Sarah slid her phone into her pocket and studied the box, wondering if she'd left it there and forgotten about it. No, she'd never seen it before.

"It was on a shelf in that little room, behind some other stuff," Jamie said. "The really dark room, not the bathroom."

Sarah lifted the top and looked through the contents: small posters, ticket stubs, a diary. She opened it. Angie's name was inscribed on the front cover. Sarah closed it and picked up a letter. It was from Manny.

The girl's parents hadn't approved of Manny, but every teenager wants keepsakes. Afraid her parents might find them, she'd kept them at Caro's house. But why not in her room? Caro wouldn't have snooped. But maybe the girl didn't know that, had thought they'd be safer in the basement.

At the bottom of the box, Sarah found a photograph of the girl. A man stood behind her, his face in the shadow thrown by the banner hanging above them: *Bon Voyage, Caro.*

Manny had changed shifts with somebody so he could see Angie that night, the same night Sarah had gotten a glimpse of the two of them in the garden.

Why had Angie printed the photo? Maybe she'd wanted to keep it, but not on her phone, where her parents might find it. She'd had plenty of time to hide it in the basement while she cleaned up the house after the party.

Sarah's thoughts flashed back to the day Angie had packed up Caro's things. She'd almost collided with Angie at the bottom of the stairs. The girl had been nervous, stammering something about going to the kitchen for a drink. Had she really been on her way to the basement to retrieve the photo and anything else she might have left there?

Caro had complained about how often she found the girl in that area of the house when she was supposed to be working.

Somebody tapped at the back door. The man to mow the lawn, finally. Sarah started to put the photograph back in the box, then brought it closer, to get a better look at Angie's boyfriend. She gasped and almost dropped the picture. It was him—the man who had broken into the house, the man who had chased her in the car.

She pulled her phone out of her pocket.

A flicker of movement in her peripheral vision drew her attention to the door leading outside. She hadn't locked it after Jamie came in the house. It creaked open, and a man stepped inside. The landscaper? Had he tapped on the door, and getting no answer, opened it to look for her?

No. It was the man from the sketch. Sarah took a step backward, watching his face. Judging from his startled expression, his unanswered tap had led him to believe the house was unoccupied.

She'd wanted to find him, but not here—not in the house with her and Jamie. And she didn't need to find him anymore; she knew who he was.

He hesitated, his gaze traveling from Sarah to Jamie, standing between them, and finally to the photo Sarah held. His jaw tightened and his gaze hardened. A lightening bolt of fear charged through Sarah. She drew in a ragged breath, motioned toward the front door and yelled, "Run, Jamie!"

The man–Manny–charged toward her. She turned to sprint up the stairs, to give Jamie time to get out the front door, but he ran down, to his hiding place in the cellar. A dead end.

If she could get out the front door, she could scream for help. Maybe the landscape guy would be there. No, she couldn't leave Jamie.

They'd never make it down the stairs before the man caught them. She had to lure him away from the stairs and give Jamie time to hide.

She ran through the living room, toward the front door. The man followed, angling to cut her off. She dodged around a sofa. Her arm hit the cherry-wood trim on the back, and her phone skittered away. She had forgotten she was holding it.

She squeezed between the sofa and a bookcase. Grabbing a book in each hand, she threw them at the intruder. He ducked and, gasping for breath, she turned back toward the kitchen and the knife block on the counter.

It was too far; she'd never make it.

Jamie had left the basement door ajar. No sound of clattering footsteps came from the stairs. He had reached the bottom. He would head for the wine cellar and the bomb shelter.

She didn't have time to search for a weapon. The man was too close and she couldn't outrun him. She plunged down the stairway so fast she was afraid she might miss a step and fall onto the concrete below.

Jamie hadn't turned on the light. Smart boy. He would hide in the bomb shelter. Did Manny know it was there? Yes, he'd know. Even if he hadn't seen it, Angie would have told him about it. But it wasn't easy to find if he hadn't been inside; there was that blank wall, then a sharp turn he wouldn't see until he got close.

She should have come down to look at Jamie's "castle." She had no idea how well it would hide the boy.

She looked back. Manny was right behind her. She turned away from the wine cellar, edging into the dark end of the basement. Manny came after her. She would soon be trapped, with no way out and no place to hide. She had to find a way to slip past him and double back.

She had rarely ventured into the basement beyond the wine cellar, but she remembered an old oil furnace somewhere on her right. During a childhood game of hide-and-seek, she'd discovered she could slip behind it, then out the other side. Its rusty-brown circumference had been huge, at least from a child's perspective. Was there enough space for her to get behind it, to hide until Manny got past her, then circle back? Could she even find it in the dark?

She angled to the right, one arm outstretched.

Manny moved slower now. That might gain her a few minutes, but they must be close to the end of the cellar.

Had she already gone past the furnace? Footsteps scraped on the concrete behind her. She sent a silent prayer to keep Jamie safe until Dee and Dave got back. But that might be too late for her. She increased her speed.

She touched the rough iron surface of the furnace and slid to a stop. She sidled around it with soft, careful steps, and waited, her heart pounding so hard she was afraid Manny would hear it. He'd slowed down, probably listening. She waited, taking shallow breaths.

"I know you're here," he said. "Come out now and I won't hurt the boy."

He was close, just on the other side of the furnace. Near enough to feel it, to know it was there?

"I promise. I just want to talk to you." He was so close, she shuddered. If he turned her way and took a few steps, he would probably touch the furnace.

She inched the rest of the way around, careful to keep her clothing from brushing the rough iron surface. She took one short step, then another, barely lifting her feet, inching back toward the stairs. Every nerve in her body screamed at her to run. She took another tiny step.

Was he still standing by the furnace, listening? Just a few more paces and she'd be in the open, able to move a little faster. If he was still by the furnace, she had gained some precious time. Enough to get outside and scream for help. Or should she head for the kitchen? If she could get a knife, she might have a chance. At the least, she could face her attacker well away from Jamie.

Muffled footsteps, too close, told her she'd never make it.

She took several deep breaths, trying to calm her nerves. The only edge she had was the darkness and her familiarity with the basement's layout, something she hoped he didn't have. She had to be close to the wine cellar. Had Jamie closed the door? She took shorter strides, still stepping softly, one arm again outstretched to lead the way.

She never felt the door, but a drop in temperature told her she was inside. Another few steps and her fingers touched metal. She ran her fingers over the edge. She'd reached the first wine rack. There were several rows, the end of each attached to the wall. One of the corridors between them led to the old bomb shelter.

She ran past it, noisy now, wanting Manny to know she hadn't veered into that corridor. She moved past it, to the next one, and edged into that aisle. It was a dead end. All of them were, but she hoped to use that to her advantage. The small space at the end of each, where the shelves joined the wall, were tight, but she had squeezed through them when she was a child, and she wasn't that much bigger now. At least, she hoped she wasn't.

It was tight. The rough wall scraped her bare arms and back, and the wine rack dug into her breast. For one heart-lurching moment, she thought she couldn't do it, that she was stuck. A dull clang told her he had bumped against the other end of the rack. He was moving toward her.

One more desperate push and she squirmed into the next aisle. He would find a dead end and a space too small to crawl through. What would he do then? Find his way to the next walkway between the shelving? Or take the one leading to Jamie?

She had to draw him away, but she couldn't try squeezing through another end space. She might not make it next time.

She had to get on top, out of his reach.

When Caro, barely five feet tall, had the wine cellar built, she had insisted the wine racks be no higher than her head. There would be space on top. Not much, but enough for Sarah.

The back aisles held less wine than those in front, so there would be open bottle slots. She might be able to use them to climb. There would be more light there, too, through the window at the end. Not much this late in the day, but enough to at least see his shape, and more importantly, to see the tops of the racks. He wasn't likely to be looking up, as long as she made no sound.

Choosing the section nearest the wall for stability, she groped along the rack until she felt several empty slots. Reaching about a foot higher, she found another. Time to climb.

Near the top, she let her foot nudge a bottle. It rocked a little, clicking against the metal. Had he heard?

She stayed motionless, listening. Nothing. She waited. A faint shuffle, then another, a little closer. He was moving her way. Good. She was drawing him away from Jamie.

She climbed to the top, careful now, not touching any bottles. Crouching in the narrow space under the basement ceiling, she listened for footsteps.

As long as she could hear him, she could follow. If he left the aisles on either side of her, she'd have a problem. The space at the top was too cramped for her to stand and jump to the top of another rack. She could barely see them, anyway. She would be trapped. He could run from one corridor to the next faster than she could climb down one rack and up another. She had to finish this quickly, from the rack she was on.

He was headed her way, more sure-footed now, familiar with the configuration of the shelving. He would think she had no way out of the corridor. Sliding a wine bottle from the rack, she waited, trying to judge the distance by the sound of his footsteps.

His movements were slow and cautious. She held her breath, afraid he would hear her labored breathing. She had to connect with the first blow; she probably wouldn't get another chance.

He was close. She drew her arm back, slow and easy, so she didn't make a sound. Finally, he was directly beneath her. She swung the bottle hard.

He ducked at the last instant, and the blow grazed his shoulder. He thrust his arms upward, reaching for her. His fingers brushed against her leg, and she pushed away, just out of his range.

A bottle clinked against metal as he pulled it from the rack. She sensed the rush of air just as it hit. Pain numbed her right arm, diminishing the impact of her second swing. Too bad, because she'd been on target with that one. It hit the side of his head.

He knew she was on top of the shelving now; she'd lost her advantage. She crawled along the rack, toward a dimly lit area, moving so fast she feared she might tumble over the edge. She stopped when his figure was only a dark shadow against the encroaching darkness. Crouching, she waited, working her arm and shoulder.

Something heavy slammed into her chest, knocking her off balance. She scrabbled for something to hang onto. One hand caught the edge of the rack. Grasping it, she teetered on the shelf's edge. She pushed backward far enough to regain her balance.

Quick footsteps moved toward her. Glass clinked on metal just beneath her.

She slid a bottle from its slot, drew her right arm back like a tennis racket, and swung the bottle as hard as she could. He fell, and the sweet aroma of aged wine filled her nostrils.

She teetered, the momentum of her swing pulling her forward. She reached for something to hang onto, but couldn't find it. Arms flailing, she fell on top of him.

He'd cushioned her fall, but one of her arms slammed into the concrete. Searing pain jolted up her shoulder.

He stirred and moaned. She grabbed a broken bottle. Holding it by the neck, the jagged edge toward him, she tried to stand. Her left leg gave way. She grabbed for a shelf, still clutching the bottle. Teetering on her right leg, she tried again to put her weight on the left. She couldn't do it.

She had to hold on, for Jamie. There was nobody else. Dee and Dave hadn't been gone long enough.

Manny jerked her right leg out from under her. Lights flashed, then faded into gray. Hoping Jamie had inherited at least a little of his mother's psychic abilities, she willed him to stay where he was until Dee and Dave got back. Then she slipped deep into darkness.

Chapter 33

The lights were on, so bright Sarah blinked. She couldn't move her leg. Had the man fallen on top of it? "Jamie, where are you?" The words trembled on dry lips.

"Jamie's fine," somebody said, and she turned her head. She was in a bed–a hospital bed.

Dee stood beside her. "Jamie's fine," she repeated. "He stayed in his hiding place, just like you told him. The first officers on the scene didn't even know there was a child in the house until we arrived. I was frantic, thinking he was lying somewhere in that basement, hurt so bad he couldn't call out, or worse, dead. But Eric knew where to find him." She smiled. "In the castle."

"What about Manny?"

"He's locked up. They haven't figured out all the charges yet." She gave Sarah some water. "You're supposed to just take a few sips."

Sarah didn't say anything until she'd worked the water back into her dry throat. "You said first officers. How did they know to come, that we were in trouble?"

"Nine-one-one call from one of your neighbors. She was out jogging when a woman flagged her down, insisting she'd seen a man breaking into your house, then heard a woman screaming. The neighbor said her first inclination was to shrug the woman off; she looked like she was homeless. But with Caro's death and the recent break in, she decided she'd better make the call."

"I never screamed." But it was probably the only way Maudie could think of to get the police there quickly. Had she and Danny followed the man to the house and seen him go inside?

"Do you know who the homeless woman is?" Dee asked. "The police haven't been able to locate her."

"I know who she is," Sarah croaked. "My guardian angel. She saved my life." Sarah motioned to Dee for more water and took a sip. "You said you didn't find Jamie until you got back. He must have been so scared, poor little guy, staying hidden all that time, then hearing all those unfamiliar voices when the police got there."

"It wasn't that long. We heard the dispatcher on the police scanner. Dave did a U-turn, and we headed back. Got there just a few minutes after the patrol officers."

A nurse came into the room. "How are you feeling, Mrs. Wagner?"

"Sore, and my leg feels stiff."

She laughed. "That's because it's in a cast. You broke your left leg, dislocated your right shoulder, and have a nasty cut on that arm."

"Not to mention scrapes and bruises on the rest of your body," Dee added. "When we first got there, we thought you were covered in blood. Turns out a lot of it was wine." She set the glass on the bedside table. "Though there was no shortage of blood."

"Well, you're doing fine now," the nurse said, "but we're going to keep you overnight. The doctor thinks you'll be able to go home tomorrow."

Dave came later that afternoon, carrying a plastic bag and a vase of yellow Shasta daisies. "They don't have much in the gift shop, but I thought you might like these. I'd have come earlier, but Dee had me on kid-sitting duty."

"How is Jamie doing? Is he okay?"

"Worried about you." He smiled, and Sarah fought the urge to reach up and trace his lower lip with the tip of her finger. "Don't tell Dee," he continued, "but I think you've displaced her as Jamie's hero. She's just a cop. You climbed up on wine racks and fought off the bad guy. You're Superwoman."

Sarah shuddered. "Super scared. He was the brave one, not turning on the lights, staying hidden so long."

"You're both my heroes," Dave whispered, brushing a lock of hair from her cheek. "I'm just glad you're okay. It could have been so much worse. Sarah, I—"

A man in hospital scrubs pushed back the curtains. “Hi, Ms. Wagner. I’m Vic Carlton, from Physical Therapy. I need to go over some stuff with you, if this is a good time.”

Dave rose, pulling a book from the bag he carried. “I brought *The Source*. It’s the only one of Michener’s books I wasn’t sure you’d read.” He put it on the table beside the bed. “I have to go, anyway, and relieve Dee. I promised to watch the boys while she goes shopping.”

“Shopping?” Dee didn’t seem like the sort of woman who would ask Dave to babysit so she could shop.

“For you. Something to wear home from the hospital.” He nodded at the cast, bent and brushed his lips across her forehead. She watched him leave, wondering what he’d been about to say before Vic Carlton interrupted.

Dee came early the next morning. “They’re going to let you go home,” she told Sarah. “I assume that’s your aunt’s place?”

Sarah nodded. She wasn’t sure she’d ever be able to go back to the house she’d shared with Scott.

“I couldn’t find many of your clothes at the house, and nothing that would fit over the cast,” Dee said. “ So I got you a couple of inexpensive summer skirts and tops. I hope they fit.”

“Thanks, Dee. That was thoughtful of you.” It was the sort of thing Laura would have done. Sarah worked a button-front sleeveless blouse over the bandage covering most of her upper-right arm.

Dee stood back and cocked her head. “It’s too big. You’re even smaller than I thought.”

The skirt was too big, too, the hem falling against her ankles, but it had a tie at the waist Sarah could adjust. “I think I’m going to be sporting a new look. And no ‘flip backs’ with Jamie for a while.”

“Dave’s at your aunt’s house, watching him and Eric, and Sam and Laura are on their way home.”

“So much for their romantic getaway.”

“I don’t think it was too romantic. Sam called me at 6:00 this morning, wanting to know if you and Jamie were okay. He said

Laura started getting some strange vibes yesterday afternoon. She'd never had anything like that before."

"No, Laura has dreams. Oh, God, don't tell me. She dreamed about us."

Dee nodded. "Something about Jamie folded up in a dark box and you running away from him. When she saw you covered in blood, falling to the floor, she made Sam get up and call me."

Sarah laughed. "I'm surprised they're not here."

"I told Sam you were both okay, and we didn't need them to get in an accident on the way home. I made him promise that they'd have breakfast before they start back. But I'm surprised she hasn't been on the phone to you."

"My phone is somewhere on the living room floor, and I'm not sure it's even working."

"We'll look for it. Ready to go?"

Sarah nodded, and the nurse wheeled her down the hall, Dee walking beside her, carrying crutches and a bag of Sarah's belongings.

It wasn't over. Not yet. Not until she found out why Laura didn't tell her about the boxes.

Eric and Jamie ran to greet her at the front door, then skidded to a stop when they saw the cast. She smiled and held out her un-bandaged arm. "I'm okay. I just need a couple of hugs, one at a time. Then you can be the very first to sign your names on my cast." Not that she could imagine anybody else doing that. Laura's family was all she had left.

"I'm gonna stay with you next time, Auntie Sarah," Eric said. "You and Jamie got to have a real adventure. I didn't even get any ice cream. Or pizza, either."

Sarah struggled to keep from laughing. She couldn't think of a response.

Dave said, "Well, we can fix that right now." He picked up his phone. "What kind of pizza do you guys want?"

"There's ice cream in the freezer," Sarah said, watching Dave's slender fingers tap keys on his cell phone. "Chocolate and vanilla bean. And, Dave, you'd better order enough pizza for Laura and Sam, too. They should be here soon."

They timed their arrival well, pulling into the driveway at the same time the pizza arrived. They hugged Eric and Jamie a little tighter than usual and hung on to them a little longer. Sarah's hugs were shorter, encumbered by the cast and bandaged arm.

By unspoken agreement, they gathered in the kitchen, making small talk while they finished the pizza. When they moved into the living room, they left the boys perched on stools at the kitchen counter, eating their ice cream.

Sarah hobbled to the sofa, sank into the thick cushions, and propped her crutches against the arm. Only then did she ask the question that had been bothering her. "Why did he come after me? I didn't show anybody the sketch."

Laura frowned. "What sketch?"

"The one you made of the man who broke into the house, the guy we thought killed Caro. I planned to show it around the neighborhood, to see if anybody knew him. But Maudie talked me out of it. She said it was too dangerous. She and Danny were going to try to find out who he was. So why did he come after me?"

"Who is Maudie? And Danny?"

"Remember the day we went to the store and found the egg cartons with one egg missing?"

Laura nodded, and Sarah launched into her story, watching their faces as she told them about her encounters with Maudie and Danny. Laura looked appalled, Sam and Dave interested, and Dee amused.

"You really gave them Scott's sleeping bag?" Sam asked, grinning.

"You've developed some interesting sources," Dee said. "Sure you don't want to join the police force?"

"She's done more than that," Dave said. "She helped me solve that frustrating burglary case I told you about." He stood so he could face all of them. "There have been a lot of burglaries in this area recently, but they didn't fit the usual patterns," he explained. "The crooks seemed to know which houses to hit, exactly what was in them, where the good stuff was located, and how to get in and out quickly."

"Sounds like an inside job," Sam said. "People who worked in the houses."

"Exactly. But I could never make a connection between any of the workers and the burglaries. They always had alibis, usually working at other jobs. We figured somebody was coordinating the whole thing, but couldn't find any proof. Then I got a lead: a man who worked at Caroline Brenhauser's bon voyage party."

"Manny," Sarah whispered.

Dave smiled at her. "No, Manny's friend Roberto."

The name seemed familiar. "The one Manny traded shifts with, so he could see Angie?"

Dave nodded. "Exactly. Roberto was pretty antsy when I first talked to him, so I decided to give it another try."

"That's the possible lead you were telling me about?" Dee asked.

"Yes, and he was scared. He'd had some time to think about it, and was afraid he was going to be charged with Caro's murder. He said he never worked that party, Manny did. And, because their boss didn't know about the shift, Manny didn't have an alibi for the night Caro died. The man behind the operation, Julius Rasmuson, hired a lot of people—some legit, some undocumented, and some shady. He sent one or two of the crooked ones out on every job. They cased the house—what was of value, where it was located, the security, that sort of thing. If they could, they unlocked a window that the owners would rarely open. If there was a security system, they watched for somebody entering the code. Sometimes, they were able to hide a small camera to record the keystrokes, kind of like thieves do on ATM machines. Later, he sent others out to do the actual burglary, so there was no connection. Manny screwed up when he changed shifts because he didn't tell Rasmuson, and he got assigned to the burglary, too. For the first time, one of the people who worked at a house had no alibi for the burglary of that same house. And, as it turned out, for the murder."

Sarah had watched her cousin's face while Dave spoke, but it betrayed nothing. Laura shifted in her chair, reaching for Sam's hand. "And he killed Caro?"

"Not intentionally. According to him and his partner, she surprised them on the upper floor. She ran, probably trying to get out of the house. Manny claims he was yelling at her because she was going straight for the railing, so she was looking back at him when she crashed through."

Sarah blinked back tears. "So it was a burglary, after all. Even though the sketches were never missing."

Laura stared at her, eyes wide. "What do you mean they weren't missing? Did they turn up somewhere? We searched every inch of this house."

"Including the cubbyhole under the stairs where I found them right before I discovered what Scott had done."

"I looked in there. I pulled everything out so I could see what was in the boxes."

"I know."

Laura frowned at Sarah. Silence settled over the room. Sam opened his mouth to speak at the same time Laura scrambled to her feet. She ran to the stairs, jerked open the cubbyhole door, and stood, staring at the unmarked boxes. "Those weren't here. Not when I searched." She pulled them out and opened them. "Oh my God, everything is here. All of it." She spilled the contents of one box onto the carpet.

Sarah, watching her cousin's face, was convinced. Laura hadn't known the boxes were in the cubbyhole.

"How did they get there after we searched?" She thought about Scott, the way he kept disappearing the day before Caro's memorial service. But what could he have to do with the boxes?

"Sarah?" Sam spoke slowly, like he was thinking as he formulated his words. "Dave said Manny changed shifts so he could see his girlfriend."

"Yes, that's what Angie told me."

"Did you tell her you were looking for the sketches? That you suspected the person who took them had murdered your aunt?"

"Yes. Yes, you did," Laura said, looking up from the contents of the boxes. "The day we did the walk-through. Remember? We found her video game and CDs, and when we stopped for lunch on our way to Sam's apartment, you called her."

"And I asked her if she knew where Caro might have put the sketches, told her we thought they were connected to Caro's death." The girl seemed so young, so naïve. "Was Angie part of it, then?" Sarah asked.

"I don't think so," Dave said. "I doubt she knew what her boyfriend was doing. She was just making conversation, telling him what was going on and he took it from there."

"So the day he broke in and scared Laura, he wasn't taking anything. He was putting something back," Dee said. "He and his partner had already loaded those boxes into their vehicle, which they'd parked in the garage, beside Caro's Lexus. She got a ride home, so she wouldn't have gone in there—wouldn't have seen their vehicle. After she fell through the railing, they took off."

"Later," Dave added, "Angie told Manny you and Laura had connected the sketches—in those boxes—to the murder. He couldn't get rid of them. They'd be traced back to him. He was probably in a panic, not knowing what to do with them. Then, when the crime scene tape was gone, he saw an opportunity. He broke into what he thought was an empty house to put them back, not knowing you'd already searched the place."

Laura nodded. "He was standing at the bottom of the stairs when I saw him. I thought he was on his way up, but he must have just closed the cubby door."

"But why would he do that?" Sarah asked. "Why not just destroy them?"

Dee shook her head. "They couldn't chance even a fragment being found because they'd done something else before they left the house. Remember the wine on the deck? They had set the scene to make it look as though Caro was drinking. I suppose they thought that would lead to a determination that it was an accident."

"Not very bright," Dave said, "if she didn't have any alcohol in her system."

"Maybe in their world everybody has a few drinks every night, and that would be enough to cover it. Who knows? Nobody said these guys are the sharpest needles in the folder." Dee grinned and continued. "As far as they were concerned, they were in the clear. Then Angie tells Manny that Sarah and Laura think somebody broke in because the sketches are missing—the sketches that Manny still has."

Dave laughed. "For Manny, the solution is a no-brainer. He thinks the house is empty; the crime scene tape is gone. He knows how to get in; he's already done it once. All he has to do is find out from Angie where Caro might have stored something like that—a place where it might have been all along."

"And he chased me to get my camera, because he thought I'd taken a picture of him," Sarah added. "One to match the photo Angie kept in the basement room, which not only would have identified him, but placed him at Caro's party. I guess that was Angie's private area, a place where she could keep things safely hidden from both her parents and Caro."

"And Manny wanted that photo,"

Sarah, watching his face, nodded. "The day Angie packed up Caro's things, she was trying to get down to the cellar to get it, but I kept her upstairs, working. I was downstairs, between her and the cellar door. When she left that day, she thought I was leaving, too—going home—so Manny assumed the house was empty again." She shivered.

Laura reached inside the box.

"Don't touch anything," Dave said. "We need his fingerprints."

"Dave, I already did, when I found it," Sarah said. "I took some of the things out."

"There's a piece of paper in there," Laura peered into the box. "It looks like a receipt of some kind."

Dave asked for a baggy and a pair of tweezers. Laura raced to get them. He fished the paper out with the tweezers and dropped it into the baggy. "Did you touch this?" he asked Sarah.

She shook her head. "I didn't even see it."

He held it up to the light and grinned. "Good. It's a receipt from a gas station. It's dated the same day he broke in. So it couldn't have been Caro's. And it has a credit card number on it. It must have fallen from his shirt pocket when he bent over to shove the box in here. Gotcha, buddy."

Sarah's mind was racing. "Angie overheard me talking to Scott, telling him I was going to show the sketch around. That's why

Manny came after me. But that was Tuesday. Why did he wait until the weekend?"

"Maybe she didn't see him until then, didn't have a chance to tell him," Dave said. "She wouldn't have thought it was important. Apparently, she never saw the sketch, didn't know it was him."

Laura walked toward Sarah. "He killed Caro, and he almost killed you." She sank down beside her cousin, gathered her in her arms, and cried.

"I think it was something of a draw," Dave said. "Sarah was down, but so was he, and she still had that broken bottle clutched in her hand, ready to use as a weapon." His eyes sparkled, and he smiled at Sarah.

She had to stop watching the curve of those lips, wondering what they would feel like on hers.

"Auntie Sarah!" Eric stood in the doorway. Did he have blood on his hands? Sarah struggled to rise, then saw wine stains on his knees.

"Oh, Eric, you've been down in the basement. You shouldn't go down there, honey. Not until we get all the broken glass and spilled wine cleaned up."

"Did you break all those bottles?" he asked, his tone accusing. "You told us not to climb up on the racks. 'Specially on the high shelves. Didn't she, Auntie Dee? Remember? She said all the best stuff was up there."

"And it is, Eric, it is," Sarah said, smiling. "I found a very good bottle of wine up there."

Chapter 34

Laura rose from the sofa. "We'd better get you boys home. It's going to be past your bedtime by the time we get there."

"Not me," Jamie said. "Somebody has to stay here and take care of Aunt Sarah. She can't even climb the stairs by herself."

Sam laughed, and Sarah tried to swallow the lump in her throat. She'd worried that Jamie might be so traumatized, he'd need therapy. Instead, he was concerned about her well-being. "I'll be fine, Jamie. I have my crutches."

Dee sank onto the sofa cushion Laura had just vacated. "I've got an idea I'd like to run by you, Sarah. My condo is being painted this week. I was planning to ask Sam if I could bunk at his place for a few days." She gestured toward the rest of the room. "But this is more my style. Would you be interested in sharing it with me for a while? I'm a pretty fair cook, but you don't know me very well, so if you don't want to do it, just say so."

"I think it's a great idea. But one of the bedrooms is an art studio, and another is Caro's office. I've been sleeping on the daybed in my old bedroom." Sarah hesitated. If Dee used Caro's room for a while, it might be easier for Sarah to move into it later. It wouldn't be so much Caro's room. anymore. "Angie has packed up Caro's things and stripped the bed. There are clean sheets and blankets in the linen closet. But the bathroom hasn't been cleaned yet."

"Why don't we bring the daybed down here?" Sam asked. "There's a bathroom close by."

"That's another great idea," Sarah said. "If Laura doesn't mind bringing my stuff down here, I'll have everything I need."

It didn't take long. Sam and Dave carried the daybed into the alcove and set it up. Laura hung the skirts and tops in the coat closet and moved the rest of Sarah's things into the guest bathroom. "I need to get you some more clothes." She studied the cast and bandage. "Loose ones, to fit over all that."

"I can pick some more up tomorrow," Dee said, "now that I have a better idea of her size."

"You're going to have some good company," Dave said, as he told Sarah good night. "Not just Dee." He nodded toward the bookcases that lined the walls. "You have Michener and Follett, among others." He smiled, kissed her on the cheek and left Sarah wondering if her face looked as warm as it felt.

After Dee got Sarah settled for the night, she went back to her condo to pack a bag. They got to bed late that night, and Sarah didn't awaken until daylight filtered into the room. She smelled coffee and cinnamon.

Dee brought a plate into the alcove and set it on a table beside the daybed. "You like cinnamon toast? I figured it's fast, and you won't have to come to the kitchen to eat it. I also found a thermos, so when you finish your coffee, you'll have a couple of refills handy." She went back to the kitchen for the thermos and a mug of coffee. "I don't know what to do about lunch. I can make a sandwich and wrap it up, or try to swing by—"

"There's a box of protein bars in the cupboard. Bring me a couple of those, and maybe an apple or a banana, and I'll be good."

"Can you manage okay for the rest of the day? I can bring something back for dinner."

"I'll be fine. Thanks, Dee. I appreciate all this."

Dee grinned. "I expect to get paid in fine wine. I'm dying to try some of those bottles—the ones from the top shelves—the really good ones." She waved as she went out the front door.

She came back that night with take-out Thai food and several large bags from the shopping mall. "They're probably too big," she said, "but they have to fit over the cast. I didn't figure you'd be wearing them once it comes off, so I hit the sales rack."

By late in the week, Sarah found herself looking forward to Dee's return from work every day. They had dinner, sipped Caro's wine, and had several long conversations. Sarah learned about Dee's years as a military policeman, her tours of duty in Iraq, and Jason Callender, the young husband she had lost.

Sarah told Dee about her mother and Richie, and finally, late one evening, about her father and Anna.

Dee stood at the kitchen sink, looking out into the night. "Loss like that does something to you—something other people don't understand." She turned to Sarah, who sat on one of the kitchen stools, where she had plenty of room for her cast. "You're never quite the same after that, are you?"

"No. I guess that's why I stayed with Scott. I couldn't bear to lose anybody else. I don't have many people left."

Dee hugged her. "Never stay with anybody who doesn't treat you well. And you have more people than you think. That's how you manage loss. You find other people who care about you, like Dave and me. We both admire you. You showed a lot of courage down in that basement."

Sarah pulled her crutches under her arms. "It wasn't courage, Dee. I was scared to death. It was love. Love for Jamie."

She had nightmares that night. She was back in the basement, hiding from Manny, who had found his way into the room where Jamie hid. She awoke with a strangled cry and sat up, hoping she hadn't awakened Dee. The house was quiet, but she couldn't get back to sleep. She sat alone in the darkness, trying to figure out what she was going to do with the rest of her life.

She worked at her computer the next morning, exploring options, and making calls. By late afternoon, she was back on the daybed, nodding off as she tried to read through some of the material.

She didn't realize she'd drifted off to sleep until a loud noise awakened her. Somebody was pounding on the front door. Her laptop slid to the floor when she shifted her legs off the daybed. She hobbled to the door and opened it.

The arm Scott had raised to pound on the door dropped to his side. His gaze took in the cast and bandage. "What the hell happened to you, Sarah? Did they hurt you?"

She gaped at him, surprised he was there, confused by his question. The loan sharks. He thought they had hurt her. Had they really threatened his family?

He stepped toward her, his arms open, but she edged away, inadvertently giving him room to step inside. He closed and locked the door and repeated his question. "Did they hurt you?"

"No, it was the man who...the man who killed Caro." She stumbled over the words. She had accused Scott of killing Caro, had believed him guilty. "I'm sorry I thought you did it."

"It doesn't matter now. I just wish you'd had a little more faith in me. I told you I didn't hurt her. You should have believed me."

Nothing had changed. Everything was going to be her fault. "You told me too many lies, Scott. How could I possibly have any faith in you?"

Anger, quickly suppressed, flashed across his features. She'd known him too long, watched for that surge of anger too many times for him to hide it. Experience had taught her to diffuse it, but she didn't want to fall back into old patterns. That was finished. Yet, the cast made her vulnerable.

She had taken a step back toward the daybed but realized she couldn't rise from it easily. She turned instead toward the kitchen, maneuvered to one of the stools and perched on its edge, holding the crutches between her and Scott. "I thought you were in jail."

"I'm out on bail." His face was calm now, the anger hidden. "But we can beat this thing, Sarah. Talk to Laura. If the two of you don't testify against me, my lawyer thinks maybe I can win. I'll keep going to AA and we'll be fine."

She stared at him, speechless.

"Sarah, I'm sorry I lied to you. I just didn't know what else to do. But that's all over now. I can get help with my gambling problem. We can start over." He reached over the crutches, trying to get an arm around her shoulders.

She leaned away from him. "No, we're not going to start over. You not only lied to me, you stole my money and Caro's, and even worse, let Laura go to jail for a crime you committed."

"I told you I had to do that. I was afraid they'd hurt you."

She didn't believe him. "Scott, even if that was true, which I doubt, it doesn't matter. You got yourself into this mess, but you won't take responsibility for your actions. You're too busy blaming somebody else." *Usually me.*

Anger sparked in his eyes again, and she drew back a little farther. He put a hand on her bandaged arm. "I love you, Sarah. We can make this work. You'll see."

"I talked to Robert Gibson this morning. He's filing divorce papers for me."

His hand squeezed tighter, sending a jolt of pain through her upper arm. She pushed at his hand with her free one. "Scott, that hurts."

He tried to pull her to her feet. "You're not getting a divorce, Sarah. You belong to me."

She tried to jerk free. "I don't belong to anybody, and you can't keep me if I don't want to stay." She winced as his grip tightened.

He released her arm long enough to grab the crutches and throw them to the floor. He turned back to her, one arm raised.

"Stop right there. Lower your arm and step back. Now."

Dee stood at the bottom of the steps, in uniform, her gun drawn and aimed at Scott. Her voice was calm. "I said now."

Scott stepped back and lowered his arm. He glared at Dee, then turned his attention back to Sarah. "If you don't want to lose half your money, you'd better reconsider that divorce. You've forgotten, this is a community-property state."

Sarah smiled. "I didn't forget. Mr. Gibson assures me that inheritances are not community property. So you're out of luck, Scott. Now get out and stay out. Mr. Gibson also has a restraining order ready to file, just in case."

Dee escorted him to the door, warned him not to come back, and locked the deadbolt. By the time she got back to the kitchen, Sarah's entire body was trembling. "I was so scared."

Dee grinned. "You hid it well. I was proud of you and the way you handled him."

Sarah inclined her head toward the stairs. "How did you get over there? I didn't hear anybody come in."

Dee shrugged. "I saw the Explorer parked in the driveway, and figured you two might be talking. I didn't want to interrupt, so I went up the patio stairs instead. But when I got to the end of the hall, I realized the conversation was getting loud and ugly. So I came down."

Sarah started laughing, a nervous giggle that finally dissolved into hiccoughs.

"What is so funny?" Dee asked, smiling.

"I—I just..." Sarah took a deep breath and swallowed. "His face, when he saw you with that gun. Scott likes to be in control, and I think he just lost it. In more ways than one." She collapsed against Dee, laughing.

She was going to miss Dee, who had stayed with her an extra week, long after the painters had finished work on her condo. Sarah wished she could stay forever, but Dee had a life of her own. She'd spent enough time babysitting Sarah.

Dave had visited a half-dozen times and Sarah, watching him and Dee together, had smiled. Their relationship was much like Sarah's and Laura's, stronger than friendship. She had marveled, wondering how it had come about, until she realized how close she felt to Dee after only two weeks.

She was going to be lonely without them, but her arm had healed. She could get around much better on her crutches and didn't need anybody there on a daily basis.

"Let's have everybody over one last time before you move out," she told Dee. "We can keep it simple. The weather is beautiful, so we could grill some steaks and bake some potatoes, and eat on the–in the garden—set up a table and some chairs out there." She didn't think she'd ever be able to use the patio again. "That won't be much work. I can sit at the counter and make a salad."

"Great minds think alike," Dee said. "I was just going to suggest something like that."

They gathered that Saturday, a warmer-than-average May day, with the temperature in the high 70s.

"It's perfect," Laura said, surveying the yard, "and the garden is beautiful with all the azaleas blooming."

"I love this Mediterranean climate," Sam said. "I never want to live anywhere else. Mild winters with dry, hot summers, and a delta breeze at night. What's not to like?"

"The fog?" Dave asked, smiling as he helped Sam set up the folding table.

"Well, there is the wintertime tule fog."

"Are we going to stand around talking about the weather?" Dee asked. "Dave and I have an announcement to make." She handed him a beer, and Sarah felt a twinge of something she couldn't define. Had she misjudged their relationship?

"I made detective," Dee said, and Sarah felt a rush of joy. Dee lifted her wine glass. "And—" They waited, smiling, while she drew out the moment. "Dave got a promotion."

"But that means you'll have to work with Matt Coleman," Laura said.

"Yeah, there's that. But if Coleman doesn't change his attitude, I suspect his next assignment will be patrol,"

Dee hugged Sarah, then raised her glass again. "I propose a toast to Sarah, who helped us catch a murderer, solve a robbery, get Laura out of jail, and get Dave and me promoted."

"I'll drink to that." Sam drained his glass of iced tea, set it on the table, and nudged Dee aside. "My turn." He enfolded Sarah in both arms. "Thank you for never giving up on Laura, and for fighting so hard to protect Jamie. I owe you."

Jamie cocked his head to one side. "Is Aunt Sarah a hero or something?"

A wisp of smoke floated toward Sarah, carrying the scent of grilled meat. She drew in a long breath. "The real heroes were Maudie and Danny, and I still haven't thanked them." She tapped the cast with her fingers. "But as soon as this comes off, I'm going to find them. Then, Laura, do you think you could find a house for them, a small one somewhere close to the supermarket?"

Laura stopped setting the table and turned toward Sarah, bright red napkins in hand. "You mean, to buy? You're planning to buy them a house?"

"Just a small one, but there would have to be a fund for utilities, too."

"You don't have the money." Laura flushed. "I mean, you only have the money in your trust fund," she stammered.

"Robert Gibson has already approved it. He thinks it's a small reward for their help in finding Caro's killer. Besides, I'll have the money as soon as my divorce is final."

"You're actually doing it?" Laura cocked her head to one side, her look appraising. "You're just full of surprises, Sarah. I never thought you would leave Scott. But I'm glad. Does that mean you'll be living here, then?"

"No. As much as I love this house, it's part of my past, not my future, and I need to move on with my life. But I'm going to hang on to it. I still can't bear to give it up."

Dee turned to look at the house. "I suspect you'll be back in it eventually. I can't imagine anybody but you living here. This house is a part of you."

"What are you going to do, Sarah? Where do you go from here?" Dave's voice was soft, his eyes warm, but Sarah's gaze was on the gentle curve of his lips.

"New York."

With a sharp intake of breath, Laura dropped the napkins. "New York? Sarah, why? That's so far away."

"Not nearly as far as Paris, and they both have excellent design schools." Sarah tried to smile, but her lips trembled. She hesitated for a moment, looking into her cousin's stricken face, then continued in a soft voice, "I've been too dependent on family, on you and Caro and Scott. Hung on too long, even when it wasn't good for me. I need to learn how to stand alone, find my own way."

Laura picked up the napkins and used one to blot the tears coursing down her face. "But you'll be back? When you finish this design school, you'll come home?"

Sarah, unable to speak, nodded.

Dave's gaze met hers. "We'll be here when you get back," he said, "waiting."

NOTES FOR MY READERS

Love, Murder and a Good Bottle of Wine is the first book in the Wagner and Callender mystery series. You can find *Snowbound*, the second book, by going to Amazon books and typing in either the name of the book or my name.

If you'd like a free short story about Dave Wheeler and how he met Dee Callender, visit my website at chrisphipps.com and click on the Free Short story menu.

Word of mouth is crucial to every writer's success, and reviews are one of the best ways to show your support. I appreciate every one I get, even if they consist of only a line or two. If you enjoyed *Love, Murder, and a Good Bottle of Wine*, please consider leaving a review at wherever you purchased your copy.

Do you have a question for the author? Email chris@chrisphipps.com

Made in the USA
Coppell, TX
28 March 2024